THE CHRONICLES OF THE FALLEN:
THE FALLEN RESURRECTION

Book 1

C. E. TRACY

This book is dedicated to all those friends and family who helped me achieve this dream. Your help has been unbelievable appreciated. You will never be forgotten.

Prologue

Aaron opened his eyes and all he could feel was darkness. It stuck to every inch of his skin, completely encasing him. He blinked once, twice, but the darkness remained. He tried to move, to wipe it from his eyes, but it held him fast. Panic rose in his chest and his heart began to beat faster. He wrestled with it, kicking out and scratching at it as best he could. Nothing changed. He tried screaming, but the darkness muted the sound. He couldn't breathe. The darkness had wrapped itself around his throat like two sturdy hands attempting to drive the life out of him. As he panicked, a stirring in his brain caused his fear to flutter. Something carnal had awoken inside him as he struggled. It was as if as his human mind began to falter, an animalistic will to survive took over. He strained with every ounce of mental and physical energy against the overwhelming black.

Suddenly he was free. Released from the bonds that had him bound. Intoxicating air filled his lungs in short gasps. His body went limp as he relished in the beauty of daylight. The sun nearly blinded him, but he wasn't going to close his eyes just in case the darkness returned. As he lay there, curious sounds caused him to stir. He pushed up onto his elbows and gasped before closing his eyes tightly, willing the darkness to return. All around him towered an army of grotesque creatures. Scorpion-tailed locusts took quick peeks at him with faces more suited for human bodies. Lion–fanged leopards batted each other with bearlike paws. Positioned close to him stood four statuesque abominations: a lion, a calf, a man-like figure, and the largest eagle he had ever seen. Each had six wings and was covered with eyes. They stood perched like they were his private guard, ready to protect him at all cost.

Aaron could feel the blackness taking hold when suddenly all the eyes on the sentinels focused on him. Fear beat off the desire to faint and he stumbled backwards, trying to get as far away from these monsters as possible. He only managed to take a few steps when the ground beneath him began to tremble. The eagle swiftly rose into the air, grasping Aaron's arms in its talons. It lifted off just as the ground disappeared beneath him. An object came speeding from the hole, passing within inches of Aaron's face at a speed that nearly ripped his clothes off. The other three guardians immediately took to flight to fend off the unknown attacker. The eagle flew him away from the conflict as the air was quickly filled with gruesome screams and the clang of weapons.

The sounds had significantly lessened before the eagle set him down. Before it even had a chance to turn and defend the boy, a shower of boulders rained down on them. Aaron dove and cowered on the ground practically beneath the now unrecognizable animal. He could feel the thuds of stone hitting the carcass and hear the sickening crack of bones breaking. It made him nauseous, but fear of his own death kept him from puking. Finally the shower stopped.

Panic fueled him as he jumped up and tried to make a run for it. He made it to the base of a small hill when a massive wall of stone rose up from the ground blocking him. He instinctively veered to the right but ran into another wall that had risen up directly after the first. Behind him he heard the sharp grinding as a third wall raised parallel to the one he'd run into. He was trapped.

He turned around and made to run out of the box when a winged apparition appeared, landing by the mouth of the trap.

'Let me go!' he cried, completely confused at what was going on.

The creature chuckled. 'You know I can't do that. You control these creatures, these abominations. To stop you stops them.'

'I don't know what you're talking about,' Aaron shouted at him. How could he control these things? He couldn't even so much as control what his hair did.

'Denial till the end then? Figures.'

The winged man started towards him. Aaron didn't know what to do or where to go. Fear froze him in place. Time slowed as his captor sailed through the air, bringing his arms up to strike Aaron down. Just as the angel's fists were inches from his target's face, something plummeted from the sky and crashed into him. Aaron dove to the side as the ball of winged bodies whizzed passed, obliterating the back wall of the trap.

When they stopped rolling, the lion pinned its prey to the ground. It roared triumphantly before going for the killing blow. The fiend, who had been unsuccessfully trying to get the lion off from him, instantly went limp. Its arms collapsed onto the earth as the lion shook it viciously. When the lion released its grip off its prey's throat, it roared in agony as its teeth crumbled into dust. The man pushed himself onto his hands, laughing as the lion stumbled away pitifully. Before the animal could get very far, two slabs of stone erupted from the ground, completely crushing the creature.

The winged man stood and dusted the dirt from off him. Aaron couldn't move. He'd just seen two creatures break through a stone wall, one have its jugular ripped out - but not really - and the other get pulverized between two rocks. What kind of nightmare was he in?

A tiny pebble bounced against his head and onto the ground. He looked at the wall next to him and then at the winged man, who was now walking towards him. The man pointed at him and smiled. 'Goodbye,' he said calmly, sharply closing his hand. A crack ran through the wall, webbing out in all directions. Aaron clawed at the ground trying to regain his footing, but his panic made him clumsy. He slipped and fell on his back, screaming as the wall collapsed on top of him.

Chapter 1

Aaron bolted up in his bed. He stared around the room confused, wondering what had just happened. His heart beat erratically until he realized he was still in his room. He felt the wall next to him for reassurance that it was still standing and not crushing him. 'Must have been a dream,' he grumbled before closing his eyes and curling into a ball underneath the warm covers. He'd just begun drifting into blissful sleep when his door burst open and painfully bright light invaded the cracks of his eyelids.

'Time to get up man,' an annoyingly cheerful voice said. 'The girls are going to be here in like 30 minutes.'

Aaron groaned in irritation. "Go figure," he grumbled voicelessly. "Of all days to wake up early it had to be today." He slowly opened his eyes and glared at the neon red 6:00 am grinning wickedly at him. Every cell in his body screamed to just go back to sleep, but begrudgingly he ignored their millions of enticing calls. This was only his second date with this girl and no matter how tired he was he wasn't going to ruin his chances. He unwillingly hauled himself out of bed and into the shower.

The two girls arrived at the apartment a few minutes later than predicted. They left the engine running and watched as the boys loaded up a cooler with lunch, water and other snacks before gathering the miscellaneous hiking gear they might need. Once everything was unceremoniously crammed into the trunk, they made one final sweep to ensure nothing was left behind. Satisfied that they had everything, they were on their way.

Aaron's date, Sharon, was an avid outdoor enthusiast. It was this passion for nature that had initially piqued his interest. You see Aaron wasn't too fond of nature. He'd had way too many unfortunate experiences whilst out in the wild. Whether it was getting injured, lost, or otherwise made uncomfortable, anything bad that could happen always happened to him. In order to keep these from occurring, he opted to refrain from any outdoor activities. Despite his previous encounters, he'd somehow let her convince him that it would be fun. So here he was, exhausted and apprehensive as they drove towards the Boulder Caves. "What could possibly go wrong?" he tried reassuring himself.

'You doing alright back there?' a feminine voice called back, disrupting his thoughts.

'Um, yeah. I'm fine,' he replied as cheerfully as possible without sounding cheesy.

'Are you sure?' the other girl, Agnes, asked, her nasal voice only slightly hiding the mocking tone.

"She must have told her friend," he thought, rolling his eyes. Aaron grimaced. 'Yeah, I'm just tired,' he replied flatly.

'Alright,' Sharon said, not sounding entirely convinced. 'So did everyone sleep alright?'

Her attempt at making small talk felt contrived. It was something someone said when they had nothing else of importance to say but didn't want to deal with the silence. Aaron could hear it in her voice so he turned away to stare out the window and brood. He had no real reason to, just that he was beginning to feel strange. A knot was forming in his stomach and he couldn't figure out why.

'Hey man. You alright?' Tony asked, his eyes narrowing in genuine concern.

'Of course I'm fine,' Aaron snapped, looking back to glare slightly at his roommate. He was beginning to get annoyed. 'I said I'm tired.'

Aaron turned away again and concentrated on the scenery as it swiftly blurred by. He had lied. He really wasn't fine. He hadn't lied about being tired though. That he was very much. As for being mentally all right, he was not. He was growing anxious. Plus he couldn't help thinking about the dream he had. It had felt too real. Almost like a premonition. But he didn't believe in that sort of mumbo-jumbo, so it had to be something else. There had to be something else unnerving him. But what?

The awkward silence lasted for a few minutes before dissolving into nothing. The conversation was soon forgotten and everyone focused on other thoughts. To distract himself from the dark thoughts of his dream and the unease at being out in nature, he concentrated on his studies. Genetics to be precise. This was his first year at Franklin Pierce University and his primary focus was animal gene splicing. His relatives had ridiculed him for such a ridiculous scientific venture, but such mythological creatures as the sphinx and the chimera fascinated him. He had always wondered if such creatures could be created. If so, he wanted to be the one to create them. These thoughts always bolstered his courage whenever he felt weak.

The sun had fully exposed itself from behind the horizon by the time they arrived at the caves. Sharon had claimed that the earlier you went, the less people there were. It seemed reasonable enough. Plus, the fewer people around meant the less embarrassed Aaron would feel if something happened to him. Sure enough, as they pulled into the parking lot, there was not a single car in sight.

THE FALLEN RESURRECTION | 7

'That's strange,' Sharon mumbled. 'There are usually at least a few people here.'

'Maybe there's a holiday we didn't know about,' Agnes replied.

'Doubt that, but this is perfect,' Tony snorted. 'Just means we get the entire place to ourselves.'

Laughing, he punched Aaron hard on the arm, quickly jumping out of the car before he could retaliate. Aaron darted after him, chasing him unsuccessfully around the empty lot. Tony taunted him nonstop, purposely staying an annoying arms-length out of reach. Aaron picked up a couple rocks and chucked them at him in frustration.

'Hey, hey, hey,' Tony laughed, ducking behind a tree at the edge of the lot. 'That's cheating dude.'

'So?' Aaron replied, ricocheting another stone missile off the tree his roommate was hiding behind. 'Maybe you shouldn't run so fast.'

'Like that's gonna happen.'

'Then I get to use rocks.'

'Seriously you guys?' one of the girls yelled at them. 'Let's get inside the park first and then you can try and kill each other.'

'Momentary truce?' Tony called from behind the tree.

'Fine,' Aaron conceded, feigning disappointment as he dropped the rocks. 'Saved by a girl.'

'Whatever man,' Tony denied as he caught up to him, putting him in a friendly headlock and ruffling his hair. 'I was about to bring you down when they stopped us.'

'That I highly doubt,' Aaron scoffed, digging his fingers into his friend's side, causing him to spasm and let go.

Back at the car, the girls smiled and shook their heads in mock reproach. It had been highly amusing watching the two boys play fight around the lot, but they were here to explore. Roughhousing could come later.

Aaron's initial anxiety about being back in nature quickly subsided after they entered the park. The hike through the caves was relatively simple including crawling through the narrow paths of the nearly claustrophobic 'Hall of Ships'. Even without a hardhat he remained uninjured. No twisted ankles, no hands in unknown substances, and also no stains on his clothes. So far it was as if nature was trying to make up for all the problems it had caused him in the past.

After a refreshing lunch in the full heat of the afternoon sun, the girls made a proposition. As they had all seen pretty much all there was to see in the park, they now wanted to hike around the mountainside. There was still plenty of sunlight so there was no real risk of getting lost in the dark and the girls had brought a map of the area. This was exactly what Aaron had been dreading. Hiking in a park within a controlled environment was one thing, but traipsing off into unknown terrain was a no-go.

'I'd really rather not,' he voiced nervously, his heart beating franticly.

The others turned their heads slowly to stare at him. Sharon looked put-off while Agnes was livid.

'And why not?' Agnes argued. 'It's not like anything bad is going to happen. Don't be such a baby.'

'Hey. Don't!' Sharon admonished. 'I told you about his past experiences.'

'So? Why should his fears stop us from enjoying ourselves? He just needs to man up.'

'Excuse me?!' Aaron erupted. Who did this girl think she was? 'You need to learn how to be empathetic as you obviously have no idea how to interact with normal people.'

'You're the one who's pathetic you...'

'Hey, hey, hey guys,' Tony interjected, inserting himself between them. 'Let's all just chill out. I'm not usually the one who plays the adult, but come on you two.

There's no need for trash talking.'

'But...' she began, but was quickly hushed by a look from Sharon.

Tony paused a moment to ensure that neither one of them was going to say anything else before continuing.

'Now dude,' he said, turning his attention to Aaron. 'I get how you feel about being out here and all, but honestly when was the last time you went hiking?'

Aaron looked at the ground and thought for a minute. 'About ten years ago I think.'

'See man? Don't you think it's about time to give it another shot? Seriously. What's the worst that could happen? It's still light out and it's not like we're the first ones to hike here. Alright?'

Aaron wasn't thrilled about it, but his roommate did have a point. It had been so many years. Maybe it was time to give it another shot.

'Fine,' he said glumly.

'Awesome,' Tony said, patting Aaron on the back. 'Let's get going then.'

Begrudgingly, Aaron followed the other three. Despite his resolve to give it a shot, he still felt apprehensive. Something about this place was unnerving. He hadn't said anything, but he didn't like it there. Something felt wrong. It was almost suffocating how wrong it felt. But as he had already agreed to go with them, he knew he couldn't back out now. What would his date think about him if he did?

Much to his relief, the hike was relatively easy. The further they walked, the more sheepish he felt at making such a big deal of it. Maybe this was the time things would turn out for the best. So far nothing bad had happened. Maybe his bad luck was over. He hoped so. Despite not liking the place, the day was turning out pretty good. A turn for the worst would not be ideal.

From the start of the hike, Aaron walked a few paces behind the others. This was largely because of his not wanting to be distracted. He wanted to take extra precaution about where he stepped. This was not to say that he wasn't paying attention to them and what they were saying. At first the conversation between the three was nothing but idle banter, but the deeper into the forest they went, the more the talk turned to the history of the area.

'Do any of you know how the caves were found?' Sharon asked the other two. Aaron was apparently too far back to really be included in the conversation.

'No idea,' Tony replied, not totally interested.

'Wasn't somebody injured when they were found?' Agnes remarked.

'Well yes and no,' Sharon answered. She was beginning to sound more like a tour guide now. 'In the mid-19th century, two brothers were out fishing by the river when one of them suddenly disappeared.'

'Disappeared?' Tony scoffed. 'This is starting to sound like some campfire ghost story.'

Agnes laughed. 'Doesn't it?' she agreed.

'Well it's not,' Sharon chided, 'as neither of them dies in some ghastly manner. One of the brothers fell into a hole and landed 15-feet below in some shallow water in what is now known as the Shadow Cave. From that point on, this area has been a very popular tourist spot.'

'Sounds fascinating,' Tony mocked. 'Oh! You know what'd be really cool? If one of us stumbled upon another cave while we were hiking!'

Sharon cast him a withering look. 'While that would be "cool", that is highly unlikely. This area is not known for real caves like the Mammoth Cave in Kentucky or the Cave of the Winds in Colorado. We mostly only get the caves made from collapsed boulders.'

'It'd still be cool,' he sulked, walking away from the trail.

'You probably shouldn't just wander away from the

trail like that,' Sharon called after him.

'Why not? As you said, it's not as if there's going to be any unknown caves to fall into.'

He turned around to continue walking and then disappeared suddenly from view. Aaron, who had at this point caught up, and the two girls stared in horror at the spot where Tony had just been standing. They stood there confused before a splash brought them out of their stupor. They quickly ran over to the area where he had just been standing. Gaping up at them with jagged teeth was a hole that Aaron's date swore could not have been there before.

Sharon pulled a flashlight from her pack and shone it down inside the hole. It was difficult for her to tell exactly how deep it was, but from the faint rippled reflection she saw, it was safe to assume that the base was covered with water. That was comforting to some degree.

'I can't find him,' she announced worriedly.

Aaron inched toward the edge of the hole and peered inside. 'Hey man. You down there?'

Agnes was just about to offer some snide remark when they all felt the ground shiver. Their eyes widened fearfully as they quickly realized what was about to happen. They attempted to scramble back away from the edge, but weren't quick enough. In a shower of stone, dirt and bodies, they plummeted down into the darkness.

The water was shockingly cold as they hit it with a sharp splash. It was like a glacier had melted just before they fell in. Aaron sunk only a few feet before being able to claw his way to the surface. Breaking the water, he was greeted by darkness with a single point of light that wasn't doing much good at brightening up the cave. It took a matter of minutes to get accustomed to the dim darkness. Before long he was able to make out some shapes that looked oddly human-like standing above the water.

'Aaron is that you?' Tony's voice echoed before a blinding beam of light shot him in the face.

'Yeah it's me,' he cried out painfully. 'Get that light out of my face please. I'm blind now.'

'Sorry man. Swim over this way. There's some kind of walkway.'

As Aaron waited for his eyes to readjust, he calmly doggie paddled his way in the direction he recalled the light coming from. He could now hear the girls' voices, which confirmed he was going the right way. After a short swim, his hands connected with a solid piece of stone, which he was able to climb up on to. The stone felt oddly smooth and angular, like it had been purposely placed there rather than having been created naturally.

'Have you made it over here yet?' Sharon called out to him, not realizing he was a mere five yards away from them.

'Yeah I'm right here.'

'Damn it man,' Tony exclaimed, once again blinding Aaron with the light. 'Don't sneak up on people like that.'

'Will you stop shining that stupid light in my face! I would like to use my eyes still.'

'Guys stop,' Sharon said, snatching the light from Tony. 'Where are we?' she asked as she began shining the light around the room.

'No idea, but I can guess it's not a known cave,' Tony answered, vaguely trying to hide the irony. As he began surveying the room he added, 'and good thing your flashlight is waterproof.'

'How're we going to get out of here?' Agnes asked, starting to hyperventilate. 'No one is going to know where we are and if they don't know where we are how will they find us? And what if we can't find a way out? Are we going to die down here? I don't want to die down here. I have a paper due next week and who will take care of my cat?'

While the other two tried to calm her down, Aaron sat on the ground relatively calm. He found it mildly amusing that he wasn't the one freaking out. Go figure something like this would happen, but at least it wasn't only happening to him. Despite their circumstances seeming pretty dire, something about the cave was strangely peaceful, like the strain of containing an earth-shattering secret had finally been lifted. Not to mention the knot in his stomach was finally gone.

As Agnes began to calm down, Aaron stood up and began slowly inching his way along the walkway. While Sharon had been bathing the room in light, he had sworn he'd seen the mouth of a tunnel at one end of the room. Rather than interrupt the calming session, he decided to use the time effectively and investigate it himself.

He had almost reached the end of the walkway when he heard his roommate call out to him. 'Yo man, where'd you go?'

'I'm over here,' he replied, keeping his back turned just in case he was to be blinded for a third time.

'What're you doing way over there?' Tony asked after bathing him in light

'I think I saw an opening somewhere over this way,' Aaron said, pointing in the direction he thought he'd seen the opening.

'Well wait for us to get over there.'

Aaron rolled his eyes, but waited impatiently for the other three to get to where he was. Once they'd caught up to him, he led them over to where he believed the opening was. Sure enough, tucked behind a large boulder was an almost perfectly circular tunnel mouth.

'How'd you see this?' Sharon asked.

'I don't know. I just did.'

'Should we follow it?'

'It's not like we have many other options,' Tony answered.

It was true. Unless they were able to find another

tunnel somewhere else in the room, this was the only real option they had. With Tony leading the way, they began walking down the corridor. They followed the strange tunnel, which looked oddly manmade, deeper and deeper into the hillside. Aaron's heart thudded in his chest and he could swear it was echoing. He was so nervous he could barely feel that the knot in his stomach had returned. He honestly couldn't wait to leave this place behind. He never wanted to leave the city again.

They made one final turn before stopping at what appeared to be a dead end. Agnes had nearly begun hyperventilating again when a sight caught them all off guard. Set in the middle of the back wall was a doorway. The four of them stared in perplexed silence before cautiously moving forward to investigate the strange oddity.

The double doors were ordinary, made from dark red wood and paneled with different kind of white wood. It was fashioned with two large, circular iron handles. In the centre of the door was a large circular mural. The inlays were composed of many different shades of wood depicting an intricate scene. On the right door was the image of four angelic creatures in front of a strange gothic castle. With them stood a small group of other humanoid beings. On the left door were pictured four decrepit creatures swirled in darkness and flanked by what seemed like innumerable concourses of minions. Near them stood a single humanoid figure surrounded by strange creatures, like someone had played mix-n-match with various animals. It appeared as if it was the final scene before some epic battle, one that history books seemed to have omitted or even more likely not known.

The knot in Aaron's stomach twisted painfully as he stared at the scene. There was something oddly familiar about the figure standing with the creatures. Hadn't he dreamed this? He tried to remember but his memory was cloudy, like someone or something was keeping him from remembering.

   While the others stared at the scene, Tony walked up to the door and grabbed one of the heavy, circular iron handles and yanked with all his might. It groaned defiantly, but didn't budge. He gritted his teeth, propped his leg against the other half of the door and tried again. The veins in his forehead and neck bulged close to explosion, but still the door remained closed. Aaron, who was finding everything amusing now, was about to lend a hand when an irritated screech came from the hinges as the door final relented. Tony tugged it open just wide enough for them to fit through singularly before it obstinately stopped.

   Sharon was the first to enter with the others following quietly behind her. She shined the light around and they were disappointed at the starkness of the room. It was empty save a large sarcophagus in the centre. Tall iron candlesticks stood guard at each corner with the remnants of ancient wax winding like an ivy ghost down the cold, gray, soulless metal. The walls were bare with the exception of one cubbyhole where a lantern could easily be placed.

   The four huddled at the head of the tomb, taking in its ornateness as Sharon bathed the sarcophagus in light in order for them to see it better. The top of the case was carved similar to the tombs of royalty. Smooth alabaster stone depicted the carved figure of a man. His eyes were shut and peaceful while his hands rested gently at the base of his stomach, clasped at the fingertips hiding the exposed navel. The lower half of the man was draped diagonally with a blanket of rose granite, beginning right below the clasped fingers, cutting across the left calf to the right ankle, exposing both unshod feet. He strangely appeared to be resting on a bed of interwoven feathers.

   The sides of the tomb were curiously carved with more scenes of angels. The north side held a scene of winged men dallying with normal women. The east side showed a group of winged men being thrust out of the presence of some higher being. The west side showed a scene of a winged man being attacked by dogs and wingless men wielding swords and axes. The south side depicted a scene of a winged man with unknown offerings in his hands kneeling before a lavishly dressed being.

'I wonder what's inside it,' Tony questioned as he gently rubbed the lid.

'Well I would guess someone's body genius,' Agnes replied dryly.

Tony rolled his eyes and turned to Aaron. 'Hey man. You wanna give me a hand with this lid?'

'Maybe we should just leave it how it is,' Sharon mildly objected.

'There's no harm in opening it just a little to look inside. Now come on Aaron.'

Aaron shrugged his shoulders and walked over to where his roommate was waiting.

'Now you stand at that corner,' he said, pointing to the opposite corner from himself, 'and on the count of three we'll push. Ready? One, two, three.'

Both boys pushed as hard as they could, but nothing happened. Not even a speck of dust went out of place.

Agnes laughed mockingly. 'Seems it obviously wasn't meant to be opened.'

Tony ignored her and put his shoulder to the lid again.

'C'mon,' he said, motioning for Aaron to get in place. 'Let's try one more time. One, two, three.'

The two boys made sure their hands were only on the lid and pushed like their lives depended on it. Again nothing, but they didn't stop. The veins in their foreheads were beginning to swell when they felt the lid give slightly. They stopped to catch their breath before giving it a final go. With a third solid push, the lid slid off easily, as if it had been greased. With a crash it landed on the ground and broke into two massive chunks, spraying dust and specks of granite into the air.

'Now look what you've done,' Sharon coughed, waving the dust out of her face.

It looked as if she was going to actually chastise them, but her curiosity got the best of her. Once the dust had settled enough, they all gathered around to look inside. Instead of housing a rotting corpse, the sarcophagus revealed a locked trapdoor.

'Would you check that out,' Tony remarked self-satisfactorily. 'The whole tomb thing was a trick. But how do we open the lock?' he asked after noticing a large, heavy metal padlock.

'Looks like another dead end,' Aaron grumbled, sitting down dejectedly next to the box.

'Wait a minute,' Agnes called out. 'Shine your light back over by the lid. Did any of you happen to hear something other than stone breaking a minute ago?'

'Like what?' Aaron asked.

'Like something metallic.'

'I didn't.'

'Neither did I,' Tony added.

Sharon shrugged her shoulders when they looked at her. Agnes rolled her eyes in disgust and snatched the flashlight out of Sharon's hand. She shined the light in the pile of debris and was able to faintly make out a dull reflection. She nudged a couple chunks of granite aside with her toe before bending down to pick up a tarnished brass key.

'I think I found the answer,' she said as she walked back over to the sarcophagus.

Tony moved aside so she could climb inside the tomb. She placed the key in the lock and gave it a determined twist. As if it had just been oiled, the lock popped open unhindered. She tossed the lock onto the pile of rubble and moved back as far as she could to let the boys open the trapdoor. With a reluctant groan, the door gave, letting loose the putrid, musty air it had been holding for who knows how long. Agnes got hit full force with the smell, which made her cough violently. The other three quickly covered their faces, blocking out most of the stink. Tony smiled wickedly behind his shirt, which he was using as a mask.

Once they had grown accustomed to the smell, Agnes shone the light inside. Dangling into the darkness was a scary looking rope ladder. They all eyed the ladder warily, nobody wanting to test out its stability. Tony let out a determined breath before kneeling down by the side of the opening. He gently lowered himself down in, hanging on to the edge as long as he could. Aaron and Sharon watched in unease as he disappeared into the hole while Agnes continued to shine her light inside. They relaxed only after he called up to them to come down having safely reached the bottom.

Once they were all together again, Tony sniffed the air. 'Why does it smell like oil?' he commented.

'Hey!' Agnes exclaimed. 'Maybe it's a lighting system like you see in the movies.'

'Maybe,' Tony said. 'Did anyone happen to bring a lighter?'

Sharon sighed and dug through her pack, producing a lighter. She handed it to Tony who tried it out to be sure it worked. After a tiny flame caught, they began searching for the origin of the smell. As luck would have it, a few feet away from the ladder stood a basin filled with the oil Tony had smelled. Igniting the lighter, Tony cautiously lowered it towards the liquid, quickly retracting his hand as the flame caught.

In true cinematic fashion, lines of fire spider-webbed between basins, bathing the cavern in light. What lay before them made their jaws drop in wonderment. The four found themselves in a vast cavern containing treasure of all kinds, art, as well as books. The treasures glittered alluringly in the light, tempting them to take at the least a coin as a memento. It was like being Aladdin in the Cave of Wonders. There was more wealth in that room than all of them together could have imagined seeing in their entire lives.

'This is incredible,' they all gushed, the glittering gold reflecting in their eyes.

'Try not to touch anything,' Sharon cautioned, trying to remain rational.

'Are you serious?' Tony complained. 'It's not like this place is going to be booby-trapped.'

'Do you really want to test that theory out?'

With this thought in mind, they did their best not to disturb anything as they moved from one end of the room to the other.

Aaron was maneuvering through a canyon of furniture when something caught his eye. Well it more or less caught his mind's eye. He had barely even noticed the ring, but something in his mind clicked and made him do a double take. It was resting on the arm of a plush-looking armchair. The band was fairly ordinary with no ornate decoration or gilding. The head contained a dark stone, like obsidian, in which was etched the likeness of the three-headed dog Cerberus. It was definitely strange seeing something like that here, but before he knew it, he had picked it up and slipped it onto his finger.

He was twisting it around on his finger admiring the way it looked and felt when he heard Agnes call out, 'Everyone come quick!'

He never even considered taking the ring off but hurried to catch up with the others. When he exited the maze of treasures, he found the others gazing mesmerized at something in front of them. He followed their gaze and instantly knew what had transfixed them. In front of them was another sarcophagus placed parallel with the south wall. It was mounted a few steps up, making it stand out from the rest of the treasures in the room. Unlike the previous tomb, and they all could tell this from wherever they were standing, this one actually contained a body.

The sarcophagus appeared to be made entirely of glass with silver accents artistically arranged around the box. It was mounted on top of an alabaster pedestal similar to the style of the one they had previously crawled through. The glass casing seemed to be like that of a lid, placed gently over the top of the body rather than having had to awkwardly place the body inside it.

While the discovery of this mausoleum was remarkable, the biggest surprise came once they reached the casket. The body inside the glass looked unnervingly similar to the carved figure on the previous tomb. The skin was white and appeared smooth, almost fake looking. The eyes were serenely shut and the fingers were clasped, gently covering the exposed navel. A real red blanket was draped diagonally across the lower portion of his body, exposing only his unshod feet and partial left calf. The most unsettling thing about the body was the fact that it looked fresh, as if it had only recently been laid in place.

Then they saw the wings.

Chapter 2

Tyler was gazing perplexed into his electron microscope when the lab door came crashing open, causing the already cracked wall behind it to cave in a little further. Pieces of plaster and sheetrock fragments crumbled onto the white and black tiled floor as the door bounced off it. He glanced up disconcertedly to stare at the now slouched figure of his twin brother Mark, who was clutching the satin black top of the nearest lab table struggling to catch his breath.

He rolled his eyes as he stared at his brother. These types of dramatic entrances were very common for Mark. They usually landmarked some trivial moment in his life made somehow dramatically important. For instance, last week there was some sort of video game release that he'd been impatiently waiting for. Tyler had been putting the finishing touches on his latest experiment when Mark came crashing through the doors, in the exact same fashion as he had now just done. Throughout the years, Tyler had grown accustomed to these entrances and now responded to them as if Mark had entered the room like a normal human being. If it hadn't been for this, he might have made some irreversible error in his experiment causing him to have to start over.

With these thoughts roaming around in the back of his mind, he stared impatiently at Mark, who was still working on catching his breath. After another minute or two, Mark finally raised his head and looked at him. Tyler was surprised to see Mark's face lit up with a smile he had never seen before. Normally, with his burst appearances, Mark looked like a puppy that had just received a new bone; a type of retarded happiness reserved for children or the mentally challenged. This time there was something different about his smile. He looked somewhat mischievous, as if some grand scheme of his was now coming together. In truth, it was pretty creepy.

'Well, what is it?' he prodded impatiently, abruptly breaking the crystalline silence that had formed between the two brothers. 'I have more important things to be doing right now.'

Mark's strange smile parted to say three small words, 'It's been found.'

Despite the vagueness of his statement, icy chills ran down Tyler's spine merely from the tone of Mark's voice. He sounded different. Sinister. Like a mad scientist whose creation had just come to life. Tyler stared at him, strangely intrigued, as a tiny ember of fear began to smolder in his chest.

A sudden slamming of a door somewhere along the hallway jolted him back to reality. He almost laughed out loud at the ridiculous thoughts that were running through his head. He reassured himself that while his brother was indeed acting stranger than normal, he had nothing to fear from him. Mark had always been the weaker of the two brothers and that in some sense comforted his ego for the time.

Reverting back to his former sense of suave indifference, Tyler smirked and replied, 'what are you on about? What's been found?'

Mark's grin grew wider as he stood there. Tyler

was beginning to grow impatient as the seconds ticked away. He couldn't tell if Mark was coming up with a clever story to tell him to waste his time or if what he had to say was so important that he needed to draw up so much suspense that Tyler would explode, more from anger than from excitement.

He was on the verge of disregarding this waste of his time as some attempt of Mark's to keep him from finishing his experiment when he spoke.

'They found the fallen angel!!!' he announced with so much gusto that Tyler had to wipe drops of spittle from his perfectly bronze cheek.

Tyler rolled his eyes for a second time and shook his head, trying not to display his immense irritation at the incomprehensible drivel he was forcing himself to listen to.

'Are you serious?' he responded, adding as much sarcasm as he could muster. 'You interrupted my research to tell me this?'

Mark couldn't help but look somewhat crestfallen as his brother berated him. In his defense, Mark countered him saying, 'This finding is just as important as your tedious research,' adding just as much sarcasm to the word "tedious" as Tyler had just given him. Mark knew he was striking a nerve as he watched his brother's debonair gaze instantly flare into an inferno of anger.

'Just as important as my tedious research?' Tyler spit, each word dripping like ice above a flame. 'How could the supposed finding of a "fallen angel" be as important as my "tedious" research?' he questioned, daring Mark to contradict the value of his research again.

'Because it proves so many things,' Mark spat back angrily. 'For one, such a finding could help theologians prove the existence of God. Second, in the scientific world, anthropological scientists can more accurately timeline mans existence, evolutionists can totally be disproved and genetic engineers have an entirely new specimen to pick apart. It is simply the greatest find of this age.'

Tyler's eyes burned holes in Mark's skull the longer he spoke. He hated to admit it, but the finding of this "being" was indeed a major find. But how important could this thing really be? The more he thought about the angel being overrated, the less irritated it made him.

'Well how can anyone be so sure that this is actually a fallen angel?' Tyler asked, his anger cooling while an unconscious spark of interest began to spring to life.

'Are you serious?!' Mark answered. 'You haven't seen it yet have you?' It was as if someone had just told him they had never heard of peanut butter.

Tyler raised his eyebrows in response, shrugging his shoulders indifferently. 'Should I have?' he asked.

Mark began laughing hysterically. He just could not believe what he was hearing.

'I can't believe you're serious,' Mark said between bouts of laughter. 'They've had the body in the university genetics research lab for the past two weeks.'

Considering that was where he was supposed to be this whole time, it made perfect sense to him why he hadn't seen it yet. He had been coming to this particular lab because it afforded him the peace and space he required to concentrate.

Tyler rolled his eyes. 'Well I still don't see how people can believe that this creature is a fallen angel.'

Mark's face reddened as he prepared to burst into another bout of laughter. Before he could open his mouth, Tyler pointed at him, an overly stern expression on his face, and crossly said, 'don't laugh. It's getting really old and I'm not in the mood. Just tell me.'

Suddenly Mark's countenance changed. His previously jovial character morphed into one of mischief and secrecy.

'You remember the legend grandpa used to tell us when we were younger?' he asked, staring blankly in Tyler's direction, as if trying to remember it himself.

'Vaguely,' Tyler replied, with a quick wave of his hand.

'Well if you can remember, the legend speaks of a fallen angel, exiled from the heavens and sentenced to keep watch over mankind. Upon being sent to earth, he was able to retain all his gifts and powers but one: his gift of immortality. But even without this gift, he was still able to live a really long time.'

Tyler couldn't help but look at his brother with a skeptical eye. Mark began pacing the floor excitedly as he continued.

'The legend states that after he died, his body was kept secret deep within the catacombs of the Vatican. Little by little, word began to leak about the possession of the angel. In order to protect their secret, the church moved the sarcophagus to England around the end of the 13th century. More specifically, Westminster Abbey. Although it remained safe there for the next 300 years or so, rumours began to spread up from Rome like wildfire. Coincidently, it just so happened to be around the same time the first pilgrims were leaving to the Americas.'

Tyler couldn't believe what he was hearing. It sounded too incredible to be real. An angel being hidden by the Catholic Church and then transferred across continents? Could it really be possible? Mark had stopped pacing and was staring blankly at the wall, still talking.

'This could not have been a more perfect opportunity to quell the rumours of the angel and at the same time protect it from anyone who would try to steal it. At their first chance, the Bishops and Priests at Westminster packaged the sarcophagus into a crate and shipped it over here along with one Priest in charge of its arrival and safekeeping.'

'Ok. Well that's very interesting and all, but why is the angel so important? I mean why the big fuss over hiding the body and keeping it a secret?' Tyler asked, impatient and excited at the same time.

'I'm getting to it,' Mark replied, without missing a beat. 'Once in America, the Priest had the crate loaded up and driven to a secluded part somewhere in the northwestern part of New England, where it was buried deep in the earth and a humble church built over the top of it. As luck would have it, a handful of the new immigrants to this country had heard rumour of the transport. Before long, those who believed the rumours tracked the Priest to his church. They frantically searched the building, but found nothing. In anger, they killed the Priest and burned the church to ground, forever destroying any hope for future generations to find the angel. Or so they thought.'

Mark paused for a moment to catch his breath before continuing. 'Now, to answer your question about why the church was trying to hide the angel, it's very simple really and rather disturbing. The legend behind the angel is that he will one day resurrect and his resurrection will usher in the end of the world. There is more of the legend, but the last part is missing.'

Tyler heard everything Mark was saying, but didn't want to believe it. It all seemed too fantastical to believe. If what Mark was saying was true, then it really would be the greatest scientific and archeological find of this century. The unearthing of a figure of multi-continental legend would most surely trump any other find for many centuries to come. While this was a dreadful thought, Tyler couldn't help but believe that while this might pose a problem later, right now it was no bother. He still hadn't even finished his experiment.

'How much longer is it going to be here?' he asked. Despite being a rival for scientific attention, he didn't want to miss such a valuable opportunity.

'Well, they're still performing tests so I'm assuming it'll be here for quite a while,' Mark replied, his eyes still aglow with mystery.

Tyler's eyes widened momentarily as he suddenly realized what was happening. Somehow he'd let himself be drawn in to the seemingly fantastical world of myth, magic and legend that Mark surrounded himself in. He paused for a second to regain his composure and took a deep breath. Smoothing out his pristine lab coat, he looked back at Mark, his cool, debonair manner once again smothering the embers of something other than rationality.

With an air of disregard, he coolly said, 'Thank you for informing me about the body. Once I get an opportunity, I'll head over to the lab to check it out. Now, if you'll excuse me, I need to clean up my things as I need to leave.'

He turned his back on his brother and began returning the Bunsen burner, the glass pipettes, the selection of chemicals he'd been using, and the other odd pieces of equipment to their respective places. When he finished with that, he grabbed the sprayer with all-purpose spray, some paper towels and began wiping down his work area. As he cleaned and put things away, he didn't need to turn around to know whether Mark was still there or not. In his mind he could see him glaring at him with the icy, dejected stare he always gave him whenever he reacted this way to his excitement.

It never ceased to amaze him that he treated his brother so cruelly. Although they were twins, they could not have been any more different. Tyler had always been the more rational of the two, his hobbies and interests being geared towards those things with reasonable explanations. Mark on the other hand found his interests among the realms of magic and mysticism. If it had anything to do with the worlds of fantasy and illusion, you could bet he had heard of it and liked it.

It wasn't only their hobbies and interests that separated the two boys. In appearance and mannerisms they were worlds apart. Tyler, the first-born, had always been the more popular of the two. He was your all-American boy with sandy-blond hair, deep blue eyes and a fair complexion. He had played football and baseball in high school as well as been part of the science and chemistry clubs. He excelled at most anything he did and was highly liked by all, especially the girls. He never had any problems getting dates to any of the school dances or social events. It was as if he had an endless supply of women at his disposal.

Where Tyler seemed all-American, Mark fit in perfectly with the gothic/emo scene. He had jet-black hair, emerald green eyes as well as a fair complexion. Despite his deeply tanned skin, the darkness of his hair always seemed to make it seem whiter than anything natural. Sports had never really appealed to him as well as most things involving large crowds. He tended to be more of a loner, which directly resulted in his being shunned by the majority of the community. Despite this, he was the smarter of the two brothers. His main problem lay in the execution of his knowledge. Whatever he set his mind to he excelled at, which was whatever he liked, including at school. If he didn't like the subject or whatnot, he wouldn't do it. It was a surprise to most people that he had even graduated from high school.

As one could suspect, the appearance of sibling rivalry was something of a given. Not that Tyler had much to worry about. He had always been the good child whereas Mark had always been that of a rebel. Not that Tyler was a perfect child either. He just didn't give his parents as much trouble as Mark did. Mark just couldn't seem to pick good friends. Most of the friends he had during high school were now either in jail, dead or in the military.

Tyler shook his head in exasperation as he

thought for the millionth time over the multiple differences he and his brother shared. He turned to toss the dirty towels into the bin and noticed he was alone. "Strange," he thought. Normally, Mark's exits were just as pronounced as his entrances. He shrugged his shoulders indifferently and quickly made the finishing touches on his cleaning before grabbing his bag and jacket from the coat rack by the door. He turned off the lights, locked the door and listened for the gentle click signifying it was securely shut.

As he walked down the overly illuminated white hallway towards the exit, he kept thinking about his relationship with his brother. It wasn't as if they hated each other. It was just that they had never had the twin bond most people talk about. There was no special link connecting the two. It was as if they were mere siblings, and barely even that. There had always been resentment of each other from both sides. Mark resented Tyler for being the favourite and more popular of the two. Everyone noticed him and had always referred to Mark as "Tyler's little brother."

A faint smirk appeared on Tyler's lips as he thought about that. It wasn't a cruel smile, just one that showed remembrance of a significant event. Mark hated being referred to as his little brother. Minutes separated the two by birth, but in those minutes a wall had been built between them that had gotten increasingly stronger and thicker throughout their 22 years of life. Mark had always been considered second rate compared to Tyler despite his many achievements. "It's no wonder he rebelled," he thought.

He exited the chemistry building and stepped into the dim brightness of the already setting sun. He could hardly believe it was barely five pm and already getting dark. He descended the steps in front of the entrance and took an immediate left, cutting across the Lehmann plaza in the middle of the University campus.

Tyler resented Mark because he tried to be so different. At least to him it seemed that Mark was trying to be different from him. "Maybe it wasn't that either," he pondered. Maybe he resented him because he was different. Having a brother was supposed to be awesome. He was supposed to be your best friend, your partner in crime. Somehow, Tyler had gotten the raw end of the deal. Having a brother had been more trouble than it sometimes seemed to be worth.

He stopped under the shade of a towering oak tree to readjust the books in his bag that had become uncomfortably uneven. He wiped the sweat from his forehead and gazed into the sky. It had been a particularly beautiful day with no clouds, but even with the sun setting, the heat could still be felt. He'd rather deal with the constant heat any day than the stress of having a brother.

Even with them both being at the same university, Tyler still felt the cold hand of resentment. He'd been the first to be accepted to St. Matthew's University. Although mostly unheard of, it was in fact the top school for genetic research in the country. Since this was what he was studying, it seemed like the ideal place to go. He was about to begin his second semester when guess who came knocking on his door? Mark. Not exactly what he'd been expecting. Come to find, Mark had followed him there for some mysterious unknown reason, which kind of creeped him out. Mark had been accepted with relative ease and even though he got good grades, he seemed to have kept the same ideals he'd had in high school. He rarely went to class, rarely worked, but still somehow managed to keep up and stay afloat. On top of it, Tyler felt like he was trying to prove something with his antics.

He shouldered his bag and tried to focus on something else. Thinking about Mark only depressed him. He had tried to have a close relationship with his brother, but those times were long past. Tyler just wished that something would happen to change their current situation. Anything would be better than this constant battle between them.

A little ways past the oak tree, Tyler entered a parking garage on the northwest side of the campus. He walked through it and emerged before a vast black sea of asphalt that at this time of evening was practically vacant. He was on his way to pick up Helen from soccer practice. It was a daily ritual that he never failed to fulfill. She was the main ray of sunshine that could brighten up any gloomy day of his life and today her positivity was very much needed.

He quickly crossed the lot and reached a short chain link fence over which he jumped with relative ease. He walked along the track towards the girl's soccer team, which was practicing on the north end of the field. As he neared them, he quickly spotted the "47" on the back of a midsized, light-brown haired beauty.

Helen was the single best part of Tyler's life. He sat in the stands and stared at her, thinking how genuinely lucky he was. Now Helen and Tyler were also very different, but somehow their differences had brought them together. While he was so precise in everything he did, she was not. In some senses, she was more similar to Mark in that she was hardly rational at times. With her it was refreshing. Everything didn't feel like a competition. He could be himself and she herself. Neither of them needed to be any different because when it came down to it, what they had was enough. He loved her because she fulfilled a part of him that he couldn't.

Unlike the two brothers, Helen had come to the university on a soccer scholarship. And like lots of sports figures, she had no real idea what she wanted to do with the rest of her life. She had always excelled at soccer and had no other desire than to play professionally. She had no plan B in case she never made it. This was completely unlike Tyler, who had the next ten years of his life planned out to a T and got incredibly flustered whenever something happened that he hadn't factored in. Helen could never live like that. She was spontaneous and reckless, living life on the edge of her seat. Whenever an opportunity to explore, travel or be crazy came up, she took it. Her personal philosophy was to live each day to the fullest and that's exactly what she did.

While Tyler sat on the cold metal seat in the stands thinking about her, he watched as she checked her pink banded watch, a gift from him, and then began looking around. When her eyes finally landed on him, an enormous smile split her face. She jogged over to where he was sitting as he exited the stands and walked to the fence that separated the track from the inner field. Once they reached each other, she leaned over the fence and planted a large kiss on his slightly startled face.

'Someone seems glad to see me,' he teased, brushing a stray hair from in front of her sky blue eyes. Her eyes were the one thing that made him catch his breath every time he saw her. They were the type of color begging for a double take in order to fully appreciate their brilliance.

'Well I was beginning to miss you since you're late,' she chided, winking at him with one of her startlingly beautiful eyes.

Tyler rolled his eyes and began to apologize. 'Sorry about that. Mark came to me with something somewhat relevant today and I lost track of time.'

Helen smiled and eyed him cautiously. 'You were interested in something he had to say? Are you feeling ok? Are you coming down with something?' she mocked, jokingly pressing her warm, sweaty, grass smelling hand against his cool, slightly moist forehead.

'Very funny,' he laughed, swatting her hand away. 'It's just that he was telling me about the "newest member" to the genetics department.'

'Oh really now? It must've been very interesting for you to have kept me waiting here,' she jibbed, smiling to show she was teasing him again.

Tyler just smiled at her, shaking his head in response.

'Ok, ok I'll stop,' she said, reaching her arms around him, pulling him into her embrace. 'I'm just glad to hear you took an interest in something he had to say.'

'Well for the most part,' he offhandedly commented, groaning inwardly after he said it. Now he'd have to do some explaining.

Helen pulled away from him to look him in the eyes, a puzzled expression on her face. 'What do you mean "for the most part"?' she questioned.

Tyler sighed and took a deep breath. 'Well you know how he can get when he gets really excited. The way he was going on about this "fallen angel" nonsense, you would have thought someone had found a dragon or even an alien!' he ranted.

'Fallen angel? As in the legend of Arakiel?' she asked, more puzzled than before.

Tyler looked at her in sincere surprise. He didn't like to think critically of Helen, but she was the last person he would have expected to know about such things.

Exasperated, he cried out, 'How is it that everyone knows so much about this legend except me?!'

Helen gave him a defiant stare, somehow sensing his true thoughts.

'Come on,' she said. 'My parents happen to be ministers. Despite the fact the legend comes from the Catholic Church, it's popular in this region because it's here that the sarcophagus of the angel is believed to have been buried. My parents have loads of literature on this region and each book is riddled with references to the legend, including a map of where the old church was rumoured to have been located.'

Tyler was startled by her knowledge of the angel. He sheepishly looked at the ground as he tried to come up with something to say. He knew he was wrong to have judged her and was even more embarrassed that she had known his real thoughts. He lifted his head to apologize for casting such misplaced judgment when he heard her ask the question he knew he was going to have to face.

'You got him all worked up and excited and thinking you were actually interested in what he had to say didn't you? Then you brushed it off when you realized you were becoming interesting in the same thing as your brother. That's what happened right?'

They seemed like innocent enough questions, but he knew she would see through anything other than the truth.

'I was interested, but it just seemed too fantastic to be real,' Tyler tried to reason. He would have rather been placed on the rack or even in an iron maiden than endure the agonizing glare he was now receiving.

Helen shook her head in disgust. 'Why can't you just for once actually care about what he says? Stop living so rationally and try to remember what it was like to have an imagination. Try being a real brother for once instead of only caring about how you view the world. You aren't the only person in it or can you even see that?'

He tried to come back with some response to save his dignity, but nothing came. She was right. It had been a very long time since he really cared about what his brother said. It wasn't his world so he had never put much concern to what it might possibly hold for Mark. He could try and reason that his brother did the same to him, but Mark actually talked to him about stuff, even if it was stuff that he didn't care about.

When he looked back up, Helen was halfway back to the team.

'Helen!' he called after her, but she didn't turn around. 'Helen c'mon. Come back.'

He knew it was pointless to try and reason with her. One thing that scared him about her was her temper. When she got angry, it was best to just leave her be and let her calm down. It was a hard lesson he'd had to learn a couple times. Disheartened, he turned around and slowly walked back down the track. Once again he felt as alone as his car in the empty parking lot. This wasn't the first time they'd had this argument. It was becoming a regular occurrence now. Every time Mark came in with news, like today, which seemed to happen more often recently, Tyler and Helen fought. He hated that they fought, but why couldn't she see how difficult it was for him. He wanted to try, but something inside him just couldn't do it.

In anger, Tyler kicked a stone that was in his way. Considering the day he'd been having, it should have seemed clear that nothing good was going to come from anything he did. Being a rather large stone, instead of bouncing a few feet and stopping, it shot across the asphalt and bounced right into the side of his car, which was only about 20 feet away.

'Dammit!' he shouted, now angry with himself. He jogged the remainder of the way to survey the damage. Thankfully, no real harm had been done.

He jerked the keys out of his pocket and unlocked his door. He yanked the door open, chucked his bag inside, climbed in and slammed the door shut. Now what was he going to do? Mark was angry with him, and now Helen was as well. He would have liked to call either one of his parents, but he knew he would hear the exact same thing everyone else was telling him.

Frustrated, he started the car, revved the engine and sped towards the exit. The only place that seemed to calm his spirit whenever he got into one of these moods was St. Stephen's Cathedral on Hummock's Hill. It overlooked the town and offered a spectacular view of the area. Not to mention it was the home of one of Tyler's most unexpected friends, Father Michael. Exiting the lot, he turned right onto the one-way street surrounding the University. In the final remnants of the setting sun, Tyler began the five-mile stretch to his destination.

Chapter 3

Father Michael waved goodbye as the last of the remaining stragglers started their cars and drove out of the lot. He let out a sigh of exhaustion and leaned up against the solid doors of the church. While the service was no more stressful than any of his others, he was still somehow overwhelmingly tired. Part of it had to do with dealing with the emotional baggage of one of his dearest friends, but the rest he claimed had to do with the upkeep of the cathedral and the mental strain of keeping its secrets.

The towering cathedral of St. Stephen's had received itself an enigmatic place in the history of Rochester, New Hampshire. Being a nearly two-century old cathedral idyllically placed on a hill outside the city, one would never suppose it to have a sketchy history. It was a well-known fact that St. Stephen's was not the original cathedral built when the city was first founded in 1720. The original cathedral, also situated outside the once smaller city, had dwelled in relative peace until one night when the citizens were woken by the sounds of glass breaking and the acrid smell of smoke. To their horror, the cathedral was engulfed in flames and there was nothing anyone could do to save it.

A month after the destruction of the cathedral,

the leaders of the town decreed that the ruins of the cathedral were to be removed in hopes that the escalating gossip and rumours would be dispelled and the construction of a new cathedral could begin. On the day they were to begin cleaning up, they were shocked to find the lot barren, as if nothing had ever been there. Word also arrived that same afternoon that the Church would be sending people to construct a new cathedral.

Where the original cathedral had been located just outside the city boundary, the new cathedral was to be rebuilt further away on Hummock's Hill to stand as a reminder that a house of God could never be destroyed. It was supposed to stand as a symbol of perseverance and strength. While it would seem as such, the people were more perplexed with how long it had taken to build the new house of worship. Reconstruction was not to begin until five years after the ashes of the previous cathedral had cooled and been swept away.

As the years slowly passed, the citizens of Rochester patiently waited for construction to begin. Most had given up hope that it would ever be rebuilt. Then one silent morning in the spring of 1805, hammering could be heard coming from Hummock's Hill just as the sun began to peek up above the horizon. By midsummer, a beautiful new cathedral stood proudly on the hill. Its presence once again struck hope within the hearts of its worshipers.

"What an incredible building," Father Michael reflected as he pressed his hand thoughtfully against the weathered stone. His home was truly a remarkable edifice. Whenever he got thinking about the place, it always amazed him how he could have been so lucky to end up working in such a unique location.

Before Father Michael had come there, only four priests had occupied St. Stephen's. Each man was there for a total of fifty years before, as if on some "life" timer, they mysteriously died. Then, as if the deaths were expected, a new priest would arrive early the following morning, ready to take over. That wasn't the only strange thing. Despite each priest coming from a different country, each spoke the same five languages, was gifted in music and was fairly young and fit.

Father Michael had begun his service three years ago after the untimely death of the previous priest, Father Desmond, a stern figure who had originated from a tiny mountain village in the eastern regions of France. The people in his ministry were quite unsure of what to make of Father Michael at the beginning. For starters he was completely different from Father Desmond. The difference was like night and day. Father Desmond was a figure of authority and composure. He had an air of importance while at the same time maintaining some semblance of humility. No one really knew Father Desmond. From what the younger generation had been told, he had always been like this. So when the day came that he died, no one knew quite how to react. Some were glad while others just felt nothing. He had never made a difference in the lives of his parishioners for them to really feel a void with him gone.

Father Michael was his exact opposite. During his first service he made it quite clear he intended on visiting and getting to know each one of the members. Throughout his 36 years of life, he had developed an innate ability to connect with people of any age or background. This ability to bond with a person was unlike any other priest they had ever met. Not only was he able to make himself more emotionally accessible to people, but he made going to church easier. People felt welcome and special. It was for this exact reason that Tyler was on his way to St. Stephen's.

It had been by freak chance that Tyler and the priest had met. Since Tyler wasn't Catholic, he had never attended a sermon by him. In fact, other than admiration for the beautiful building, he knew nothing of the history of the cathedral or its priests. Likewise, Father Michael knew nothing of Tyler. He knew each one of his parishioners and their families, but outside of them he knew relatively few.

It was during the spring semester of Tyler's second year that these two strangers would meet. Since St. Matthew's University was a Catholic school, a large variety of religion classes were offered. Those in their first and second years of school were required to take at least one religion class per semester. Tyler ended up registering later than he should have and got stuck in a Medieval Bible course.

The fourth week into the semester, an announcement was made that a guest lecturer would be coming to teach the class for the entire following week. The professor, Dr. Lechner, was a member of Father Michael's congregation and was pleased to discover that their new priest was quite the scholar, having Masters Degrees in both Medieval History and Theology. It was for this reason that he had invited the priest to lecture.

Something about the man intrigued Tyler. He had an air of humility despite his massive amount of knowledge. Plus his way of understanding ancient religious text was pure 21st century thinking. That alone made Tyler consider becoming Catholic just to attend his sermons. This impression led to the two having a couple very in-depth and personal discussions. Once Father Michael's guest lecture week came to an end, he made a general invitation to the class to come visit him and the cathedral at any time. He reiterated this invitation to Tyler personally as they said their goodbyes after class. Tyler took his invitation seriously and from then on visited him every week or so.

For Tyler, St. Stephen's was a place of peace and an asylum from the chaos and stress of his life. Throughout the last couple semesters, he had come to visit the place more frequently with each passing week. It almost seemed as if he had moved in he was there so much. The visits never bothered Father Michael because with each visit their relationship had grown. It was now at the point that Father Michael viewed Tyler more of a younger brother than merely a friend.

It was no surprise to him to see headlights hurriedly winding along the hillside towards the cathedral. 'Uffa!' Father Michael thought. "Here comes more stress." He grimacing slightly at what could possibly be bothering Tyler this time. Not that he disliked spending time with him. On the contrary. It was just that Tyler had been coming over around 6 p.m. every day for the last week or two to vent. It begins to take its toll after a while.

He shook his head gently, letting his shoulder length chocolate brown hair sway back and forth from the momentum. He enjoyed accompanying his members outside, as he was able to get some fresh air and bask in the dimming light of the setting sun. Now, as he watched the headlights rapidly approaching, he sighed and walked back inside to prepare some tea for his guest.

The pot of water had barely been put on the gas stove when he heard the faint echo of agitated footsteps descending the cold granite stones that led to his quarters. He quickly went to the tiny cupboard next to the stove and pulled two chipped floral saucers and teacups that had been donated to the ministry some 30 years before. He had just set them on the table when he faintly heard a timid knock coming from the slightly ajar thick oak door.

'Come on in Tyler,' Father Michael called out, hurrying even faster to finish the preparations.

If Tyler had wondered if things could get worse, he wouldn't have been surprised to find out they would. Nothing could have been more embarrassing for him at that moment than the oak door. Even with it being partly open, it still posed a burden. He had to use all his force just to get it to scrape along the floor obstinately. On top of it, the rusty hinges mocked his struggle.

He had barely gotten the door open wide enough for him to squeeze through when Father Michael offered some helpful, albeit late, advice. Without even looking up from his preparations, he called out to him saying, 'If you push it firmly and quickly there won't be as much of a squeak.'

Embarrassed by all the noise he was making, Tyler gripped the handle and proceeded to swiftly and firmly close the door. Instead of a gentle click of the door shutting, he miscalculated the distance and ended up slamming the door shut. The walls and ceiling groaned in disapproval. He closed his eyes and took a deep breath. It was apparent from the expression of disgust on his face that he was even more embarrassed than he had been trying to open the door. Letting out his breath slowly, Tyler rolled his eyes and began cursing himself for the racket he was causing. He maneuvered slowly around objects making his way towards the middle of the room.

Father Michael's basement quarters were fairly roomy unlike the usual housing situations for priests. Along the front wall ran a bookcase crammed with books of all sizes and thicknesses. It was made up of two wide units with two thinner units between them. Each section had six shelves and each shelf was labeled. Most of the shelves housed religious books, but the odd shelf was home to a great deal of mystery novels, historical books, classics and even fantasy series. Each shelf was in meticulous order as well. The books were arranged according to size, author and then title.

Most of the rest of the apartment was laid out like any normal studio room. The division for the living room and bedroom was mostly nonexistent while the workout area and kitchen were designated by their floor differences. In between the workout and the sleeping area was a protrusion from the wall. This was his bathroom.

It was very uncommon for a priest to have a workout area, but Father Michael had specially requested these items. Despite his busy life as a priest, keeping physically fit was immensely important to him. In the corner hung a punching bag while a bench, free-weights and a medicine ball lay strategically placed in the small space. Huddled by the wall were also a treadmill and an elliptical machine. Unknown to the community, in his younger days, Father Michael had been quite the fighter. He had studied various forms of martial arts and excelled quite naturally at kickboxing.

Along the left hand wall stood piles and piles of miscellaneous church paraphernalia, boxes of information pamphlets for tourists as well as boxes of hymnals and other church material. A bunch of other boxes were piled into some extra pews that had also been stored in the basement in case of future use. Father Michael had been meaning to sort this gigantic pile of garbage, but had just not gotten around to it yet.

Tyler reached the table in the kitchen and immediately sunk down into one of the four metal folding chairs surrounding it, resting his head on the solid wood with a nearly audible thud. Father Michael let out his breath slowly and turned his lips into a small knowing smile as he removed the kettle from the stove and walked over to the table. It was no surprise to see Tyler like this. It had been the same type of entrance every day for the past week. Reaching the table, he poured tea into the two cups, set the kettle down on a well-worn, knitted yellow potholder and sat down.

'What happened today?' he asked as he added two lumps of cubed sugar to his tea from the bowl that sat in between them.

Tyler let out his breath dramatically and raised his head. His eyes had a look of such unrest that worried Father Michael. He could see that things had worsened since the last visit.

'I just can't do it anymore,' Tyler exclaimed. 'It seems that no matter what I do it's never good enough.'

Father Michael understood Tyler's agitation all too well. He needed to calm him down if he expected to be any help. Reaching across the table, Father Michael pushed the container of cubed sugar towards him.

'Season your tea and just take a few minutes to relax. We have as much time as you need,' he said, smiling warmly at Tyler.

Tyler rubbed his face with his hands before dropping two cubes of sugar in his drink. As he stirred the tea with the small spoon Father Michael provided for him, he watched the granules of sugar swirl around in an almost hypnotic manner. Somehow the revolving was putting his anxious mind at ease.

Once Father Michael noticed Tyler's face relax, he said, 'Once you're ready, slowly tell me what happened.'

Tyler took a sip of his tea, took a deep breath and let it out gradually before beginning.

'It's the same story like every other time. Mark is driving me absolutely insane and I swear I'm beginning to think he's doing it on purpose. On top of it, Helen is getting on my case about it and that's really starting to get old. It's like she doesn't understand how difficult it is for me to understand him. We're nothing alike and never have been. How can she expect me to just spontaneously disregard my thoughts to understand him? It doesn't work like that. It's not that I don't want to it's just that there's something in me that doesn't care about the things that interest Mark. Then there's school and my upcoming exams plus my experiment is so close to success that this added stress is making it hard to concentrate. I'm about ready to explode!'

As Tyler ranted on about his day and the imposed stress from things important to him, and yes Mark was important to Tyler whether he was willing to admit it or not, Father Michael tried his best to pay complete attention to him. Truth was, Tyler's stress was starting to affect him as well. It's a common fact that those things you surround yourself with directly affect you. Since Tyler had been around so much with his ever-mounting stress, it had begun to weigh heavily on Father Michael as well. Despite his days consisting of seemingly monotonous but needed activities, such as dusting relics or visiting members of his congregation, he found his thoughts dwelt mainly on Tyler and his problems rather then the things he needed to be thinking about. Father Michael pondered silently about why Tyler's problems affected him so much. He was so deep in his thoughts that he barely registered Tyler say something offhandedly. It instantly brought him out of his contemplative stupor.

'...And then there's this thing about the discovery of a supposed "fallen angel" that everyone but me seems to know about. What could possibly lead people to think this character is even real?'

'What did you just say?' Father Michael asked, quite surprised. This was the first time he had heard anyone from this region mention the old legend. What made it even stranger was it was a twin talking about it. Could Tyler really be talking about what he thought he was? Father Michael was more concerned that he was only hearing about this discovery for the first time. He should have been informed about it being found ages ago. Shouldn't he have? Either way, he had only heard him distractedly so he couldn't be sure he was referring to the Legend.

'What did you just say?' he asked again, a bit more subdued.

'About what?'

'About the fallen angel. What do you know about it?'

'Me? Nothing really. It's just everyone else like

Mark and Helen seem to know a lot about it and it's kinda annoying. How do they both know all this stuff about it and I know nothing? Why do you want to know?'

'No reason. It's just interesting to hear about it from a younger generation, considering it's an ancient legend that most people around here seem to have already forgotten about.'

Of course that wasn't exactly true. It was still very much present, primarily spoken about during tours. Hearing about it now was very significant and he really wanted and needed to know what was going on. Even though he liked and trusted Tyler, he knew he couldn't tell him his concerns without causing him to worry and maybe even become suspicious. He was going to have to shrewdly get the information from him.

'Well what's it about then?' Tyler inquired leaning forward, resting his arms on the table. 'Mark told me some things, but knowing him, he probably embellished it in some areas.'

'What exactly did he tell you, so I know what is true and what he embellished?'

Tyler looked down at his tea and scoffed. 'He was acting pretty crazy, but what I got from it was that an angel was exiled from heaven and cast down to earth. Nothing much changed except he lost his ability to live forever. When he finally died, his body was kept hidden at the Vatican before being transported to England and then eventually here to America. Once it got here it disappeared.'

'Is that all he told you?'

'More or less. The last thing he said was that the resurrection of the angel would bring about the end of the world. Is that true?'

Father Michael stared at him thoughtfully for a moment before standing up and motioning for Tyler to follow him. He stopped at the giant bookcase at the front of the room. After searching for a few seconds, Father Michael pulled a rather large, ancient looking leather bound book from the second shelf of the first bookcase marked 'Religious Mythology.' From the look of the partially cracked leather and the thick layer of dust that lay upon the top of the book, Tyler could tell it hadn't been opened or touched in a very long time.

Holding the book away from himself and Tyler, Father Michael roughly blew as much dust off the top as he could. The remainder he wiped off with the long sleeve of his robe. Once it was as dust free as he could get it, he handed the book to Tyler. Tyler was confused at why he was giving the book to him, but instinctively reached out and took it. For as large as it was, it was surprisingly not that heavy.

'What is this?' he asked, turning the book over in his hands, finding the cover void of any indication of content.

'In this book you will find as much information about the Legend of the Fallen Angel as there is available,' Father Michael answered. 'I would go into some detail about it with you, but regretfully I just remembered I have an evening mass to attend to and my time is actually rather limited tonight. Keep it as long as you need as I already know everything the book contains.'

'Ok. Thanks.' Tyler replied, sticking the book under his arm. 'Well then I won't keep you any longer. Thanks for the tea and for listening to me.'

'It's no problem. You know I'm here for you whenever you need.' A promise he was forcing himself not to regret.

After Tyler grabbed his bag, Father Michael accompanied him from his quarters, up the stairs and out into the parking lot. His face gradually changed from his usually jovial smile to a look of intense concern as they walked.

'What is it?' Tyler asked once they reached his

jeep, somehow knowing what he was going to tell him.

'Well, I know you've been told that you should try to understand your brother and be nicer to him, and I agree that you should try it. But I just had a thought, maybe you actually shouldn't try.'

'What do you mean I shouldn't try? That's what's gotten me in this mess in the first place.'

Father Michael knew it was risky meddling with things he was uncertain about. But if he was right, this rivalry was going to be needed, although not the anger and frustration.

'What I meant was don't try to resolve your problems with Mark right this second. You have so much weighing on you at the moment that you need to focus on one thing at a time. Take small steps. You don't need to accept everything about him in one sweep. Try just listening and go from there.'

'Ok. I'll try," Tyler said skeptically. "Well I'll get going now.'

'Alright. Have a good night.'

'Yeah you too.'

Father Michael stood gazing into the night until Tyler's taillights disappeared into the densely wooded hillside. Getting the information from him had been easier than he had expected. With no questions having been asked, he knew he was in the clear. "I just hope he can get this issue resolved," he thought as he turned and entered the cathedral. "It would be a real shame for him to crumble apart right now when he is so close." Taking one final look into the darkness, Father Michael disappeared back into the cathedral.

Chapter 4

It was almost nine o'clock by the time Tyler reached his apartment. Rather than going straight home, as he was prone to do, he drove around in the countryside. It had been too dark to enjoy the scenery, but something about being away from civilization, being close to nature and the stars, had a strange ability of putting his mind at ease. It helped him put complex situations in better perspective.

Rather than focusing on the current predicament with his brother, the majority of his thoughts surrounded the mysterious leather bound book, which sat in the passenger seat. There was something foreboding yet oddly familiar about the book. The rational part of him knew that there could be no possible way the book could seem familiar. This was the first time his eyes had ever laid sight upon its fragile pages. Then there was the other part of him, the part he was constantly attempting to squelch, telling him this mysterious book had been waiting for him. The longer he drove, the stronger this hidden irrational side fought to be heard. By the time he reached home, there could be no denying it, this book was meant to be sitting in his hands at this moment. He just didn't understand why.

As he got out of his car, he reached over and

grabbed the tome. He was so absorbed in his thoughts that the sudden vibration in his pocket nearly caused him to jump out of his skin. In his fright, he fumbled with the book for a few seconds trying to get a better grip but was unsuccessful. He could only watch in panic as the book slipped from his grasp and crashed open-faced on the pavement.

'No, no, no,' he cried out, quickly kneeling down. He gingerly pulled up on the spine and was relieved to find that none of the pages had broken loose. He brought it up to his chest, holding it securely with both arms. Just before it reached his chest, his heart nearly stopped for a second time when he heard something metallic clatter at his feet. As terrifying as this sound seemed, the metallic sound confused him. What kind of object had been hidden within the book's pages and why was it there?

He stooped down once more and reached out to pick up whatever had fallen to the pavement. Right next to his shoe was a strange medallion. He grasped it by the thin chain from which it hung and held it up to the light. It was a peculiar little ornament, unlike anything Tyler had ever seen. The metal was slightly tarnished and had the colour of gold. On one side of the medallion was an engraving of a strange looking bird. It looked like a cross between a dragon and possibly an eagle, or maybe a phoenix. Circled around the creature were words written in what he could tell was Latin. He had seen enough of the language from his religion classes to be able to recognize it when he saw it. He just didn't know what it meant. The other side of the medallion was blank except for a small indentation in the middle. With no way to know what the medallion was for, he wrapped it in his hand and went inside.

The lights were out when he walked in the door, which meant that Mark had not yet come home from wherever it was he went after school. It was possible he was working, but where was a question Tyler couldn't answer. Navigating his way through the dark, he made his way from the front door to his bedroom and turned on the light.

His room was a good size smaller than Father Michael's. It contained a single sized bed, a cheap entertainment center with a 30-inch television - both donated by his parents - an antique oak dresser, a small bookcase and a ragged looking desk. Everything in his room was meticulously organized. Much like the priest, Tyler's books were arranged alphabetically according to size, author then title. There were no dirty clothes lying on the floor and no pen, pencil, piece of paper or notebook was out of line on his desk. Ironically, this was probably the only area where the two brothers were alike. Both were complete neat freaks. Nothing in the house was dirty and if it was, it got promptly sanitized.

He hung his backpack on the hook on the backside of his door and set the old book on the desk. Before sitting down to examine it, he completed his usual ritual upon returning home. He hung up his jacket and changed into more comfortable clothes, depositing the worn garments into the dirty clothes hamper on the left side of his closet. As soon as he was done, he sat down at the desk. He unwrapped the chain from his hand and placed it next to the book. He hoped, besides explaining the whole legend, that the book could explain what the medallion was for.

He reached out to open the book when his pocket vibrated for a second time. Because of the near disaster with the book, he had completely forgotten about the text. He pulled his phone and smiled knowingly when he saw whom it was from. '**Hey Baby. Sorry about getting angry with you earlier. I know you're trying. Forgiven? Love you.**' There was no way he could stay angry with Helen. Especially after seeing the picture message she sent him. 'It's ok. I'm sorry for making you angry. Am I forgiven? Love you too. And thanks for pic naughty girl ;)' he replied. He set the phone down but it vibrated just as he pulled his hand away. 'lol. You're welcome and of course silly boy. Time for bed. See you in the morning. Night.' He sighed gratefully, happy that at least things were patched up between them. Now he was able to put the phone down and focus on the book.

At first he was a bit cautious about touching it, thinking that it might break by the slightest twitch of his hand. Especially now that he had already dropped it. Once he opened the cover, he was intrigued to find that the pages looked as if they had just come off the printer's block. The ink even smelled fresh. Regardless of how new it looked, he tentatively turned the pages. In the front he found no Table of Contents. This was inconvenient. Now his only option was to skim each page to find what he was looking for. Whatever that was.

As he turned the pages, he got more and more distracted from looking for anything in particular. He was no history or literature buff, but he could at least appreciate beautiful objects and this was one of them. Each page was exquisitely crafted. The intricately handwritten pages were expertly formed. The letters were small and clumped together making some lines look like single words. The style of the letters was angular and blocked, much like the much-coveted gothic script. This random bit of information came from a documentary on the History Channel he had watched some time ago on the evolution of handwriting. "Gotta love the History Channel," he thought, smiling to himself.

Page after page of ornate words and intricate illustrations mesmerized Tyler and drew him in. With each turn of a page, he became more and more intrigued. He read about the myth of the Holy Grail and the rumour of its life sustaining abilities as well as the alleged marriage of Christ. Each page gave compelling evidences to their truthfulness as well as evidences to discount any remote possibility of realism. Along with the data came facts that tied each myth to the next showing how they were intricately intertwined to each other, creating a complex web of mythological deception. Or so it seemed to him.

Without realizing it, hours had passed since he had first begun to read. He had intended to only skim the first twenty pages or so and then head to bed, but the more he read the more interest he developed until all concern of time vanished. As the night drew on, without realizing it his head began to nod. Within minutes, his head was resting on the opened book and he was fast asleep.

His head had barely came to rest on a beautifully depicted portrait of an angel enshrouded in flames when a peculiar, barely audible sound floated into his bedroom through the crack under the door. The sound wouldn't have even registered to him if it hadn't been for the strangeness of it. It almost sounded like a gust of wind rustling leaves or pages with the faint tinkling of chimes. Not to mention the sharp, spicy fragrance that accompanied it.

'Mark?' he called groggily, his brain barely registering the possibility of his brother just getting home.

He waited, silently, listening for a reply but heard nothing. He lifted himself quietly from his chair and cautiously twisted the doorknob to open his door. He didn't know who or what was out there, but he didn't want to alert them to his presence, even if it was Mark. He wasn't ready to face him yet.

As he stepped into the hallway leading to the front of the house, he noticed the door separating the two areas was shut, something that never happened. To make matters even stranger, a faint glow was flickering at the base of the door, much like the usual calming glow of a candle. But this wasn't calming. This was unnerving.

When he reached the door, he placed an ear up to it hoping he would be able to hear something that would give him some hint to what was producing the eerie light. Nothing. Not a peep could be heard. He knew the only way to find out what was lurking behind the door was to open it. Not knowing what to expect, he had to make a choice: he could either quickly yank the door open in hopes of catching whatever it was off guard or he could inch the door open and attempt a peek at what this thing might be and go from there. Now Tyler considered himself somewhat of a sensible person. Yanking the door open to catch the thing by surprise seemed like a pretty rash decision and most likely the most dangerous of the two choices. With even more caution than he had already been exhibiting, he reached for the doorknob. He took a deep breath and twisted the handle to the right.

He eased the door open slowly a couple inches. It wasn't enough to make a good enough observation, as he could see nothing but light. Even after his eyes had grown accustomed to the brightness, he still saw nothing. He blinked a couple times, just in case his eyes were playing tricks on him, but each time he opened them, he still saw the same thing, nothing. There was nothing but light. He opened the door wide enough for him to scan the whole room from behind it, but still he saw nothing. There was no being or object anywhere in the room producing the brilliant light. It was all very puzzling. "What could be creating this?" he wondered, chewing on the inside of his lip like he always did when something profoundly confused him.

As he was mustering up the courage to investigate the anomaly, he felt something whisper in his head, 'Come closer.' His skin paled at the sound of those words. He had not only heard them, but they had felt as if they had been directly injected into the regions of the brain that responded to direct commands. As soon as he felt the words his body responded. Because of the racing of his brain and his complete terror, he forcefully commanded his body to remain in the spot he was standing, which was now strangely right inside the living room door rather than right behind it. "How'd I get in here," he wondered, terror and confusion battling for dominion inside his head.

The voice resonated through his brain a second time. 'Come closer!' it said, more forceful than before. This time, rather than intense fear, a strange sense of curiosity began to build within the pit of his stomach. What phenomenon could possibly be able to speak words with such force and reaction into someone's head? Was it the same anomaly creating the light or something completely separate? If it was creating the light, how was it able to do so?

Before he could stop himself, he maneuvered through the furniture and into the center of the room, stopping directly at the light's edge. The light was so brilliant and so perplexing that he wanted so badly to reach out and touch it, to bask in the warmth of its mysteriousness. He raised his hand to caress the light, but stopped when the voice came again. This time it was more soothing and coaxing than stern and forceful. 'Come into the light,' it said, causing all his fear to melt away with the gentleness of its tone. Without a second's hesitation, Tyler walked directly into the brightness.

He felt a shock of warmth and immense peace wash over him as soon as he entered the light. It enveloped his body and his mind, helping him reach a level of relaxation he had never felt before. All concern about his brother disappeared, stress for exams vanished, worries about his experiment were gone. He was in pure bliss and never wanted to leave. As soon as his whole being was possessed by this joyful sensation, he felt a tiny prick at the tip of his right big toe. Although it was a tiny prick, compared to the fantastic feelings he was having, he might as well have been stabbed in the foot with a rusted fork.

Almost simultaneously with the first prick came a second one, this time on the left big toe. Then, like falling into a vat of needles, one by one the pricks began to consume every ounce of his flesh, starting with his toes, rising to his knees, then hips, his arms and up to his torso. He tried to cry out, but the pain was so extreme that his voice got caught in his tense throat. With each prick, it felt as if a drop of blood had been squeezed from that pore. His eyes spun wildly in their sockets as if searching for something to turn off what was causing him this pain.

Once the pricks reached his torso, Tyler felt his feet lift off of the carpet and dangle lifelessly in the air. It was as if he had lost all control of his body. He felt like a puppet, an unwilling toy to some demonic presence. As he hung there, something began to materialize in the air a few feet in front of him. His mind could barely conceive what was going on, let alone that the pricks had ceased. He was so terrified that his brain simply froze. All he could do was watch in suspended horror and anticipation for whatever it was that was manifesting itself.

At first the mysterious apparition seemed to be a mere void in the light. It was hard to tell if the light was being sucked into the void or repelled by it. Either way, the void where the light had once been had taken on a grayish colour. From within the grayish mass, the colour began to swirl like batter being poured into a mold. Faster and faster the gray swirled, producing a variety of other colours, which seeped and oozed towards various parts of the mass. Tyler watched this kaleidoscopic performance, noticing an outline had taken shape. Slowly, fingers and toes began to take form as well as facial features.

Within a short space of time the apparition had

completely solidified. Tyler immediately noticed an oddity in its form. For the most part the creature had the shape of a regular human being. Even with those similarities, something seemed off about this particular person. The figure opened its eyes and extended its wings. This was definitely not the oddity he had seen. With one swift motion, the figure wrapped its wings around him until they both stood face to face, suspended in the air mere centimeters from the other. Tyler felt the voice again and quickly recognized the source.

'Your time has finally come,' the being voicelessly whispered.

"Who are you?" Tyler cried out mentally, hoping the being could hear his thoughts.

'I am a representation of your future.'

'WHAT?!?' he exclaimed, remembering the oddity he had noticed.

The being blinked, its eyes flashing like fire. It came across as some semblance of a smile.

'In this form I am merely a messenger, sent to impart the first clue for your journey: "The first in mountain hidden deep, inside the secret golem's keep." May you succeed on your quest, for if you don't, all is lost. I'll be waiting for you in the darkness.'

Before Tyler could ask what it meant, the pricks began climbing up his neck, working towards his head. The moment the pricks reached his eyes, he felt his throat slacken and found his voice. Unable to bear the pain any longer, he let out a blood-curdling scream that dispelled the light and loosed his body from his suspended state. With no energy left to catch himself, he crumpled unconscious to the floor.

Chapter 5

Tyler's sleep was abruptly interrupted by a loud banging on his door. 'Tyler? TYLER! What's going on in there?' Mark called through the door, obviously worried. 'Tyler answer me!' he called again, banging on the door a few more times for added emphasis.

Tyler rubbed his eyes sleepily and reached over to unlock the door. The lock had barely clicked open as Mark came rushing into the room.

'Are you ok? What happened? I thought someone was killing you in here,' he rambled, obviously distressed.

'What are you on about? I'm fine.' Tyler yawned, grumpy from being so rudely awakened.

'Are you sure? When someone screams the way you were, it's usually because something awful is happening.'

'What do you mean I screamed?' He remembered vividly the dream from last night. Was it really a dream? It had felt so real.

'Holy shit! You're bleeding too,' Mark exclaimed, rushing from Tyler's room to get some tissue.

Tyler felt something cool and moist congealing on his upper lip. He pressed his fingers to his mouth and felt something wet and sticky. Pulling his fingers from his face he found them stained red. "I never bleed," he thought as he stared at the blood. As he stared in confusion at his red stained fingers, he suddenly remembered the book he had been lying on. He frantically scanned the pages searching for any noticeably out of place red splotches and was relieved to find none. A sudden itch on the tip of his nose caused him to pause. Before he could scratch it, he felt the itch drip off his nose and watched in horror as the tiny drop of blood plummeted towards the page.

A tiny flash of movement took his attention momentarily from the drop of blood. Hadn't the medallion been face up? Now it was flipped over, slightly tilted by lying on the chain. He looked back to the drop and watched as it suddenly veered away from the page, landing squarely on the medallion. Before it even had a chance to splatter, it was sucked up through the indentation in the back of the medallion. The blood coursed through the metal through invisible veins, which glowed brightly as the liquid flowed through them. As quickly as the veins appeared, once the blood was gone, they disappeared. Tyler's eyes were wide with alarm as he stared at the medallion. He picked it up cautiously and spun it around in his hands. Everything about it looked the same. There were no visible signs of blood or the veins that he could swear he had just seen. "I need more sleep," Tyler thought as he laid the medallion back onto the book.

Mark returned quickly with some toilet paper and handed it to Tyler. He wiped the blood from his beneath his nose in a robotic, hypnotic manner. The combination of the strange dream and what he had just witnessed brought on a state akin to shock. Could it really have caused his nose to bleed like this, or was it some freak chance occurrence? Was he so tired that his eyes were playing tricks on him? He had to be going crazy. No sane person would be seeing what he thought he was seeing.

'What time is it?' he asked, tossing the stained toilet paper into the bin, which stood between the desk and the door.

'Around nine I think,' answered Mark, reflexively looking at his wrist, which was normally clad with some expensive looking watch.

'NINE!?! Crap,' he exclaimed, jumping from his chair. Before he even reached the door, he felt the room start spinning. He had to grab a hold of the doorframe in order to stop himself from collapsing.

Mark rushed forward a few steps and stopped. 'Are you sure you're all right?' he asked, frowning slightly as he watched Tyler tremble.

'Of course I'm all right. Why shouldn't I be?' Tyler retorted. He took a couple deep breaths as he rested against the doorframe.

'Well for starters you almost just collapsed because you have no energy which always happens after your nose bleeds. Secondly, your screaming sounded like you were in a lot of pain.'

Tyler was glad he was facing the hall and not his brother at that moment. His face had twisted into an expression of pure irritation. He knew what his brother was saying was true and that made the situation that much worse.

'Well I'm fine,' he snapped. 'I just need a minute.'

Mark said nothing in response, which made Tyler roll his eyes in annoyance. "How could someone who looked and acted so badass hardcore be such a pansy when it came to family?" he wondered snidely as he pushed himself off the doorframe and slowly eased his way down the hall towards the bathroom.

By the time he finished with his shower he was feeling more like his old self. There was nothing that a nice hot shower couldn't cure; at least in some cases. When he emerged from the misty bathroom he found

Mark's door closed with music blaring so he didn't bother knocking. As the warm water had cascaded down his nicely sculpted body calming his aching nerves, he realized that he had been unjustly rude to Mark. Was there really anything so wrong when a sibling acted concerned? His natural reaction to his brother had been of annoyance when it should have been reassurance. But Mark had not seen or felt what he had dreamed. It had felt so real and he had even bled. Again he wondered if it had merely been a dream.

He quickly dressed and prepared to leave. As he opened the door to his room, he gazed at the book and medallion on his desk, wondering momentarily what exactly he should do with them. Acting on impulse, he clasped the necklace around his neck tucking it under his shirt. He tucked the book under his arm and headed out the door. When he got into his car, he set the book on the backseat resisting the sudden urge to look through it again. He was intrigued to find out more but he knew if he looked at it now he would never get to Helen's on time. Besides, he still was curious to discover the significance of the medallion, which felt oddly warm against his skin.

As he drove from his apartment across town, he sent Mark a text apologizing for acting so harshly towards him. No response. This surprised him since Mark almost always responded quickly. Maybe he had hurt him more than normal this time. If only he had known that this was only the beginning of the last normal day of his life, he might have tried a little harder to be reconciled with his brother.

Unlike normal Thursday morning traffic, the roads downtown were completely congested. Not only were the streets jam-packed, but he was also stuck in a dead zone. He was unable to call or text Helen to let her know he would be late. All he could do was inch forward praying that he would eventually get reception. By the time he had made it through the traffic jam, gotten reception and arrived at Helen's house, she was long gone. She as well was not responding to any of his texts. Resigned to having everyone mad at him, he went to the one place where he could close out all his outside distractions and focus: the lab. He would have considered going to see Father Michael, but he was getting the sense he was becoming a nuisance.

The refreshing aroma of disinfectant greeted him as he walked into the lab. He instantly felt relaxed and at home. The smell assured him a pristine environment to continue his experiment. Yesterday his results had narrowed the correct combination of chemicals exponentially. Today, if he had no interruptions, he should be able to correctly create a cocktail that might change genetic science for decades to come. He felt sure of it. He immediately set himself to work retrieving microscopes, pipettes, test tubes and the other various objects vital to his experimenting.

Once his workstation had been set up in the precise order necessary, he pulled his notes from his satchel. Within these notes contained a record of all the failed experiments and near hits that would direct him towards the right chemical composition. Hundreds upon hundreds of these experiments yielded no results while a handful of his most recent experiments generated minimal success. While the little successes were truly remarkable, they provided him with no real reason to celebrate. He would only be happy once he had complete success.

Hours passed as he mixed various chemical concoctions, but was met with little result. He was beginning to become frustrated. He turned to his notes to see if he was missing something. He knew the key to success lay somewhere within, but he couldn't find it. He read through page after page of the failed experiments until finally he stumbled upon something he had originally and purposely ignored. Opened on the table in front of him lay the description of the discovery of restriction enzymes found by Daniel Nathans, Werner Arber, and Hamilton Smith in the 1970's. He had intentionally avoided the use of the restriction enzymes because while they separated the DNA, they only separate the strand into palindromic sections rather than simply separating the entire strand into two long segments.

Tyler stared in defeat at the page of various restriction endonucleases when something began to stir in his brain. He realized there really was a way to manipulate the restriction enzymes into separating the strand into two pieces rather than multiple sections. Ripping a blank sheet of paper from his notebook, he began jotting down a complex formula, uniting his findings with the proven findings of his predecessors. It took him about an hour to completely compose his new formula, but once he put his pen down, a smug look of triumph had replaced his early appearance of defeat.

Excitement tingled through his frame like electricity as he cautiously mixed the chemicals together. Never before had something so profound been discovered as his composition for genetic manipulation. If it indeed proved successful, his name would be remembered for eternity. Such a concept caused him to nearly overpour the nitrogen. Such a mistake would have ruined the solution. Too much nitrogen would have caused the DNA to freeze instead of limit mobility. He resumed his concentration for the remainder of the mixing to prevent any more near disasters.

Once the finishing touches had been added to the compound, he placed a couple drops into a test tube. With this done there was one last thing to do: add a drop of blood to extract DNA for testing. He pricked his pointer finger with a sterilized pin and squeezed a drop of blood into the mixture in the test tube. After wrapping a band-aid around the wound, he placed the tube into the centrifuge and patiently waited a few minutes as the machine did its job.

He eagerly paced the floor as he waited for the whirring to stop, signaling completion. After two minutes, a sharp beep sounded and the whirring ceased. He excitedly withdrew the test tube and strode quickly over to his microscope. Taking a pipette, he extracted a few drops from the tube. He placed them onto a glass slide and stuck them on the stage. What he saw took all words from his mouth. Suspended in the matter were two separate strands of DNA. His experiment had worked!

Tyler's brain was reeling from the shock of this miracle that he hardly registered the sudden crashing of the laboratory door, signaling the arrival of Mark. Upon receiving no kind of greeting, good or bad, it hit him that something profound had recently occurred.

'So, did the master scientist finally succeed?' he snidely asked, pushing Tyler to the side so he could peer into the microscope. 'Did you actually crack it?'

Tyler just stood there looking completely amazed as he watched Mark gaze seemingly perplexed down the lens at a messy array of particles. When he didn't receive an answer, he looked back up to see Tyler gazing at the wall as if something interesting was posted on the bare nothingness of the blank white space.

'Hey Captain Oblivious,' he exclaimed, a bit annoyed, 'I'm talking to you.'

'Oh sorry,' Tyler said vaguely as he turned his attention slowly from the wall to Mark. 'What were you asking?'

'I was asking if you had cracked the gene code and now I'm wondering exactly what it is you've got going on here.'

Tyler walked past him over to the microscope where he flicked a switch, which projected the image of the Petri dish onto the blank wall behind it. He walked around the table and began pointing out the various objects in the picture.

'What you're looking at is a strand of DNA or in other words deoxyribonucleic acid. It is common knowledge that each strand of DNA is made of four nucleotides......'

'Yeah ok. I know this already. What does this lecture on basic genetics have to do with this jumble on the wall?'

'If you be patient, I'll tell you.' Tyler gave him a stern look before continuing on. 'As I was saying, DNA is made of four nucleotides: Adenine, Cytosine, Thymine and Guanine. Each has its mate one could say. Adenine pairs with thymine and cytosine pairs with guanine. Each strand forms with its mate a double helix in which the genetic material runs. The matter at hand is that if one could split apart this double helix into two separate strands, then one could in theory create a new genetic code by mimicking an existing genetic code. By introducing it to a separate, synthetic DNA strand, one could reassign genetic characteristics or infuse new ones before any were formed. Of course you'd have to split the strand up a little more so you don't just recreate the same strand.'

'So are you saying that what you have projected on the wall is a separated DNA strand?'

'Exactly!'

Mark could hear by the sound of his voice that Tyler couldn't believe he had cracked a code that scientists had been trying to crack for decades. Even Mark was in a state of shock. If this were real, then he wouldn't have stolen the samples in vain. The next step was finding out how Tyler had done it.

'So what exactly did you do to cause this reaction? What could you have possibly discovered that decades of scientists couldn't?' He was trying his hardest not to sound too suspicious, but his inquisitiveness didn't seem to faze Tyler.

Tyler gazed in pride at the separated strands, trying hard to ignore Mark's condescending attitude. 'Well, all I did was combine chemicals with certain separating and combining properties.'

'Combining properties? What are they for?'

"This is going all too easy," Mark thought. "He seriously doesn't suspect a thing." He needed to play his game carefully though. Even though at this moment Tyler wasn't suspecting anything sinister, he could easily let something slip and reveal his true intentions.

'You can't seriously think that separating the DNA is the only part? Within the same "cocktail" you could call it, one has to put the desired genetic structure to be combined. The chemicals with the combining properties ensure that the two strands will fuse together.'

Of course Mark knew this.

'Well what chemical compounds did you use to create this "cocktail"?'

Once the words had left his mouth, Mark knew he had asked the wrong question. Tyler creased his eyebrows in an inquisitive stare as if Mark had asked him for his bank account number or some other personal information. Mark was going to have to play the wildcard now.

'I'm not giving that information out until I first know it's successful and then get it patented,' he said as Mark tried hard to hide the utter disappointment at this response.

'But hasn't it already proved successful? I mean the DNA strand split. What else do you need to know? This means you've won. You're the best. Isn't that what you want everyone to know? How much better you are?' Mark sarcastically spat at him.

'Excuse me?!' Tyler replied, very offended now. 'What are you talking about? I'm not trying to prove anything?'

'Of course you are. You always are. Always needing to stand out and be noticed.'

Tyler began to fume. He was about to reply with some nasty comeback when he remembered what Helen and Father Michael had been telling him. He needed to be nicer. More understanding. Right now he needed to try.

'Listen. If this is about this morning and yesterday, I'm really sorry. I don't know what else to say. I honestly can't give you a definitive list of components because the experiment isn't complete yet. If you want, we can run through the final steps together. What do ya say?'

Mark glared at him in superficial anger, impressed at his own performance. 'Fine,' he answered as he walked over to his brother's side.

'Now, as I was going to say, it has only proved partially successful,' he admitted as he walked backwards away from the projection, biting his lip as if contemplating his next move. 'What I need to do now is create a new genetic code to introduce to the host strand. Then I need to add the combining "cocktail" in order to see if it works as well. Only then, once it has been completely joined to the host strand, can this experiment be deemed successful.'

'Does it need to be human DNA or will any type of DNA work?'

'Not sure to be honest. Personally, I'd rather not use human DNA, but otherwise it shouldn't matter much.'

Mark smirked as he turned way from his brother. The timing couldn't have been more impeccable. Here was the perfect opportunity for him to exploit the stolen samples as well as his brother's ignorance. He reached into his back pocket and extracted a vial, which emitted a strange blue aura, and held it up. The strange light caused

Tyler to turn and stare at his hand.

'Here's your sample,' Mark said deviously.

'What is that?' Tyler asked, eyeing the vial apprehensively

'Did you not just hear me say, "here's your sample"?'

'But why is glowing?'

'Does it really matter? You have a sample now so all you need to do is test it out.'

'Mark?' Tyler began, looking at him seriously. 'Where did you get this?'

'Ugh. What is with all the questions? Fine. I found it downstairs in one of the labs. It looked cool so I took it to check it out.'

Tyler stared at him incredulously. 'You're joking right? You stole this?'

'More like borrowed. But seriously, what is the problem? Would you rather take hours to figure out some new form of DNA or just use what I gave you? Simply choice really.'

'I'd rather not have to resort to stealing to complete my work. Really Mark, you are unbelievable.' Tyler chastised.

'Oh quit the holier-than-thou act. Are you gonna use it or not?'

Tyler stared at Mark angrily before snatching the vial out of his hand. Mark genuinely smiled back at him. Tyler turned the vial around in his fingers, inspecting it. He popped the lid off the vial and poured the contents into a new Petri dish, which he had taken from a drawer next to him. He placed the dish on the stage of the microscope, adjusted the view and began inspecting the contents. He looked into the microscope and didn't speak for what seemed like ages. At times he would pull his little notebook out of his back pocket and jot down this and that. Of course Mark had no idea what it was. Tyler was enhancing the zoom when he gasped.

'Tell me right now where you got this!!' he shouted angrily. 'You didn't just find this in a lab downstairs at all. There is no way.'

So many responses filtered through Mark's mind, but it all boiled down to one thought: 'Why should I tell him when he won't even tell me the contents of his genetic cocktail?'

'Of course I did. Where else would I have found it?' he lied, hoping he sounded convincing enough.

'Quit lying to me Mark. This isn't a game.'

'Duh. Why don't you just calm down and tell me what you found,' he said condescendingly. 'I've been dying to know what it is.' From the look on Tyler's face, he was about to explode, which made Mark giddy.

'Fine. At first glance, this DNA sample appears to be perfect. Every protein and nucleotide has no irregularities and they fit together as if they were formed as one piece. Taking a deeper look, I noticed that there are certain proteins that don't exist in current DNA strands, which means that this sample is either from some other planet or else it is very, very old.'

From the look on Tyler's face, Mark knew he'd been figured out.

'So which one is it then?'

Mark took a deep breathed and sighed. 'Alright fine then. It's from the past,' he said nonchalantly, putting lots of emphasis on sounding annoyed.

Tyler looked at him as if expecting him to go on. 'What?'

'And where did you get it?' Tyler asked him like he was talking to a child.

'I extracted it from the angel myself.'

'You're not serious?'

'Why do you keep asking me if I'm serious?' Mark asked, now really annoyed. 'Of course I'm serious. It's not like it was difficult to do either. Anyone can wear a lab coat and look like a scientist. Carry around a clipboard and a pair of goggles and you disappear. It was thrilling. Like pulling an "Ocean's Eleven," except in a lab.'

'Are you crazy?!' Tyler shouted at him. Then lowering his voice, he whispered harshly, 'If someone were to find out we're both going to end up in jail.'

Mark just smiled at him.

'What are you smiling about?' he snapped, turning his back to him, trying to hide his worried expression. 'This is a serious mess you've gotten us into and I really don't see any real way out.'

'I do,' Mark whispered.

Tyler ran a hand through his hair and turned back to Mark. 'How do you presume we resolve this predicament?' he questioned, blocking any other emotion from surfacing save disconcert.

Mark's smile widened as he began to explain.

'It's simple really,' he stated, 'what you are going to have to do is continue with your experiment. Test the sample and see if it combines with the separated DNA strand. If it works, the next step may be risky, but as you have noticed, it's going to be a necessary one. If the sample combines as you predict, you are just going to have to inject the sample into yourself.'

Mark watched in morbid fascination as Tyler's body went rigid as the insanity of what he had just said sunk in.

'You have gone insane haven't you?' Tyler exclaimed. 'Of course the sample will combine. I have no doubt about that, but inject myself with it? It could kill me and what would you do next? Claim me as some mad scientist bent on creating the perfect human and failing? I don't think so.'

Tyler shook his head in anger and frustration. Deep down Mark knew his brother knew it was the only way, but he couldn't bring himself to going through with it.

With a mask of sincerity, Mark put his hand on Tyler's shoulder and said, 'I know this is a tough choice to make, but what if it succeeds? What if the combined DNA alters your genetic structure and you become the perfect human being?'

'I don't care about that. I would rather live than be perfect. There is no way you are going to convince me to do it. You should do it if you think it's the only way.'

Mark gave him a reassuring smile and said soothingly, 'Oh stop overreacting. Nothing is going to go wrong. You are too smart to have made any mistakes. And besides, if I tested it out on myself and died, things would still be bad for you.'

'Fine. I'll make a compromise with you. I'll test it out and see if it works, but that's it. Once we see that the sample combines, I'm pouring it down the sink.'

'Down the sink?' Mark sneered. 'You disappoint me. I figured you more of a real scientist than this.'

'No. You figured me to be more suicidal than this. Sorry to disappoint you, but I'm not.'

Tyler turned his back on Mark and began preparing the strands. As soon as they were ready, he combined the sample with the cocktail. Once all the elements were put together, he siphoned all the contents of the petri dish into another test tube and put it in the centrifuge. They both waited impatiently for the whirring to stop. Tyler just wanted this whole affair to be over. Mark couldn't wait for it to begin. Once the beep sounded, Tyler pulled the tube from inside it and after preparing a slide, inspected the results.

'It worked!!!' he exclaimed, more excited than he had intended.

He hit the same switch as earlier to project the contents of the dish onto the wall.

'Look here,' he exclaimed. 'The sample you gave has split apart and connected with the test sample. I was afraid because of the foreign proteins and age that it would be rejected, but it wasn't. In fact, it appears to have realigned itself to compensate for the differences.'

'This means your assumption was correct?' Mark asked.

'Yes. This means that now genetic manipulation can become a reality. Do you know what this could mean for medical science? This is amazing!!!'

Mark couldn't help but admit that he found this all fascinating and somewhere inside himself he was sure he was really happy for Tyler. There was still one step of his plan left to complete and he wasn't going to be happy until it was done.

'This is truly amazing and we'll go out and celebrate to commemorate this advance in science, but there is still one thing left to do.'

'I told you already I'm not doing it. You be my guest, but if something bad happens don't blame me.'

Mark had hoped it wouldn't come to this, but it had. If Tyler wasn't going to take it willingly, he was going to have to force him. He walked over to his brother and grabbed the test tube out of his hand. He pulled out a syringe and withdrew a healthy dose of the mixture. He placed a tourniquet around his arm and waited for his veins to expand.

'Looks like I'm going to have to be the brave one,' he mocked, taking one final glance at Tyler.

'Whatever. I can't believe you're actual going to do this.'

Mark suddenly laughed. 'Of course I'm not going to do it. I can't you believe you bought this whole thing.' He laughed even harder.

'What are you talking about?'

'Did you really think I would test out your experiment on myself? No. I'm here just to make sure you do.'

'What?'

Before Tyler could react, Mark lashed out and

stabbed the syringe into his brother's neck. It had only slightly pierced the skin, when Tyler backhanded his arm sending the syringe flying. It landed in one of the sinks a few tables away. Mark turned to retrieve it, but Tyler kicked him in the back sending him sprawling. He crashed into the wall and nearly collapsed. Growling, he turned and ran at Tyler, tackling him and slamming him into the other wall. Pure rage fueled both of them now. They punched and kicked each other till lines of blood splattered on the floor. When Tyler finally laid Mark out on the tile, he backed away.

'Why are you doing this?' he shouted at him. 'Do you really want me dead?'

Mark gurgled maniacally as he staggered up from the floor. 'No. I don't want you dead, but I do need you to finish what you started.'

'Why is it so important? Is this all really worth it?' he asked, motioning to the damage they had down both to the room and themselves.

'You couldn't possibly understand,' Mark laughed. 'That's why you need to be shown instead.'

He ran at Tyler once more. Just before he reached him, he faked left and twisted around him, catching him off guard. He raised his arm above his head and jabbed the syringe again completely into his brother's neck. This time Tyler couldn't deflect his hand. He gasped in shock as he felt the contents of the needle enter his bloodstream. He collapsed onto the tile as the empty syringe tinkled evilly next to him.

'What have you done?' he cried as tears freely flowed. He was terrified. He didn't want to die.

Mark limped over to the wall and slid down it. Now all he had to do was wait. He wondered how long the reaction would take. Hopefully not too long.

With each tick of the clock, Tyler's head pounded. It felt as if a gong was being sounded in his head. Every sound around him was amplified exponentially. He heard scratching in the walls, voices coming from who knows where as well as a multitude of other sounds. He tried to speak, but the sounds in his head blocked his ability to find his own voice. Sudden fear formed in his eyes as the room around him began to change shape. Fire broke out in his entire being like thousands of tiny pinpricks again and again. He looked at Mark who just stared at him with a sincere expression of concern before the floor came racing towards his sweat drenched head.

Chapter 6

Mark drove slowly to the hospital. He was trying to come up with a believable enough story. He knew he was going to be questioned once he got there, but he couldn't seem to come up with anything. All his mind would do was replay the image of his brother collapsing onto the floor. It was by far the worst moment of Mark's life. The problem was, he couldn't decide why. A part of him was agonizing over the possible failure of the experiment while the more rational side was worried about losing his brother. It was a surprisingly short battle with his rationality narrowly beating his selfishness. He checked Tyler's pulse and was relieved to find its steady rhythm. It was strangely slow, like he was merely sleeping rather than being on the verge of death. When Tyler didn't respond to being shaken, Mark called 911.

The response time of the paramedics was impressively quick as well as their efficiency. Within ten minutes, an ambulance had arrived. The EMTs gently and speedily checked Tyler's vitals before carefully securing him to a stretcher. Then they were gone, leaving Mark behind to gather Tyler's belongings and clean up some of the mess their brawl had caused.

Mark stared at the room and sighed. He almost considered leaving it for the janitors, but then a thought struck him, "what if someone were to find Tyler's notes?" If that happened then all the research his brother had done might be attributed to some thief who had no idea what it all had cost. He couldn't let that happen. He might be willing to use his brother as a guinea pig, but was he really that callous to let his brother's work be lost? He groaned and slowly began picking up the mess.

It took him a lot longer than he expected to get the room looking less like a bomb went off in it. He wiped off the countertops, swept up the debris, and bleached the floor where a pool of his brother's blood had been. The hardest part was wiping up all the chemicals. He had to put on this funny rubber coat, which covered almost his entire body, just so he didn't get any of the chemicals on him. He also couldn't just use any rag to clean them up. Whenever chemicals were spilt, an absorption spill kit was required to be used. It was tedious and time-consuming, but finally he was done and off to the hospital.

By the time he arrived at the hospital, he had a pretty solid story. He had even more time to polish it searching for a parking spot. Parking was a ridiculous waste of time. It took almost as long to find a spot as it did driving there. Once he parked, he rushed into the front lobby. When it was discovered whom he was there for, he was assaulted with a barrage of questions. He replied as matter-of-factly as he could, but his answers never seemed to satisfy them. When asked what had happened, he told them they were in the lab as Tyler was conducting experiments and then he collapsed. It was the truth, kind of. Of course he had to leave out most of the truth. He was also asked if Tyler had exhibited anything out of the ordinary prior to his collapsing. The only thing Mark could tell them about was the random occurrence of the bloody nose that morning. Everything else was normal. After that, all the questions they probed him with had to do with medical history, basic information and insurance.

When the nurses had extracted all the information from him they needed, Mark was directed to a waiting area. He was going to have to wait there until his brother was issued a room. Rather than just sit in boredom, he made a few phone calls. The first was to his parents to let them know Tyler was in the hospital but that he was going to be fine. They wanted to fly out there, but he reassured them that Tyler had merely caught some virus or something similar and there was no need to fuss. He promised that if anything serious developed he would let them know. That seemed to pacify them, but it was obvious they were still very concerned. Good thing they didn't know the truth. They'd kill him for sure.

The second call was to Father Michael. The priest answered at the third ring and without even waiting to find out who was on the other end asked, 'How is he?'

Mark was slightly surprised that Father Michael knew who was calling him and stammered, 'Well they haven't told me much, just that he's breathing but unresponsive. I just got here about ten minutes ago though. They haven't finished taking tests yet, but I'm sure he's gonna be fine.'

'Good. Well as soon as I'm finished tonight I'll be there to check up on him. Thank you for the call.'

Father Michael abruptly hung up. Mark stared in confusion at the phone while the dial tone buzzed in the background. "How had he known?" he wondered.

The third call went to Helen. She was very angry when she answered the phone. Apparently, Tyler was supposed to pick her up after practice, but had never shown up. She ranted and raved about how inconsiderate Tyler had been lately. This wasn't a surprise to him considering the way his brother was always treating him. He waited rather impatiently for her to end, but she didn't. Finally he forcefully interrupted and blurted out that Tyler had collapsed at the lab and was now in the hospital. Mark couldn't help but feel a little guilty knowing he had sounded harsher than he intended. He waited to hear some sort of response but all he got was silence. When she finally spoke, he could hear her trying to suppress her emotions and not cry.

'Is he alright?' she asked, her voice wavering slightly.

Mark sighed. 'I don't know. He's alive, but not responding.'

'My dad's on his way to pick me up. As soon as he gets here I'll have him take me straight to the hospital,' she replied, a hint a relief unmistakable as she sighed. 'Oh, and thank you so much for letting me know. I really appreciate it.'

'Yeah no problem.' Mark shut his cell phone brusquely, abruptly ending their conversation.

He normally had no issues with Helen, but right then her abrasiveness had struck a chord with him. It made him wish he had been the one injected. He shook his head in exasperation, banishing the thought from his mind. What was done was done and nothing could change it. All he could do now was wait and hope for the best. It was a struggle to decide which best he hoped for most. While he hoped for his brother to be all right, he also hoped that the experiment hadn't been a total loss. Of course both would be ideal.

Waiting proved to be the biggest challenge. As time dragged on no progress seemed to be made and no questions were getting answered. During the first few hours after Tyler's arrival, a severe fever set in and his body rejected all medicinal aid. The fever became so intense after twelve hours that he had to be submersed in an ice bath. Within a quarter of an hour the ice had completely melted and a dense mist had filled the room.

The baffled doctors ran to and fro between phone calls to various other hospitals and experts in hopes to find some way to bring the fever down. They had never experienced a virus so resilient before. No matter what they tried nothing worked. The only thing they could determine was that whatever it was, it wasn't contagious. Once Mark, Helen and Father Michael learned this, they never left Tyler alone.

Three long days passed before the fever broke and Tyler regained consciousness. During that time, Mark and Helen alternated shifts sitting with him with the occasional visit from Father Michael. Despite his busy schedule, the priest always offered to relieve whoever happened to be sitting with Tyler. As the fever waged war on his body, the three could do nothing but wait in unbearable gloom, offering silent prayers, hoping that no lasting damage was done.

Unbeknownst to Helen and Father Michael, a battle had started inside Mark's body. He knew testing out the cocktail was going to be risky, but now he wondered if such a venture was really worth it. As he watched the baffled doctors conduct tests and probe his brother's pain-riddled body, a part of him wished he could just confess to what he had done in hopes it would somehow aid them in curing Tyler. Then there was another part of him. A secret part that up until now he had been able to suppress. It whispered things to him that he wanted but knew he shouldn't have. It was this voice that was speaking to him now. It urged him to stay silent. What good would revealing the truth do them? He needed to see this through to the end. Only then could their destiny finally unfold.

On the evening of Tyler's third day in the hospital, Helen showed up unexpectedly to sit with her boyfriend. Mark was glad to have someone to keep him company. They spoke quietly for a while, until he couldn't sit anymore. He stood up to stretch and nearly collapsed from exhaustion.

'How long have you been here?' she asked after

helping him back into his chair.

Mark rubbed his eyes and thought about it. 'I'm not sure,' he replied. 'Since last night I think?'

Helen immediately pulled her mobile out of her purse and dialed a number. 'Yes hello? Can I get a taxi at the front entrance of the hospital?'

'What're you doing?' Mark asked half-heartedly as he tried to take the phone from her. He put Tyler in this mess and he wanted to ensure that he survived it. Even if it was for selfish reasoning.

She swatted his hand away and gave him a stern look. 'Twenty minutes? Perfect. We'll see you shortly then.'

She closed her phone and put it away. She turned back around and found Mark glaring at her quite fiercely.

'Don't give me that look,' she scolded. 'You need to get home and rest. When was the last time you ate?'

'I'm fine,' he tried to tell her but she wouldn't have it.

He had no other choice but to let her help him downstairs to meet the taxi. Besides, he was too weak and tired to fight any further with her. When they exited the front doors, the taxi was already waiting there. She got him situated inside and used her credit card to pay the bill. She gave the driver the address and waved as they left. She watched the taxi exit the lot and suddenly make a right instead of the left that led home. "Maybe he's having him stop for food first?" she thought as the taxi soon disappeared in the evening traffic.

Back upstairs she positioned a chair close to the bed and sat down. It was slightly uncomfortable, but since his hand was right there, she felt a little less scared when she held it. Shortly after she sat down she was fast asleep. She had unsettling dreams about dragons and never-ending roads in the sky, which caused her to thrash around gently. Some were so startling that she would bolt up in terror, as if she believed for a split second that she was somewhere less desirable. She was just waking from another terrible dream when she felt a slight increase of pressure to her hand.

'Tyler? Baby? Can you hear me?' she exclaimed excitedly, drawing herself nearer to him in case he responded. She gently placed the back of her hand against his forehead and was pleasantly surprised to find a regulated temperature.

Her lips curled into a huge joyful smile, which disappeared quickly. As she brought her face in front of his, his eyes opened very wide and rolled back into his head as his body twisted in pain. His mouth opened to scream, but no sound came. His hands clawed at the metal bars on the sides of his bed as his back arched a foot off of the bed. Helen jumped from her chair in panic and ran to the door. Yanking it open, she propelled herself into the hallway.

Not far from Tyler's room stood the nurses station. It took Helen a matter of seconds to reach it. Every time she had passed the station prior to now there had always been an abundance of nurses chatting idly. But this time, when she really needed them, the station was bare. She frantically paced back and forth, racking her brain as to where a nurse or another nurse station might be. Her only option was to check another floor for help.

She quickly made her way to the stairwell at the end of the corridor. Before she reached it, the door opened and three nurses – one male and two female – traipsed through, laughing as if one of them had just recited the punch line to a particularly funny joke. The clatter of feet on linoleum brought their laughter to an abrupt stop and they all turned to greet the person who was rapidly approaching them.

Helen rambled incoherently, panting in exhaustion. 'Tyler...pain...his eyes...hurry...need help...'

The older looking of the two female nurses gently

put her hand on Helen's arm.

'Take a deep breath and tell us what's wrong,' she instructed, looking at Helen in confusion. Once Helen had relaxed a little, the woman tried to find out the problem. 'Who is Tyler, where is he and how is he in pain?'

Helen opened her mouth to reply when an ear-piercing scream echoed through the dimly lit, silent corridor. All four of them stared down the hall as the scream reverberated off the linoleum and stucco, slowly dying down to an eerie silence.

'Was that him?' the nurse nervously whispered.

'I think so, but just a minute ago he wasn't able to make a sound.'

Another scream echoed through the halls. As they stood there in terrified silence, a door thirty yards down the hall exploded off it's hinges as the room's inhabitant came barreling through out into the hallway.

'TYLER!!!' Helen cried out in disbelief.

A third animalistic scream reverberated throughout the hall as they watched Tyler cautiously from the end of the corridor. They stood frozen in their spots as they watched him move sporadically towards them. He had only made it the short distance to the nurse's station before collapsing and writhing around on the floor in pain.

Seeing him crumple to the floor seemed to jar the nurses from their stupor. They raced to his side to make sure he was okay, but he was making it difficult. His thrashing around made it near impossible for the three nurses and Helen to keep him in one place. It was as if some new reserve of strength had been opened during his fever.

Tyler writhed around on the floor muttering unintelligibly. They all did their best to calm him down but he just moaned louder. The male nurse tried in vain to find out what was wrong.

'What happened to him before he was admitted?'

'I'm not sure. All I was told was he was in the lab when he collapsed,' Helen answered.

'Could he have ingested any dangerous chemicals or spilled them on his skin?'

'I don't know. He never really told me what he was working on. The person you should be talking to about that is Mark but I sent him home a few hours ago.'

While Helen answered his questions, the young female nurse ran into the nurse's station to call for a doctor. They had no other option. She had just finished dialing the final digit when she heard her name being called urgently. 'Mary, quickly! We need to get him on his back but he won't let us.'

Mary dropped the phone, missing the cradle, and darted around the chairs to exit the nurse's station. She made it out just in time to see the male nurse get dealt a powerful kick. He flew backwards landing in a heap further back than humanly possible. He must have been knocked unconscious because he didn't get back up. Mary turned her horrified gaze to Tyler and let out a scream that turned Helen's and the older nurse's blood to ice. They turned to see what Mary was staring at and gasped.

Sensing a lack of resistance, Tyler ripped his arms free and attempted to stand. He growled as he tore the top portion of his hospital gown from his body and began clawing at his upper back. Helen and the nurses stared in confusion as something where his shoulder blades should have been began pushing against the skin. Despite all Tyler's attempts, his arms could not get at the right angle to tear the area of skin causing him the pain. He scratched vainly causing rivulets of blood to flow down his back, which quickly ebbed until he tore through the skin again. Helen could hardly fathom what she was seeing. How could he heal so quickly?

From both ends of the hallway commotions began

to sound as patients left their rooms to investigate what all the noise was about. Before any of them could get close enough, hospital security and a doctor came running through, blocking the direct route to the disturbance. When they arrived at the nurse's station, they all froze and stared in disturbed silence. They watched Tyler squirm, attempting in vain to release the objects trapped beneath his skin.

The doctor was the first to gather his wits. 'We need to subdue him and if one of you has one, I need a knife. If not, I need one of you to take the nurses and find me a scalpel.' He shouted orders to the security officers who quickly broke free from their trance-like state and began to surround him. If Tyler noticed the circle of men he didn't show it. He continued growling and scratching at his upper back.

Taking advantage of Tyler's distraction, the security guards rushed forward. It took all the strength they could muster to secure him against the floor. He had ungodly strength, which made it a struggle to restrain him. As soon as the officers appeared to have him under control, the doctor went forward and knelt next to Tyler's left shoulder with the knife one of the guards had given him. He instructed one of the nurses to grab him a bottle of alcohol and a lighter and set to observing his back. In true old school fashion, as soon as he had the requested items, the doctor poured the alcohol on the blade and then used the lighter to finalize the sterilization process. Once the instruments were ready, he patiently waited until the objects under Tyler's skin began pushing up again.

'Now, once I've made the incision, be prepared to take him out if necessary. I have no idea what might come out and we can't let him infect anyone else,' the doctor instructed, making sure the officers acknowledged their understanding.

When the first bump appeared, the doctor

brought the knife down a few inches above it and stopped the incision a few inches below the spot. As quickly as he could, he repeated the procedure along the right shoulder blade once the second bump appeared. He waited for something to appear, but when he looked back at the incisions, he found them healed. He cut into Tyler's back again, but once again the wounds healed almost instantly. He looked bewildered at the boy as he tried to figure out a way to keep the wounds from closing.

'You four. You are going to have to help me,' he said, motioning to the closest of the guards. 'What I need you to do is pull the skin apart as soon as I cut it.'

The doctor made the incision as before and moved back as the guards held the skin apart. They fought valiantly to keep the wounds open as the skin attempted to repair itself. Suddenly Tyler ceased struggling and the skin relaxed. Nobody moved. Then one by one the guards cautiously let up and backed away from him. Tyler moaned as he lay there on the cold floor. Then something extraordinary happened. As he struggled to right himself, his skin began to emit a strange aura. Its brilliance outshone the brightest candle, giving Tyler an angelic appearance of innocence. His face contorted in pain and he gasped, falling to his knees. Cries of fear came from the chorus of onlookers as the slits stretched open to let something out. The cries quickly changed to gasps of disbelief when the objects from his back extended fully to reveal two full-feathered wings.

Once the wings had fully extended from his back, the slits healed, making it look as if the wings had always been there. Each wing stretched between five to six feet from his back to the tip and was covered with soft, white feathers. The feathers were the purest shade of white any of them had ever seen. Even the pristine white walls of the hospital paled and seemed somewhat tainted in comparison.

Tyler tried again to right himself but struggled as

the light reflected off his now angelic face. Never had anything so painful felt so right, so beautiful. What has happening to him? It took him a few minutes, but when he finally stood straight, he stared proudly and defiantly into the crowd. A single tear dropped from his chin and splattered on the floor. The world seemed to disappear and all he heard was the single teardrop hit the ground. It felt like a trigger, releasing something he couldn't have controlled if he wanted to. Without warning, a strange surge of raw emotion erupted from his body and spread out in all directions.

The nurses, security guards, doctor and Helen were the first to feel the effects of this eruption. As it passed over their bodies and entered through their pores, undiluted healing power cured whatever ailments they were suffering from. On it went continuing on to the other patients. Sudden murmurs of surprise sounded as people began to excitedly jump around and praise God. Patients in wheelchairs could suddenly walk, bedridden patients were able to move around, wounds were closed, scars were healed, sadness turned to joy and pain became gratification. Anybody with a malady, be it physical, mental or otherwise, felt the exhilarating feeling of freedom as the wave passed over them. It was like their prayers had attained a physical manifestation.

The hospital staff watched the people celebrating their miraculous healing as the security guards eyed Tyler warily. Not sure of how to respond to this sudden situation, the guards once again prepared to subdue him. They slowly formed a line between him and the crowd, drawing their weapons in case he tried anything drastic.

Helen, who had been watching the excitement of the healed, turned and gasped as she saw the guards' reaction. 'Tyler run,' she cried out as she placed herself between him and the guards.

Tyler too had noticed them and had quickly evaluated his options. He was somewhat surprised at his clarity of mind, considering he had just sprouted wings. It seemed as if his only mode of escape would be through a window. Problem was that they were three stories up and he had no idea how to use these wings. Plus the eruption had drained a significant amount of his energy, but as he eyed the guards he knew he had no choice. The room closest to him was open, so he made for the opening, not knowing if he was being pursued or not.

He crashed through the thick hospital window and plummeted into the cool, summer night. The people heard the breaking of glass and turned to find the angel gone. They rushed to various windows, pushing and shoving each other to look out and see if it was he who had broken the window and whether he was really flying or if he was now dead or injured on the ground thirty feet below. At first there was no sign of him on the ground or in the air and then all the sudden he soared passed the windows and away from the building.

He drifted awkwardly across the night sky. He had no idea where to go now. Not that it mattered. All he wanted was to get as far away from the hospital as possible. Before he could get far, he felt the same sensation as before in the hall. A second surge of raw emotion erupted from him, depleting the rest of his energy. His eyes rolled back into his head and his body went limp as he plummeted to the ground.

Chapter 7

Agent Erickson's overly polished black dress shoes clicked monotonously as he strolled through the nearly empty, over-lit, white corridors of headquarters. In his hands he held the file he had been called in to examine. Today should have been his day off, but as it always seemed to happen, the office could never make it through one day without requesting some service from him. Today's request was of the utmost urgency as no one could make heads or tails of the situation. Normally, he would provide assistance via webcam from the comforts of the den in his modest estate in Lexington, Virginia, but today his presence was required and so he begrudgingly complied.

Occupying an elevator alone, he let himself relax as it descended into the bowels of the building. He leaned back against the polished chrome and steel interior pondering about what he could be needed for this time. The last couple cases had been high profile military espionage cases of which his past military service had been needed. Thinking of these cases brought a faint smirk to his lips. Had they really known what his military expertise was, they might have more use for him. Be that as it may, the less they knew of him the better it was for him and everyone around him.

A ding announced the arrival of the car three floors down from where he started. He turned left and walked up to a lone, whitewashed door and ran his security card through the electronic lock. A green light flashed allowing him access to the room. As he entered the room, lights automatically began turning on thanks to motion sensors located on all sides of the door.

The room resembled that of a typical storage room. The ceiling was widely spaced with hanging bulbs and the floor was bare concrete. The back and left wall were lined with steel and wood shelves which contained cleaning supplies, office supplies and other various odds and ends that found this as their semi-final resting place. Along the right wall stood boxes of miscellaneous material stacked from floor to ceiling. In the middle of the wall of boxes was a small, square box, seemingly misplaced amongst the much larger ones surrounding it. Erickson walked up to this box and tapped gently on the 'T,' 'S' and 'U' of 'This Side Up' on the front of the box. As if waking up, the box jiggled and slowly extended itself from its place amongst the bigger boxes and opened up to reveal an impressive array of security equipment including a retinal and fingerprint scanner, voice box, keypad and keycard swipe.

Erickson placed his chin and his forehead on their rests and waited momentarily for the scan. A thin, blue strip of light shot across his eyes first up, then down, then side to side before disappearing as quickly as it had come. A green light displayed at the base of the box flicked on, announcing a pass. He then placed his hand next on the fingerprint scanner. A cool, clear liquid filled the pad and congealed slightly around his fingers, processing his fingerprints. Again the green light flicked on. Leaning in close to the voice box, Erickson clearly stated, 'Agent Samuel Erickson I.D. 5673448.' Again a green light flashed. Lastly he typed the day's password, j-e-l-l-y-f-i-s-h, into the keypad before swiping his keycard.

After the last green light flickered on, the small box closed and retracted back into its place. The room gave a small shudder as a section of the floor rose up, revealing a second elevator, which traveled deeper beneath the building. It looked large enough to carry two normal sized passengers comfortably. Erickson's upper body was practically the size of two normal people. He squeezed into the car once the doors opened and pressed the number -6, waiting impatiently as it slowly made its way down three more floors.

When the elevator finally reached the sixth sub-basement level and opened its doors, he was temporarily blinded by the reflection of the lights off the solid white room. He nearly tripped on the elevator door as he stumbled out of the car. He blinked away tears as his eyes adjusted to the light. 'Why does every room need to be white,' Erickson grumbled.

He took a few minutes to let his eyes adjust to brightness before continuing. He located the door behind the elevator and walked down a long, narrow hallway, which ended at a large observation room. As he neared the room, he noticed an oddly familiar figure standing in its centre. An involuntary chill ran down his spine as he tried to remember where he knew him from.

As he neared the room, the man turned around and greeted him warmly.

'Hello Samuel. Been a long time. Have you been crying?' he asked jokingly. Erickson was blinking more than normal from the bright light, which had caused his eyes to water.

He stared at the man blankly. Humour was a complete waste on him. He found most attempts to be foolish play-on-words or observations, exactly what the man had just tried doing. Stupidity wasn't funny. Ever.

The man sighed. 'Ever the serious one I see. Shame.'

'I'm sorry, but might I ask how we know each

other?' Erickson responded. He was more concerned about whom he might be working with rather than whether he could laugh or not.

The man averted his gaze momentarily to the floor while the corners of his lips drew upwards into a thin, ominous looking smile. He found something in Erickson's manner amusing.

'Let's just say the time of "The Fallen" has finally arrived.'

If his response surprised him he made no sign of it. Erickson just nodded his head in acceptance and turned his attention to why he had been requested on his day off.

'So what matter of dire urgency am I here for?'

'Have you had a chance to look through the file you received?'

'Not yet,' he replied. He stared absently at the folder still clutched in his hand. 'I normally have no need to sort through meaningless files when verbal explanations suit me much better.' Reading files was a waste of time. No one could accurately understand the gravity of a situation by staring at words. The tone in a person's voice and look in their eyes were more accurate portrayals. Plus you could tell whether the information was the truth or a lie.

'I see,' said the man, nodding, appreciating his honesty. 'Follow me then.'

The man led Erickson through the room, maneuvering through a small group of lab-coat clothed observers, over to a large window centered on the back wall. What Erickson saw when he reached the window made him regret not at least glancing through the file when he'd had the opportunity.

'Is that what I think it is?' he questioned. He'd thought the comment on "the time of The Fallen" was some code to explain that they were on the same side, not a statement of fact.

'Amazing is it?' the man answered, his eyes twinkling in amusement.

'Of course it is! Does anyone else know about this?'

'Other than those here, only a small group of people from a hospital in Rochester, New Hampshire, but they have been properly handled. We were alerted to his presence by a series of 911 calls made a few nights ago. Apparently, our new friend here came crashing through the roof of a townhouse not too far away from the hospital.'

Erickson stared blankly through the window at the figure in the room. He felt uncharacteristically giddy at the sight, but was strong enough not let it be seen. It was still a beautiful sight to behold a creature of such magnificence. This was a truly defining moment, because it proved all his work had not been done in vain. Breaking into the Vatican's library, sneaking around in the private areas of Westminster Abbey, all in search of clues for the location of something he wasn't sure he believed in until now.

'What's going to be done with "him"?' he asked the man, not turning his view from the angel.

'Well for the last few hours our physicians and scientists have been attempting to conduct tests on "it", but have been met with certain resistance.'

'What kind of resistance? He's confined to a chair so how much resistance could he be giving?'

'The file explains the resistance, but as you prefer visual and verbal explanations, follow me and I'll show you.'

The man motioned for the agent to follow him. He walked around Erickson towards the left side of the window where another electronically locked door stood. After swiping his card, the door hissed open and the man walked through, pausing briefly to make sure Erickson was following him.

Erickson was a little anxious as he walked through the airlock. These types of rooms always unnerved him. He heard the door click tightly behind him. It was indeed a dream to witness such a finding as this, but at the same time he wasn't sure what to expect. Nothing like this had ever been found in the history of man so it was safe to presume the creature to be highly unpredictable and volatile.

He found himself growing ever more astonished with the creature the closer he got. The only article of clothing still attached to the angel's frame was the tattered remains of a hospital gown. It was attached around his waist by the frayed remnants of string, covering the extremities of the obviously male creature. Everything about it was anatomically perfect. Its body looked as if it was chiseled out of pure marble. The porcelain skin was smooth and practically blemish free. Well-defined muscles rippled and accented its lean frame. Its face radiated with an aura of perfection. The entire structure of its being was symmetrically flawless. It was the perfect specimen of the ideal human and perfect male.

'He's perfect,' Erickson marveled as he walked slowly around the figure, which was securely strapped into a medical chair.

'Yes it is, but its perfection is causing our scientists and doctors quite a few problems. Watch this.'

The man took a syringe and walked over to the silent, unmoving figure. He uncapped it and attempted to stick the needle into its upper arm. When the needle struck the skin, rather than insert smoothly as with a normal human being, the needle shattered into several pieces leaving the skin unmarred.

The musical tinkling of the broken needle on the floor caused the angel to stir and slowly open its eyes. It squinted against the blinding lights directly above its head and attempted to raise an arm to shield its eyes. When it found it couldn't move its arm, the angel struggled vainly to rise from the chair, automatically causing the straps holding it in place to tighten. Once it realized it was bound in place, it began to thrash around wildly, creating a sharp grating noise as the chair wobbled back and forth.

'What're you guys doing to me?' the angel asked through gritted teeth, visibly angry. 'Why am I strapped to this chair?'

While the angel thrashed around, Erickson and the man slowly edged away from it in order to protect themselves. Erickson had learned early in life that the safest way to escape when you were being attacked was to never turn your back. Even though the creature was secured in the chair, they were still unsure of what it was capable of. They kept eye contact with the angel until they had backed into the wall closest to the observation room exit. Once they hit the wall, they turned and made a run for it. They were just about to the door when its plea stopped them.

'Please help me.'

It's appeal sounded so pathetic, helpless and sincere, that it caused them both to pause and consider helping it. They turned back around and found the angel staring them firmly in the eyes. His gaze was so powerful that they stood there unsure what to do next. For the next five minutes an awkward silence filled the room as the three of them, as well as everyone in the adjacent room, stared at each other.

Erickson was the first to speak. 'Who are you?' he asked as he did his best to mask his unease.

The angel just stared, his eyes filling with defiance.

'I asked you my questions first. Answer mine and then I'll tell you who I am. Not that you don't already know.'

Erickson was about to speak when he was silenced by a sharp, clearing of the throat. The man stepped around him and into the view of the angel.

'You were brought here in order for us to run some tests on you. The straps are for everyone's protection since we are incapable of knowing what threat you could pose to us.'

The angel listened quietly, clenching his fists open and close as if trying to gain circulation back into his hands.

It sighed. 'Alright. I understand the precautionary detail, but to be honest I'm no threat to anyone. So could you please release these straps? I can barely feel my hands.'

Erickson smirked amused and the man chuckled softly.

'Nice try, but until we figure out exactly what you are, you will remain restrained. As soon as we believe you pose no viable threat, then you will be released.'

The angel's countenance darkened as he began to understand his situation. Erickson's unease grew slightly as he stared between the man and the angel. It was like watching a battle of wills and not knowing which one to bet on. Then, the angel's expression changed. The discontented stare completely disappeared to be replaced by a look of total indifference.

'Fine then,' it replied, as if totally unconcerned. 'If that's the way it's going to be, I'll just have to break out.'

The man scoffed loudly and began to laugh.

'Don't be ridiculous?' the man guffawed. Incredulity filled his voice at the ridiculous notion. 'The straps binding you are a tightly woven polymer fabric specially made to be able to hold up to 3000 tons and can only be cut by a diamond saw. The window here,' he said, walking over to thick observation window to the left of the airlock, 'is two feet thick and made of bulletproof plexiglas. The rest of the room is made of cinder block and concrete, 6-feet thick and completely solid. I'm sorry my friend, but you are completely contained and have no possible hope of escape.'

The angel chuckled; a sound similar to the gurgling of a mountain stream and smooth like crystal.

'You seem to think that these restrictions apply to the likes of all creatures. If you couldn't tell, I'm not quite the same as other people.'

A faint resentment trailed in the wake of his words, as if he had not always been like this. Erickson watched him intently, still wary of the creature and his proclamation of escaping. According to it, the extensive reinforcements placed around this underground station would not be enough to contain him and if that was the case, they were in big trouble.

The man, who continued to be so sure of these protective measures, stared in defiance at the angel. 'If you think you can escape then by all means go ahead, but I guarantee you won't be able to,' he challenged.

'What are you doing?' Erickson exclaimed, grabbing the man's arm. 'Are you trying to get us killed?'

'Don't worry Samuel. It won't be able to escape. We are perfectly safe.' He calmly pulled Erickson's hand from his upper arm.

The man turned back to the angel and motioned with a nod for it to go ahead and try. The angel took a glimpse around the room, surveying it, taking note of every crack, crevice, strength and vulnerability. Once he'd gotten a general feel for the room, he turned his attention to the straps securing him at the chest, waist and calves. Recalling the strength and structure of the straps, the angel focused intently on their centre.

As Erickson watched the angel, he found himself distracted at what he could swear was someone humming. He glanced around the room but saw no one.

'Do you hear something?' he asked the man, who was also looking around the room.

The man never even had a chance to answer the

question before the humming began to reverberate throughout the room as well as in their heads. With each second the sound became louder, but strangely didn't cause them any discomfort. In was like the incessant drone of a low flying plane as it got closer. Once the humming reached an impossible crescendo, the angel began to exude a pale glow, which glowed brighter and brighter as the humming plateaued. Within a minute, the room shone with a heavenly light, purer than any of the iridescent bulbs proclaimed to emit. Erickson shielded his eyes from its brightness until it suddenly wasn't there anymore.

He looked to the angel and found him still sitting in the chair with the straps still holding him. He smirked, glad that the restraints had proven themselves. Then he watched the angel begin to smile. It was confusing. Why was it smiling when it couldn't even break free of its bonds?

'What are you smiling about?' he asked.

'Oh nothing. Just wondering the best way to say goodbye.'

Suddenly the straps around the angel disintegrated as it burst through them. Erickson and the man collapsed in fear. It had been years since he'd felt this feeling. Not since his first mission in the Baltics where he'd been victim to the wrath of a double agent that had gone rogue. It debilitated him. He couldn't see. He couldn't breath. All he could feel was a knife, gently gliding against his jugular and down his chest, not cutting him, but invoking mental torture of what they might do to him.

He heard the sound of feet moving closer. His heart beat as fast as hummingbirds' wings. What were they going to do to him? He was about to lose consciousness when he felt hands on either side of his head. A cool, calm feeling began to seep into his head, rapidly permeating through every pore of his body. From the calm came the most exquisite feeling of ease he'd ever felt. Every pain and ache he had been feeling simply vanished.

As Erickson sat there marveling at his new pain-free disposition, he quickly realized the hands were no longer on his head. He opened his eyes and found his vision had been restored and his breathing had returned to normal. He looked straight ahead to where the angel was standing. It stood in the middle of the room staring at him. He turned his gaze from the angel to where the man had been and found him laid out on the floor. He started to stand to go to him but the angel motioned for him to stop.

'He'll be fine,' it said. 'Before I leave, I just wanted to answer your question. My name is Tyler Morris and I have become the fallen angel of legend, prophesied to return. I don't know why it's me or why I'm here, but I know that through me this world will either be saved or destroyed.'

Tyler quit speaking. His wings unfurled spreading out over ten feet from tip to tip. Erickson stared in disbelief. They were a strangely impressive and humbling sight. Tyler gave him a nod and turned to the large observation window. It resembled one of those windows found in aquariums, just a whole lot more indestructible. All the inhabitants of the room had crowded to the window to watch the action, but now began to back away as Tyler's attention focused on them.

He nodded towards the window and concentrated on the two foot thick unbreakable glass. The people behind it began to panic and stumble away as a small vibration ran across the surface in a rippling fashion. Seconds later, the window groaned defiantly and gave. Screams came from the room as the window shattered into billions of tiny razor-sharp shards. The screams quickly subsided as the people put down their arms when they didn't feel anything. Many of them gasped when they saw the shards of glass had not sprayed throughout the room, but were floating as if suspended in a gelatinous layer of air. Suddenly the pieces swept away from their frame and into the room, forming a cylinder around Tyler, looking similar to the rings of Saturn.

Erickson watched in trepidation as the pieces of glass began to orbit the angel. At first they rotated slowly, gently reflecting the light into brilliant, dancing rainbows strewn about the room. Soon they began to spin at a breakneck pace, blurring the image of Tyler within its core. The tip of the cylinder arced into a point as the orbiting glass and Tyler started rising off the floor. Once they reached the ceiling, the concrete and cinder block practically disintegrated at impact and within minutes he had disappeared from view.

Other than a few shocked cries coming from the levels above, dead silence echoed around him. When he finally regained control of his being, he moved to right beneath the hole but found it vacant. Tyler, the mysterious resurrected fallen angel, was gone.

Chapter 8

As soon as Tyler disappeared from view, all the people in the observation room began freaking out again. The sounds of their agitated voices sounded like an oncoming train in Erickson's ears. The dull rumbling caused his head, which had only moments before been ache-free, to begin to throb.

He had to use the wall to steady himself as he tried standing. It took everything in him to ignore the commotion and his aching head so he could stay upright. Once he had gained his composure and felt steady, he let go of the wall and brushed the dust and debris from out of his hair and off his clothing. A sudden jolt ran through his body as a tiny sliver of glass, which had been caught on the sleeve of his jacket, stabbed into the palm of his hand. Two miniscule droplets of blood oozed out of the wound and pooled in the hollow of his hand as he stared in perplexed astonishment, mulling over the events that had just transpired. Somehow, Tyler, this "fallen angel," had defied all manner of possibility and had escaped when it was believed no hope was to be had. Could this really be what he and The Brethren had been searching for these last few years?

Erickson knew he needed to arrange a meeting with The Brethren as soon as possible. Pulling the sliver of glass from his hand and shaking off the blood, Erickson took a quick glance around the room. About 3 yards away lay the body of the man facedown, covered in dust, cement pieces and shards of glass. Erickson rushed over to him and was relieved to find him still alive. He did a quick one over to make sure there was no physical damage to the man before gently patting him on the face three or four times to revive him.

'You all right?' he asked when the man opened his eyes. The man flinched at the brightness of the light but was more concerned about the destruction.

'What happened?' he groaned, staring dumbfounded at the scene that lay before him.

'Well it would appear as if the creature, whose name is Tyler by the way, accepted your challenge and escaped.'

'You must be joking?' the man stated, stunned.

'Do I seem like the joking type? And even if I were, right now would be rather poor timing to joke about such things. I have no idea how he did it, but he removed himself from his bindings, shattered that window and bored his way out through the ceiling.'

The man stared in astonishment at the gaping hole in the ceiling. He appeared to be fine so Erickson got up, brushed the dust from off his knees and turned to leave. He had more important things to do than sit around and babysit.

'If you're doing alright, I have a pressing engagement I must be present at.'

'Yeah, yeah I'll be fine,' the man responded absently.

Erickson passed through the frightened throng in the observation room and made his way from the lower levels to the main entrance. Once he passed through the main terminal and out into the sunlight, he pulled his mobile out of his pocket. He turned it on and pressed the number one on speed dial. A few rings passed before a rich baritone answered on the other end.

'Yes Samuel. What can I do for you?' the man asked.

'I need to request a meeting with The Brethren right now,' he stated abruptly as he waved his free arm. A taxi stopped and he quickly got in.

'Why the sudden urgency? Have you found something?'

'Yes. A fallen angel has just escaped from an impenetrable security cell at headquarters about fifteen minutes ago.'

'Alright. You shall have your meeting. Be there in 1 hour.'

'Perfect. I'll be at the meeting place shortly.'

Shortly was an understatement. Throughout the duration of their conversation, he had already traversed half the distance. The rest of trip was relatively uneventful and traffic was surprisingly sparse.

The taxi arrived on the outskirts of a rundown factory in the lower east end by the docks a short time later. Erickson paid the driver and sent him on his way before squeezing through the fence and entering the lot. Walking past what appeared to be the main entrance, Erickson turned the corner and walked up to a dumpster and paused. He made sure no one was around before putting his shoulder to the dumpster and pushed it a few inches. This activated a hidden mechanism, causing the dumpster and a small portion of the wall attached to it to swing out, revealing a hidden passageway into the darkness.

Fluorescent lighting flickered on as soon as he entered the passageway. Illuminated before him was a staircase leading below the main level through the side of the abandoned factory. Before beginning down the stairs, Erickson touched a password into the keypad by the mouth of the entrance. The dumpster rolled back into place against the wall and move the few inches deactivating the sensor.

From the bottom of the stairs, he followed a short hallway into a large, circular, cavernous room. Even though he had been in this room many times, he still felt a sense of wonder every time he entered. The chamber had been housed in a secret grotto found accidentally after a hurricane had damaged the side of the above factory, leaving its opening exposed.

The walls of the cave were formed of solid granite, which glistened brilliantly in the flickering torchlight. From these walls hung thick strands of dark green, red and bright yellow moss. He had always wondered why The Brethren left the moss when it seemed so out of place amid the expensive upgrades. Amongst the strands of moss hung the banners of their order, a hooded figure holding a sword and a cross, encircled by eight odd angelic figures. Four of them represented the four elements while the other four he didn't recognize. The only significant attribute was they each bore a different colour: red, white, black and a pale green.

On the ground, black onyx and white marble had been laid to even out the rigid ground, giving the floor a checkerboard look. On the east end was a two-foot opening about eight feet from the ground that let in a small waterfall of seawater that outlined the perimeter of the room. It disappeared into another opening at the base of the west wall. Set in the back of the room was a semicircle of twelve chairs made of mahogany and cherry wood with burgundy satin cushioning. They were placed on a stage behind a wooden partition, which was intricately carved with scenes of an epic battle and the fall of angels from heaven. Between each chair stood a tall iron candlestick, each with a white ornate candle burning brightly.

He stood at the entrance admiring the dark beauty of the cavern until he heard a sharp tapping echo throughout the room.

'Samuel. Please approach the council,' came a nasal, high-pitched voice from the dark shadows of one of the chairs.

Distracted from his gazing, Erickson entered the room and sank to one knee before the semicircle.

'Welcome Samuel Erickson: Agent of the U.S. Government, faithful follower of our order and most trusted liaison. For what purpose have you called us, The Brethren of the League of the Damned together? We have been informed it is a matter of some urgency. Please rise and state your case.'

Erickson rose. A faint glimmer of a smile formed in the flickering of the candlelight as he took a deep breath.

'Brethren. As of this afternoon, confirmation of the existence of the Fallen Angel has been made.'

A commotion broke out from amongst the hooded figures. He could slightly make out more of their faces as their movements caused the flames to flicker revealingly. It surprised him to find only a handful of the darkly beautiful chairs filled. It could only be assumed that the meeting had been too short notice for all of them to make it.

'How can you be sure it isn't some hoax?' another voice called from the shadows. 'There have been so many rumours of such phenomenon in the last fifty years. Is it possible it could be another false lead?'

'I know it isn't a hoax sir because I've seen it with my own eyes.'

An awkward silence filled the room as the gravity of his reply sunk in. For a matter of uncomfortable minutes, Erickson stood in the middle of the room, waiting anxiously for any one of The Brethren to make some sort of response. After the first couple of minutes passed, a hooded figure, which sat in the center of the semicircle, stood and spoke.

'Samuel Erickson. This information pleases us greatly. We, The Brethren of the League of the Damned, charge you now to seek out and locate the Fallen Angel. Once you have found it, you are to follow it and report back daily of your findings. This task is one of utmost importance as the Angel is the key for our success. Now go. We shall prepare your travel arrangements and any accommodation requirements you might need. Go and Godspeed.'

Nodding his head in understanding, Erickson cast one last look into the darkness of the stage before turning and retreating out of the room. Finally. The beginning of the end had come.

Chapter 9

When Tyler broke through the final layer of sheetrock and concrete, he found himself in unknown surroundings. The rays from the noonday sun reflected off the towering glass skyscrapers bathing the rooftop in semi natural light. He released his control of the glass shards, letting them crumble onto the rooftop where they glistened in the sunlight like thousands of clear, uncut diamonds. He shielded his eyes to get a better look around him, but was deterred by the neighbouring buildings which dwarfed the one in which he'd been bound. He peered over the ledge but didn't get any better clues. Some eight to ten stories below him, the sidewalks were bustling with midday activity as thousands of people rushed to unknown destinations. The only thing he could figure was that he was downtown somewhere.

He shook the remaining shards out of his hair and off his skin before climbing onto the edge of the building. Where could he possibly be? He knew he couldn't stay on the rooftop for much longer. He could swear he heard sirens in the distance as well. The problem was, how could he escape from these people if he didn't even know where he was? Especially in the middle of the day. He needed to remain hidden, but that was now impossible. He looked upward, taking a good look at the height of the surrounding structures and determined that his best shot at figuring out where he was would be by looking down from atop any one of those buildings.

Without any regard for being seen, he took to flight, reaching the tops of the high-rises in a matter of minutes. He rose from the midst of the claustrophobic cluster of buildings and floated gently on the wind, letting his wings bask in the unfiltered radiance of the sun. A gentle breeze tossed his unkempt hair to and fro and the warm sunlight encasing his body in its radiance. His mind disappeared to a place where he felt as if all his woes were gone. Time stopped as he entered a state of bliss where none could harm him. To his dismay, a passing cloud brought this beautiful state of euphoria to a quick end. Disappointed, he returned to trying to figure out where he was.

He had barely made half a rotation when a familiar sight revealed to him his location: Washington D.C. Directly to his north stood the Washington Memorial, sticking up out of the ground like a beacon, pointing him the way home. He maneuvered through a flock of seagulls, passing over the memorial and continuing north out of the city and up along the coast.

As he flew, he felt as if he was noticing for the first time the true beauty of the world around him. It was as if he had experienced a rebirth and his eyes were finally open. All around his being he sensed the emotions of life from the explosion of birth to the sudden snuffing of death. Every plant, creature and even inanimate objects projected some wave of being that fascinated him to the point that he almost fell out of the sky when he remembered he was flying.

He was still trying to get the hang of flying. Flying itself was easy enough, it was just the freaking out part when he zoned out and then remembered he was in the air. Since the first moment he took to flight some days ago, at least it seemed like a few days ago, it had come almost naturally, like the wings had always been a part of his body. Even though his body had adapted instantly to the new addition of the wings, his brain was still adjusting. It was like riding a bike though. The longer and more often he flew, the fewer times he panicked when he disappeared into his thoughts.

He flew all throughout the day and a good way into the night along the coastline before fatigue and thirst finally forced him to the ground. Turning inland, he landed in a forest on the outskirts of a small town. He glided around over it before spotting a small glade where he could land without having to maneuver through the tightly packed trees. On the ground, he searched as quietly as possible until he found a small stream, gently gurgling through the underbrush. He quenched his thirst before nestled himself against the base of a large oak next to the stream, quickly passing into unconsciousness.

When he finally woke up, the sun was already at its peak in the sky, showering the forest with golden rays of light. He brought his hand up to shield his eyes from its brightness and looked around, marveling at the circumstances that brought him to this current place. Had it all really happened or was it all some sort of psychotic dream? Tyler felt around his back and once his fingers felt the soft downy feathers he knew it was all true.

He stood up and wiped the dirt and plant life from what remained of the tattered hospital gown that had somehow remained attached to his waist throughout all this. He was going to have to get some new clothes soon or else people would be in for more of surprise than they would already be. As he extended his arms to stretch, he could feel his back muscles pivot as the wings extended with the movement of his arms. This was quite interesting. Both times he had flown, panic had driven him to get away and thoughts on how he was able to fly hadn't really presented themselves. Now that he was semi safe, he figured it was as good a time as any to figure out how he was able to control the wings.

He moved a few yards away from the tree to a location with more space and extended his left arm straight, parallel to the ground. As his arm moved, the left wing extended as well, spreading to full length. He dropped his left arm quickly and just as fast, raised his right. The wings moved as fluidly with the arms as if they were connected. Then a thought struck him, as he had been flying, his arms hadn't been flapping. This caused him to pause a moment. "What if.......?" he thought, scratching his chin in consideration. Without moving his arms, he tried to make the wings extend on their own. It took quite a bit of concentration, but before long, he was able to extend the wings without his arms moving. It was as if they were another set of appendages that could move independently, without much thought involved. Of course these were new additions to his body so it would take some time to get the hang of them, but now that he was beginning to understand how they worked, he should be able to manipulate them like they had always been there.

Since he was continually getting the hang of moving the wings, he practiced raising one wing at a time, both together and flapping. Sometimes he found himself raising his arms along with the wings. It frustrated him the more often he did it. It took some intense concentration and self control, characteristics he had been able to develop through trying to remain rational, unlike Mark, but soon he had made significant progress. Once he felt confident with his progress, he felt it was time to try taking to flight.

As he was preparing to take off, he heard a twig snap to his left. He pivoted towards the sound and found himself staring into the eyes of a boy no older than 10 years old. He was standing, barely visible, behind the oak tree under which he had been sleeping the previous night. Tyler should have been frightened that the boy might have brought others with him, but as they both stood there, frozen in the speckled sunlight, neither one of them seemed afraid.

'Are those real?' the boy asked, hobbling out from behind the tree, his crutches pushing the foliage out of the way as he walked.

Tyler stared at the boy, a little perplexed.

'Yes they're real. Aren't you afraid of me?' he asked as the boy came within arms length of him.

'No.'

'Why not?'

'Because if those wings are real than you're an angel and angels are good. Right?'

His logic seemed sound and struck Tyler to the core. This boy really had no idea who he was, but because of his wings he assumed he was good.

'Well I am an angel, but not the kind you think I am,' he said, dropping to one knee in front of the boy. 'I'm a fallen angel.'

'Does that mean you're bad then?' the boy asked, inquisitiveness filling his eyes.

Tyler laughed. 'You know, I really don't know what it means. This is all relatively new to me. By the way, what's wrong with your legs?'

The boy sighed and hung his head.

'What's wrong?' Tyler asked dropping to both knees, concerned his question had been a bad one.

'Nothing. When I was born my legs came out deformed and the doctors haven't been able to fix them. I'll never be able to walk normally.'

Tyler looked across at the boy, compassion filling his being.

'There's something else isn't there?'

The boy looked up, doing his best to look tough as a tear

slipped down his cheek.

'I was hoping you were a real angel cause maybe you could fix my legs.'

His honesty caused Tyler to choke back tears. What could he do? As he stared at the boy, he wished there was something he could do but he wasn't sure if there was. It was true he was now an angel, but could he really heal someone's physical deformities? He had eased the agent's suffering, but that was so small compared to changing the state of the boy's legs. If he didn't at least try he knew he would never forgive himself.

Putting his hand on the boy's shoulder, Tyler said, 'Well this is what we're going to do. I'll try to heal your legs, but don't get your hopes up. Like I said, all this is new to me so I don't know if I can.'

The boy smiled and nodded his head eagerly in understanding, wiping away his tears with the back of his hand. Tyler put his hands on both the boy's shoulders and closed his eyes. In his head, he tried to access the ability to heal. He searched throughout his mind, but felt nothing. He tried concentrating really hard, but all he felt was the heat from the sun, and the heat of embarrassment. As best he could, he sent his psyche throughout his body searching for that strand of power that had made him able to heal. It made no difference how deeply he searched it somehow eluded him. After a few minutes with no outcome, he gave a sigh of defeat, letting go of the boy. He hung his head in shame.

'I'm sorry,' he said, feeling honest regret.

'It's ok,' the boy said, putting his hand comfortingly on Tyler's shoulder. 'At least you tried.'

A sudden commotion came from the surrounding foliage as a mob of people appeared through the trees, entering the tiny clearing in which they stood. As soon as they saw Tyler, they stopped, obviously confused. Once they saw the boy with him, their bewilderment turned to panic. They all started speaking at once, calling the boy to them, but daring not to come much closer to the monster, whom they believed could possibly harm the child.

Tyler stood up behind the boy, who had already turned around to face the throng. Putting his hands on the boy's shoulders once more, a sudden swell of courage poured over him. His wings extended to their full length, catching the full power of sun, which was now shining intensely in the clearing. He raised his face to meet the light. As the sun warmed his face, he felt a peace come over him and he began to smile. The peace spread through his veins like pure sunlight, causing his skin to take on an ethereal glow. It was as if the warmth of the sun had triggered an angelic switch in him.

He knelt back down and whispered into the boy's ear, 'Are you ready?' Seeing the boy give a tiny but resolute nod, he wrapped his wings around him. As he enveloped the boy, he began to chant a sweet but haunting melody. The mysterious melody lulled the mob, which had been cautiously moving closer, into a mesmerized silence. As he chanted, he grew brighter and brighter until the brilliance of the sun couldn't compare. Then the brilliance was gone. Releasing the boy from his hold, Tyler turned and ran, jumping into the air and taking flight. Within a few beats of his wings he had disappeared from the view of the crowd.

Chapter 10

    The sun was beginning to dip below the cloud line when Rochester came into view. Tyler had been flying up in the bulky clouds as a precautionary measure. He figured the further up he flew, the less like a man with wings he would appear. He floated serenely amid the white bulky masses, letting the wind casually blow him in the right direction. He could have made it to Rochester hours earlier, but as it was, he felt no dire need for urgency. So he took his time.

    The sun was waving its last goodbye before sinking beneath the horizon when he arrived at his destination. There were still a few cars left in the parking lot of the cathedral when he arrived, so he perched himself inside one of the bell towers and waited patiently for the parishioners to vacate the premise. Boy did he have to wait. It wasn't until the last specks of daylight had been eaten by the oncoming darkness that a slender stretch of light appeared, disappeared, appeared again in the form of two piercing beams, which then faded into the surrounding hills. He waited a few minutes longer to ensure no one returned. Once the coast was clear he sprang noiselessly from the tower. As he circled around towards the front of the building, a flutter of movement at the edge of the field, where the lush sea of green dramatically formed tall stalks of yellow silk, caught his eye. He turned his head towards it but any movement had ceased. He circled around once more out of curiosity, but when nothing remerged, he continued on his way, landing semi-awkwardly in front of the entrance.

He did his best to make no noise as he slowly eased the massive oaken doors open a crack. He had it nearly opened and shut without incident when an earsplitting squeal sounded for a split second as two well-worn and ungreased sections of the hinges connected. Cursing himself, he quickly slammed shut the door and disappeared into the darkness of the vacant chapel.

Father Michael was sitting at the table in his dining area reading the newspaper when the high-shrilled squeal pricked his ears, followed by a slam, which shuddered the walls. Creasing his eyebrows in curiosity, he got up from the table and walked over to the stove where a kettle of water was quietly waiting to boil. He pulled the top off but found the water still reverently sitting on the bottom as if telling him there was no way it could have made such a bothersome noise.

Grabbing his jacket and a flashlight, Father Michael crossed the room, quietly opening his door. He noiselessly ascended the spiraling staircase leading to an alcove just off the entrance of the chapel. He took a few steps into the oratory and peered around. With enough light coming from the various stained and unstained glass windows, he was able to see his immediate surroundings without much difficulty. He found nothing out of the ordinary so he began to retreat back down the stairs.

Just as he was placing his foot upon the top step, a muted, metallic clang echoed throughout the hall, much like an empty tin can would make on a tile kitchen floor.

'Who's there?' Father Michael called out. He cautiously entered the chapel again. 'I know someone's out there.'

Silence answered, giving him no clue to who or

what was now hiding in the darkness. Shadows groped at him from every corner, clutching at his imagination, making him see monsters and demons in their two-dimensional plane. He pulled the flashlight from his jacket pocket and shined the beam around the room, illuminating ever crack and corner, dispelling any notion of imaginary horror. Everywhere he looked, he found nothing. No sign of intrusion, no disturbance of dust, no book or chair out of place. Nothing.

When he reached the end of the pews, he noticed the sacrament table at the front of the chapel seemed slightly empty. The ceremonial wine goblet, which normally stood on the left side of the table, had gone missing. He scoured the immediate area, but found nothing. He even looked under the table. Although, how could a chalice of such a light weight have managed to roll behind the heavy nylon table covering, which nearly reached the floor? He knelt down and checked under the pews. Again nothing. It was as if the chalice had simply vanished. A muted sound, no goblet. Only him and the darkness. Well himself, the darkness and some intruder that had yet to make itself known.

A muffled, rustling sound came from behind him. Father Michael turned quickly and shone the light into the apse, but found not a soul. He slowly shone the light around the alcove a second time and was perplexed when the light rested on the chalice, sitting upright in the back of the room. It was close to the massive stain glass window depicting the Lord Jesus in full figure with arms outstretched, welcoming all those who wanted to be spiritually fed into his fold.

He walked up to the vessel, knelt down and picked it up. Turning it around in his hands, he quickly inspected it, insuring that it hadn't been damaged. He let out a quick, short sigh of relief upon finding the goblet still in pristine condition. Of course he still had no idea as to how it had gotten in the apse, bit at least it wasn't damaged.

He was stepping to turn around and replace the cup when a chill ran down his spine, sending shivers racing across every inch of his being. It was as if a presence had suddenly become aware, taking up the entire room within its consciousness. Father Michael was caught so off-guard he froze in his tracks, seconds away from passing out from the sheer weight of it. It felt like time stopped. He waited, expecting something, anything to happen.

He didn't have to wait long. A gruff voice growled in his ear, 'You feeling lucky, punk?'

'What?' Father Michael asked, a little baffled by the question, struggling not to collapse.

The gruff voice chuckled rather maniacally, causing all colour to recede out of Father Michael's face. That would be if you could have seen it in the dark.

Again the gruff voice spoke. 'Well do you?'

'I...I...I don't believe in luck,' Father Michael stammered, now beginning to tremble. Was he going to be killed in his own parish? "It hasn't even been fifty years yet," he thought, randomly remembering the service of a priest in this cathedral. "Pull yourself together", another voice in his brain chastised. "You're a fighter remember, so act like it." It had been many years since he had needed to fight. The adrenaline needed to trigger such a response was relatively high. If it came to that, what would he be able to do?

The voice let out a chilling laugh, which bounced multiple times off the cold granite walls. 'Well that isn't going to do you much good now is it?' the voice growled, obviously pleased with the response he had given.

Suddenly a light bulb went off in Father Michael's brain. He twisted around the flashlight in his hand. Maybe the perp didn't know he had it. Highly unlikely, but possible. He would simply use it a club and brain the villain. He just needed to time it right. With this new resolve, he was determined to not go down without a fight.

He gripped the handle of the flashlight in his right hand and the chalice in his left. He hoped to catch the perp unaware. Crying out wildly, he turned sharply, swinging both objects in a wide arc to where the voice sounded like it had come from. Despite the sturdiness of the attempt, neither object connected with anything solid and with the momentum, he slipped off his feet and crumpled to the floor. Just before he hit the ground, instinct kicked in. He ducked and rolled into a crouch.

The voice chuckled mockingly, amused at the spectacle, but did nothing. Father Michael ears picked up the sound and turned his head slightly in the direction. He shook the flashlight gently but was dismayed to find he had somehow managed to break the tiny bulb, rendering it useless other than as a baton. He immediately slowed his heart and calmed his breathing. If he was to survive this, he needed to relax. Years worth of training came flooding into his memory.

His ears perked as he heard a tiny scuffle to his right. Whoever it was, they were barefoot. He felt a tiny gust of wind and heard a shuffle in the air now directly in front of him. What kind of creature was this? He could sense its presence mere feet away from him now. He closed his eyes and let the beast inside take over.

He lunged to attack, jabbing with the flashlight rather than swinging it. The creature sidestepped it easy enough but wasn't prepared for the roundhouse kick that sent it sprawling into the pews. It noisily tried to get up but the priest was there in a second pile-driving his fist into the demons chest. Before he could connect, the creature grabbed his arm and pushed off the ground with its feet, twisting around his arm and disappearing into the rafters.

'Come back down here and fight,' the priest shouted up to it. 'This is what you want isn't it? Well

I'm not going to be that easy to kill.'

'Who said anything about killing?' the creature said from above him. 'Killing you would be pointless as I need you alive.'

'Why? What is so important about me?'

'Do you really want to know?'

'Of course.'

With a thud, the creature landed a few feet away from him. It chuckled, this time inquiring, with a loud, gravelly and menacing voice, 'Would you like a light to see me better?'

Before he could utter a response, every candle in the room burst into flame. The darkness disappeared and exposed the demon that had been causing Father Michael all this fright. 'Che cavolo?!?' the priest gasped in confusion at what stood turned with its back to him. Here was a man with the wings of an angel. There could be no other description. Not even birds had that magnificent of wings. Each feather radiated strength and shone with an indescribable brilliance that even the candles seemed to bow to their beauty.

'Would you look at that?' the creature spoke, breaking Father Michael's fascinated concentration. 'I had no idea I could do that.'

The creature seemed obviously pleased with this new discovery and sat there marveling for a moment before turning around.

'Tyler?!' Father Michael gasped. He couldn't be totally sure if it was his friend he was looking at. 'Is that you?'

The intense light from the hundreds of fiery candles cast an aura of radiant purity around his being that seemed more natural than a mere byproduct created from the flames light. His sandy blonde hair waved in some unfelt breeze, giving it the affect of holy fire. His once tan skin now had the appearance of pearl, smooth with a smoky translucency that seemed to absorb the surrounding light into its very core rather than reflect it. His seemingly constant stressed out demeanor, along with tired out expression and sad, puppy dog eyes, were all gone, replaced with an angelic serenity not possibly found on this world. This new, but old Tyler stood before him, bathed in flickering candlelight. He could almost not believe what he was seeing. It had only been the previous week that Tyler had been venting all is stress about Mark, but now one might think he had never had a stressful moment in his entire existence.

Father Michael picked himself off the floor and asked once again, 'Tyler? Is that really you?'

Smiling mischievously, he replied, 'Of course it's me. Who else would it be?'

The priest suddenly burst. 'La sapevo! Sapevo che dovevi essere tu. Non posso credere che sta accadendo, durante la mia vita!' Father Michael spun around in unbridled glee.

'Um, Father?'

The priest stopped reveling to look at his friend.

'Sì? Uh I mean yes?'

'What were you just saying?'

'Nothing for you to worry about.'

'You weren't surprised about this were you? About me becoming an angel?'

Father Michael laughed uncomfortably, purposely not answering the question. Tyler was acting so casual and spontaneous. It suddenly bothered the priest that he was acting unconcerned. If he only knew how many people in the last 300 years had attempted to find what he had now become, he would not be acting so carelessly. The problem was he didn't. Father Michael sighed, knowing that he was going to have to be told.

'Tyler,' he began, trying his hardest not to be as casual as he usually was with him. 'This house is one of the most sacred buildings belonging to the Church. Here is housed the very essence and understanding of your past and our future. The secrets found here would cause the very undoing of the delicate balance of what is known and of what is meant to remain hidden.'

Father Michael's voice resonated through the rafters and off the high vaulted ceiling. The richness of his tone mixed with his thick Mediterranean accent gave his message a much deeper and more profound importance than he would normally have been able.

Tyler stared amazed at him, surprised at such power of speech.

'Where'd you learn to speak like that?' he inquired, his eyes wide with delight. 'You seriously had me on the edge of my seat there. Did you memorize that or did you just make it up right then?'

Father Michael stared at him with the same dumbfounded expression that Tyler was giving him. Was he serious?

'Tyler!' he admonished, 'this isn't a joke. This is serious. The very future of humanity is at stake here!'

Tyler lowered his eyes to the floor, crestfallen. 'Sorry Father. I was just impressed.'

Father Michael dropped and shook his head in exasperation.

'No Tyler, I'm sorry,' he said, sitting down in a pew. 'It's just that there is so much at stake now that you're here. I personally am amazed that it really is you. I would have never thought that in my lifetime, the Fallen Angel of legend would arise. I had my suspicions and hopes, but nothing was ever sure. To have this happening now is all very surprising and unbelievable for me, as I'm sure it is for you.'

Tyler turned and walked to the first pew and took a seat next to the priest. The red velvet cushion of the pew felt like sitting on a tangible cloud. He hadn't realized how exhausted he was. He'd been flying almost nonstop for the last couple days and then playing his prank had drained him to almost empty. Of course

Father Michael didn't know this so he couldn't blame him for being cross.

'You're right Father,' he agreed. 'This whole ordeal has been very surprising and confusing to me. First off, why me? Better yet, how? I have so many questions that I know are never going to be answered, because it's not as if you can get a face to face sitting with the Creator to find out why these things are happening. There are also these new powers I have that I have no idea how to use, such as healing and I'm guessing I can control fire. By the way,' he said as he leaned forward in the pew, 'do I have control over all the elements or just certain ones? I've been wondering that since the whole candle thing. Anyway, there are also these creepy guys who I don't feel right about.'

'What do you mean "creepy guys,"' Father Michael asked. 'Describe them to me?'

'Ok. One of them was a bigger guy. Kind of like your typical henchman. Broad shoulders, very Asian features, I assume very dangerous.'

'And what about the others?'

'There was just one other guy and he's harder to figure out,' Tyler said, biting his lower lip as he remembered him. "He was tall and thin. Slightly wrinkled. I'd say about mid to late 50's. His hair was like salt with some pepper, white with a random strand of black. His eyes were the colour of cold steel; gray, hard, lifeless. It felt as if he'd been alive much longer than he looked and much longer than a normal human being ought to. He just didn't feel natural to me.'

The priest glared at the floor and muttered angrily under his breath. 'Merda.' He stood abruptly catching Tyler off guard.

'Come,' he said. He reached out a hand to help Tyler up. 'If your descriptions are correct, we have very little time so we have to hurry. They most likely already know you're here. There was a story on the news today about a boy who was miraculously healed by what the citizens called an angel. That, I'm assuming was you and if they saw it, they know which way to look for you. Though they could probably figure out you'd be heading to the safest place you knew anyway.'

Father Michael rushed up the center aisle, his dress gown billowing behind him. At the end of the pews, he turned to Tyler and with a nod of his head, requested him to blow out the candles. With a sharp thrust of his wings, as well as blowing with his mouth, the candles flickered angrily for a moment before extinguishing themselves.

Once they both were inside his quarters, Father Michael locked the door and placed a three-inch thick round steel crossbar across it, securing the room. This concerned Tyler as he had yet to realize the gravity of the situation. The priest turned off all the lights save a new, unbroken flashlight, which he had pulled from a drawer in the nightstand by his bed.

Tyler stood by the door as Father Michael went and stood in front of the bookcase, trying to remember the combination. There had been some system to activating the shelves, but he couldn't seem to remember how it started. He began rummaging around through random stacks of books, muttering sharp foreign words randomly. There appeared to be no particular rhyme or reason to any of the books he unsystematically picked up then put back down. Certain ones he picked up he would put back in their places and then pull them out again about a half-inch while others he'd move onto another pile to get them out of the way.

'Is there anything in particular I can help you find?' Tyler asked, standing there in confused silence.

'No no no,' responded the priest, half mumbling to himself. 'I just need to trigger a series of books rather than just one in order to activate the lock mechanism. Makes things more complicated for those working against us.' He chuckled.

The more he spoke, the more confused Tyler got. Who is "us"? And whom are these people working against this mysterious "us"? What did it have to do with him? So many questions were now running though his head that he couldn't help but slip in a thought that maybe becoming this "Fallen Angel" wasn't such a cool thing after all. It seemed more stressful then enjoyable. Especially now. Not that he enjoyed being an angel, just that as there was nothing he could do about it, he might as well make the best of it.

'Aha!' exclaimed Father Michael triumphantly, releasing his hold on a book from the next to bottom shelf. Groaning, he picked himself up off the floor and dusted off his robe. 'That should do it.'

'Should do what?' Tyler asked, beyond confused now. He moved closer to see what the priest had done.

'Just wait. It should happen any moment.'

'What should happen? Have you never done this before?'

'Well, I've never needed to before, now have I?'

Tyler opened his mouth to preach about the necessity of foreknowledge when a grinding noise came from behind the bookcase. It sounded something similar to a large stone being dragged along a gravel-strewn floor. They both took a few steps backwards as the two middle sections of the bookcase suddenly slid towards them and then in opposite directions, revealing a circular doorframe. Engraved in the granite around it, was a saying written in some ancient looking language.

מעבר לדלת זה שקרים את האמת מעבר לכל היגיון'. What does that mean?' Tyler asked, having snatched the flashlight from Father Michael to take a closer look.

'Impressive,' Father Michael commented as he moved into the light. He ran his fingers along the cold, lifeless stone, feeling the grooves of which Tyler had spoken. 'You even said it correctly. It's Hebrew and means, "Beyond this door lies the truth beyond reason."'

'I'm assuming we're going to be going in there.' Tyler stared in apprehension at the door, visibly blackened with age. It was hard to tell in this light if it was made of stone or wood, but for some unknown reason, it had darkened considerably while its surroundings had remained the same. Or maybe it was just a dark door. Something about it struck him as odd, but he couldn't tell why. He was wondering why he couldn't make heads or tails of anything when Father Michael simply walked right through it. He disappeared into the darkness that just moments earlier had seemed like a door.

Tyler's heart beat erratically in his chest. He had every reason to feel apprehensive. Firstly, he was alone in the darkness, as the priest had taken the flashlight with him. Secondly, he should have been able to see some residue of light from the flashlight, but once Father Michael disappeared into the doorway, all light ceased. It was like a giant black hole. It unnerved him. He'd never really been a fan of the dark, and walking into the epitome of darkness was daunting. He didn't want to seem like baby, so he summoned up his courage and put those thoughts of insecurity out of his mind. With his arms stretched out before him, he walked forward into the blackness.

On the other side of the black hole, Tyler found himself in a well-lit tunnel running at a slight, but noticeable decline. He followed it down until it opened up into a magnificently huge cavern. Massive milky tan natural columns rose to the ceiling with veins of vibrant reds, oranges, yellows, greens and blues. Adolescent stalagmites and stalactites rose and hung from the floor and ceiling, glistening majestically in the fluorescent light. The sound of trickling water somewhere in the cavern echoed hauntingly and added to the humid atmosphere prevalent in the air. It was so humid in fact, Tyler had barely stepped into the room when he was cascaded by tiny pinpricks of water, which clung to his skin and the remnant of his clothes like glue.

In the middle of the cavern was a large pool of water. The water was a resilient sapphire blue around the edges which rested serenely against the bright emerald ferns and mosses cluttered around like patches. Towards the centre of the pool, the water lost it's resilient blue to become ominously black. "Did that lead to another cavern under this one?" he wondered.

Hugging the wall was a walkway, which led along the cavern wall into a separate alcove. Tucked away inside was a humid free glass enclosure. The hidden room was nearly square with the remaining wall part of the cave. The entrance to the room jutted out a few feet and reminded him of the entrances one went through before entering a sterilized room. First he had to step into a small passageway, which sent out gusts of warm air, ridding his body and clothes of the pesky dots of condensation. He was nearly knocked off his feet when the first gust of air hit him. Had it not been for the gusts of air on all sides, he would have toppled over. After he was dry, a vacuum switched on which sucked all the humidity out of the air, leaving the room dry and ready for him to leave.

Once inside the room, Tyler found another bookcase, directly opposite the entrance, with books that looked hundreds of years older than the ones in Father Michael's room. Spaced out around the room, computer monitors lined the walls, each with the same image on its screen: a map with an arrow clearly marking Rochester, New Hampshire. In the middle of the room was a series of objects in glass cases atop pedestals made of blood-veined marble. He felt like he was in museum-esque estate with the ornate carpet under the pedestals and the assortment of burgundy velvet and mahogany reclining chairs, sofas and end tables.

'What is this place?' he asked, gazing around the chamber.

'This room houses the entire history of Arakiel and his Grigori, also known as The Watchers.'

Tyler stared blankly at Father Michael, who was riffling through some papers at a desk in the left corner. After a few moments of silence, the priest turned to look at him. He shrugged his shoulders admitting without words that he had no idea what he was talking about. 'So, who were they?'

Father Michael dropped the papers he had collected and turned and stared at him in disbelief.

'Didn't you read the book I lent you?'

'I started to, but then I had this crazy dream and before I could get back to it this happened.' He left out the bit where the book was. The priest didn't need to know it was in the back seat of his car. Probably covered in debris.

'Wait. What do you mean you had a dream? What was the dream about?' Something in his manner denoted that the dream was somehow important.

As quickly as he could, Tyler recited to Father Michael the curious dream. He breezed over what the person said, highlighted the excruciating feeling he'd had, and ended with the bloody nose he had when he woke up that Mark had stressed about. The priest absorbed everything he said. It concerned him that he was just finding out about it.

'I wish you would have told me about this dream after you had it,' he exclaimed once Tyler had finished. He moved to another desk and began vigorously rummaging through papers. It had somehow remained hidden from his view until Father Michael practically sprinted to it. 'If I had known about the dream I could have been more prepared for this meeting rather than winging it.'

He continued ranting under his breath while he rummaged through drawers and files until at last cried, 'Trovato! Here it is.' He walked back over to Tyler and thrust a piece of paper at him. 'Here is what I could have prepared you for if you had told me.'

'How? I thought this was the first time you'd been in this room.'

Father Michael smiled mischievously. 'True I was instructed not to enter this room until the appointed time, but that doesn't mean I wasn't privy to the information in here. Like this document. Now read.'

Tyler took the aged, yellow piece of wrinkled paper from Father Michael's hand and quickly perused the contents of the page. It was a prediction made by a Shaman from the Karuk Indian tribe of California. What he had in his hand was almost a word for word description of the dream he'd had. The creepiest part of it all was how the prediction concluded accurately that the one who had this dream would become a fiery creature of the sky and would come claim what was rightfully his.

'What does it mean when it says I will be coming to claim what is rightfully mine?' he inquired, handing it back to the priest.

'All in good time,' he answered, his creepy smile growing broader. 'There are some other matters to attend to before we get to that. First off, I need to give you a quick briefing of your past.'

'Is that really important?' Tyler asked, breathing out sharply through his nose.

'Of course it is. Without knowing your past, how can you expect to truly succeed in your future? Now sit down.'

Father Michael walked over to the bookcase and after a few minutes of searching, reached in and gingerly selected a particularly ancient looking text. Placing it delicately on one of the mahogany end tables, he took a seat in the plush armchair next to it. He motioned for Tyler to sit down in the one diagonal to him, as he had yet to move from where he was standing. As soon as Tyler took his place, Father Michael lovingly picked up the antique manuscript.

'This book contains an extensive history of who you are, why you fell, where you have been and what you have done for your entire existence. It also contains the full legend and other vital bits of information. Let's begin then shall we?'

'We aren't going to be going over the entire book are we?' Tyler moaned, eyeing the book in dread. It was not a tiny book.

'No of course not, but there are some things we have to discuss.'

'Why do we have to discuss them?'

'Because I'm required to.'

'Who says? Is there some guide book you were given on how to educate a fallen angel?'

'As a matter of fact yes I was. Well not really a guidebook per se, but rather training.'

'What kind of training? Who gave it to you?'

'Enough with the questions!' Father Michael exclaimed, abruptly closing the book on his lap. 'There are some things I need to tell you and that's all there is to it. You need to just listen and things will explain themselves.'

When he got no response from Tyler, he took a deep breath and began.

'Alright. As time is already short, I will give you the condensed version. Your predecessor went by the name Arakiel. He was one of twenty leaders of the Grigori, also known as The Watchers. They were all cast down to this earth in order to watch over the inhabitants as penance for their betrayal. As time went on, it was recorded that they lusted after and then procreated with mortal woman. The flood of Noah wiped out their spawn, an evil race of cannibalistic giants who terrorized all creatures. After that act of uncontrolled passion, they were completely cut off from the presence of God, which also ended their immortality. One by one, they were hunted down and destroyed. While they still had their powers and long life, their numbers were too few to handle every attack. In order to preserve their race, they went into hiding. Arakiel was entrusted with the secrets of their whereabouts as well as all their names and special abilities. It has been said he also had a record of their descendants, but that has never been confirmed.

'Arakiel evaded capture and death for centuries until the creation of a wide spreading church appeared on the earth. In the dark of night sometime in the fifth century, after observing the leaders of the church and determining whom the head of the church was, Arakiel stole into his room to request an audience. Being the last known fallen angel, Arakiel was protected until his death in the eighth century at some undeterminable, but very old age. The records which he had brought with him were kept deep within the library of the now Vatican City, lost to myth and legend, but very true nonetheless.'

'So how did the legend start?' Tyler asked, now very enthralled in the story. 'If he was so protected by the church, how was he found out? I'm sure by this time all the angels had been forgotten about.'

'You're right,' Father Michael acknowledged. 'By the time Arakiel died, memory of the fallen angels had all but become a tiny speck in earth's history. No, it was more malicious than that. A priest had been discovered having secret relations with a local member's daughter. They were both publicly revealed and excommunicated. In his rage, the exiled priest began sharing church secrets to anyone who would listen. This didn't last long before he mysteriously disappeared, but at his mention of the body of a fallen angel being held in the catacombs of the Vatican, controversy sparked and grew like untamed fire in a water-parched forest. Hence the need for the body to be moved until it reached its final resting place.

'As for the legend, Arakiel revealed the prophecy to Pope Adrian I as he lay on his deathbed. The Pope had it written down and kept safely hidden, its contents being known only to a select few people. How this lowly priest stumbled upon the prophecy no one knows. Once the body was moved, copies of the prophecy were made to be kept with the body at all times.'

'So what exactly is this prophecy?' Tyler asked. He stood up to stretch his arms, legs and wings.

'The prophecy consists of most of the things you already know. At some point, the fallen angel will resurrect to usher in a premature end of the world. That's what you know right?'

'Yeah. More or less.'

'Well it's a bit more complicated than that. The prophecy is that the Grigori will be gathered and their souls awoken to either usher in the Apocalypse by doing nothing, consisting of the destruction of the human race, or they shall be used in an epic battle of good versus evil, saving mankind and ushering in an era of rebirth and earthly purity.'

Father Michael looked up from the book and was met with a look of complete terror from Tyler. His skin had drained of all colour, looking about as white as the feathers of his wings. His eyes were wide and filled with angst.

'You're starting to see now the gravity of your situation I hope. This is not merely some new life for you. The literal fate of mankind rests solely in yours or your brothers hands.'

The last couple words of Father Michael's statement jarred Tyler back to reality.

'What do you mean mine or my brothers hands? What does he have to do with this?'

'Why everything,' Father Michael replied matter-of-factly. 'You don't really think that you're going to be the only fallen angel do you? Truthfully, you are merely one face to a double-sided coin, yin missing the yang. The fate of mankind rests in one of your hands, depending on your actions. Now come. We haven't much time and you still need to know about the Temple of the Fallen, its key and the League of the Damned.'

Tyler stood there in shock. He couldn't believe that Mark was also going to become a fallen angel, if he hadn't done so already. It was as if fate was playing some cruel joke on him. The one time he could forget about him, now he had to worry about him coming and trying to screw everything up. This just couldn't seem to be getting any better. At least he understood better why Mark was so adamant about his experiment succeeding. "He probably couldn't wait to not be human anymore," he thought, rolling his eyes in disgust.

Sensing an impatient stare, he turned and found the Father standing by one of the computers next to the desk he'd first found him at. He ambled over to the desk and waited to hear another long, but provocatively interesting report.

'First you need to know about the Temple of the Fallen. Within this temple lies the Flaming Sword spoken of in Genesis when Adam and Eve were cast out of the Garden of Eden. With this sword the saving of the world will be accomplished, if that is the choice you make. Either way, it is only possible if one has the key to enter it as well as the knowledge of the temple's location.'

Father Michael typed something onto the screen, which brought up a 3D image of the key to the temple. The image played in a steady stream of seven pieces combining into a single piece.

'As you can see, the key has been broken up into seven pieces. The cleverness of this key is that each piece can be attached with any of the other individual pieces to be used as weapons or armour. Each piece contains some form of power and when attached to another piece that power grows. Only once all the pieces are combined can the object be used as the key to the temple.

'Naturally, there is also going to be some opposition. The key pieces are located at various holy sites. Each site will have a guardian, a keeper and a set of trials, so be wary. Each location and its obstacles will be unique and different so you cannot rely on past experiences to get you through. Along with obtaining the key, you will obtain a vital clue for the location of the next piece. Once the last piece has been found, the location of the temple will be revealed, although we believe we know the general region.'

Father Michael discontinued the image, bringing up a set of personnel files. 'Now, as you know, you are being pursued. The large man, who is no doubt a henchman, belongs to an evil society known as The League of the Damned. They have been around for centuries, waiting and actively pursuing any lead they can get to obtain the key. The group was formed by the exiled priest as a means of revenge before he disappeared. They will do anything to get what they want and what they want is power. The eerie man you spoke of is one of their most dangerous henchmen. He used to be one of their leaders, a group of twelve men known as The Brethren, but stepped down to take a more proactive hand in the search. It is a better-known fact that he is a brilliant, callous surgeon, unconcerned with moral ethics and disregards life. He is ruthless and cruel, so you must always be careful.'

He clicked out of the files, which contained short bios of known affiliates with the League. 'Now that I have overloaded you with all this information, you need to get going.'

'Um ok?' Tyler mumbled, somewhat caught by surprise by the abruptness of the announcement. 'How am I supposed to survive out there? Where am I even supposed to be going first?'

Father Michael turned back to the computer and brought up a picture of the west coast with a single spot marked with a large red dot.

'Where is that? It that where I'm supposed to go?' Tyler asked, leaning closer to the screen to find the name of the place.

'Yes it is,' Father Michael answered. 'Mount Shasta is the location of the first piece of the key. It is a holy site for many of the Native American tribes in the region. Be very careful there. While your arrival has been prophesied, that was a long time ago. It is highly likely that no one remembers it and would see you as a threat and a desecrator.

'As for your survival, I have had an emergency pack made for some time now. You will take it with you. It has everything you will need, including a tent and a sleeping bag. Now, let's get out of here and get you some clothes.'

Chapter 11

Erickson sat comfortably in a private jet as he was flown from D.C. to Portsmouth, New Hampshire. The forecast had called for clear skies and the news was ripe with stories of a mysterious figure with wings. Sightings had been off the chart since the breakout occurred; the most miraculous one being the healing of a 10-year old boy with deformed legs in New Jersey.

After Tyler's escape and Erickson's commission to find him again, he had taken the time to quickly glance over the file. Right then, the most important detail he discovered was that the boy had been transported from Rochester, New Hampshire. When the report of the healed boy came in, it was confirmed that the angel was trying to head back to familiar surroundings. He made a phone call to switch his flight to the closest airport in the area.

Now that he was sitting in a comfortable armchair like seat, he used this luxury of free time to study up on his current mission. He opened up his briefcase and pulled out his laptop. He spread out the file on Tyler and a few books from the county library, including a couple from private archives in various other locales.

Once he had arranged his source material into a workable environment, he set to work on understanding his target. The first place he began to study was the file. He started there to better understand the person. From the first couple of pages the boy seemed fairly normal. He was raised in the Midwest by rural, middle-class parents, had a twin, graduated in the top 5 percent of his class and was avidly involved in many various extracurricular projects and pastimes. After the pages on his pre-university days, things appeared more interesting and complex. He studied genetic manipulation and was quoted as wanting to be the one who cracked the genetic code.

There was also information on the twin brother, Mark. He appeared to be the smarter of the two, but lacked ambition and social skills, unlike Tyler. Strangely, his whereabouts were currently unknown. A small note was scrawled in the margin. "Brother possibly involved with terrorist group." Interesting.

Erickson decided to study something else for a while as he was getting little results from the file on the angelic part of his being. Instead, he turned to one of the books in a pile in the top corner of the small table in front of him. The first book he picked up was called "Forgotten Legends of the Northeast." Within its pages held the lost horror stories of the last few generations; those tales told to children to amaze or terrify them. Scrolling down the table of contents, Erickson soon located the tale of a Fallen Angel. He flipped through the pages until he found it.

As he read, his hand instinctively reached to play with the cartilage of his left ear. His fingers gently caressed three notches evenly spaced apart. The grooves almost appeared like birthmarks but were nothing so quaint. He'd had an abusive father who found it more satisfying to teach his children lessons by marring them then by actually teaching them anything. Pain was his only lesson. Erickson had learned it well. At least how to deal with the physical pain.

By the time he had read through the various descriptions of the angel and other miscellaneous websites on the matter, he arrived in Portsmouth. Quickly stowing his belongings, he prepared for landing and the last leg of his journey. He procured a rental car shortly after exited the gate and quickly maneuvered through traffic out of the airport. Entering the freeway, he traveling northeast towards Rochester. Within two hours and minimal traffic, he pulled into the city limits with a decent amount of sunlight left to get an adequate view of city. On the opposite end of the valley, the dull glare of the emerging streetlights reflected off the magnificent structure of a cathedral on a hill.

Shortly after entering the city, Erickson came upon a somewhat respectable looking motel. He pulled into the mostly empty parking lot and parked close to the office next to a tan early '80s model station wagon. He paid for a standard single room on the farthest end of the lot. When he opened the door, he was greeted with a mid '70s style room. The carpet was creamy brown shag, which looked like it had been there the entire time the motel had been in business. Certain patches, especially around the bases of the furniture, looked significantly dingier and the room emanated a mildewy smell. He figured that if he were to tear up a section of the carpet, the boards would be rotted through and mold would be everywhere. The rest of the room looked as if they chose the two most dismal and mismatched colours and bathed the room in it. The bedding, draperies and wallpaper were the same creamy brown as the carpet, but were layered with green circles the colour of vomited spinach.

He shook his head in disgust as he carefully set his bag on the edge of the bed before setting to secure the place. Despite his access to some of the most advanced technology in the world, Erickson preferred the simple means of security. Some of his methods were hand-rigged to his specific standards while others he arranged as is.

First from his bag he pulled his specially rigged battery packs. Each one contained enough volts not to electrocute someone, but just enough to deliver unpleasant sensations. He attached these to the securely closed window latches as well as to the door handle. The door handle was always risky in case the motel manager showed up, but in his mind it was better to be safe than sorry.

Next, Erickson removed a small leather pouch that contained a couple dozen metal jacks. They had been a gift from his only real friend as a teenager. They used to play with them in a series of mock trainings and now they provided him a valuable service as deterrents. These weren't your normal jacks with the dull edges and easy to bend metal. They were formed from reinforced steel as to not to be able to bend when stepped on. The ends of the tines came to perfect points and were long and sharp enough to puncture through at least an inch of thick leather, plastic or rubber soles and into the base of the intruder's foot. He was surprised that neither of them had seriously injured themselves with these. He placed them a couple feet away from the door, giving the intruder enough space to open it and enter without alerting the perp to their presence. He also placed them directly under the windowsill.

These preparations were merely precautionary and more out of habit than anything else. He wasn't really concerned with anyone breaking in. As this mission was strictly reconnaissance, he was not all that worried about anyone working against him. Regardless, if anyone was after him and if they happened to make it passed these traps, he had other weapons at his disposal. Those were simply used as a last resort. His fists were usually enough to do the trick. Erickson hadn't made this far in his career without spilling some blood, but the body count was relatively low compared to some of his contemporaries. This was most likely due to the fact that blending in to his surroundings was his specialty. He wasn't called the chameleon for no reason.

Once he finished securing the room, Erickson pulled out a map he had bought at the airport and plotted his next move. He placed Tyler's file next to the map and pinned the places mentioned in the file. University here, work there, apartment shared with brother here and girlfriends house there. His daily routine consisted of visiting most of the places at least once a day. Then, sporadically, he would visit an old parish on the outskirts of town. Sometimes he would go for days in a row and then go a week or two before visiting again. As this seemed out of the ordinary, Erickson figured this would be as good a place to start as any. Logic states that if you are trying to hide from someone, the last place you would go was the places you frequented the most. As time was of the essence, he grabbed the map, his jacket, a gun he'd stashed underneath his pillow, his camera, and stuffed them into a small rucksack with some other necessary items and left.

He parked his rental car outside a diner at the base of Hummock's Hill before ascending it. Dressed in the dark greens, browns and blacks of military fatigues, Erickson melted into the oncoming night, moving quickly through the gold and green fields directly below the cathedral. It was during the final moments of sunset, right before the night began its reign, so he moved very carefully.

By the time he made it through the fields and onto the grass the darkness had taken hold. He broke the border of the lea and had only gone a few paces on the grass when he looked up to the cathedral in time to see a shape jumping from one of the towers. The shape spread its wings and circled the building, descending towards the front. He saw the angel turn its head suddenly in his direction. He instantly dropped and flattened himself on the ground.

Seconds after he had blended in with the grass, the angel reappeared. It slowly made its way around the side of the building as if searching for something it thought it had seen. When it was confident there wasn't anything out of the ordinary, it hurried on its way. Erickson didn't move a muscle until the angel had disappeared from view. As soon as he felt it was safe again to move, he picked himself off the ground and quickly ascended the hill.

Now that he knew his target was here, he was going to have to play it that much safer. He was not in the habit of underestimating his enemies and this was no different, despite the obvious physical differences. The main problem was how he expected to not underestimate him when there was nothing anyone knew about him. All he could go off was that the angel had escaped an extremely high secure facility already, so he was going to need to perform extreme caution if he expected to learn anything tonight.

He made it up the rest of the hill without further incident. He flattened himself against the side of the cathedral when he heard a loud crack and felt the walls shake. "The creature must have gone inside," he guessed, before quickly making his way around to the main entrance. Once he got there, he placed his ear against the door in an effort to determine whether or not contact with the angel had been made. As he figured, the wood was too thick. He was still able to hear a muddled voice coming from behind the door. Whoever it was close as he could barely make out what he was saying.

'Who's there?' the voice inquired. 'I know someone's out there.'

Erickson made to retreat from the area and then stopped. He hadn't made a sound, which meant that whoever the person was talking to was inside the chapel. It was strange, but the voice had seemed somewhat guarded, like they had no idea who was there. Wasn't this guy supposed to be the angel's friend? Perhaps he was playing a prank on the man. Or better yet, perhaps he was more dangerous than he had originally anticipated. He hoped there wouldn't be a need for a cleanup crew. The last time he had to deal with one of those they nearly had to be cleaned up themselves.

He placed his ear against the rough oak door again and strained to hear any movement at all. For a few minutes he heard nothing. The longer he heard nothing, the more confident he felt it would be safe to enter. Of course he also wondered if something had happened to the priest. He pulled out his iPhone and quickly located a blueprint of the cathedral. Unlike any other cathedral, this one appeared to only have one entry point. At least one that regular people knew about. This was not ideal. It meant that his only option was to enter the building as quickly and quietly as possible and hope that no one was standing close enough to notice his entrance. Taking a few deep breaths, he counted down from three and in one swift motion, tugged open the door, spun inside and yanked it closed behind him, stopping it noiselessly a centimeter before its resting place.

Inside the cathedral, Erickson crouched at the base of the giant oak doors letting his eyes grow accustom to his now hidden surroundings. Black, shapeless masses soon began to solidify into recognizable objects, walls, chairs and columns. From the back of the chapel, voices drifted lazily, a mumbled mess followed by a sudden, crashing as something broke. He immediately began searching for a place to hide as the sound of destruction intensified. Directly to his left, he noticed an opening next to a thick column. He moved towards this opening and stopped just beyond the column. It was silent now with the exception of the occasional raised voice. He strained to catch more of what was being said when he heard a voice resonate against the marble and granite walls.

'Would you like a light so to see me better?' the voice inquired. Erickson disappeared further into the opening. Suddenly the room lit up as if the sun had taken up room inside it. Erickson's hands instinctively flew up to his eyes to protect them from the blinding, brilliant light before he realized he was still hidden in the shadows. It was a relief that the opening had been so close to him. Had it not, he might very well have been discovered and being seen now would have severely jeopardized the operation.

He closed his eyes and concentrated on the hushed voices he could faintly make out. He could understand the occasional word, such as the angel's name, and then he heard a whole phrase resonate from the chapel. Otherwise, all he heard was muffled silence. It bored him sitting there listening to them. It reminded him of being back in school. He was never that good of a student. The only reason he made any attempt at going was because of sports. He needed good grades in order to play. He thought it was a stupid rule. He was really good at football and wrestling. His talent should have satisfied any scholarly requirement, but it didn't. So he begrudgingly went to class and did the bare minimum in order to stay afloat and play.

He was straining to listen again when he felt something tickle the back of his neck. He brushed it away lightly not breaking his concentration. Then he felt something skitter across his forearm. He nearly screamed. His eyes widened in horror as he clawed at his arms, trying to get rid of whatever was on him. He was deathly afraid of spiders. As a child, his father had punished him by locking him in a closet. A brown recluse had bitten him and he'd nearly died. Since then, spiders were his number one enemy. He didn't care if they were endangered or not.

Once he was sure the evil insect was either dead or gone, he calmed his breathing and returned back to listening. He was able to catch the last few comments about himself, "broad shoulders, very Asian features, I assume very dangerous." While this was certainly true, it was not good that the angel had associated him as an enemy. The Brethren were not going to like this as all. Hopefully they didn't take him off the case.

He heard the priest call for the angel to follow. "This isn't good," he thought as he edged towards the lip of the alcove. Just as he made it around the corner, the lights shut off and a single beam nearly shot him in the face. He stumbled backwards back into the opening. He hadn't registered the stairs directly behind him when he'd initially come in and nearly cursed out loud when he abruptly learned this crucial fact. Due to his athleticism, he had fairly good reflexes and was able to catch himself after a few steps and avoid an unmistakably painful end.

He quickly righted himself before cautiously and hurriedly descended the stairs. At the base he found a door, presumable leading to either the Father's quarters or a storage room. He really didn't have time to think about it as the sound of footsteps on the stairs were getting closer and he was not too keen on getting caught. He entered through the door and into what he now saw was a rather large living area, and one that was also practically void of anywhere to hide. As he raced through the maze of objects, he was rather disappointed to find his only option was under the bed.

He reached the far side of the bed just as the door on the other side of the room opened. He dove to the floor without a moments thought. As luck would have it, the bed was raised off the ground, but not by much. As his upper torso was quite broad, Erickson knew that there was no way he would be able to fit underneath it. All he could do was lie there in hopes that they stayed on the other side of the room.

Since he only had a few inches to see through under the bed, not to mention the other furniture obscuring his view, he had no clue what was happening. It was highly inconvenient for him at the moment, but what could he do. After a few minutes and some scuffling around, some of which sounded alarmingly close, the lights went out. The voices were more audible now, but he wasn't able to make out any of the words, as the acoustics in the room were slightly worse than in the chapel.

A grinding noise infiltrated his ears making any other sound completely imperceptible. "What is that?" he wondered. The sound lasted only a few seconds before being replaced by a short sliding noise. Whatever it was, nothing in the room could have made a sound like that. At least nothing he had noticed. Once the sliding stopped, he heard the murmuring of voices for a few minutes before they too disappeared. A chill unexpectedly traveled down his spine. His senses instantly perked. He only had chills when something big was happening. He needed to know what it was, but he had to be patient. He first had to be sure whether or not the two were still around.

Minutes felt like hours listening to the smothering silence. He felt unnervingly alone. He tried peeking out from the side of the bed to see if anyone else was in the room. It would have been near impossible to see them in the darkness though. He fumbled around in his rucksack producing a small but powerful flashlight. While shining it around, it only took him a few seconds to determine the source of the grinding. Two sections of the bookcase had opened, revealing a strange black abyss.

It was soon apparent that there was no one else in the room. He quickly made his way over to stand in front of the abyss. Something in the recesses of his mind pulled at the strings of memory as he stood there. It looked strangely familiar. He'd seen a phenomenon like this somewhere before. The memory of it skipped merrily through his brain, darting ever beyond the tips of his mental fingers. Perhaps he had merely dreamed about something like it.

It was no use trying to remember where he'd seen it. What was more important was figuring out how to get passed it. He chided himself for not having had a better vantage point to see how they'd gone through it. From his military training he'd learned to be very cautious of anything that appeared either too easy or too good to be true. This entrance seemed far too easy and at the same time terrifying. The fluid motion of the abyss created a hypnotic effect that simultaneously tugged certain parts of his psyche, accentuating feelings of remorse and guilt. The longer he stood there staring into its inky recesses, the further through his being the guilt spread, bringing him close to tears and abandoning his mission. Memories of the atrocities he'd witnessed flowed through his mind like a river from a fractured dam.

Not willing himself to succumb to this heightened guilt, he grasped at whatever strands of courage he had remaining and stepped into the abyss. It was like passing through a trial by fire; one that purified the soul before one could enter the other side. He gasped when he passed through, finding he had complete control of his conscience again. He turned and marveled at the mysterious substance. While it appeared dense, passing through it was as if passing through a fine mist. The touch of it on his skin was gentle and somewhat healing, although it hadn't seemed so when he was standing on the other side. He now felt regenerated and awake. It was weird but amazing.

When he'd fully gained his composure, he looked around and found himself in a brightly lit passageway. He could see about thirty feet before it turned. He couldn't help wondering where exactly he was being led to as he cautiously began following it. At least there was only one direction. A maze would have done his head in. Shortly after turning passed a sharp corner, the passageway ended and opened up into a magnificent cavern. He stared in amazement at the incredible sight before him. He might be a strict, military trained man-for-hire, but he still had the humility to appreciate and be in awe of the wonders of the world.

A sudden commotion to his right caused him to fall to a crouch and whip out his gun. He'd moved it from the bag to his hip after he'd arrived at the cathedral as a safety measure. Nothing appeared. The room was empty. He hated being out in the open like this, but he didn't have much of a choice. Against the wall he noticed the thin pathway running along the outer rim. It disappeared after about twenty feet into a crevice in the wall. The crack was barely wide enough for his stocky frame to squeeze through without needing to angle himself slightly. It ran only a few feet before widening out and revealing a good-sized enclosure. It was roughly the size of the laboratory where he'd first encountered the angel. This one looked much more inviting, other than it was encased entirely in thick glass. The room was roughly thirty square feet. The far wall was an entire bookcase, running from the floor to the top some fifteen feet high. The other three walls were lined with computers. It looked like a mini library.

In the centre of the room were three red-veined marble pedestals, each containing some unknown object secured behind large bell-shaped glass lids. These pedestals were surrounded by a variety of red lounging chairs. In fact, there was a lot of red in that room. Almost a nauseating amount of red actually. At least it wasn't pink. That would have worried him.

The angel was standing closest to him, more or less in the middle of the room. He was standing in front of the priest and appeared to be telling him something important as the priest was standing with his arms folded, staring intently at the angel with a concerned expression. They were both so engrossed in the story that they hadn't noticed his entrance into the cave. It gave him the perfect chance to locate a hiding place. There weren't many options, so he was stuck with hiding next to the glass behind one of the computer consoles.

Rather than risk getting seen by crossing across the mouth of the cavern, he stuck to the shadows on the right side. As he crept he took another quick glance around the cave. He found it strange the remarkable amount of light, considering it was underground. He hadn't been able to see any noticeable light fixtures and it wasn't bioluminescent light from lichen. It was more like fluorescent light one would find in any home or building. Either way, he was grateful for it as it made him practically invisible in the shadows it created.

He found a small enclosure on the side opposite the men that was just large enough for him to squeeze into. It kept him reasonably concealed and enabled him to have an unhampered view his target. From his bag, which he had laid out in front of him, he pulled a stethoscope. He had considered bringing with him a small drill and microphone but as he'd been unsure where he would be listening he opted rather to bring the stethoscope. It was good that he did. Even as unscientific as he was, he could still tell that the room was pressurized and the air controlled. He knew this from the entrance of the enclosure. Had he bored a hole into the glass, the pressure in the room would instantly and noticeably drop, giving him away. Plus the stethoscope was completely old school and that's how he preferred it.

He placed the buds into his ears and tentatively placed the chestpiece against the glass. He half expected a blast of voices to explode into his ears, which had happened all too often. Thankfully this time they didn't. Quite the opposite in fact. The voices were very faint and he had to concentrate very sharply to make out every word. 'This is really getting old,' he grimaced. Didn't these people know how to speak louder than 30dB?

Ridiculous. Because of this, he was going to have to take mental notes of everything said. Normally he would have his pad of paper next to him to jot down notes, but right now, as with this whole case, this was nowhere close to normal.

It didn't take long for his arm to begin losing feeling from holding up the stethoscope. It almost felt like his entire body was falling asleep out of boredom. For the last while, he had been straining to hear something vital, but the entire time he listened to them argue and then begin a history lesson. He hated history. Sure, to not know history is dooming yourself to repeat the mistakes of the past, but the only thing that had ever interested him about the past were the heroic warriors, such as Achilles, Julius Caesar and Genghis Kahn. They were cunning, noble and great leaders, the true men of their day. That was when he was a child though. In this moment he had no desire to learn history. He needed to know where the angel was going next and when. Although, he heard a part of him say, "it's good to at least understand what it is that you're following." He pushed that thought out of his head.

He was finally succumbing to the boredom when, '...the literal fate of mankind rests solely in yours or your brothers hands,' whispered softly through the chestpiece. His surprise was equal to if not greater than the angel's. There was going to be two of them?! He could be pretty sure The Brethren had no idea there was going to be more than one angel. He was further surprised to hear that his role was known, although rather crudely described. He was no henchman. Also the identity of the strange man and the society he worked for were detailed. Not even he had known exactly whom he worked for. To him they were merely a paycheck.

Finally he heard it. "Mount Shasta is the location of the first piece of the key." At last he had what he had come for. It was time to go.

Chapter 12

All the windows were rolled down letting in a refreshing cool breeze as Erickson drove away from the cathedral. He was more than happy to be away from there. Getting out had proved an even greater challenge than getting in had. He hadn't realized that the door had been barricaded, trapping him in. There was no way for him to leave without making it obvious that someone had been there. Once again, his only option was to hide by the bed and wait for them to exit the room before sneaking out after them. To be honest, it had proved good that he hadn't been able to leave. He was able to learn the next destination the angel planned to take before departing for Mount Shasta: Helen's house.

Who this Helen was interested him greatly. She had been described very little in the angel's file, mainly a small paragraph claiming she was his girlfriend. It was a strange thought thinking that such a creature had a human girlfriend. Then again, if he understood things correctly, the boy hadn't always been a winged being so it would be normal for him to have a girlfriend. Then why wasn't she mentioned more? The less a person is mentioned normally means they play a very minor role in the whole scheme of things. That or their role wasn't known or wasn't meant to be known by him. The angel's plan to visit her put it into his mind that perhaps she was a larger player than she'd been made out to be.

As soon as he got to his rental, he called The Brethren to report his findings. What he said seemed to satisfy them. They urged him to continue following the creature as they vaguely eluded that time was running out. He tried to ask what they meant, but was only answered by a dial tone. He tossed his phone onto the passenger seat in disgust. His cases usually never bothered him, but something was beginning to stink with this one. He also never asked questions or even cared with any of his previous cases, but with this one he found that the more he got involved the more complex the story became. For one who never got involved before, he was beginning to regret taking this one on. What did The Brethren mean that time was running out? Was it because the angel was bad or was it that they had an ulterior motive? He'd heard what the priest said about them and initially that hadn't fazed him, but with all these questions beginning to mount, he wondered if he should back out now before his indifference was compromised.

He sighed. That was a bridge he'd have to cross later. Right now his primary concern was locating the address for this Helen. He pulled into the parking lot of some obscure diner somewhere in town. Once he was parked, he pulled a briefcase from beneath the passenger seat and extracted the angel's file. After skimming around a bit he found her name, Helen Saunders. He remembered pinning her name into a map at the motel. If he remembered correctly, she lived close to the university campus.

From the briefcase he pulled a slim, silver laptop. He navigated to the internet and began searching databases in search of the girl's address. He was annoyed to find five exact matches in the greater Rochester area, but it could have been worse so he didn't let himself get worked up. After another couple minutes of searching he was able to knock off three of the five. One was recently deceased and the other two were middle-aged woman. The other two remained mysterious and their records somehow eluded him. He didn't have time to do more searching so he was just going to have to go by on both of them and hope that one of the two was the right one.

The first address was the closest so he went by on her first. He was quite pleased when he pulled into a brightly lit student-housing complex. Referring back to the address, he drove around the lot until he located flat X217. It was located on the second floor of the three-story condo style apartment. The outside of the flats was very manicured and tidy. The gray stucco looked like it had been recently repainted as well as the raised white edges. The lawns were very well lit and neatly trimmed. The grass was a luscious and a healthy green and the houses were lined with a vast array of colours coming from daffodils, snapdragons, tulips, marigolds and other flowers. Palms trees were added to give the area that special exotic quality. He half expected some deer or other animals to appear.

The lights were on in every flat but the one he wanted. Naturally. He was pulling out to leave and check out the other address when a car pulled up. His luck couldn't have been more potent tonight as a girl exited her sporty, but pink, Prius. She walked up the cement stairs and entered the apartment. The lights in the living room flicked on giving Erickson the sure signal that this might be his girl.

He got out of the rental and ascended the steps. He knocked gently on the door and recited in his mind exactly what he was going to say to her as not to arouse suspicion. After a few seconds, the door opened revealing a petite, skinny, red-haired girl whose skin was speckled with millions of brown splotches. He was about ninety-five percent sure this was not Helen Saunders. People who looked as the angel did most certainly didn't date girls who looked like her. Sure it was harsh, but it was true.

'Hello. I was hoping that I might be able to speak with Ms. Saunders,' he said silkily, each word purring.

The girl eyed him warily. 'She isn't here right now. She never is on weekends. And isn't it a bit late to be knocking anyway?'

'Right,' he responded, trying not to let the disappointment sound in his voice. 'Sorry about the hour. It's just of dire importance and I needed to get a hold of her as soon as possible. Do you happen to know where it is that she goes on weekends?'

His silky smooth approach was obviously having no effect on this girl. "There must be something wrong with her head," he thought. His schmaltz usually worked with women, and even some men. Could he risk adding more charm?

The girl's eyes narrowed even more and she began edging the door shut. 'What's so important that you can't wait until Monday when she gets back?'

Her voice was filled with contempt as she spoke. It wasn't a surprise that she was suspicious of him. It just meant that he was going to have to lay it on that much more. "Time to pull out all the stops," he concluded as he straightened the suit jacket he'd donned before coming to her door.

'It has to do with her boyfriend,' he replied, eying her to see how she responded. He was taking a huge risk here, because how was he to know if Helen really had a boyfriend or not. Sure the file said she did, but files were not always up-to-date.

'Tyler?!' she exclaimed, falling completely into his trap. He had nicely said the right thing because the girl got all jittery with excitement. 'Is he ok? Where is he? Will he be coming back soon? We've all been worrying about him since she said he'd been hospitalized and then disappeared. There are so many rumours about what happened that night and.....'

'Tyler's fine,' he said, cutting off her unbridled rant, himself pleased to have found what he needed. 'We just need to affirm a few facts with Ms. Saunders before he can be released. So where is it that she goes on weekends?'

'She goes to her parents house at 37 Berry Street not far past Hanson Park. Oh she is going to be so excited!!!' she exclaimed, jumping up and down, stopping quickly to keep her glasses from falling off.

'Thank you for your help. You've been most gracious,' he said with a coy smile and a wink. 'Oh and one more thing. I'd like to keep it on the down low. Please don't alert her about this. I wouldn't want her to get her hopes up prematurely. Ok?' The girl nodded her understanding.

It seemed almost ironic to him that when he checked the second address he found it was exactly the same as the one the girl had given him. He plotted this new address into his GPS and headed off. The nice thing about travelling at night was the lack of traffic. It took him about a quarter of an hour to get to Berry Street. The road led him into a seemingly perfect suburban neighborhood one would see in horticulture magazines. Even in the hazy light of the contaminating yellow streetlights, Erickson could see that each lawn was immaculately cut and decorated with strategically planted shrubbery and flowers. Dotted around the yards were fountains, benches and other ridiculous oddities meant to beautify rather than pollute the natural attraction of the already magnificent landscape.

Helen's house was no exception. The house itself was a two-story monstrosity made of compacted stone decoration at the base and stone columns surrounded by walls painted a pale off-whitish colour that invaded the rest of the building. At least it looked off-white. To offset the hideousness of the colour, the house was designed with the first story consisting mostly of large windows. There appeared to be more square footage of window space than there was of actual wall space.

The yard, like most houses on this street, was littered with decoration. From the meager light, he had the vague impression that a rainbow had vomited on their lawn and most way along the street. It felt as if the people on this street had gone out of their way to make this the most colourful neighborhood ever. Roses appeared to be dipped in paint and large, primly pruned lilac bushes and chrysanthemums were crowned at the base with marigolds. Honeysuckles artistically climbed the walls competing against the bright green and pink leaves of ivy found stealthily creeping along the columns of the house. By the time he reached Helen's house he could understand why the rainbow had been sick, as he himself was beginning to feel queasy. He shuddered at the thought of what this horror street of colour made a person feel like in the daytime.

A single light was on in the second story of the house when he pulled up. The curtains were drawn to not attract too much attention, but if anyone had been looking close enough, it wouldn't have been difficult to notice the shadow of a figure with wings standing a little ways behind the shades. He parked his car across the street out of the direct light and surveyed the scene.

It was plain to see that he was going to have to climb on top of the garage to get as close as possible. A straightforward front approach was simply out of the question. Not that he couldn't, just that even an idiot would know the best way to get caught would be to climb where anyone could see you. He was going to have to approach from the back, furthest away from her window and hopefully somewhat easier to access.

If possible, the back of the house had more windows than the front did. At least the back was nowhere near as decorated. It actually looked more or less like they had completely forgotten about finishing it. A large hole, which resembled the beginnings of a swimming pool, lay uncovered with shovels littered all around it. Tire tracks in the trampled grass could be seen vaguely in the moonlight.

It would have appeared that his luck was beginning to wane. The back yard angled low, giving Erickson very little chance of being able to climb up the back of the garage. He quickly checked the unfinished pool in the hopes that a ladder had been left out as well. Much to his dismay, he could tell from the angle of the bottom of the hole that no ladder was going to be needed. With no means to help him climb the back, his only choice was to somehow climb the side.

As if the Fates were willing him to have some sort of fighting chance, the side of the garage had an a/c unit as well as a couple sturdy, plastic garbage cans. The most sensible option would have been to stand on the a/c unit, but it only rose about three feet off the ground forcing him to have to jump another couple feet to even be able to grab onto the ledge. The problem was that the roof was covered with terra cotta tiles, which were not the easiest things to walk on or the sturdiest to climb. Plus there was a higher chance of his being seen as it was practically underneath Helen's window. No. The most practical choice was to take one of the larger garbage cans and place it closer to the back corner. The only problem with that choice was that on one side of the can there were wheels. Sensible for it's normal purpose, but highly problematic for what he intended it for. To give him the best chance possible, he placed the side with the wheel away from the wall. He would have to make sure he stood closer to the wall to keep it from rolling.

There was a three-foot walkway of cement along the side of the garage ensuring the garbage can was on level ground. He attempted to mount the can, but quickly found that the edges of it were not as sturdy as they looked. Not only did the edges bow from his weight, but they also tilted off balance. He tried to spread out his weight, but stepped backwards first. The bin tilted slightly catching the wheel, tipping him off. He jumped and successfully landed on his feet while the bin clattered on the walkway, spilling its contents all over. Naturally, it had to be filled with tin cans. He quickly scooped the cans back into the bin and lifted it upright. He scanned the area to see if anyone had noticed. All was quiet. He was about to give it another go when he heard voices above him.

'Should we go out and check on it?' a female voice questioned.

'Nah. Besides, if there's a mess, I'll clean it up my way out,' a male voice, obviously the angel's, replied.

He heard the window slide shut and slowly let out his breath. He was going to need to be more careful now that they were alerted to some presence. He placed the bin back against the wall and looked around for some sort of handhold, but the walls were mostly bare, especially where he was standing. When his eyes landed upon the second garbage can, a brilliant idea seized him. He wheeled it over and laid it gently on its side up next to the first can then stood on it. The plastic bowed from his weight but held him and was high enough for him to climb on top of the first can successfully without tipping it over. The lid felt dangerously close to collapsing so he had to quickly make it from the can onto the top of the garage. He was now high enough that all he needed to do was grab the edge and hoist himself up. As the roof was only slightly angled, there was less of a chance of one of the tiles breaking free and sending him back down painfully.

Even with things now looking back in his favour, it still took all that he had to get up onto the roof. He hadn't done pull-ups in years and despite his toned physique, it proved to be quite the challenge. He even considered swinging a bit to bring one of his legs in range to pull himself up that way but when the tile under his right hand slid a centimeter, he decided against it. He was just going to have deal with it and dead lift himself up. It took a few minutes, but sure enough, all that muscle was proving its worth. Soon he was over the edge and breathing heavily on the roof. He lay there a few moments catching his breath before making his way as quietly as possible over to the Helen's window.

The white, silky curtains were parted a couple inches, just far enough for him get a view of most of the room. To his disgust, she was your typical girl. Her room was a bright shade of nauseating pink. Amongst the sea of pepto-bismol were the painted figures of fairies, unicorns, and rainbows, symbols of feigned reality portrayed in extravagant detail along the walls of her morbid paradise. About a foot below the top of the wall was a shelf that ran the entire breadth of the room, filled to the brim with stuffed creatures of all types and species alongside barbies and plastic ponies. Erickson was so overcome by nausea at the sight of her room that he was barely able to notice the two figures on the left. They were sitting close on a bed of the same putrid neon pink that plagued the rest of the room.

'...to Mount Shasta? What are you supposed to do there?' she whined.

'It's the location of the first piece of the key,' he replied, as he gently caressed her sand-coloured hair.

'Hmph. I still don't understand what's going on?' she snorted in frustration. 'Why did it have to be you? Why couldn't it have been your brother? He's the one who's always so dead set on being different.'

The angel laughed violently and then clasped his hands over his mouth as she looked at him angrily.

'Be quiet!' she hissed. 'You'll wake up my parents!'

The angel just smiled at her.

'What?'

'I can't believe you're being negative about my brother. You're the one who's always telling me to be nice to him.'

'Well it's true,' she said defiantly. She folded her arms and turned her back to him, trying to hide a faint smile at the same time.

The angel laughed again, this time much quieter. 'Ah come now. You know I understand.' He wrapped his arm around her middle, drawing her back to him causing her to giggle giddily.

Oh how this display of young love disgusted him. "I wish they'd just be done already," he groaned inwardly. He too had once been a young lover, but that was buried deep in his past and this display was not something he wanted to remind him of it.

'Besides,' the angel began, 'didn't I just tell you that he's also going to become like me? So it really doesn't matter. Both of us would've become like this one way or another.'

'If you say so,' she said, her eyes closed as she serenely pressed her head against his chest. 'I have something for you though.'

'Yeah? What?'

'Here you go.'

'Oh wow. Thanks! How'd you get this?'

'They gave it to me after your infamous escape.'

Erickson wasn't sure what they were referring to, but from their shadows, he could tell she had given him some sort of necklace.

'Oh!' she said suddenly, righting herself rigidly. 'Did I tell you about the boy in the news?'

'No. What boy?'

'A young boy from a small town in Jersey was miraculously healed by what he says was a "Fallen Angel."'

The angel just stared at her in disbelief.

'So he was really healed?' he asked, his voice low and wavering slightly.

'Yes he was. The whole town was in shock and expressed their gratitude to the "mysterious winged apparition who disappeared in a flash of light leaving them momentarily blinded and a boy with an incurable ailment healed."' She recited the last bit like she was reading it. 'That was really you then? You are their "mysterious winged apparition?"'

'Yeah it was me,' the angel choked. He wasn't doing well keeping his emotions hidden. 'I can't believe it worked.'

Suddenly, the angel got up from the bed.

'Um I need to use your bathroom.'

'Sure,' Helen said smugly, smiling as if she knew the real reason he was running out of the room. 'Let me check quickly to see if the coast is clear.'

She was gone for less than a minute before she returned and beckoned for him to follow her. This was the moment Erickson had been waiting for. Pushing up on the upper edges of the window frame, he was happy to find it not latched. He quickly worked it up a few inches before being able to stick his large fingers underneath it to raise it up the rest of the way. He quickly climbed inside and looked around the room trying to locate the pack he'd seen the angel leave the cathedral with. When he found it, he unlatched the top and reached into his jacket pocket, pulling out a small, round, silver button, approximately the size of a snap button and the width of a dime. He reached into the satchel and was fastening it to the side when he heard the handle on the door turn. He pulled his hand out of the bag, not caring whether the button was attached or not. He flipped the top of the bag shut and dropped it to the floor before darting to the window, climbing out as quickly as he could.

He had just pulled his foot out the window when he heard a loud gasp.

'Tyler! Somebody just climbed out the window!'

He stumbled slightly rushing to the edge of the

roof. He jumped awkwardly down to the secure pavement and raced to his car. Before the angel had any chance to see who it was, he was in his car and zooming down the street, his headlights off so he could disappear into the darkness. He didn't slow down until he reached his hotel on the other side of town, only turning his headlights on when he could no longer see Helen's house or neighbourhood.

He parked in his room's parking spot but didn't get out of the car for a few minutes. "Tyler huh?" he thought as he begun to put the pieces together in his mind. It was all starting to make sense to him now. The angel had told him his name at the facility and it was in his file, but for some reason he had thought it was simply an adopted name rather than his real one.

"Well boy," he thought, "how about you let Papa Erickson keep watch over you for a while." He pulled his laptop onto his lap and clicked it on. He navigated through a few programs until finally pressing enter one last time. A map of the United States filled the screen with a flashing dot by the southeastern corner of New Hampshire, where the state and Maine connected.

'Got you.'

Chapter 13

Following the disturbing events of the night, Tyler felt it necessary to leave as soon as possible. Now that his girlfriend's house was no longer safe for him to stay at, the only option was to leave straightaway, as he should have done in the first place. After checking to see that everything was still in the bag and that nothing had been added, he kissed Helen goodbye and left.

The night was cool and calm as he flew through the moonlit darkness away from Rochester. When he left he'd been agitated and angry, but somehow, by simply flying his anger transformed into ecstasy. How he wished that everyone could have wings and experience the joy he felt from flying. Life would be so much easier this way.

Despite the joy he felt flying, the journey to California proved to be long and somewhat boring. He felt it wise to keep hidden during the day and travel only at night. Finding hiding places also proved to be a challenge. Most of the time, it wasn't possible for him to find refuge in a forest and he would have to seek out caves, sheds, and one time he even hid in the rafters of an abandoned barn. It seemed the closer he came to reaching his destination, the more difficult it was becoming finding proper seclusion.

Somewhere in the Midwest he decided to take an

extended rest. Something had been bothering him since he met with the priest. How was he able to control fire? Father Michael never answered that question. Did he even have an answer? Probably not. In that case he was going to have to figure out how to do it.

The nice thing about being in the Midwest was that the landscape already looked burned. If he happened to create something catastrophic, most people would be none the wiser. He didn't plan on doing anything over the top since he wasn't sure what he could do. To be safe, he made sure he was away from any roads before he began practicing.

The first thing he tried doing was produce a flame. He tried snapping his fingers, rubbing his hands together, but nothing happened. He pointed at objects and commanded them to light up. He tried to find the fire inside him to bring it forth but was only disappointed. He even tried saying fire in whatever languages he could think off. It was useless. Nothing he did seemed to trigger whatever switch needed to bring forth fire.

He sat on the ground resting his head on his hands. He closed his eyes and imagined what he would do if could have manipulated fire. He pictured the barren wasteland around him ablaze from fire that spread from him on the ground. The flame then morphed into soldiers; his own personal militia of fire demons. They gathered around him before they all were drawn into a giant orb.

Tyler smiled as he thought of being able to do all those amazing things. He wiped his forehead, which was now dripping sweat. It had suddenly gotten much warmer. He opened his eyes and darted swiftly away from where he was sitting. Suspended in the air was a giant ball of fire. How had it gotten there? Had he created it? He looked at his hands and flexed them. He reached out to the orb and closed his hand. The sphere stayed the same.

It flickered calmly as if waiting for him to figure it out. He thought about the fire going out and suddenly the orb was no longer there.

Was that all it took? When he had lit the candles at the chapel, he had only thought how cool it would be to say the phrase and then somehow create light. He imagined the candles lighting up and was amazed when they did. It had never occurred to him that it only took his imagination to create the flame.

Testing out his theory, he imagined a ball of flame in his hand. He stretched his arm out and as he thought it, the ball of flame appeared. He imagined flame in both hands and it was so. It was amazing. He had unwittingly figured out how to use his new power. He now just needed to hone it and test it out some more. If all it took was his imagination, in theory he could do almost anything he wanted.

For the remainder of that day he trained. He produced fire in all manors of ways. He flicked sparks, threw fireballs, he even tried breathing fire as a joke. It mostly worked. His throat felt very raw afterwards so he decided not to try that very often. By the time night came, he had become very proficient in generating fire in small measures.

The next day he tried working it in larger methods. He created larger fireballs and attempted molding the fire into objects. His first attempt fizzled into nothing. It was supposed to be a dog but it wouldn't solidify. He tried multiple times, but it never seemed to improve. Each time it began to take shape, but then a gust of wind came and it dissipated into nothing. It was making him angry, so he focused on something else. He tried making whips out of fire. These were easier to make. They consisted of one strand of fire coming from each hand. He concentrated on the stability of it and flicked it. The first flick wasn't very hard so it kept its shape well enough. He tried it again harder and lost it.

He made some progress though so he was happy.

He couldn't waste any more time developing this new power and had to move on. Each day he flew hard so that when he finally landed to rest he could get in a little practice time. In the short time he had, he could see tiny improvements in the forms he created and the stability. He learned that it wasn't only in his imagination. It was a combination of his personal strength, his mental strength, his emotional state and his surroundings. In the desert the fire was easier to create. In a forest, not so much. He had to concentrate harder and strain physically to even produce a spark. The more he practiced though, the easier it came. He was sure that when the time came, he would be ready to use it.

The sun was rising on the morning of his seventh day traveling when Mount Shasta came into view. It towered like a beacon in the sky and all he wanted to do was cry out in joy. He was so tired of travelling. Within a few hours he entered the city limits. By this time the sun was well above the horizon so he was forced to seek refuge in a seemingly abandoned apartment complex. All of the doors he tried were locked, but he kept looking. Before long he found one that wasn't.

The apartment smelled rank, as if more than one creature had died and was decomposing there. With what little sunlight was filtering through the dingy, dust infested blinds, he surveyed the dismal surroundings and groaned in distaste at what he found. The carpet, or what appeared to be carpet, was severely stained and large sections of it looked as if some animal had either eaten it or simply destroyed it for lack of anything else to do. The '70s style flower wallpaper was peeling off the sun-spotted wall and looked no worse than the carpet from the obvious sign of consumption by vermin and bugs.

He went into the kitchen area and was met with the same state of disrepair and destruction as he had found in the living room. Cabinets sagged with warped and termite eaten wood. Some of the cabinet doors dangled dangerously looking like they'd been nearly ripped off their hinges. He didn't even bother looking in the fridge. Most likely it was overrun with mold and rotten food. He tried the faucet in hopes that water was still running, but quickly shut it off again when something similar to brown sludge came glopping from the pipes.

The bedroom was no better, but at least it held a mattress, disgustingly spotted with heaven knows what. He dropped his bag next to it and collapsed onto its cushy goodness. He was too exhausted to really care and right now anything was better than the hard ground. He stretched himself out on it and was soon fast asleep.

A loud crash woke him from his peaceful sleep. His brain was slow to recover but could still register that more people were seeking refuge in the apartment. The voices were low and hard to understand until one if them suddenly gasped.

'Somebody's been here!!!' exclaimed a person with an annoying, nasally, high-pitched voice, presumably a woman.

'Keep it down!' a duller, gruffer voice replied. 'They might still be here. How do ya know someone's been here?'

'Because there's shit in the sink.'
'Literal shit or garbage?'
'Literal shit.'
'How can you tell?'
'Cause it smells and looks like it.'
'Probably just came from the pipes.'
'I dunno. It looks a lot like diarrhea.'

As the two continued their nonsensical dialogue, Tyler quickly came to his senses. The arrival of the two squatters proved to be quite the inconvenience. He looked frantically around the room, but only found a window and the closet. The window was an immediate no-go as he risked being seen by more than these two.

Plus it wasn't big enough to fit through. His only option was the closet.

He quietly slid off the mattress, grabbed his bag, and made his way over to the closet door. The closet was one of those with the two sliding doors, but only one of these doors was still on its runner. The other had fallen backwards into the closet, resting against the shelf at the top. That was not a good thing. As he inspected it, he noticed that if he could just push the door's base in about an inch or so without making too much noise, he would be able to slide open the other door with no problem.

He reached for the door, taking a quick moment to listen. When the voices sounded no closer, he grabbed both sides of the door, pulled it away from the shelf, lifted it up and moved it more than enough inwards. He placed it as gently as possible back against the shelf and slid open the other door just wide enough to fit himself through.

He had just slid the door shut when he heard the man say, 'Hey. You didn't shut the bedroom door when we left did ya?'

'Why would I 've shut it?' the woman asked, annoyed.

'I dunno. It's shut and I didn't shut it so either you shut it or yer so called intruder is in there now.'

'Oh be careful!' the woman squeaked, as she crashed into who knows what.

'Be quiet!' the man hissed. He was just outside the door now. Tyler listened intently as the squatter cautiously turned the doorknob.

Tyler sank as low as possible into the shadows of the closet in hopes that the two might be disheartened when they entered the room and found it empty. Boy was he wrong. While he hoped they would just leave, he knew the couple was going to make the same deduction that he had made: that the closet was going to be best place to hide.

The couple looked rather perplexed when they entered the room and found no trespasser there. They both crossed over to the window, the woman, as bravely as possible, creeping just slightly behind the man, as if attempting to hide in his shadow. When they found the window still locked and no sign of disturbance to it, they immediately turned to the closet. It was truthfully the most logical place to hide.

After they crossed in front of the bed, the couple was no longer in Tyler's line of sight. All he could hear was their bated breath and the shuffle of their feet across the stained, browning carpet. The sound of their breathing was uncomfortably close to the door now, as if they were trying to hear a sign of his existence before exposing it for real.

An explosion from somewhere in the house caused the woman to shriek and the walls to shudder. Before the couple or he had any chance to comprehend what was happening, a barrage of policemen began filing into the room. The cops were shouting things incoherently to the couple who, once they'd come to their senses, were shouting just as incoherently back. Feelings of fear and anger gradually swept over him as the cries of the couple turned from surprise to anger, fear and desperation and the shouts of the policemen became frantic.

He tried to sit there silently and wait out the invasion. He was most likely forgotten about so there was no need to expose himself. As he sat there, something very indistinctly began gnawing away at his core. It was a strange feeling, slightly painful, an ache that progressively spread throughout his being. As the tension outside the closet intensified, the stronger the ache became until he felt it suffocating him. He could feel each individual emotion as separately as the next. Each one was trying to overpower the others in a battle of wills. Fear, anger, anxiety, pain, each one real and heartbreaking. They crushed into Tyler's chest like an anvil and were absorbed into his pores, poisoning his essence.

Before he could stop himself, he screamed and flung aside the working sliding door, causing it to break free from the slider and shatter against a wall. The room fell silent as he stepped from the closet, his cheeks tear-stained and pale. Mouths gaped as many in the room made the sign of the cross.

'Please stop fighting!' he cried, as fresh tears streamed down his face. 'I can't stand the anger. It feels like poison to my soul.'

No one spoke. A deafening silence had filled the room as all eyes gazed at where he had suddenly appeared. A few sharp breaths sounded at first, but then nothing. The unrealistic possibility of an angel standing before them could barely be comprehended by most there. Many stared in disbelief while others, such as the woman with the high voice, brought a hand to their mouth as tears began streaming down their cheeks. Could they sense his purpose and feel his purity? Or were they simply confused at his presence?

Before any of them could react, Tyler walked through the line of officers, never flinching as he felt the many hands clutching at his wings, as if by touching they could deduce whether they were real or not. Some murmured barely audible prayers at his passing, but all heads bowed in reverence as he walked by.

Then he was gone. No one spoke nor moved for the space of a few minutes. His presence had seemed like a dream, or insanity, brought on by the many hours of unrelenting stress. But, as if left for confirmation, lying calmly on the floor of the closet was a single, perfect, white feather.

Chapter 14

It didn't take Tyler long to locate another hiding place. With all the policemen inside the one apartment, rather than simply flying off, he continued down the hall, trying the other knobs as he passed until he found another one unlocked. He quietly shut the door, locked it and quickly did a one over on the apartment. He wanted to make sure that this time there was no sign of any other occupants, such as a mattress. Once satisfied, he laid himself down on the floor and fell asleep.

When he awoke, the room was pitch black and thankfully the only person in the place was himself. He stood and stretched. The journey was really starting to take its toll on him. He felt beyond exhausted despite having slept for more than eight hours. Then again, he usually felt worse when he slept longer than normal. He reached down for his bag and made his way out of the house. This was the last leg of his journey so he had better get a move on.

Before he left the apartment, he pulled a map from the front pocket of the satchel. It was of the northern California region. Marked boldly with a big black X was the address where he needed to be heading. It wasn't so much an address as coordinates to a specific area. He followed it as best he could until he reached the outskirts of town towards the southwest and continued out into the Shasta National Forest. Despite the clarity of the night's sky, the shadowy forest below him made it nearly impossible to determine where he was heading. It was going to be slower, but to save himself from missing it, he landed in the first clearing he came to and walked the rest of the way.

The surrounding atmosphere was a lot more pleasant than he had expected it to be. The air felt clean and was ripe with the smell of pine and fir trees. The soil beneath his feet was cool in the clear night air and felt full of life. An unrushed breeze wafted through the branches of the trees, bringing with it the aroma of distant flowers, the chattering of hidden animals and the promise of serenity from the toils of a stressful day.

He was taking a moment to take in this marvelous sensation when he heard the faint crack of a nearby twig.

'Who's there?' he called out, only to be answered by the mocking silence.

He stood motionless for a few seconds listening. The air was still and he heard nothing other than the remote hooting of prowling owls. He had barely begun walking again when a voice as coarse as desert sand drifted ominously out of the surrounding darkness.

'It's about time you got here.'

'Who are you?' Tyler cried out, creating two orbs of fire, one in the palm of either hand. This was the first time he considered using his power as a defense mechanism. He needed to be sure to not let his mind think anything too drastic. The fire cast a wide arc of light through the surrounding foliage, but revealed no intruder.

'Quite impressive. I see you've been developing your various gifts. Although, it would have been more impressive if you'd made your hair fire as well,' the mysterious voice commented before it laughed in mockery.

'Show yourself!' Tyler exclaimed, 'or else I'll do far more than make my hair become fire!'

The orbs in his hands flashed brightly and moved away from his hands before elongating, growing legs and arms. The creepy fire clones floated ominously at his side, waiting for his command to attack. From his feet, snakes of fire slithered through the trees. As if the fire had tiny claws, the tendrils climbed up trunks, stopping dangerously close to the fragile leaves and needles and latched onto rocks like veins of magma.

'Alright, alright,' the voice replied. A stones throw away, a figure emerged from behind one of the trees. 'No need to get all wound up. Besides, I'm not who you should be worried about.'

'What do you mean by that? And who are you? Why were you following me?'

The mysterious person laughed and moved towards him, theatrically walking into the light. Tyler was surprised to see how young the person was. There stood a young man of no more than 15 years. He looked about the same height as himself, but as he was standing somewhat downhill from the kid, it was safe to say the boy was slightly shorter. His hair was jet black and seemed to disappear completely in the darkness behind him. For as dark as his hair was, the boy's skin was only a few shades darker than his own, at least that's how it looked in the flickering light of the veins of fire encircling him.

What made this young man's appearance even stranger was he was dressed straight out of some country western movie. On his feet he wore a simple pair of sandals with what looked like leather laces. On his legs he wore a lightly decorated pair of leather chaps attached to the strap of his hopefully sturdy loincloth. Across his chest and back he wore what seemed to be a painted vest made from either long beads or some type of bone. His face, upper arms and abdomen were painted with runic symbols, which looked oddly familiar to Tyler.

'My name is Mem Loimis,' the boy proudly announced, 'but those who know me usually call me Kahit. And I wasn't following you. I was already here.'

Tyler stared at the boy skeptically. 'Well, aren't you up a little late? It's after midnight.'

The boy stared at Tyler with a smug grin on his face, the dim firelight reflecting off his light gray eyes.

'Of course it's after midnight. You don't think it would've been better for us to meet in the middle of the day do you?'

'Us meeting? You must be confused. If I were to be meeting someone they would be much older. Besides, how would you know whether we were to be meeting or not?'

'Because I'm the one you're supposed to be meeting with. You missed the old man by about two weeks.'

Tyler stared at him in disbelief. What was this kid talking about? Father Michael never mentioned him meeting with anyone. Besides, would the person he was entrusted to really be a mere teenager? Could things possibly get any worse? He immediately ceased those thoughts. The last time he thought things couldn't get much worse he became a fallen angel on a quest to save the world.

The boy sudden laughed. 'Yeah I wouldn't think things like that either if that happened to me.'

'What?'

'Uh nothing,' the boy said, looking away awkwardly. He sighed and turned back, looking Tyler more confidently in the eyes. 'Look. I know this is weird. It's not the greatest for me either, but neither of us have a choice so just deal with it. Now can you turn off the fire please?'

'Fine,' Tyler said, extinguishing the flames and rubbing his temples. 'I guess I'm just gonna have to take your word as there is no one else around to refute it. It's just that you're so young!' he spat out.

'Hey! Don't give out on me yet. I may be young, but as your Spirit Guide I have all the wisdom and knowledge of the Ancients as well as nature.'

The situation was now proving even more ridiculous. Not only was he to trust his way to a teenager, but one who could supposedly commune with the dead and trees. He knew he shouldn't have questioned if things could get much worse.

'Fine. Fine,' he exclaimed. 'It's appears I have no choice. If you are who you say you are and you are in fact my supposed "Spirit Guide" - why I even need one is beyond me - then please lead the way. Time is of the essence.'

Kahit smiled broadly and took off through the trees. Tyler walked a few paces behind the boy, still unsure of so many things. Not that the boy made any attempt to answer any of his questions either. All he did was smile and make animals noises, which Tyler was sure he got responses to. The further they walked, the more and more curious he got and the more questions began filling his mind. Who was this kid? What was a Spirit Guide and why did he need one? Where exactly were they going and was the kid even sure they were going the right direction?

All of the sudden, the boy stopped and turned around.

'Fine. If it'll ease your mind, I'll answer all your questions,' the boy said with smirk. 'But on one condition. Stop referring to me as either kid or the boy. Just cause I'm younger than you, doesn't mean I'm a child.'

'What?' Tyler sputtered.

'First, who I am I already told you. I'm Mem Loimis, but you can call me Kahit as most people do. A Spirit Guide is someone who is preordained to a certain task of assisting a person through their life. Why you need one is because your journey is not going to be easy and you are going to need whatever help you can get. And lastly, yes I know where we're going and yes, we're going in the right direction.'

With that being said, he turned back around and continued walking.

'Now wait,' Tyler said, jogging a few steps to grab Kahit's arm to make him stop. 'First off, you really sounded grown-up just then. Secondly, how did you know I had those questions? Who are you really?'

'I've told you twice now, I'm your Spirit Guide,' Kahit said, obviously annoyed at Tyler and his incessant questioning.

'Telling me you're my Spirit Guide doesn't tell me anything. All it tells me is that you are a guide, not how you read my mind and how you knew to meet me here. I'm not going another step until you explain.'

Tyler meant it. To show he was serious, he planted himself on the ground and stared defiantly up at Kahit. He knew he was acting like a child, but if it was the only way to get the answers, so be it.

'Fine,' Kahit exclaimed. 'It looks like I'm gonna have to be the adult here.'

'Good. Now start talking.'

After a brief pause to gather his thoughts he began. 'A Spirit Guide is a being generally known by a specific person. The common belief is that they knew each other in a former existence and the one was sent to help guide the other on the specific path that they chose for themselves. In your case it's quite different. Neither one of us knows the other and I'm pretty much 100 percent sure that we never knew each in other in some prior existence. My destiny has somehow been linked with yours and I was guided to this spot at this time. My calling is that of a Spirit Guide, but who I was to aid specifically was a mystery to me and my mentors.'

'So how can you be sure that I'm the one you're meant to guide?'

'Because I heard you.'

An uneasy silence fell between the two as Tyler took a few seconds to let all the information sink in. If what he was saying was true, then Kahit was just as new to all of this as he was.

'So,' he said, clearing his throat, 'you're telling me you heard my thoughts, which is how you were able to know the questions I had? And you never had that happen with anyone else before?'

'Nope. No one. I knew you were on your way and once you arrived I knew where you were heading. I wanted to be here when you arrived.'

'That is so strange,' Tyler said as he hoisted himself off the ground.

'You're telling me. And it came at the strangest time.'

'What do you mean?'

'Well, I was getting ready for bed when I felt the weirdest feeling, as if something in my brain was waking up. Suddenly my room disappeared and all I could see was bright light. It really hurt my eyes. Then I heard a voice in my head. I felt him say, 'Come closer' and then you appeared. I could feel your fear. It felt exactly how I was feeling. When you finally came into the light, I felt sharp pains all over my body. I could see your lips moving but nothing made sense. It hurt so fricking bad. Then it all disappeared. When I woke up I had a bloody nose.'

Once again Tyler was dumbfounded. How could it be?

'What day was that?' he asked, trying to dissuade himself that it was even possible.

'It's not going to matter what day it was. I already know you experienced the same thing, but you looked different.'

'Yeah, I was still normal then.' It was difficult not

to feel bitter about it. 'There's one problem though. I was dreaming when all this happened. The whole experience with the light was only a dream.'

'It might have felt like a dream, but it wasn't. It was real. Ever since then, I've heard and felt you. Now, since we've settled this can we continue? As you said earlier, "Time is of the essence."'

They walked silently for the next half hour until at last they arrived at a meadow. They stopped by a giant boulder stuck solidly in the ground.

'Why are we stopping?' Tyler asked, inspecting the rock.

'Because we're here.'

'Here? But there's nothing here.'

'Well what'd you expect? A big door wide open with an invitation for everyone to come claim its treasure?' The mockery in Kahit's voice was only slightly masked.

'No, but at least a clue to the entrance would've been nice.'

'That's why you have me,' Kahit said as he turned his back on Tyler.

He, more annoyed than anything else, rolled his eyes and stared at Kahit as the boy walked around him to the boulder. He placed his hand gently onto the stone and began chanting. Tyler struggled to hear what he was saying, but the words sounded like they were in some strange, foreign language. Probably his tribes' dialect.

Kahit pulled a piece of chalk from his pocket and proceeded to draw five points on the stone with lines all meeting in the center. As the lines were being drawn, the chanting grew more melodic, as if he was chanting some ancient tribal melody. Lastly he drew a straight, horizontal line from the second to the fifth point and a perpendicular line from the first point to the base, creating a cross.

When the drawing was complete, Tyler noticed

something about the air. It was still. There had been a constant breeze throughout the night and now all of the sudden it was gone. It felt like the chanting had lulled the entire world to sleep, as all was still and silent. There was a strange eeriness in the silence, as if the forest sensed what was about to happen and waited, in reverence, for the door to finally open.

The last symbolic motion Kahit made was touching his forehead with the fore and middle fingers of his left hand and then his chanting ceased.

'The way for you to go has now been prepared. All that's left is for you to open the door.'

'How do I do that?'

Kahit turned and looked at him with a comically mischievous grin. 'With burning touch by hand of flame, to pass the gate erase the frame.'

A relatively simple riddle, but Tyler still stared at him as if he had no idea what he was talking about. "With burning touch by hand of flame, to pass the gate erase the frame." He turned back to the rock and thought about it. Walking up to the stone, he gently placed his finger to it, tracing the drawing as if etching it into his memory. It seemed fairly obvious what he needed to do. Erase the drawing with fire. But did he just throw fire at it or did he have to physically use his finger to erase the outline?

Tyler turned to discuss his thoughts with Kahit, but found himself alone.

'Kahit?' he called, but got no response. He was gone. Disappeared into the forest without a sound. Go figure. Once again he was alone to figure things out.

He turned back to the stone and focused on the drawing. He was to erase the frame by burning it off the stone and that would somehow unlock the door. But how was he to burn it off? Was he required to only burn the lines of chalk or could he engulf the entire face of the rock in fire? Did he only get one shot at this or did it even matter? Since he had no one to answer these questions, he was just going to have to take the hypothetical route that he only had one shot.

He took a few steps back and raised his arm, extending his fingers towards the boulder. He concentrated hard, focusing all his energy on the five outer points until there position was burned into his memory. As he stared intently, he could feel the heat beginning to build behind his eyes. The fire slipped like acid into his bloodstream, carving a path down his arms to his fingertips. The fire inside was sharp and vivid, but rather than bring pain, brought a sense of power, which bolstered his confidence. As soon as the fire reached his fingertips, it leapt forth from them, as if impatient to get where it knew it needed to go. Each finger of flame attached itself to one of the five points on the stone. As soon as all had connected, they erupted into massive flames, eating away the lines of chalk, leaving nothing but the charred, smoldering remains of their existence.

Once the drawing was gone, Tyler waited in silent anticipation for something to happen, but nothing did. Five minutes passed and then ten, but a door never appeared and the stone stayed the same as when he got there.

"How could this have happened?" he thought. Did he not do it right? Maybe there was something he forgot to do, but it was as if the fire had done it and not him. If something had been forgotten it hadn't been intentional.

The longer he waited the angrier he got. Finally, in a fit of rage he turned back to the stone feeling the fire once again racing through his veins. He began beating the stone with his fists, which had suddenly burst into flames. The fiercer he beat the more nothing happened. The stubborn stone yielded nothing. In a last fit of despair, with tears of frustration running down his face, he moved backwards as he formed a fireball the size of a large globe and threw it with all his might against the stone.

The fire splattered against it, clinging to it like mud. It glowed there expectantly, stationary in the still air. A slight tremor rippled through flame. Suddenly it began seeping into the cracks and crevices of the rock. The rock glowed with an ethereal luminosity as the fire disappeared inside it. Like having ingested something rancid, the stone began to quake and shiver as the fire wormed its way into its core. Like an infected wound, the stone began to swell, vibrating violently. Tyler knew this wasn't going to end peacefully so he ran and took refuge behind the nearest tree and not a second too soon. As soon as he got behind the tree, the boulder exploded, catapulting white-hot nuggets of melting rock across the immediate vicinity of the forest.

The tree he stood behind shuddered painfully as it was attacked with the shrapnel. Branches, leaves and chunks of bark flew around the clearing as he did his best to cover his bare skin. As the final remnants of stone clattered to the ground, he cautiously peeked out from behind the tree. When nothing else came at him, he stepped out to inspect the damage. To his dismay, a hazy mist of dirt and dust blocked his view. "A breeze would be helpful right about now," he mused. Much to his surprise, a faint cool breeze suddenly picked up and began dispersing the dirty cloud.

The movement in the air worked wonders to the stagnant air. The dusty cloud swirled hypnotically as the breeze gently encouraged it to leave. As the dust and rubble settled, Tyler moved closer to inspect the scene. In front of him lay a narrow passage, dark and foreboding that led straight into the earth. He was not too keen on going into the tunnel, but as this was where his path had led him he knew there was a good reason for him to follow it. He created a fire orb in his hand before squeezing his way through the entrance.

Once he made it through the tight opening, the tunnel opened up nicely to allow for comfortable movement. The air was damp and earthy, but otherwise the flow of air seemed consistent. The light from his makeshift torch revealed the upper portion of the walls and ceiling were formed from the natural rock layer while the lower portion of the walls and floor were packed earth. As he walked further into the tunnel, the walls changed material. Sometimes the floor and base of the walls were stone with the ceiling dirt while other times, depending on the direction he was going, one wall and half the floor and ceiling would be stone while the other half would be dirt. It was as if the creature that made this tunnel gave no concern to the stability of it and the material it was tunneling though.

The trek through the passageway was long and boring. He walked through it as quickly as he let himself, but it never seemed to end. A small part of him wished he'd trigger a booby-trap just so he'd get to do something other than walking. He rounded a turn and stopped. He had often heard the expression "Trapped like a rat in a maze," but he never dreamed that one day he would become one. Before him stretching out more than two football fields in length and width was a maze hewn from solid stone. From where he was standing he could make out a variety of dead ends, but as to which road led to them, it was nigh impossible to distinguish in the darkness it melted into.

He stepped down the few steps into the maze and found a torch attached to the wall. He extinguished the orb in his hand and pulled the new torch off the wall. Holding a torch was a lot easier than creating one. He didn't have to concentrate so much on keeping it lit or the right amount of brightness to see well. He quickly lit it and was dismayed to find it didn't cast its light very far. Maybe the fire orb was the better choice.

At the edge of the torchlight he made out a faint

glittering. He walked towards it a found pedestal with a bowl of liquid. It seemed very strange to have a liquid-filled pedestal just randomly placed with no real purpose, unless of course it was some archaic light fixture. Rather than risk dousing the torch in the liquid, he flicked a tiny spark into it and smiled as it burst into flames. Now he could really see his surroundings.

As was the case with most mazes, this one had two possible starting points: a left and a right one. Neither one looked particularly promising. He bit his lip in confusion. There had to be some sort of clue to which way he needed to go. If not he could be stuck here for ages and never find a way out. His eyes widened as he had an unexpected thought. That wasn't completely true. Of course he could easily find his way out. All he needed to do was fly. He didn't know why he hadn't thought of it earlier. He stretched his wings and took to flight, reaching the ridiculous height of the walls quickly. Seriously, did they really need to be that high?

He had barely breached the top of the walls when he heard a chorus of twangs. It was like the sound a blowgun made. He tilted his head thinking about it and felt a sudden breeze flutter passed. He instantly dropped as a multitude of arrows whizzed over the spot where he had just been. That ruled out flying over the maze. Go figure the one place he didn't want a booby-trap there was one. On foot it had it be.

When he landed on the ground, he brushed his cheek and it stung. He looked at his hand and saw a streak of blood across it. He hadn't realized how close to death he'd just been. He stared at the fire as the shock set in. Was he going to die here? Had he really only made it this far to fail? Would his brother have made it any farther? His brother. The thought of Mark succeeding where he might not snapped him out of his stupor. No. He wouldn't let Mark be better than him.

He set to looking for a clue to start the maze. On

the wall shimmering in the firelight was a plaque. He walked up to the wall to get a better look at it. It contained what appeared to be some sort of riddle, which he hoped was to help him start the maze correctly. It read:

Left or right but which is right when not a clue to help is left. But left strategically is left a hint, that's right, to choose the right. So now at last we here are left, of which of these two ways is right. Be it left or be it right you are left to choose what's right. I'll stop the tease and tell you right, the way you need to go is left.

Tyler was dizzy by the middle of the strange riddle. It was as if some deranged person was let rampant on a piece of paper. How was he supposed to make any sense of this drivel? Left or right? Neither way looked particularly promising. The riddle was making no sense to him either. He was just going to have to make a choice. So he chose right. Right, left, right at the intersection, follow the path, straight through the next couple of intersections, right, left, left, left, right, right, right and so on. On and on and on he went through the endless maze until finally as he rounded what he hoped to be the final corner, he saw a faint flicker of light. Excited to be at the end of the maze, he ran forward and stopped in disappointment. He wasn't at the end at all. He was once again at the beginning. He had just wasted who knows how long and had made it absolutely nowhere.

He took a seat on the bottom step and groaned. Things were definitely not going well. He looked up and inadvertently glanced at the plaque. He started to look away when something made him pause. "Could it have really been so simple?" he thought. "It's impossible." Looking once again at the plaque, he read the final statement and was thankful no one else had been there to see what an idiot he was. "I'll stop the tease and tell you right, the way you need to go is left." He was supposed to go left. It had told him plain and simple, but with its awkward wording and the fact he'd stopped reading too early, he'd been expecting the direction to be right rather than the actual direction being left. Now that he knew the correct course he needed to be going, he stood up and started on the left path.

On his way, he made many wrong turns, but kept on going. Occasionally he would find other pedestals, although none of them revealed more clues to which way he should go. Other than making it easier and quicker, it really didn't matter. He had no other option but to continue on. Something kept telling him that he was so close to his goal. At least this time he was sure he was on the right part of the maze. Without that reassurance, it would have proved an even more daunting task.

After what felt like many hours later, he made the actual final left turn leading to a doorway out of the maze. He had never felt as grateful as he did as he exited the labyrinth. He'd never been good with mazes and that was by far the worst he'd ever encountered. Especially as it was a physical maze rather than one on a piece of paper. Now that he was out the room, he needed to know what lay before him as once again he was faced with relative darkness. At least he had a torch to dispel some of the gloom.

Looking around him he was able to tell that he was no longer in a tunnel or anything else as confining. By the entrance he found another pedestal. From it led narrow channels that ran along the base of the wall and seemed to reflect the light. Instantly he thought of the various scenes from movies where treasure seekers enter the dark room and without considering whether the liquid might be water or not, stick their torches into the channels of fluid, which luckily end up lighting the room. It seemed plausible enough and before Tyler could stop himself, he dunked the torch right into the liquid. To his luck and surprise, the liquid was flammable. The fire spread from the pedestal down the canals, snaking along the walls, brightly lighting a rather large cavern.

The room he found himself in was stunning. He felt like he'd entered into an Egyptian tomb. The ceiling stretched at least a hundred feet high and was dotted with jagged stalactites. Six columns ran along both sides of the room. They were placed into two rows of three flanking an obvious pathway. The columns had a traditional look with ornate capitals and bases very similar to the Mediterranean works found in Greece and Italy. In front of each column was a statue in the form of a Golem, a giant mythological creature made of inanimate matter. They were traditionally very holy creatures and very prevalent in Jewish folklore, but how Tyler knew this surprised even himself.

The Golems themselves were shaped in different positions. The first two were kneeling with their hands out in the offering of a sword. The next two were standing straight with their heads bowed, their foreheads up against the hilt of their sword, which tip was slightly buried in the dirt. The last two were standing tall with the left arm extending their swords with the tips of both touching.

A sight suddenly caused Tyler's heart to race. He couldn't believe just how close he was to accomplishing his quest. In the distance, just beyond the two standing Golems, was a platform. On top of it he could see something resting on two stands of glimmering metal. He smiled in triumph. Within his reach was the first piece of the key.

Chapter 15

Erickson was feeling pretty clever with himself as he parked his car in a secure little outlet just off the dirt road leading into Shasta National Forest. This was probably one of the easiest reconnaissance missions he'd ever been on. All because of his planting a small tracking device. His usual method of tracking consisted of weeks of grueling legwork following targets and mapping their daily habits. He wasn't so lucky with this case. He was forced to resort to more modern methods and he had to admit, he was starting to be converted to some of these modern-day gadgets. Tyler had never once suspected that Erickson, the random trespasser, had planted it in his bag rather than take anything. After he almost got caught, he wondered if the boy would find it. He wouldn't have understood what it was considering it looked like a small silver disk, similar to the size and texture of a dime. He'd wondered if Tyler would keep it if he found it? The answer seemed to be yes since here he was.

He'd been following closely since the angel left on his cross-country jaunt to California. At first he pursued him during the day, stopping once he came within a mile of where Tyler had hid himself. As they neared their destination, he had to make the sudden switch to sleeping during the day and following at night. It wasn't easy, but it had proved to be a good choice. If he hadn't he would now be sleeping while Tyler located and acquired the key. Either that or he'd be far too exhausted to function at his normal capacity.

The angel wasn't too difficult to find once Erickson got there. The forest was bathed in lustrous moonlight, which made it easier to spot the boy walking through the trees. He found it amusingly sinister to be walking through a forest in the middle of the night, trailing the boy by about fifteen meters or so. He deemed it far enough away not to be heard and close enough that he could follow without getting lost. There were a few times he crept closer and Tyler stopped to call out as if he had heard something. All he would have heard was noise. There was no chance of him being seen. The chameleon had come out to play and "Follow the Leader" was the game. There was something animalistic in the pursuit, even if it was only to gather information. Like cat and mouse, although this time the roles could very well be switched. Be that as it may, the chase was uneventful. That was until the stranger showed up.

He appeared as if brought in by the wind. One minute it was only he and the boy and then about 25 feet ahead of him the stranger appeared. It was difficult to make out anything about the new guy. He moved like a shadow, similar to himself, but he strangely seemed to be made of shadow rather than mimic it. Erickson would never have noticed the newcomer had he not looked in the stranger's direction as he was moving through the trees. The stranger hid himself a couple yards from Tyler and yet the angel couldn't seem to figure out where the person was. Devious and at the same time evilly amusing. If this person meant to do the angel harm, he sure wasn't wasting any time getting himself killed. He must not know how dangerous this creature was.

A sudden explosion of light nearly exposed his position. He froze where he was. A normal person might have run for cover, but he had full confidence in his transparency. It would be easier to see a stick insect on a branch than him right now. He was cloaked in simple fitted black attire, which was accented with muted greens and browns. Whatever skin was still exposed had been painted to resemble underbrush. He had even put in coloured contacts to hide the whites of his eyes and a mouth guard to hide his teeth. He loved the feeling of disappearing behind his handiwork. It made him proud as no one had found him yet.

The scene before him was comically mesmerizing. It was truly a sight seeing the boy manipulate fire. The flames moved effortlessly at his every whim, morphing from orbs into two humanoid figures. They floated ominously at his side while lines of fire began snaking through the leaves from his feet in all directions. Some of them climbed up trees like painful ivy, coming close enough to the stranger that its flickering light reflected gently off his face. It was a young face, much too young to be running around a forest at this time of night. His skin seemed to contain a reddish hue. It could have been from the fire though. It was darker than Tyler's but resembled more of a dark tan than actual dark skin. Possibly Native American, Latin or European descent.

Erickson wasn't prone to intervening when his targets were in trouble. Usually he could call on some passerby or the police, but this time he didn't have that luxury. He prepared to make his move but stopped when the stranger casually strolled from behind the tree. The two conversed for a while before the angel extinguished the fire. "Smart move," he thought. "Don't ever lower your guard until you're sure it's safe." Once the fire was out, they conversed for a short while longer before the boy began leading Tyler deeper into the forest. He was going to have to remember the boy as well as Tyler's ability to create fire. The Brethren were going to want to know about these new developments. They might be important. This was thrilling for him. He hadn't had this exciting of an opponent in ages.

He moved silently behind them, keeping sure to stay an even safer distance behind the two. He marked various trees to give him a trail to follow back to his car. The boys stopped only once to have a somewhat lengthy discussion and then moved on before stopping one last time in front of a large boulder stuck firmly at the base of a wooded hill in a small clearing. He watched curiously as the newcomer proceeded to pull out an object and begin drawing on the stone. Erickson ducked behind the dense brush patched around the outline of the glade. He tried to push the braches apart to get a better look at the boys, but stopped. There were so many thorns that even the gloves he was wearing were tearing. He was going to have to try somewhere else.

He found an opening only a few feet away from where he had been. It was wide enough for him to see the entire clearing and still remain hidden. The kid had already finished the drawing by the time Erickson had found it. He found the opening just in time to see the kid vanish when Tyler passed in front of him. It was like one of those magic tricks where the magician walks through a door and does not appear out the other side. Those tricks were always provided with some sort of explanation on how they were performed, but this, this trick was real. The boy simply evaporated into the night air. Tyler appeared just as surprised when he turned to find the kid gone.

He thought the angel would be daunted by the sudden disappearance of the boy, but if he was he didn't show it. He just went back to figuring out what he was to do. He stood there captivatedly before taking a stance with one arm in the air pointing at the stone. Watching the fire pour out of Tyler's body captivated Erickson. The veins in the boy's arm glowed brilliantly, starting at his shoulder before flowing down to his fingertips. The agent stared wide-eyed as the end of the boy's fingers suddenly spewed lines of fire that snaked through the air to the rock. It was a magnificent display, but if it was supposed to have an effect it failed.

Erickson watched in amusement as Tyler didn't move for a good fifteen minutes after the fire died out before going awol. He physically attacked the rock with his fists before unleashing his fury in a truly destructive manner. Creating a massive fireball, he let it loose on the stone, which also had little effect. From the size of the thing, Erickson was glad it was the stone receiving Tyler's fury and not himself.

He turned away from the scene momentarily to relieve the cramp that had been building in his thigh. When he turned back, he found the angel gone. "Where'd he go?" he wondered. He looked at the stone and immediately felt his heart sink. The boulder had somehow swollen to twice its normal size. Even with his blending ability, he knew that blending in to the background was going to do him no good when the stone exploded. Just as he ducked behind a tree, the rock exploded, showering the area where he had just been with jagged pieces of stone, each one incredibly hot and sharp.

He waited patiently until the clatter of flying stone died down. Peering cautiously from behind the tree, he was disappointed to find a stationary cloud of dirty fog. He looked to where Tyler had run and saw no one. Could he really be so lucky? Perhaps the angel hadn't been quick enough and had gotten knocked out by a chunk of stone. "That would definitely make things easier," he mused. A gentle breeze wafted the cloud away and he was pleased to see an entrance. He edged out into the open. The Brethren would be sure to reward him greatly if he beat the angel and stole whatever he was after. He started for the entrance but stopped when the angel suddenly appeared. Disappointed, Erickson melted back into the scenery.

Once the dust had settled, he watched Tyler create a small ball of flame before entering the cave. Erickson pulled out his flashlight and quickly followed. He had to be more careful in the tunnel than he had out in the forest as there was nowhere for him to hide. Since the tunnel appeared to have no branches, he was able to remain further back and still keep an eye on the angel.

He followed Tyler down endless corridors till finally the boy turned a corner and stopped moving. That is to say the light didn't move. Erickson patiently waited for the angel to move on but he didn't. Other than a fluctuation in the light, nothing happened. This puzzled the agent. Creeping up to the opening, he pulled out a mirror he'd brought with him and looked around the corner. Tyler was gone. Down a few steps on the ground was a pedestal containing a bowl of fire.

'Stupid,' he whispered angrily to himself. Now he'd let Tyler disappear. He pulled out his mobile to access the tracking app, but was disappointed to find no signal. Was it really that big of a surprise? They were underground. Now what was he going to do? Of course he knew what he was going to do. He was going to perform a manual search. How far could the angel have gone anyway?

He put away the mirror and moved around the corner into the room. His heart sunk as he stared at the room before him. It was a massive cavern made up into a maze. He could not have picked a worse time to lose his target. How was he ever going to find him? He groaned and walked forward towards the entrance. He attempted to read a plaque he found but stopped as he started to get dizzy. It was written in some foreign language he had never come across before. Being as he had been places most people would never imagine being, he'd encountered many languages and dialects. He pulled out his phone and snapped a quick picture of the plaque.

Since he couldn't read the plaque, he was going to

have to toss a coin. Before he had a chance to decide which direction to go, he caught a dim flicker of light out of the corner of his eye. He hurriedly climbed back up the stairs. To the far right of the room, he was barely able to make out a faint yellow circle moving slowly through the maze. "How had he gotten so far?" he wondered as he visually attempted to follow the path he had taken. "And so quickly?"

Erickson had always been good at maze puzzles. He rarely made a mistake and could complete even the most difficult of puzzles rather quickly. He knew he had only a short window of opportunity to gain the lead. He attempted to plot the course Tyler was going to take. To his immense pleasure, he discovered the path he was on led straight back to the beginning. This was the chance he needed for him to take the lead and if possible, retrieve the prize before the angel. Satisfied with his plan, he entered the maze.

Time seemed to drag on as he encountered dead end upon dead end. 'How could I have been so hasty?' he muttered to himself. In his excitement, he hadn't even thought about figuring out the way to the end. Instead he had plunged right in, eager to win the prize. There seemed to be an abundance of dead ends rather than any that actually led anywhere. He was beginning to wish he had just called it quits before embarking on this suicide mission. He took a turn by another of the pedestals when he heard footsteps and saw the reflection of light upon the walls. He'd found Tyler; or rather the angel found him without actually finding him.

The light was coming from the corridor through which he had just come. He flattened himself against a wall and snuck stealthily towards where the light was coming and waited for him to pass. He held his breath as he sensed Tyler's presence near him. The angel paused momentarily considering if he should go left, in the direction of where the agent was hiding, right or straight ahead. Erickson waited anxiously for those few seconds before silently breathing a sigh of relief when Tyler continued going straight.

After a thousand more wrong turns, Erickson was relieved to make it to the end of the maze. He found it a lot easier to follow the angel rather than lead him. Plus, he noticed a trend with the pedestals. They were a sign that they were going in the right direction. They also stood in front of the path they were supposed to take. Too bad he hadn't figured that out earlier. He might have beaten his opponent to the prize. Now he had to lag behind for a while and watch as Tyler disappeared further into the darkness of the next passage. He would have liked to stay as close as possible, losing him once was one too many times, but without knowing if his cover would be compromised he kept further back.

Shortly after Tyler entered the passage it lit up, dramatically exposing a large, cavernous room. Erickson crept up to the doorway where he could make out twelve pillars, six on each side of the room. The angel had already made it passed the pillars and was walking up the few steps onto a raised platform. On it was some sort of table or altar with a long object held by two stands. It was hard to tell exactly what it was as he was so far away, but it was plain to see that the object was of high importance.

He watched intently as Tyler paused before reaching out to grab the object. He twisted it around in his hands, inspecting it, getting a basic feel for it. Erickson felt strangely jealous and moved to go take it from him, a rash decision he wasn't prone to making. Before he had a chance to make it through the doorway, the ground began to shake and all hell broke loose.

Chapter 16

Chills of excitement ran down Tyler's spine as he stared at the first piece of the key. It took all he had not to sprint passed the towering pillars and up the few steps to stand in front of his prize. Which isn't to say he didn't walk faster than normal. He eyed it with eager anticipation, his fingers itching to pick it up. To anyone else, the fragment looked like a simple staff, but he could feel that it was so much more. He ran his fingers across its elegantly carved olive wood body and could feel its power like static upon his skin. He had found something truly magnificent.

He gently picked it up off the two silver stands, which had held it for who knows how many centuries. He twisted it around in his hands, quickly growing accustomed to its weight and the way it smoothly cut through the air. It was like nothing else he had ever experienced before. His hands felt as if they had been the mold for the grip. His fingers were an exact fit and it moved with him as if it was part of one of his already existing appendages.

He'd only been holding it a couple minutes when the ground shook so violently he was knocked backwards over the table and against the back wall. Confused, he shakily rose to his feet. He stared passed the table and had to rub his eyes to ensure he wasn't dreaming. He could barely believe it, but the Golems were now all standing and staring in his direction. Their blank, unseeing faces froze Tyler in such a way that he couldn't even think. It wasn't until one of the Golems took its first earthmoving step that he was able to somewhat regain control of his faculties.

For a stone creation the golem moved surprisingly fast. In a few steps it was upon him bringing its large fist down, shattering the altar into thousands of tiny rock fragments. He had mere moments to register the oncoming danger and dive away, nearly averting being crushed. As if sensing it had missed its target, the empty, expressionless face turned his way and stared him straight in the eyes. Was it actually aware of where he was? Apparently so, because in two steps it was towering over him bringing down its fists in fury.

Tyler ducked nimbly between the golem's legs and ran into the middle of the room. He needed to get a game plan going or else he was going to die. He considered making a run for it, but bearing in mind how quick it was, he was almost positive the others would be just as fast. He wouldn't even be able to make it between the other Golems. His only option was to fight, but how does one fight an object that didn't even exist under normal circumstances. Now normality was somewhat a paradox, but that didn't matter. Right now he had to focus and stay alive and find some way to destroy this thing.

Calling on every ounce of energy he possessed, he summoned his only weapon: fire. As the golem lumbered towards him, he began pelting the creature with balls of flame. The golem brushed the blots of fire from its hardened shell and took a swipe at him. He dodged it easy enough by taking to flight to get out of its immediate reach and began launching more missiles. He was behaving like an annoying fly, flitting around, heaving fireballs of varying sizes. The golem was getting so frustrated, if it was even capable of being so, that it began launching its own projectiles at him, which happened to be the shattered fragments of the altar. Handfuls of jagged stone were a lot harder to evade than the single or double swings of its monstrous fists. The roof was also a lot closer than he had first thought and being impaled by one of the stalactites was not on his list of ways to die, so he quickly landed.

He was forced to revert back to his first tactic albeit with a few alterations. Snaking from his hands, lines of thick fire formed along the ground, making stinging, molten whips. Strike after strike he attacked the creature. Roaring in anger, the golem charged swinging wildly. Each strike missed him as he dodged them as skillfully as a matador. He did try catching the golem's arm, but as it broke through the line of fire, it nearly ripped his arm off. Instead, he attached the fire whip to the golem's legs. It took a few tries, but finally it stuck, causing it to trip.

As it crashed to the ground, Tyler made to attack the creature in anyway he could. He ran towards it but paused when something close to it caught his eye. Without thinking, he grabbed the wooden staff and brought it down solidly against the golems head. His blood ran cold as he realized what he'd just done. Instead of being broken, the staff resonated slightly in his hand. Smiling smugly, he brought the staff down once more solidly against the stunned golem's head. A ripple spread through its body before it shattered, spraying its remains throughout the cavern. A wave of energy slammed into Tyler and sent him crashing into a wall once again.

He quickly picked himself off the ground and looked towards the other golems. If they were surprised or even concerned he couldn't tell. They simply stood there and stared in creepy silence with the same blank expression on their faces. Without warning they attacked. Stone fists swung one after the next and it took all he had to keep from being flattened by one of the blows. He even attempted taking to flight again, but quickly abandoned that idea as the golems grabbed chunks of their fallen comrade and began chucking them at him.

On the ground he threw fireballs in an effort to distract them before taking the killer hit, but he had underestimated them once again. It only took one of them to stamp the ground and he was jarred violently, missing his mark. Strangely, the golems were in no way working as separate entities, rather they were a team with one common goal: destroy the thief. With a few moves he found himself completely surrounded with no real chance of survival. Any tactic he attempted was quickly foiled by either a stamp on the ground or a swipe by one of the other golems.

It was then that the golem's underestimated him. As one of them brought their foot to the ground, he slammed the end of the staff down sending a shockwave that even Gambit would be proud of. The golem was caught off guard, not expecting him to be able to retaliate. The force of the wave caused it to topple backwards. Tyler sprung gymnastically over his foe and swiftly brought the staff down across the golem's chest while in mid-air, causing its remains to shower its comrades with more dust and debris. The golems paused momentarily, as if contemplating what had just happened before pursuing him once again.

As they neared him, he noticed something that formed a beautiful plan in his mind. The stalactites dangled ominously directly above the golems, anxiously waiting to be knocked down, as if that had been their sole purpose for being placed there. His adversaries were now coming at him in a group, like a pack of wolves going in for the kill. He body was feeling numb and he knew he had only this one shot at getting this right. He somersaulted over the first couple and landed directly in their midst. As he landed, he drove the staff as solidly into the earth as he could. Ripples went in all directions sending the golems crashing to the ground. The aftershock of their collapsing sent him crashing into the nearest column, which was severely damaged from the fighting. As they all lay there stunned, ripples ran speedily up the walls and across the ceiling, causing the stalactites to tremble violently.

Tyler quickly got to his feet waiting expectantly for the destruction, but the stalactites simply swung on the ceiling like the crystals on a chandelier. His heart suck when he realized his plan hadn't worked. He was going to have to think of something new as the golems had already gotten back up. He readied himself for the next onslaught when the foremost, and biggest, roared and stamped its foot in anger causing the room to shake once more. Tyler stared in disbelief as the golem suddenly shattered majestically as a stalactite pierced through its head and continued through its body to the ground. He stared in admiration as more and more stalactites began falling from the ceiling, having been shaken free by the support of the golem's anger. The remaining golems attempted a forward pursuit, but one by one they all met an untimely fate as the stalactites pierced through them, leaving their shattered fragments as the only recognition they had ever existed.

Tyler took cover at the rear of the cave while the golems were decimated. He couldn't have been more pleased with the result of what he had started. Who could have thought that with the aid of one of his enemies, his plan would succeed. His joy was to be immensely short lived. The final stalactite had broken free and joined its brethren in the rubble, but debris was still falling. He began to panic as he realized that the cavern was beginning to cave in. In their fighting, the columns holding up the room had gotten damaged. He hadn't even taken into consideration that the destruction he planned on causing would also affect the stability of the already damaged pillars. Now there was nothing to keep the room from collapsing around him.

He attempted to make his way across the debris towards the entrance of the cavern, but the ceiling was caving in so fast that by the time he was able to make it to the broken golems, chunks as large as dining tables began littering the room. He retreated back to the rear of the cave praying violently that he wouldn't die by being crushed. He was working on finding a way through the debris when he saw a figure at the other end of the room. At least he thought he saw a figure. It was really hard to tell with all the dust and debris falling.

'Hey!' he called out, but the figure vanished as if it had never been there. What had he expected? If there was someone there, it wasn't as if they would have been able to do anything for him. It still would have been a nice gesture if they had tried.

He stared at the destruction that was almost upon him and started to give up hope of it stopping. It was inevitable now. He had defeated the golems and was now going to be defeated in return by them. "How ironic," he thought. Screwed once again and this time there was no one to help him.

He felt a tapping on his shoulder.

'You just gonna stand there waiting to die or are you gonna try and find a way out?'

He turned to see if someone was really patronizing him and was surprised to see Kahit.

'What?! How did you get in here?'

'There'll be plenty of time to answer your never-ending questions later. For now let's get out before we end up like the other things.'

Kahit led him to the corner of the room where hidden in plain sight was a small entryway leading to another set of tunnels. Tyler took one last look at the room falling down behind him before crouching through the doorway. The boys ran through the tunnels, making turns at Kahit's command to not run into walls. Although the vibration had ceased, they continued running and didn't stop until they were safely out in the open air.

The tunnel opened up at the edge of a beautiful lake. Its tranquil sapphire water perfectly mirrored the surrounding forest and near cloudless sky. Only the occasional fish disturbed its peaceful purity. The air was calm other than a thick cloud of dust that could barely be seen above the crest of the hill behind them. It was completely opposite, and very welcome, from the scene they'd just escaped from.

'Where are we?' he asked as he dropped his pack and the staff onto the ground. The lake reminded him of his thirst and he knelt down to take a deep drink from the clear, crystal water that lay before him.

'Castle Lake. About five or six miles from Mt. Shasta. You should probably take a swim. You look like shit,' Kahit replied, laughing at Tyler's haggard appearance.

Tyler took a playful swipe at Kahit and smiled wearily. 'You'd probably look this way as well if you'd just finished fighting six golems and somehow lived to tell about it.'

'Six golems huh?' Kahit swore in amazement as he nodded.

'Six.'

'Impressive.' Kahit smiled sarcastically. 'Now, we're talking about six, ring crazed gollums like in "The Lord of the Rings" right? Cause I doubt you could take on anything bigger.'

'Whatever,' Tyler laughed. 'You're an idiot.' He jumped into the air before spiraling and plunging into the cool, crisp water. The chilled water felt good on his aching muscles, but what he wanted more than anything was a nice hot shower. The cool water felt fantastic, but hot water pouring over him was going to be his own private heaven.

'You should come in as well,' he called to Kahit when he broke the surface. 'The water feels amazing.'

'Nah that's alright,' Kahit answered as he paced barefoot along the rocks at the edge of the bank. 'You swim in one the lake up here and it's like swimming in any of the others.'

'Suit yourself.'

He swam around leisurely until his skin began to prune. He climbed out far enough away from where Kahit was laying and sprawled himself out. He extended his wings all the way to let the water dry as the sun shined brightly in the clear, brilliant sky. It felt good to finally be out in the sun again. After nearly a week of only coming out at night, Tyler had begun to appreciate the sun and its radiance. How anyone could think of willingly living in the dark was beyond his comprehension.

As soon as his wings were sufficiently dry, Tyler rose and turned to tell his companion it was time to move on, but he was already up and mostly packed.

'I forgot you can hear my thoughts,' he said as he walked over to where Kahit was dealing with the packs.

'Not that it's that difficult to do,' Kahit replied. 'You don't have much activity going on upstairs to begin with.'

'Hey, hey, hey,' Tyler retorted, wrapping his arm around Kahit's neck and giving him a noogie. 'That one's gonna cost you.'

Kahit struggled in vain for a few seconds before disappearing and reappearing a few feet away from Tyler, rubbing his sore head where he had just been attacked.

'Whoa!' Tyler exclaimed after nearly falling over from Kahit disappearing as he held him. 'How'd you do that?'

'That hurt you know,' he moped, rubbing his

aching head.

'That's the point. It's a noogie. They don't tickle.'

'Don't do it anymore. I don't like it.'

'Well be nice to me and I won't have to.'

'I thought you were the adult here. Why are you behaving like a kid?'

'I may be an adult, but I'm a big brother first and foremost and as you are younger than me, if I have to treat you like a younger brother, I'm going to.'

Kahit smirked sarcastically, grabbed his bag and turned to go.

'Hey wait. You still need to tell me how you disappeared. That's impossible what you just did.'

'You're one to talk. You're an angel,' he quipped. 'How's that any more possible than me disappearing?'

'It's not, but at least there's a rational scientific explanation for how I became an angel. Your disappearing is like something straight from the X-men, and I can't believe I actually know that,' Tyler said. He was thankful Mark wasn't around to hear him.

'Some things just can't be answered scientifically and must be understood on a completely separate plane. Supernatural phenomenon is as explainable as religious belief or understanding.'

'Supernatural? I just can't accept that. There has to be a reason, some genetic anomaly that makes it possible for you to do the things you can do.'

Kahit laughed and smiled at Tyler. "I'm sure there is, but I'm not about to donate myself to some lab to become a guinea pig so some overzealous scientist can dissect me to figure out how I work."

Tyler was confounded by the boy. For one so seemingly young, he spoke like someone a lot older. His reasoning was not like one who was only in their mid-teens.

A faint chuckle brought him out of his thoughts.

'Boy do you have a lot to learn,' said Kahit as he shook his head. He turned and began walking, disappearing shortly into the thick foliage with Tyler quickly following after him. They walked in silence for hours, not stopping for breaks or any other reason. By nightfall they reached a humble shack on the southern border of the city. Kahit pulled a key from his bag and let them in. He dropped his bag on a chair before disappearing into a back room, shutting the door gently behind him.

Tyler settled himself down on a nicely worn orange suede sofa. He was now worried that he'd offended Kahit. Just like with his brother, he was finding it hard to understand that there could be anything other than a scientific explanation to these phenomenons. When Kahit came out he would apologize to him and explain himself. Also for giving him a noogie. He found it strange that he'd even done that. He barely knew the kid. Had he even known him for twenty-four hours yet? Under normal circumstance he would never do something like that, but he felt a closeness to the kid that he couldn't explain. Probably had to do with their mental connection. He'd have to ask him about that as well, but he never got the chance. Shortly after he sat down he was fast asleep.

Chapter 17

Erickson had barely squeezed out of the opening when the tunnel collapsed behind him, crashing in an explosive cloud of dirt and stone. It was a terrifying sight watching as the rooms around him crumbled. Throughout all his years of training and missions, never once did he ever have to worry about being buried alive. Sure he'd had to escape collapsing buildings, but making it out of buildings was a lot easier and manageable than fleeing out of the depths of the earth. He'd run like never before, all the while unsure if he was going to survive. But he made it. He was dust covered with fragments of stone stuck in his clothes and hair, but at least he was alive.

The fight he had just witnessed was incredible. If he'd placed a bet on who was going to win, he would have lost big time. Who would have thought that Tyler was capable of that much power? It was like watching David fight six Goliaths and win. It was too bad he didn't make it out. How could he? With the room collapsing like it was, the only way he could have survived was if there was another way out at the other end of the room. It was possible, but not likely.

At least he wasn't going to be leaving empty-handed. As Tyler was fighting, he had to dodge a few projectiles and was surprised when a rolled up piece of parchment ricocheted off his forehead, bouncing a few feet away from him. It was still bound with a waxen seal, so he placed the parchment inside a pocket in his jacket and continued watching the fight. He'd forgotten about it until he sat down to rest after running for his life. He pulled it out and inspected it. From the outer skin, it was definitely a material he'd never seen before. It was rough to the touch and a darker, dirtier hue than typical paper or even parchment. Perhaps it was some sort of animal skin. Whatever it was, his brain couldn't take thinking about it. Stuffing it back in his pocket, he all but collapsed on the ground.

He allowed himself a few minutes to rest before forcing himself back up. He needed to make his way back to his vehicle quickly, but it was no easy feat. He was only able to make it about a hundred yards before needing to stop, his legs aching something fierce. In fact his whole body felt as though he had been slammed full force by a bullet train. It wasn't only the run that had killed him. It was an entire physical overload. Once the room began crashing down and didn't appear to stop, he felt in his gut he needed to get out immediately. Turning around, his heart sunk as he realized the maze was blocking his most direct route out. He began retracing his steps back through. As debris fell around him, his brain seemed to shut off completely. At his first dead end, he knew he was hopelessly lost. A fear he'd never felt before gripped his heart and he was unable to stop the helpless feeling of impending doom.

Suddenly a massive chunk of stone landed to his left, crushing part of the walls that surrounded him. A funny idea struck him as he recovered from the shock of almost getting crushed. The walls were much taller than he was able to reach, but now a part of the wall was destroyed. With the destruction creating a way for him to reach the top of the walls, he could easily navigate the room from the top of the maze. A new glimmer of hope began to shine through as he realized there was still a possibility for him to survive.

Once on top of the walls he was able to better pilot the treacherous maze. The gaps were difficult to cross, but the added adrenaline helped him hurdle them successfully. When he jumped he heard the odd twang and felt a rush of air above him. He smiled. A booby-trap to keep the angel grounded. How genius.

Soon he found himself at the entrance of the maze with the room collapsing rapidly behind him. He pulled his flashlight out and sped as quickly as possible through the tunnels. With it only being one long winding tunnel, it was easier for him to navigate. As he neared the entrance he felt his legs start to give. He couldn't stop though. He could hear the collapsing tunnel rapidly approaching, like a hungry black panther and he was on the menu.

The destruction was literally nipping at his heels when he saw the narrow light at the end of the tunnel. He threw himself through the opening, forcing his way to freedom and life. It was no wonder he was in so much pain. In his will to survive, his adrenaline was so high that now that he was able to relax, all the pain was surfacing. He felt like he wanted to lie there forever and never move again, but it never lasted. After a half hour or so, the pain wore off enough that it was a lot easier for him to move about and then quickly came back.

When he finally made it to where he'd parked his car, he was less than surprised to find it not there. Sure it wasn't blocking whatever traffic might possibly be coming down the road, but it must have looked like an abandoned vehicle. Quite ridiculous considering the laptop and other material lying on the floor of the passenger side. The car was of no worth to him as it was a rental, but his possessions were vey important. He needed to locate where they'd gone. 'If it isn't one thing it's something else,' he grumbled, annoyed.

It took him a while to make it to the main road and even longer still to make it back into town. No one would pick him up and it really irritated him. He really couldn't blame them though. With the stigma against picking up hitchhikers, as well as his bedraggled, filthy appearance, he probably looked like someone who might actually kill whomever picked him up.

It was nearing sunset when he finally happened upon a shifty looking motel on the outskirts of town. Seeing as he was tired and in dire need of a shower and something to eat, he gave in and got a room. The room itself wasn't so bad, but the food he had delivered to him was something he would never wish on his worst enemy. He thought he ordered something from the Mom and Pop Native American restaurant next door to the motel, but as bad as it was, he wasn't sure what he'd ordered. He tossed the mostly uneaten meal into the bin before taking a shower with his clothes on. Once the water was running clear again, he hung the clothes to dry and passed out on the bed.

It was the early afternoon by the time he woke up. Every joint in his body ached and sitting up in the bed was even difficult. It reminded him of his second day at basic. An unhappy memory for an unhappy moment. He would have preferred staying there and just dealing with finding the angel later, but the longer he went without knowing his location, the higher chance he wouldn't get paid. Groaning painfully, he inched out of bed, got dressed and left.

Not far from where he had stayed was a Denny's. Even in all his pain, after an amazing breakfast of eggs, hash browns, bacon, sausage, pancakes, coffee and orange juice, he felt much better. While paying for his meal, Erickson inquired about the local impound facility. The cashier's brother just so happened to be the man in charge of the place. He took a paper with the address and directions and set out into town to find it. He was supposed to talk to Louis, the guys brother, who should help him get his vehicle with little hassle.

It took him a little over an hour to locate the place, which happened to be conveniently placed behind the only Wal-Mart for the next 500 miles, or so the sign in front of it said. When he walked into the impound office, he asked for Louis who was promptly retrieved.

'Howdy,' greeted a jovial individual with a noticeable southern drawl as he walked out of an office at the back end of the room. He stuck out his large, tanned, meaty hand and shook Erickson's, inquiring what he could do to help.

'Has a black, Chrysler come in recently?' he asked.

'Don't know 'bout that. Let me check,' replied Louis, who waddled over to a clipboard hanging on a hook behind the secretary's desk. 'Yeah. Came in yesterday 'round 11 am. It yours?'

'Possibly. May I see it?'

'Course. I'll take ya to 't.'

Erickson followed Louis out a side door and into the yard where all the impounded vehicles were held. Walking behind his guide, it wasn't difficult to see that the walk was a tiring task for the rather large man.

'Are you alright?' he asked when Louis stopped suddenly, obviously winded and needing a break, despite the relatively short distance they'd come.

'Yeah I'm fine,' Louis gasped. 'Just ma lungs. I've asthma. Ma doctor says I need ta lose 'bout two hundred pounds if I expect ta be getting better.'

'If it'll make things easier on you, you can just tell me where it is and I can go check it out myself.'

'I would but it's 'gainst company policy. We don't 'ave far to go anyhow.'

Louis took a few more steps and nearly collapsed. 'God. I don't 'member this walk being this difficult before,' he panted, leaning against the nearest car. 'Alright. Next row over. Clear at the end. I'll wait here.'

'Thank you. You just rest and I'll be back shortly.'

Shortly? Yeah right. Erickson knew it wasn't right what he was about to do, but he really didn't have the time to waste dallying over paperwork to retrieve a vehicle that wasn't even his. He hadn't even used his real name to rent it. If it was his own car then he might be less inclined to leave it behind, but as it wasn't, he only needed to get what he had left inside it and then be on his way.

Just as Louis had told him, he found the vehicle at the end of the next row of cars. Although the outside was a little worse for wear, everything on the inside was exactly as he'd left it. He unlocked the doors and gathered his possessions as quickly as he could. He stuck the laptop and notebooks into the satchel and slung it over his head. He did a quick scan of the vehicle and after finding it bear of any trace of him he left.

He was glad to be out of the impound lot. It made him feel dirty being there. He procured a taxi and with his destination set for the airport, he was finally able to lean back and relax. The Brethren were going to be very pleased with him. Of course he hadn't been advised to bring back anything so the parchment was going to be an added bonus. On top of that all the information he had for them was going to make his bonus even larger.

Hours and a few phone calls later, he was once again standing in the middle of the same antechamber in which he received his assignment. They were waiting on the last couple of Brethren who were late for various reasons. The waiting was no problem for Erickson. It was just the unnerving silence that caused him to feel uncomfortable. Silence was usually no issue to him, but when it came to The Brethren, the silence was like millions of ants crawling underneath his skin. It was enough to make him want to scream to drive away the disturbing quiet.

Finally the last of The Brethren took his place and the meeting was able to begin.

'So what news do you bring us?' the head Brother questioned him, his face hidden behind a veil of dark material.

'As requested, I followed Tyler,' he began before being rudely cut off.

'Who is this Tyler?'

'The angel.'

'Do not refer to him in such a manner. He is no mere mortal with the privilege of a Christian name. Do not mistake him for a creature of rationality. He is not a trustworthy beast and thus should be treated with extreme caution. You know this or have you finally gone soft after all these years?'

'I'm sorry sir. You are right. Forgive me.'

'It is quite alright. It is understandable to make mistakes in judgment after all you've seen in your service, but you must not falter.'

Something stirred in Erickson as he heard those words. Had he really gone soft? It was true that he wasn't acting like normal. Getting genuine excitement over a piece of parchment and not wanting to make life difficult for Louis and even not destroying the vehicle he'd left behind in case some scrap of information led back to him and his ghost existence. Ever since he'd met Tyler in the observation room he'd been acting differently. He felt things he'd not felt for many years and now that he was noticing it he began to feel fear; real fear that chilled him to his bones. Was he really loosing his edge or was his interaction with Tyler causing this change in character?

A clearing of a throat brought him out of his thoughts and he continued on.

'For the last week, I've been following the angel as commissioned. I know that daily contact was required throughout the duration of the trip, but when nothing of much importance had been happening, I felt it of no great necessity to trouble you all with eventless reports. Only when something vital happened did I report back. From New Hampshire I followed the angel to California and to the location of the first piece of the key.'

'Were you able to obtain it?' came a question as the room broke into a commotion.

'No. I was not able to retrieve the piece, but I was somehow lucky to come into possession of this.' With much flourish, he pulled the parchment from his jacket and presented it to the Head Brother.

'Do you have any idea what this is?' the Head Brother questioned after inspecting it for a few minutes.

'I have no idea. As you have seen, I didn't break the seal. If it's of any importance, I figured it should be left to you to open it.'

'You've done truly well. Truly well indeed. What you've brought us is of much importance and may put us one step ahead of the Fallen Angel.'

'Please forgive me for being so bold, but might I inquire as to what it is?'

If Erickson had been able to see the smile hiding behind the veil of black, he might have wished he'd never asked the question.

'If I'm correct, what you've brought us, though encoded, is the location of the second piece of the key.'

Chapter 18

Tyler jolted awake as a hand gently shook him. He looked around and felt a sudden sense of confusion at what he saw. Masks with the distorted faces of jaguars, monkeys and humans painted brightly in fearsome expressions. Along the tops of the walls were various animal heads, obvious trophies of many hunting expeditions. From the ceiling hung a light fixture made of multiple sets of antlers. In fact, much of the decoration of the room used antler, from the light fixture to the chairs and coffee table.

'We need to get going. You alright?'

Tyler turned his head towards the end of the couch he'd been sleeping on. Seeing Kahit, he suddenly remembered where he was.

'Yeah I'm fine. I forgot where I was for a sec.'

Kahit laughed. 'Freaked me out as well for the first few weeks, but I'm used to it now.'

'You live here?'

'Yeah. For about four years.'

'What about the rest of your family? You don't live here by yourself do you?'

'Does that surprise you?'

Tyler stared dumbfounded at him. Of course he was astounded. No kid should be by themselves at so young. One look at Kahit reminded him that he knew his thoughts.

'So why then? I don't believe you did this willingly.'

'No? You're partly right though. It wasn't my choice, but it's part of our tradition so what else could I do.'

'Tradition is that at twelve you live alone in something like this?' he said, gesturing at the strange choice of decoration.

Kahit laughed at this. 'Of course not. At least not for every twelve year old. As you can tell, I'm not the same as other kids my age.'

'I guess not. Unless there are others out there able to read minds and disappear that I don't know about.'

'Luckily not. I'm the only one currently able to do those things. They are some of the signs of a Spirit Guide. The signs begin to show when a boy turns twelve. Once the Elders know a boy has the prophesied signs, he is sent into solitude to become one with nature and the world around him. Normally, the Spirit Guide before him will be there to guide and teach him the ways and secrets of generations of Spirit Guides before him.'

'So where is your Spirit Guide tutor? You couldn't have graduated so quickly I'm sure.'

'He died a few weeks ago. Right before I began hearing you.'

'You don't think he died because I became this do you?'

Kahit remained quiet for a few seconds thinking about it. 'It's possible, but highly unlikely. He was an old man and I'm sure it was just his time to go. All the same, he would've loved to meet you."

It was Tyler's turn to laugh. 'Meet me? Why? So he could see how ridiculous I look and hear how I seem to hurt and offend everyone?'

'No,' Kahit said, suddenly turning very serious. 'For the last several centuries, it's been the hope and desire of every Spirit Guide to be able to be the one who helps the Fallen Angel fulfill his destiny.'

This silenced Tyler and made him feel rather foolish. Once again he had stuck his foot in his mouth. He'd certainly developed a knack for making an ass of himself.

He turned to apologize to Kahit, but he didn't get a chance to begin.

'Don't worry about apologizing. It wasn't as if this was the life I would have chosen for myself either. For many months I was a hellion and it wasn't until I finally gave in to my destiny that I was able to understand things differently. The same will happen for you. Once you do, your gifts and powers will expand far beyond your expectations, enabling you to become who you were destined to be."

He left Tyler for a minute to finishing preparing for their departure. Tyler was glad that at least Kahit was able to understand how he felt, although he had yet to understand himself fully. He hoped that before long he would be able to give in completely to this new life and maybe then he'd be able to understand his brother and his obsession with the supernatural.

'So you ready to go then?' Kahit asked, returning from the back bedroom changed and with a duffel bag that looked about ready to explode.

'Sure I guess.'

Kahit led him out back behind the shack to a shed that looked barely big enough to hold a Mini Cooper. He grabbed the handle and lifted what was in actuality a garage door to reveal a rusty looking truck that looked as if it hadn't been operated in decades.

'Don't tell me we're driving in that?'

'Have you got a better idea?'

'Well for one I have wings and I can fly. Can't

you just teleport yourself to New Hampshire?'

'Sorry, but I can only disappear, not teleport. And unless you can carry me, we're going to have to take the truck.'

'Is it even going to work?'

'We're about to find out.'

They both crossed their fingers as they worked their way through the clutter to the doors. They tossed their bags into the back and got in. Once in the cab, Tyler secured the staff behind the seat, making sure it couldn't be seen and that it didn't move around too much. Kahit pulled the visor down and a set of keys landed with a gentle clink in his waiting hand. He stuck the main key into the ignition and, waiting on the moment of truth, turned the key.

It sputtered a few times before backfiring, filling the tiny garage with smoke. He tapped the gas a couple times, causing it to rev to life at which both the boys cheered. Kahit shifted into first gear and slowly made his way out of the garage and onto the road.

They made a quick stop at a Wal-Mart with a huge sign boasting of being the only one for the next 500 miles. Not likely, as Wal-Marts were as populous as McDonald's. Since it was a long drive to New Hampshire, they were going to need a ton of snacks. Tyler had to give Kahit his credit card since the boy had no money. Kahit smiled giddily which worried Tyler slightly.

As they were parking, Tyler noticed a smartly dressed man walking across the parking lot. He looked oddly familiar. Something about his shaved head and stocky build. Then he remembered.

'Do you see that man there in the suit?' he asked, pointing to the man who was about to disappear behind the building.

'Yeah what about him?'

'If I'm not mistaken, he's the same guy I saw in

D.C. when I was being held captive there. Do you think he's been following me?'

Kahit watched the man round the corner and didn't answer right away.

'If he has been following you we need to leave like now. That is, after I go get us something to munch on.'

'There's more though. I thought I saw somebody watching me in the cave as well. It was when the room was collapsing, but I couldn't tell because of all the stuff in the air.'

'Why didn't you mention this sooner? We might be in serious trouble here.'

'We? I think you mean me. You helped me yes, but it wouldn't be you they were after unless they learned about your disappearing trick.'

'So then I'm gonna go get the supplies so we can get the hell out of here okay?'

Tyler watched him run into the store and he waited as patiently as he could. It was difficult for him not to look over his shoulders to inspect the parking lot in case the guy came back. Whoever this guy was, there was no doubt in Tyler's mind that whoever he was working for, this supposed League of the Damned, knew or was soon going to know that he had the first piece of the key.

Kahit was back in less than a half hour and they were on their way. It was all Tyler could do to not think about the man. Why was it that he felt as if something very bad had been set in motion? This nagging sense of concern at the base of his stomach wouldn't go away. Even his dreams were filled with visions of dread. Painful voids with a gnawing sense of agony and suffering with muffled screams and pain filled eyes.

Somehow, after five highly uncomfortable days, they pulled into the parking area of St. Stephen's. Father Michael was standing in front of the large wooden doors with his arms folded and a smug look of proud satisfaction on his face. Standing somewhat hidden behind him, to Tyler's unexpected pleasure, was Helen. Although it had only been nearly two weeks since he'd left, it felt as if it had been years since he'd seen either one of them.

'Welcome back,' the priest said as they got out of the truck.

'Thanks. It's great to be back,' replied Tyler with a joyful if not weary smile on his face.

Father Michael motioned them inside and let them pass before closing the door firmly behind them.

'Let's make ourselves comfortable downstairs and then you can tell us all about your trip and who this young man is,' he said, pointing to Kahit.

Tyler murmured a vague acknowledgement of Father Michael's suggestion. Now that they were inside, his complete attention was focused on one person and one person only: Helen. How radiant she looked with the candlelight reflecting off her russet locks, which in this light appeared extraordinarily like burnished gold. The whole world melted away into nothing but her and him. Her hand in his felt like a long lost friend now reunited never to part again. How perfect his world felt now that she was so close to him.

As he stared at her a different voice began calling his name. And it didn't sound too pleased.

"Hey Tyler! Are you listening? Hey! Wake up in there!"

'Sorry what?' he replied, letting his mind drift away from his daydream. 'Was someone calling me?'

'Yeah. For at least five minutes,' snapped Kahit markedly annoyed. 'All those thoughts. Gross! Can you wait till I'm at least asleep before you start thinking like that again? Unbelievable!'

Helen giggled, making a sidewise glance at Tyler as she continued down the stairs followed quickly by Father Michael.

'What're you talking about? What thoughts? I wasn't thinking anything,' he said to Kahit as they followed after the other two.

'No you weren't thinking, but your emotions were certainly running wild and seriously I thought I was gonna to be sick.'

Tyler shrugged his shoulders, still not quite sure what Kahit was on about, but it didn't bother him one way or the other. He was home and finally he could rest.

They settled themselves around the table and Father Michael set out four mugs. The tea he poured for all of them was fresh and aromatic. Tyler lifted the steaming cup to his lips, getting a gentle waft of peppermint and lemon before taking a cautious sip. He let the joyously hot liquid pour down his aching and dry throat.

'So,' Father Michael began, 'tell us about your journey. I can see it was successful.'

'Yes it was. Mostly thanks to Kahit here. If he hadn't led me there and then saved my neck in the end, I wouldn't be sitting here right now.'

'Our many thanks. Kahit did you say it was? If you don't mind my asking, who exactly are you?'

'I'm his Spirit Guide,' he replied, the obvious pride swelling his chest, which made Tyler smile and laugh gently.

'Oh are you now? I don't remember reading about any Spirit Guide's being needed.'

'Well, he has certainly proved to me more than once that he is my Spirit Guide, whether or not I believe in the whole spiel, and he has showed that he can live up to that responsibility,' replied Tyler, enjoying watching Kahit's pride swell even more. 'Although,' he said with a sly grin, 'I'm sure we could have gotten here sooner, but he got us lost a few times.'

'Wait. What?' Kahit sputtered, his pride instantly deflated. 'What're you talking about I got us lost? You were the one with the map. Yeah I was driving, but I never turned unless you told me to.'

'And it's a good thing you did or else we would probably be somewhere in South America by now.'

'South America? You're totally exaggerating.'

Kahit stuttered angrily as the rest of them began laughing hysterically. He then understood that Tyler was pulling his chain. Laughing along with them, he tossed a sugar cube at Tyler's head.

For the next few hours, they listened as Tyler told them of his adventure to California, from the encounter with the squatter couple to the sighting of the mystery man at Wal-Mart. He left out no detail and Kahit filled in when he felt that Tyler had either explained something incorrectly or left out some minor detail. It was well into the night when he finally came to the end.

'Well you certainly had quite the eventful last couple of weeks to say the least,' Father Michael said as he stood up to take the mugs and electric kettle over to the sink. 'It's time now for you boys to get some sleep. Tomorrow we'll examine this staff.'

Tyler escorted Helen out to her car, trying to preserve this time with her. He inhaled deeply, catching the faint aroma of vanilla from her hair. How he'd missed that smell. He finally couldn't take it any longer. He spun her around and brought her close, kissing her passionately.

'You have no idea how much I've missed you,' he said when they finally broke for air.

'I've missed you so much as well,' she replied, wrapping her arms tightly around his body. 'I've been lonely and worrying about you ever since that man broke into my room. I expected at the least a text,' she said with a faint air of disappointment. She wasn't happy that he hadn't contacted her the whole time, but her anger could wait until tomorrow. Right now she simply wanted to hold him close.

'I'm sorry,' he said, kissing the top of her head. 'I would have, but I stupidly forgot my charger.'

'Are you serious?' she asked, looking at his face, bemused.

'I know. Dumb right.'

She gave him a half-smile and shook her head. 'I guess I can forgive you this time. Just don't go running off anytime soon.'

'You won't have to worry about that. I'm back now and I have no plans of leaving. Especially not without you.'

'I hope not,' she said, hugging him to her tighter.

'Would you like me to follow you home,' he asked once she loosened her grip.

'No. I should be fine. I'm back in the dorms anyway. Do you want me to come back tomorrow?'

'Of course I do. Whenever you're ready come over.'

'Ok. I better go now. Love you.'

'Love you too.'

After one final, lingering kiss, Helen got into her car and made her way home. Tyler stayed outside watching until the taillights disappeared and the rest of the vehicle was eaten up by the darkness. A shiver ran down his spine. Dark thoughts filled his mind. Something bad was going to happen tonight.

Chapter 19

Helen shivered with excitement as she sped home. Tyler was back and had seriously missed her. What more could any girlfriend ask for? She smiled broadly, letting loose a suppressed giggle that she was glad no one else could hear. 'Get a hold of yourself,' she reproached loudly as she looked at herself in the rear view mirror. 'It's not like he was never coming back.'

By the time she reached the dorms, she felt as if she'd released almost all of her ridiculous pent up teenage girl emotions. As she walked from her car to her apartment, she had to force herself not to skip. "What's wrong with me?" she thought, laughing embarrassedly. She was acting like a love struck schoolgirl who'd learned that her crush actually liked her back. It was irrational for her to act like this. It wasn't as if she didn't love Tyler, just that she wasn't a girly girl. Sure she didn't mind the occasional girl's night out, but she could never be one of those stupid gossipy Cosmo girls only concerned about their clothes, hair and the lives of their favourite celebrities. They were stupid.

She kicked the front door shut and turned on the light. She turned to walk towards her room and screamed. She wasn't expecting anyone to be waiting for her when she got back.

'Daddy!' she exclaimed, reaching out to the door behind her to steady herself. 'You nearly scared me to death. What are you doing here? I thought you were still in D.C. And why are you sitting in the dark? That's kinda creepy.'

Sitting on one of the couches was her father. He was supposed to be away on a business trip and wasn't to arrive back home for another couple days. His presence worried her. Normally she would run and give him a hug, but something was wrong. He seemed somehow different. His gaze was stern and indifferent. His posture was rigid and he looked completely uncomfortable.

'Daddy what's wrong?' she asked. She was beginning to feel anxious. His expression worried her the most.

'How long has the angel been back?' he asked, his tone cold and emotionless.

'Angel? I have no idea what you're talking about.' She knew better than to tell her parents about Tyler's physical change.

She tried to walk towards her bedroom, but her dad got up and moved to block her way.

'Daddy I'm tired. Can't we talk tomorrow?'

'No we cannot. You need to sit down and start explaining things. Don't lie to me anymore. When did the angel get back?' he said with stronger emphasis.

'I told you I don't......'

'DO NOT LIE TO ME!!!' he bellowed, slapping her across the face. The force of the blow knocked her over onto the other couch.

'How I am I to protect you if you keep lying to me?' he said, this time gentler, soothing. 'We know you've been in correspondence with it. It was also seen in our house in your room. Now can you still sit there and tell me you have no idea what I am talking about?' he mocked.

She rubbed her aching jaw and stared at the floor. There was no way to protect Tyler now. How did he get all this information? "The man who broke in must have told him," she realized.

'Alright,' she admitted. 'I do know the angel. It's Tyler.'

'Your boyfriend?'

'Yeah.'

He stared at her contemptuously and then nodded, satisfied by her responses.

'Now. When did he get back?'

'Tonight, but I don't know where he went.'

'Are you sure about that?'

She nodded meekly. She hoped her pathetic humility would be believable. She'd never been very good at lying. Her hope was dashed as he pulled a slim, silver tape recorder out of his jacket pocket. When he pressed play, their conversation was vividly thrust back into her remembrance.

'You're going to Mount Shasta? What're you supposed to do there?'

'It's the location of the first piece of the key.'

Her father stopped the recorder and glared at her. She wanted to stare at him defiantly, but only hung her head in shame. She knew that lying was bad, but she was doing it to save Tyler. Besides, something didn't feel right. The man standing before her might look like her father, but somehow he was not the same man who had raised her.

'I am so disappointed in you,' he rebuked, finally breaking the uncomfortable silence. 'I had such hopes for you, but now it seems that things are going to have to change.'

'Daddy what are you talking about?' she tried to ask, but he ignored her.

He slowly, dangerously, walked around her until he was standing directly in front of her.

'You do realize we've known all along don't you?' He smirked arrogantly, pulling a strand of hair from her face. 'We've known where he's gone, who he's met with, what he's done, everything. Your lies? They were pointless. It was all a test to see where your allegiance lay. Now we know.'

He looked away from her to the window and nodded. She turned to see who or what he was nodding at and gasped. She had only seen her father so she was unaware that another person was in the room. From by the window, a second figure emerged. She gasped a second time as the realization to who it was set in. It was the man from her room. How did they know each other?

She turned back to her father and he just shook his head.

'I'm sorry. This is not how I wanted things to end up, but sadly it's the only way.'

She looked from her father back to the stranger and made a choice. If this was the way things were going to be, then she was not going to go down quietly. She sprung up from the couch and made a run for it. Putting her soccer skills into practice, she faked a pass to the left of her father and spun to the right when he lunged to grab her. She jumped over the second couch seconds before the mystery man jumped to tackle her. She ran down the hall and disappeared into her roommate's room since her door was open. She slammed the door shut behind her and locked it. Her roommate's dresser was right next to the door, so she grabbed it and tipped it over in front of it.

'Sorry,' she mouthed to both her invisible roommate and the dresser.

Once she'd secured the door, she turned on the light. She got one look before clamping her hand over her mouth to stifle a scream. Lying on the floor in front of the bed was her roommate, her body crumpled oddly on the floor. Tears streamed down Helen's face as she quickly crawled over to her. The girl's eyes were open and stared unseeingly at her. She reached over to close them when the girl suddenly blinked.

'You're alive!' she quietly gasped, resisting the urge to hug her in case her back was broken.

'I'll get you out of here,' she whispered. She reached for her cell phone, but wasn't surprised to find no signal. Their apartment was notorious for being the only house with no reliable connection. She hurried over to their only means of hope: the window. Maybe she could get reception leaning out of it.

She had just reached it when the door started violently shaking and she could hear her father calling to her.

'Helen, come on out. We're not going to hurt you. You know I would never let anything bad happen to you.'

Something in his voice made her believe otherwise. Especially considering the change she'd seen in him. He was not one to be trusted. She ignored him and peeked out the window. She reached her arm out as far as she could and waited. It kept bouncing from one bar to nothing. She stretched out a tiny bit further and nearly fell out when something heavy slammed into the door. She watched horrified as her phone tumbled to the ground. Thankfully there was grass so there was a chance it wasn't broken.

Her only choice now was to climb down and find help. That meant she was going to have to leave her roommate behind. She didn't like the idea, but there was no other way. She went back over to the girl and knelt down grabbing her still immobile hand.

'I've got some bad news,' she started, brushing the girl's hair out of her face in a reassuring way. 'I'm going to have to leave you here to go get help.'

The girl's eyes darted around frantically as she tried to get her body to move. Her lips quivered slightly as she tried to speak and tears began running down her face. It was like the typical scenario in a horror film where nobody makes it out alive.

'I'm so sorry,' she said soothingly, 'but I can't get a signal in here and if I don't go, no one will know about this.'

Helen regretted letting go of her roommate's hand, but she knew it was what she needed to do. She peered out into between the complexes. From the look of it, the coast was pretty clear. The only problem was there was no fire escape. There was a drainage pipe a foot to the left of the window and the building next to them was a good five feet away. Other than tying the bed sheets into a rope, there was no other way for her to get out. She tore the sheets off her roommate's bed and fashioned a rope to repel herself down the side of the building. As she tied the end to the base of the bed, she whispered, 'I'll be back soon,' and made her way down.

It was not a difficult task repelling down the wall. It was slightly awkward at the beginning. Normally the walk over the edge wasn't so narrow. When she got halfway down, she noticed that the rope she'd made wasn't long enough, which could have posed a significant problem. Thankfully, the rope was only a few feet shy of the ground. She dropped down the remaining distance and quickly found her phone. It wasn't broken. She clutched it firmly in her hand and ran for her car.

Once inside her car, she checked the connection on her phone. There was barely one bar, but it was stable and that was good enough.

'911. What's your emergency?'

'My roommate and I have been attacked.'

'Where are you at?'

'The student dorms on 5th and Martin. Flat X217. Please hurry. I had to leave her in there. They did something to her. She's paralyzed or something.''

She was beginning to speak faster and

sporadically. The gravity of her situation was starting to set in and she wasn't taking it very well.

'Just relax Miss. We've got people on their way. What's your name?'

'Helen. Helen Saunders.'

'Well Helen, take a deep breathe and relax. Soon everything will be all right.'

'Ok. Thank you.'

She took a deep breath and closed her eyes. That, combined with knowing that rescue was on the way, helped calm her for the most part. She had only closed her eyes for a few seconds when she heard something behind her. She opened her eyes and looked into the rearview mirror. A shadowy figure sitting in the back seat made her gasp.

'Hello again,' the man replied.

The last thing the 911 operator heard was a tinny screech.

Chapter 20

When Tyler awoke the next morning, the room was completely silent and the entrance to the secret apartment was open. It was like some unwritten sign letting him know where he was expected to go once he'd gotten up. He looked around for the staff to take with him, but couldn't find it anywhere. "The other two must have taken it down there with them," he gathered. He took a quick minute to eat some of the food left out for him before walking down the passage to the glass room, as he really had no idea what better to call it.

As he exited the air chamber, he heard Father Michael excitedly exclaim, 'Avevi ragione! There he is.' The look on his face was like a fat kid at McDonald's.

'I'm assuming Kahit told you he can read my mind.'

'Yes he did. Did you know he can also disappear? I've never experienced something so unbelievable in my entire life. Other than you that is. It's truly amazing.'

'Mmhmm,' Tyler mumbled, collapsing into one of the cushy red chairs in the middle of the room. 'What time is it anyway?'

'Around two I believe?'

'In the afternoon?!'

'Well it's certainly not in the morning,' Father

Michael quipped. 'We tried waking you up, but you were dead to the world so we left you.'

Tyler rolled his eyes. The priest was beginning to sound like Kahit. It wasn't a good sign.

'Has Helen come over yet?'

'No. Was she supposed to?'

'Yeah. She asked me if I wanted her to so I told her to come over whenever she was ready.'

'Well I'm sure she'll be here soon. The day is still young. Come take a look at the staff you brought back. It's quite fascinating. By the way, what's that medallion you're wearing? I've never seen you wearing it before.'

Tyler's hand went instinctively to his chest at the mention of the emblem.

'It fell out of the book you loaned me. Helen gave it back to me before I left to Cali. I'd completely forgotten about it.'

'Can I see it?'

'Sure,' he said. He unclasped it and handed it to the priest. Father Michael held it in his fingertips and stared at it intently.

'Do you know what this means?' he asked Tyler.

'No. I know the bird is a phoenix, but I don't know what the phrase means."

'It means, "Though fire will kill, from the ashes breathes new life." I wonder what the significance of this is?' he said as he handed it back to Tyler. 'I'll let you keep watch over it as you're the one who discovered it. You never know, it may prove invaluable to you at some point. Now let me show you what I learned about the staff.'

Father Michael led them both over to the table in the corner of the room where the staff was laying. Spread around it was some open books and several sheets of paper. On the paper were various drawings, some of the staff and some of a more ornate staff with seven arrows pointing at it.

'This staff you brought,' Father Michael began,

pointing at the object on the table, 'is the main piece of the key. According to my research,' he said, pointing this time at the books on the table, 'the staff is virtually unbreakable and causes massive destruction to whatever it strikes. Now the interesting thing about it is that the amount of destruction delivered depends on the object struck. Just because you struck the Golem with it and it shattered doesn't mean if you struck me with it I would shatter. I would probably receive a powerful blow that would send me flying back, but not kill me. I don't know what the exact outcome would be, but I'm not about to let you try it out. On me at least.

'Now if you take a look at these drawings I found,' Father Michael said, this time pulling some of the sheets of paper from under the staff and handing them to Tyler, 'you will see what the staff is to look like once all the pieces have been found. You see there are seven individual pieces and from what I've read about them, each one of them is bestowed with some amount of power. Each can be used individually or together in whatever arrangement. In order to receive maximum power, as well as later open the way to the Temple of the Fallen, all the pieces must be combined together in this manner.'

'Yeah, I remember you telling me about this earlier. You showed it to me on the computer.'

'Did I? Oh well. It's hard to remember everything. It's still good to know either way. Now let's find out where then next location is.'

'How do we go about doing that?' Tyler asked looking rather confused.

'There should have been something with the staff to give us a clue on where to go next.'

Tyler shook his head. 'No. There was nothing there.'

'It might have been attached to the staff or under it. There had to be something there!'

'I'm telling you Father there was nothing else there. And it wasn't as if I really had the chance to check. As soon as I had picked it up, a rock fist smashed the altar and nearly killed me. Once the others were all finished off, the room completely collapsed.'

'Could it be in one of the ends perhaps?'

'You're more than welcome to check, but like I said, I really have no idea.'

Father Michael inspected both ends but found nothing. He sunk in depressed resignation into the nearest chair. His face perfectly reflected the mood each of them was now feeling. Without the clue, there was no way they'd be able to find the other pieces and locate the Temple. Tyler was now beginning to wish he'd been buried in the rubble than be faced with something as hopeless as what lay before them now.

A high-pitched bell began ringing, interrupting their depressed silence. Father Michael wordlessly rose from his chair and left the room. Neither Tyler nor Kahit said anything to each other. There was really nothing to say anyway. Both of them knew it was useless now unless they went back to the cave. Being as it had collapsed, the likeliness they'd find anything was pretty nonexistent.

When Father Michael returned his face was flushed white and his body was trembling.

'Father, are you alright?' Kahit asked, rushing over to him as soon as he entered the room.

The priest thrust a sheet of paper at Tyler and said shakily, 'You'd better take a look at this.'

Tyler took the paper and read it out loud:

Fallen Angel,

As I am sure you are very aware

now, you are missing a very important document detailing the location of the next piece of the key. We have this document in our possession at this very moment. While we as normal humans would require some sort of compensation for the return of such a document, you have nothing of real interest to us, besides the first piece of the key. Instead, we have a proposition for you. As well as the document, we also have in our possession a certain young lady by the name of Helen as our honoured, albeit unwilling, guest. She shall remain so as long unless you abide by our demands. Fail to comply and she shall suffer greatly. Your presence is therefore required at Boroughman's Wharf, Dock 7 at 5:00 p.m.in three days time. Do not be late.

Sincerely,
The Brethren of The League of the

p.s. Bring the staff.

The colour in Tyler's face drained as he read the note. Could this really be happening? Shouldn't he be feeling rage at this very moment? Shouldn't he be feeling his heart racing and his temperature building from his passion or drive to retrieve her? Why was he once again feeling that same sense of impending doom; that this was not going to end well?

It was Kahit who finally broke the icy silence. 'We have to go get her! Why are you two acting like that? Shouldn't we be making a game plan, finding some way to save her as well as getting back our clue?'

Tyler, trying to shake of the feeling of despair, replied, 'what can we do though? They want the staff, but we can't give it to them. Plus they've been around for much longer than we have. There isn't much we can do to surprise them.'

'So you're just gonna admit defeat and let them win? Where's the fighting spirit you had in California?'

'Kahit's right,' Father Michael agreed, moving towards the exit. 'They may have been formed for much longer, but I have plenty of experience in tactical maneuvering and strategizing.'

'You do?' Tyler inquired. He hadn't known that about him.

'Of course I do. You don't think they would entrust this to me without giving me adequate training do you?'

'Awesome,' Kahit exclaimed. 'Plus, they can't do what both of us can. With our powers, we'll get both Helen and the clue back in no time.'

'You're right Kahit. I'm sorry. Let's get busy.

We only have two days to get there and figure out how to save Helen!'

'Attaboy,' Kahit replied, clapping Tyler on the back. 'So what do we need to do first?'

Father Michael smiled mischievously before responding.

'It's simply really. First and foremost we need to investigate this wharf. Tyler this is going to be down to you. Since you have wings, you'll be getting there much earlier than us. Take a notepad. Jot down anything strange that happens. They will undoubtedly be keeping watch on the place so you will need to be well hidden. Okay?' Tyler nodded his head in understanding. 'We'll call you once we,' motioning at both he and Kahit, 'get close to the area. Depending on how long it takes for us to get there, we'll either meet up with you there or elect a meeting point. Then we will strategize and wait for them to make the first move.'

They all got up and began preparing to leave. Tyler emotions were waging war inside him. What if things went wrong? What if someone got hurt? They had no idea what these guys were capable of. Yeah they said that she would remain safe as long as they complied, but then again, they were acting like thugs. Didn't really give much room for trust. He wished he could act as hopeful as Kahit sounded, but if the boy could really feel how Tyler felt, then he would know that hope was an unrealistic expectation.

'Tyler,' Father Michael called out.

'Hmm,' he replied, grateful for the distraction.

'Don't forget to turn your phone on vibrate.'

Chapter 21

As expected, Tyler was the first to arrive at the wharf. They'd all taken off at the same time, but the nice thing about flying is that you didn't have to take unnecessary detours. It was a straight shot. This time he pushed himself to get there fast. It surprised him how quick he could actually go when exerted himself. By midafternoon he was gliding lazily over the derelict building on the dock, drifting in and out of the low hanging clouds. It was strange being back in D.C. so soon. It felt like only yesterday that he was strapped into a chair in some government facility. Now here he was, once again in this foreign city searching for a place to hide. Directly across the street from the lot was a short alleyway. He dropped down quickly into it and set to organizing a believable enough looking hiding place. He wasn't exactly thrilled about being a lookout. It wasn't the most entertaining of responsibilities, but it was important to see who came and went and what entrances they used.

The hours ticked by slowly as the sun seemed to hold its position in the sky. It was muggy and hot, like being stuck in a massive steam room with no doors or windows. Before he knew it, the sun was gone, hidden till the following morning. Tyler pulled his cell out of his pocket, but there were still no messages. The others should have only been a few hours behind him, but they still hadn't shown up yet. He'd even attempted calling them, but it went straight to voicemail. Sure he wasn't required to remain in his position until they showed up, but only a fool would leave with nowhere to go. They were meant to call and designate a meeting point. As they hadn't done so yet, the only place he knew where they would go without letting him know would be the wharf.

The sudden shutting off of an engine caught him off guard. He stared between the slates of the stack of wooden crates he was hiding behind, straining to see who arrived. He wondered what they were doing there so late. He was grateful that a single yellow streetlight was working directly in front of the gate. In front of the barbwire topped fence sat a silver Mazda 6. He could tell what it was because he'd wanted one for years. A bald, stocky man in a crisp, black, pinstriped suit stood by the gate trying to unchain it. Once the chain had slid free, he went onto the lot and disappeared through a side door.

'Where are they?' Tyler muttered under his breath. He really wanted to see what such a nicely dressed man was doing inside a rundown warehouse at a dock that had obviously not been used for many years. He wished the priest and boy were there. Though, even if they had been, he'd never have gotten the chance to find out. The man quickly appeared again, looking both ways quite shiftily as he rechained the sliding gate. Just as he was opening the door to his car, a sudden high-pitch ring pierced through the silence and then stopped. Tyler cursed under his breath as his hand instantaneously reached into his pocket pressing any button his finger could find to make the noise stop.

'Who's there?' the man in the pinstriped suit called out.

The man pulled a gun from his jacket and began

cautiously walking across the street. The passenger door swung open and a thin, awkward looking man got out.

'What's the problem?' the second, more nasally voiced man replied.

'There's someone out there. I heard a phone ringing.'

'It doesn't matter. Come on. We don't have much time and we have a lot to do.'

Begrudgingly, the man in the pinstriped suit turned to walk away, giving the alley one last look. Tyler could feel him looking straight into his eyes, but the man did nothing. He smirked and tucked the gun back into his coat and got in. The Mazda made a u-turn and drove slowly past before speeding off down the street. Tyler breathed out a sigh of relief. His heart was beating at a ridiculous pace. He'd never even considered what he would do if he were to get caught. Now that the threat was gone, he tried to calm himself down. He needed to reach the priest. Though one thing kept rummaging through his mind. "I thought all villains drove black continental's?" he found himself wondering as he pulled his phone from his pocket.

It had never occurred before to Tyler to ever smash his mobile. It had no feelings so it wouldn't have made much of a difference to the phone. After almost getting caught because of it, he was seriously considering destroying the thing. Sliding open the receiver, he was relieved to find a missed call from Father Michael. He pressed redial and impatiently waited as a dial tone rang in his ear.

'Tyler!' exclaimed an anxious voice on the other end. 'I'm glad you called back. We've had quite the trip.'

'Where are you guys? Your call almost gave me away. I've been waiting and calling you for the last few hours, but you never answered. I've been getting worried, not to mention incredibly bored.'

'I'm sorry. I would've called earlier, but we acted

on a hunch and went by Helen's house to talk to her parents, you know, just to make sure she was really gone.'

'Well what did you find?'

'Her house was completely empty.'

'Excuse me? What do you mean it was empty?'

'There was nothing in the house. The front door was wide open and everything was gone and the place was immaculately cleaned. Tyler? Are you still there?'

Tyler had let his arm drop and stared shell-shocked at nothing as he collapsed against the red brick wall behind him. He was so confused. What did this mean? How could her house be empty? Did this mean that she wasn't kidnapped or was it actually something much worse? What was he going to do now?

'Tyler!' he heard loudly from the receiver by his side.

'Um sorry,' he replied, bringing the phone back up to his ear. 'What were you saying?'

'Don't move. We're only about a half hour away. We'll pick you up and then go somewhere safe.'

'Yeah, ok,' he said quietly and clicked the phone shut.

He wasn't sure how long it actually took the other two to get there. All he could do was sit in shock as his world seemed to further fall to pieces around him. He didn't even register when they did arrive. It'd taken them a while to locate precisely where he had stuck himself. They found him hidden and sullen behind a stack of wooden crates in an alleyway across the street from the dock. His listless stare worried Kahit and annoyed Father Michael, but they were going to have to deal with him once they got somewhere less open. They helped the lethargic angel into the vehicle and left.

About four blocks away from the wharf they found a cheap, rundown motel. The room smelled of stale seawater and looked like it belonged to the Bates Motel. Despite the appearance of cleanliness, the wallpaper was slightly damp and peeling away from the walls at the ceiling and the beds looked like even lice wouldn't inhabit them. Still, it was a place to hold up until morning when they would resume the stakeout.

Their first item of business was to help Tyler regain his senses. With a blanket draped over his shoulders to conceal his wings, they moved him into the room and sat him on the bed. Father Michael tried snapping his fingers in front of his eyes and clapping his hands by his ears, but Tyler made no movement. He just stared through him with a blank, unseeing gaze. Father Michael finally couldn't take it any longer. He picked Tyler up and took him into the bathroom. Dumping him into the bathtub, he turned the shower cold on full. That did the trick. Tyler began sputtering and gurgling as he attempted to shield his face and upper body from the onslaught of ice cold, dirty water.

'Ugh!! What're you doing?' he shouted as he spat the water from his mouth. 'That's disgusting.'

'What do you think I am doing? Waking you up. You're acting like a zombie. Questo è solo ridicolo.'

Tyler wiped the water from his angry eyes and glared at Father Michael. 'Well you didn't have to make it so frickin' cold.'

'Well, anything else wouldn't have had the same effect now would it?'

'Can you two please stop fighting and get in here? People are going to think you're having a lover's quarrel if you keep on like that. Plus you two sound ridiculous to begin with,' called Kahit calmly from the other room.

Father Michael tossed a towel at Tyler and left the bathroom. After a few minutes, he emerged from the bathroom as well. His hair and wings were still damp, but he was otherwise dry. He took a seat on the edge of the bed next to the table where Father Michael and Kahit were sitting. He pulled the table close to him, placed his elbows on it and began running his fingers through his hair.

'So what do we do next?' he asked, looking from the one to the other.

'That depends on what you have to report. What did you see?'

He hoped they weren't expecting some big answer, because they were going to be very disappointed.

'Nothing. Right before you called, two men showed up, but only one went inside and only for a few minutes. Then you called and my phone wasn't on silent and they almost caught me.'

'Why didn't they? It's not like you could run away. Not to say you couldn't get away, just if they believed they were being watched, why wouldn't they try and find you?'

'No idea why really. The second guy just told the other not to worry about it and that they had a lot to prepare. Then they left.'

'Any idea to where they could be heading for these preparations?'

'No clue. They never mentioned a location, just that they had things to prepare.'

'Do you think they'll come back tonight?' Kahit chimed in, a serious expression on his face.

'I wouldn't count on it, but then again, I don't know. I think if they were making preparations for the place, they would have brought things with them and made the preparations there.'

Kahit shrugged and stared at Tyler contemplatively.

'So here's what needs to happen then. First we all need to get some rest. It's been a long and eventful day. Whatever happens tomorrow we need to be completely alert. We'll be getting up early to stakeout the place just in case someone does come back. We have barely a day and a half to figure out who we are up against and what our odds are.'

Sleeping was very difficult for Tyler. Each time he closed his eyes, recurring visions of blackness, pain and suffering filled his mind. There were times the visions became so vivid that Kahit would whimper in his sleep and gently thrash around. It took everything in his power to drive the visions from his mind so he could at least get a few hours sleep. When he finally dozed off, his dreams were filled with faceless beings and disfigured monsters.

When they all woke up, the sun was barely beginning to peek up over the waves of the seemingly calm and tranquil ocean. Tyler parted the curtains a few inches so he could gaze out across its beauty. It felt odd feeling like it was going to be the last time he'd be setting his eyes on it. It surely wouldn't be, would it? With his thoughts partly on Helen and partly on the visions of the previous night, he couldn't help but wonder. What if what he felt actually happened? How would he be able to ensure that it never did? He had so many questions about what he was experiencing, but he had no one who could know the correct answers.

'Ready to go?' came a voice from the hallway. Tyler turned his back to the ocean as if parting with words was a sign of weakness.

They walked rather than drove to avoid raising suspicion. It was only a few blocks to the wharf and it was early enough that there was no one around to see the strange looking trio. Once they neared the building, they each broke away and took position at three different vantage points. Tyler returned to the makeshift hideout he had occupied the day before. He hadn't paid attention to where the other two were hiding. It was ok though as Father Michael had also smartly brought walkie-talkies to communicate so they didn't need to remain in each other's line of sight.

Hours came and went, but there was no activity from the warehouse or the dock. Many workers passed by in front of the alley where Tyler was, but none of them resembled the man in the pinstriped suit and none of them went onto the dock or in the warehouse. Once or twice someone would stop by the gate and he would get excited, but then they'd either bend down to tie their shoe or some other trivial action before moving on. It proved even less productive than the day before.

Once it got dark, they returned to the motel, ordered some take-out and ate in silence. There was no need to discuss the events of the day. Had anything important happened, one of them would have alerted the others, but none of them had made a sound the entire day.

Tyler tried to sleep, but once again visions of darkness plagued his mind. They were like worms rotting the core of his soul. The more they infiltrated his mind, the graver life seemed to be and there appeared to be nothing he could do to stop it. Sleep was no escape either. His dreams were plagued by creatures with shiny onyx teeth, soul-searing basalt eyes and fur the semblance of night. A pack of them were chasing him through a maze where every wrong turn ended in a vortex which fed off his fear and frustration, growing infinitely bigger the more lost he became.

He was just about to give up and throw himself into the maelstrom when a single ray of sunlight broke through the slit in the curtains. It landed squarely on his face, waking him from his nightmare. He moved his face out of the sunlight and found Kahit staring defiantly at him, as if daring him to lie.

'Something bad's going to happen isn't it?'

Tyler looked away, a look of faint resignation on his face. 'I'm not sure,' he replied. It was the truth even though something deep inside him screamed otherwise.

There was no point in all of them going back, so Kahit headed to the wharf by himself. Father Michael was hesitant at first sending a teenager to do such a speculatively dangerous job, but Tyler assured him that he would be just fine. Whether or not the priest believed him was beside the point, but he let Kahit go nonetheless. They had him take a walkie-talkie and the priest made him promise to check in every hour unless something important happened. If he didn't check in, they were going to come looking for him and he'd never get the chance to go out on his own again. He promised somewhat dejectedly.

The wait was somewhat numbing, but soon 5 o'clock was upon them. Tyler made his way quickly to the warehouse, at times almost breaking into a run as if that would in some way make this go by quicker. By the time 5 o'clock struck, he was standing in front of the warehouse, but there was no sign of anyone else. Five minutes passed and then ten. Fifteen minutes passed, but still nothing. Then his phone rang. He pulled it out and nearly dropped it when he saw Helen's name on the screen.

He slid it open nearly breaking it and excitedly exclaimed her name, 'Helen!'

'Oh come now. Do you really think it wise for me to let her call you after all this fun we're having?'

'Who are you and what have you done with her?'

'How cliché that sounds don't you think? Sounding like the tragic hero in some adventure movie, rescuing the damsel in distress? It seems so romantic, but the ending here has yet to be realized. Are you ready to comply to my demands?'

'I'm here aren't I?'

'Quite right. All you need to do is go around to the side door and you'll get what you came for.' The other end of the receiver went dead.

Tyler stuffed the phone into his pocket and made his way through the unchained gate and around to the side of the building. As his hand was reaching for the door handle, he heard tires screeching and familiar voices shouting. He turned around and watched as a black continental came speeding towards him. Kahit was waving his hands and screaming at Tyler as he followed much slower behind.

A sudden chill ran up his spine and around his throat. He tried to breathe but found his throat constricted by the strange chill that hadn't gone away. Suddenly something was placed over his mouth and his whole head was encased in ice. He tried to turn and fend off his attacker, but darkness quickly began setting in on him. He felt afraid for a moment, but felt no pain or anguish with this darkness and so he let himself fall into it. It reminded him of the vortex from his dream, but not quite as ominous. As the ice melted away, the last thing he saw was a pinstriped suit as he was roughly hoisted into the trunk of the vehicle. The lid slammed shut, leaving him to drift off in the darkness. Just before the darkness took hold, he had a strange thought. "Were those black wings I just saw?"

Chapter 22

"Who would've thought things would turn out this way," Mark thought as he poured himself another glass of champagne from the ice bucket next to him on the seat of the continental. He really shouldn't be celebrating, especially with his brother knocked in the trunk, but he couldn't help but feel a tiny sense of triumph. Tyler was caught, inconveniently without the staff on him, but with their possession of the next clue, they still held the winning hand. They really didn't need his brother. Mark had been enough for them to translate and solve the riddle. What they had really wanted was for Tyler to bring the staff with him. Of course since he hadn't, they would have a backup plan. At least he assumed they would.

Mark really disliked Erickson. He was weak, unstable and capable of changing sides. It had been explained to him how the man had been acting noticeably different since his first interaction with his brother. It was hard to believe that his Tyler could have such an effect on anybody, but it was true. As he watched him per The Brethren's request, in the beginning his overall demeanor seemed fine. It wasn't until they reached California that a real change began. His legendary volatile manner became subdued. He seemed to care how his actions affected others. He was going to need to be watched regularly to ensure his loyalty, but not at the moment. Right now everything was going as planned.

What a plan it was. "Poor Tyler," he thought wickedly. How could he ever have known that he was the guinea pig in Mark's own twisted little experiment? Well, experiments. Soon he would know who the smarter brother was. Sure he had to resort to dastardly methods to get his way, but now he almost had everything he wanted. This final test was for all those years his brother made him suffer and treated him as insignificant and inferior. Did he ever think he was never going to repay him his misery? 'What a fool,' Mark chuckled, 'thinking he was better than me.'

He wriggled about a little making himself comfortable and began reminiscing on the last few weeks. What a roller coaster ride it'd been. Tyler was lucky to have been in the comfort of the hospital when his transformation had come. Once Mark found out the change had been a success, he set out to duplicate the process. At first it had proved arduous and unrepeatable. Of course he had no idea what chemicals his brother had used to make his genetic cocktail so simply remaking the sample was out of the question. He knew Tyler had made a second sample in case the first was unsuccessful. It was standard procedure for him, but Mark had no idea where these duplicate samples were kept. There was only one person who might know where they were at: Helen.

It took a couple tries, but soon he was able to get a hold of her. At first she was very reluctant to tell him where the samples were, but if there was one thing he was good at, it was assuring people he was trustworthy. His words wound around her like an infectious disease, infiltrating her reasoning until she caved in under the pressure. Once the sample was in his possession, all Mark had to do was inject himself with the other sample DNA and wait for the desired results. It was like waiting for the ultimate Christmas present. Waiting for Tyler to unknowingly create the key to their future was bad enough, but this, this was the final hurdle to making his ultimate dream come true.

He hadn't expected the experience to be a pleasant one, but he was distressed to find how totally excruciating it was. Unlike Tyler, he was somehow able to maintain consciousness throughout the entire ordeal. Fever ravaged his body with sweat pouring from every pore. In quick recession, intense cold swept over him, his blood like a river of red ice in his veins. His skin prickled and cracked under the chill. Then back to a fever. Back and forth the extremes fought over the control of his being.

On the third day the fever broke and his temperature leveled out. This bothered him at first. Despite being weak from battling the sickness, he otherwise felt completely normal if not disappointed. "Where are the wings?" he wondered. He hadn't been there when Tyler's wings appeared so he didn't know what to expect. He hoped that Helen's horror story had been over-embellished.

It proved to be quite a disappointing afternoon. He played video games to occupy the time while he waited, but it didn't help his mood. He was packing up his things to go when the jabbing, crippling pain began. It started out as awkward jabs against the skin but shortly turned to searing torture as the skin was stretched away from his body. Paralyzed, he lay on the floor frozen in some contorted position until the pain ceased, giving him a moment's peace before another spurt of pain began. That pain was nothing comparing to the intense, white, hot agony, which incapacitated him completely when the wings broke through the skin. Had he known the pain would be so agonizing, he might never have gone through with it.

Thankfully he was beyond that now. Here he sat

with his new appendages at last with the upper hand. His wings were beyond perfect. They were different and unique and not just because they were wings on a human being. He had black wings. Not that they were a portrayal of his inner workings. Every person's soul has some portion of blackness. He believed that they were black to create a difference between the brothers. One was black, the other white, but without the foolish misconceptions that white was for good and black was for bad. True, his way of achieving his ends had been devious and forever changed his brothers life, but it was their destiny, their calling in life. Could he really be bad for helping ensure that they, mostly he, obtained their full potential?

Mark laughed out loud at himself causing the driver to slightly turn his head in case he was being summoned. 'Look at me,' he chortled. 'Look at me trying to be all philosophical and such. How not me.' In truth he was the irrational one, always prone to explosive outbursts when he got frustrated. Quite unlike Tyler who was always able to remain calm and collected, rationally assessing the problem till all was resolved in the comfort of his own organized, rational brain. How boring. Life is too conventional without a little drama now and again to stir things up.

"Where was I?" he contemplated, reverted back to his memories. "That's right. My glorious wings." He grinned, running his hand along the shining black feathers. They made him all giddy by just looking at them. Touching them sent shivers up his spine. He still marveled every now and again at their majesty. How lucky he was.

It was only a day or two before the League of the Damned contacted him. They had an interesting proposition for him. Work with them to find some Temple of the Fallen and they would give him whatever he desired. It seemed like a decent offer despite the nagging feeling in the back of his head. Being the irrational person he was, he accepted. How bad could it be? They get what they want and he gets the opportunity to ensure the world knows his superiority. Though he still couldn't figure out how they'd known he'd changed. Maybe they hadn't actually known. It was possible they simply came by to speak with him and just happened to do it after he changed. But how did they know where he was? After he left the hospital, he went straight to a rundown cabin in a nearby forest to set up. He'd only left the few times to get the samples and other supplies.

From what he understood, it should have been Erickson he had to deal with. Luckily he was on some reconnaissance mission. Not so lucky though since it was some other peon he was meant to liaison with. The guy's name eluded him, but it was something unremarkable so not worth remembering. Their little minions annoyed him greatly. What annoyed him most was that they sent him the stupidest person they had. Was it really that difficult to find smart henchmen? Though if they were smart, they wouldn't be as disposable.

Mark chuckled. He enjoyed this new sense or arrogance and self-assurance. He never used to be like this. He always had to play the unsure, meek younger sibling that no one took notice of. No one bothered him that way. Ever since the discovery of the original fallen angel, his deviousness had escalated. Now that he was a fallen angel, he was able to dismiss his previous persona and let his true character shine. "Oh well," he thought. "Better to be like this than act timid and ridiculous."

He soon tired of dealing with the go-between. He never had any answers and didn't seem to know much in general. Interacting with him was a waste of perfectly good brain cells. Instead Mark decided to find the group and deal with them directly. It didn't take him very long to discover the whereabouts of the organization. He considered being diplomatic and contacting them through rational means, but as they had sent him the stupid peon, he felt no need. He sent them a pretty clear message that they'd better arrange a personal meeting, which they did.

Less than a day passed before he received a cordial phone call, inviting him to meet with them. He graciously accepted and met with The Brethren, as they called themselves. It seemed quite silly for a group of grown men to be meeting in such medieval ways all cloak and dagger and the like, but wasn't that the way of most secret societies? He'd never really wanted to be a part of any of the fraternities on campus. Their "rituals" and such seemed no more than glorified house parties and pranks. This was the real deal.

He stood before them, acting indifferent to mask his nearly overflowing excitement. As he acted with suave indifference, he could understand why Tyler did it all the time. It felt empowering. They reiterated their proposition once again: Work with them to find the pieces of the key and help create a better world. One not plagued with the atrocities of man and devastation of man's covetous nature. He informed them that his first acceptance hadn't changed and of course he would help them. As jaded as he was, helping usher in a new era in human history was something of extreme interest to him. His brother of course would be on the other side, fighting an uneven battle that he shortly would lose. "How perfect," he thought bitterly. "I shall finally land on top and watch him suffer the humiliation of not being seen as good enough."

His first task was a short, but exhausting feat. He was to watch Erickson, who hadn't reported back in a few days. His last message was that he was heading to California after the angel and that was it. They now had no idea if he was in cahoots with the angel, going rogue or just had nothing of importance to tell. The latter was his excuse, which Mark was able to correctly confirm.

Unbeknownst to the agent, The Brethren had slipped a tracking device in with his belongings. They weren't willing to take any risks with so much on the line. The two were only a few days ahead of him so he flew nonstop. He had to fly high into the clouds in order to appear as a bird to those on the ground who were fortunate to look up and see him. He caught up with them somewhere outside of Salt Lake City, Utah. From there it was easy sailing keeping tabs on them. His main concern was in watching Erickson, but he couldn't help but dart between the two of them, sizing his brother up to see what sort of challenge he might present in the future.

Once in California, Mark had to remain extra vigilant to not give himself away while following the two through the forest. He mostly had to follow Tyler. He had seen the agent walk into the forest, but then he completely disappeared. He'd recalled Erickson being referred to as a chameleon, but his utter disappearance felt like something more. He was further astonished with the arrival a young Native American boy who led the procession through the forest, painted on a rock and then disappeared into thin air. "Who is this kid?" he wondered. "Too bad I'll never get the chance to find out." There were so many new characters in this story that he couldn't help get excited for what the adventure produced next.

He didn't have to wait long. Shortly after the boy disappeared he marveled as his brother produced a stream of magnificent fire. The display earlier in the forest had seemed like a fluke, but now he could tell it was real. It was impressive and in retrospect unsurprising. Tyler was such a strong-willed person that fire fit his personality perfectly. Mark seemed much more suited to the volatile nature of water. Being highly emotional albeit mentally peaceful, both aspects of the elemental power of water, working with the element should come natural to him.

Fire and water. Black and white. It really seemed that they were polar opposites. He was going to have to try playing with the element the next chance he got.

After Tyler so violently destroyed the stone blocking the entrance, Mark debated whether or not he should follow the other two into the narrow tunnel or just wait outside. Erickson had suddenly emerged from nowhere as if he'd been there the whole time. Better the stupid agent than him. As he couldn't be bothered with squeezing through such a tiny opening, he decided to remain outside and wait. He was grateful for the opportunity to slip in a quick nap, keeping ever on the edge of consciousness in case either of them returned. Many hours later when Erickson came catapulting through the opening and could barely walk away, he was glad he'd made the decision not to follow.

As Erickson sat there resting, he watched him pull out a curious rolled up piece of parchment. Something seemed to awaken in him as he stared at the scroll. There was something important on it and he could feel it. It was like a voice calling to a memory, but not his memory, the memories of a being much older and wiser. He also seemed to feel a warning. In the midst of the wordless voice he could feel a debilitating blackness steal through his heart, warning of impending doom.

Then it was gone. When Erickson placed the scroll back inside his jacket, he couldn't feel the voice any more. He shook the chill off that had been housing in his spine and followed the agent as he left. Nothing much else happened after that. Soon he was back in Washington reporting on what he'd seen before Erickson met with them. He reported that the agent seemed to be going soft. Rather than completely cover his tracks, he simply did the minimal cover-up necessary as not to create too much of an inconvenience. This did not please The Brethren.

They were pleased, as was Mark, about Erickson's

retrieval of the scroll. The Brethren seemed to already know what the scroll contained just not the specifics. If only they had the staff to go along with the scroll. That's when the wheels in his head began to work overtime. He proposed an unpretentious plan of abduction to The Brethren, which they immediately accepted. He'd been working on a simple cage contraption before he changed. After learning of Tyler's escape, he modified it and this would give him the perfect opportunity to test it out. Unknown to his brother, Mark was somewhat innovative. He liked to tinker and invent. What he had in store for his brother was his biggest ambition yet, at least invention-wise.

According to Erickson, Tyler was still making his way across the country. This was perfect since it gave them at least a couple days to fully prepare for the abduction. Despite giving them the idea, Mark was for the most part kept out of the planning, as was Erickson. It hadn't made him very happy, but he wasn't going to complain because things were turning out better than he could have ever planned. Especially since his brother was taking his time. Mark used the extra time to its full advantage. Using some of the peons as guinea pigs, he tested, retested and retested again until the results were exactly what he wanted. Thankfully none of the guinea pigs died, but that isn't to say some weren't seriously injured. They were mostly electrical injuries. At least the peons didn't need to worry about whether their brains worked or not.

As he understood it, the plan was very simple. Tyler would be lured to the headquarters at the dock and then be transferred to another location where they hoped to acquire the staff. How they were to lure him there they didn't divulge, but something inside was screaming that no good was going to come of this ordeal. He tried to silence the feeling but it wouldn't be quiet, which was partially why he was drinking right then and it was helping, slightly. Once they got him to the other location, Mark would have the opportunity to try out his invention. They eluded to more, but made it very obvious he wasn't privy to that information.

When the continental arrived at another abandoned building, Mark remained in the vehicle as some new goons unloaded the still unconscious body of his brother. "There seems to be lots of new degenerates around today," he noticed. Many of them looked like the brainless hulks seen in mafia movies, you know, the disposable ones that stayed on the front lines. There were others performing menial tasks, but had a sinister air about them that totally weirded him out.

He got out of the car once Tyler was safely inside the building. The sun was just dipping below the horizon, painting the sky with a cascade of blues, pinks, purples, oranges, yellows and reds, all swirling around in one cosmic kaleidoscope of colour. He stopped and gazed at the magnificent scene before him. He couldn't help but think about how if today were at some other time and in some other place, he would actually be able to enjoy it. He smiled ruefully and entered the building.

When he was inside, a few of the emotionless goons led him down a couple flights of stairs. They walked down a sparsely lit hall and into a windowless room containing a single metal chair underneath a hanging light bulb. He glanced around the room but found no one else there. He turned to ask what was going on when out of the corner of his eye he watched the door shut rapidly. The lock clicked loudly. He was now left alone stunned, locked in a room making him feel like he was also a prisoner.

'Let me out of here!' he shouted, banging on the door. The only response he got was a hollow thud from his fists hitting against the lifeless wood.

What was he going to do now? This wasn't a part of the plan, at least not a part of the plan he'd imagined.

He was not the bad guy in this situation. Tyler was. He was the one who had what they wanted. Mark had already helped them with the scroll. All they needed was the staff and he could help them get it. Why were they doing this?

'Hello angel,' came a cold voice from a couple speakers spread out across the ceiling.

'Hey!' Mark called out. 'What's going on? Why have I been locked in here?'

'Let's calm down and take a seat before you hurt yourself,' the voice responded calmly with an edge of force. 'All will be revealed as the events of the night unveil themselves.'

'I don't care about the events of the night,' Mark shouted, his rage building. 'I want to know why I'm being held captive when I'm not a threat and have nothing you want.'

The voice chuckled sinisterly through the speakers spreading an uneasy feeling across Mark's skin. 'Oh, but you are a threat angel. If I were to let you leave this room and witness what is about to happen you would provide a very vital threat and we can't let that happen now can we?'

'How would I be a threat? Why won't you give me a straight, clear answer? What's going to happen?'

A section of the ceiling disappeared revealing a small television showing a surveillance feed. In the center of the room was the cage, which was now holding his brother. Everything in the room seemed exactly as they had set it up only a few hours previous. Minus the single chair in front of the cage. Then he watched as a hooded figure was carried, practically dragged, into the room and securely tied to the chair.

'No!' Mark gasped horrified as the hood was removed. In the chair sat Helen whose head sagged forward like she'd been drugged.

'What's she doing here?' Mark screamed. 'What

kind of twisted game are you playing?'

'Game?' the voice questioned with a hint of cynicism. 'We aren't playing any games. See it more an incentive for your brother to comply with our demands. He plays nice, so to say, and the girl will not be harmed. Refuse and she will suffer. Quite simple really. What did you expect? Did you think we would just kidnap him and take the staff if he brought it? Bait was needed and what is better bait than someone they actually care about.'

That comment stung Mark sharply. His brother cared about him. They may have a strained relationship, but Tyler cared about him. Didn't he?

'Besides,' the voice scoffed, 'we have more use for both of you after this and we need to ensure that our orders are obeyed.'

'But he didn't even bring the staff. What's the point of having him in the cage and her outside it when he has to be released to go get it?'

'Angel you really are so small-minded. He is being used as bait as well. We are giving those with the staff a second chance to obey our orders. They better hurry though. The good doctor isn't prone to waiting.'

Mark wished the mystery man behind the speaker was in the room so he could rip the vocal cords out of his throat. How could he have let this happen? They might have come up with the idea before him. They may have even had an entire plan already formed when he went to them. Regardless how he looked at it, he had played a role in this and if anything happened to her, Tyler would never forgive him. He needed to get to her. But how?

A sudden drip on the top of his head interrupted his thinking. He looked up and noticed a small, saturated section of the ceiling directly above his head. As he stared at the wet patch, which periodically dripped on his face, an idea struck him. He might be in a windowless room, but there was still lots of moisture in the air. He stood facing the door and closed his eyes. He had plenty of practice manipulating water, but what he was about to do he had never attempted before. Yes he had used ice to help capture his brother, but it was a small action. This was going to be much bigger. He curved his wrists outwards slightly, bringing his hands to a slight angle away from his body. He began slowly rotating his middle fingers while he concentrated. Opening his eyes and breathing slowly in and out, he began to feel the air increase in density as water molecules began connecting, forming larger droplets, which revolved around Mark creating a water shield.

Once the shield around him was of significant size, he sent a portion of it towards the door, letting it soak up the water like a parched man in the desert. He concentrated all his will power on the door until felt a sudden chill in the air and a thud as the rest of the water shield collapsed on the ground. The shield had frozen into a block of ice which shattered into millions if tiny fragments. He picked up the metal chair, which he thought was going to freeze to his skin when he touched it, and walked up to the door. Taking one powerful swing, he cracked the wood. It took a couple more hits, completely destroying the chair beyond recognition, before the door shattered into the hallway causing an alarm to go off. Agitated voices began echoing through the hallway as the siren blared obnoxiously. He quickly picked his way through the broken door and maneuvered to where his brother and Helen were being held.

The journey was not as uneventful as he would have liked, but truthfully it wasn't unexpected. He would have been disappointed if he hadn't had to fight. At least he didn't have to wait long. He made it down a couple halls before he encounter his first attacker. The goon had barely hit the floor before the entire area was swarming with the enemy. He battled his way through the onslaught of goons, attacking with his water-power as well as ice at times. A few instances he had to resort to using his fists. If anyone had imagined what a water god would have looked like, he would have made the perfect model.

As he fought, his wings rippled, giving off the illusion of the fathomless recesses of the ocean where no light reaches. The water in the air seemed to be magnetically drawn to them giving him an infinite supply of energy. With this energy he used ice to crack the pipes running through the ceiling. From the water dripping through the cracks in the walls and the ceiling, he created orbs of water, which he used to freeze many of the goons against walls and even some to the ceiling. He formed two veins of water into whips and used them to knock other goons unconscious. When those attacks were exhausted, animals of water attacked and dispersed when defeated. Snakes, wolves and eagles filled the corridors one after the next until the pathway was clear.

He was exhausted by the time he reached the room where the two were being kept. Despite largely using his water-power, he hadn't come out unscathed, but he was proud to see the others come out much more worse for wear. He hesitated in front of the door momentarily to catch his breath. Even with all the physical protection used to block the entrance, it was very unlikely that they wouldn't be guarding the door from inside as well. He dripped a few drops of water to test for a reaction. There was no electrical current so he cautiously reached for the handle. It was unlocked so he walked right in. It was pretty reckless of him, but what else could he do.

He was surprised to find a lack of assailants in the back section of the room. It was completely empty. The only voices he heard were those coming from the other half of the room, which was separated by a short curved corridor. The main voice sounded like the man who'd spoke to him through the speaker. How that voice made his skin crawl now. It was filled with false emotion, attempting to put the person's mind at ease while delivering false promises filled with contempt and sarcasm. He was going to have to tread carefully if he expected to be successful. He noiselessly crept through the corridor until the room came into view. In his standing cage, Tyler was situated to the back of the room and off to the right and Helen was only a couple meters in front of him. The man was nowhere to be seen, but his voice placed him somewhere to the right. Where exactly Mark was not sure. Not that he wanted to know.

He was going to try and take a better look when he felt a presence behind him. He tried to twist around behind the presence, catching it off guard, but his assailant was quicker. A hand lashed out knocking him off balance. He crashed into the wall and collapsed. He tried to rise again but couldn't. His attacker delivered one final blow knocking him unconscious.

Chapter 23

When Tyler regained consciousness, he found himself standing, his hands chained to a crossbeam inside a cage of humming glass. At least it sounding like it was humming. His ears were also humming and his vision was a little blurry so he might have been mistaken. It was difficult for him to make out anything. He could make out shapes and the basic outline of pillars, but not much else.

"Where am I," he wondered, wishing he could rub his head with his chained hands. It took a few minutes, but soon his vision was clear enough for him to be able to check out his prison. There was nothing remarkable about the place. It was cement he reckoned as he looked at the gray walls, ceiling and floor. There were chains hanging from the ceiling as well as sheets of plastic, which outlined the cement and iron pillars holding up the building. It was plain to see he was being held in the basement in some unfinished or abandoned building. He wished Father Michael or Kahit had been able to follow them, but he knew it was a vain wish. They had decided to leave the car behind at the motel leaving them no time to get it before he was long gone.

The cage he was in was strange as well. He was imprisoned standing up chained to two plastic posts. He was curious about the buzzing he was hearing so he spit on the glass. It crackled and sparks erupted onto his face. At least now he knew what was making the noise. He flicked a spark at it and the glass absorbed it. His eyes widened as the glass shimmered. How was that even possible?

A sudden commotion erupted as two men walked into the room dragging something. They set down the object on a chair he hadn't noticed and secured it. His head tilted as he observed the object. He could see now that it was a person. They weren't moving so they were most likely drugged, but he couldn't figure out whom the person could be. Then his blood went cold. It couldn't be. As the two men were leaving, one of them turned and pulled the hood off the person's head. It was Helen.

'Helen!' he shouted, but was quickly silenced as the sound echoed painfully through his cage. There was no way he was able to talk to her. Like him, she was alone, except she was caught up in something that had nothing to do with her. Fear gripped him as thoughts ran through his head about what he would do if anything were to happen to her. He was afraid because he didn't believe he would be able to control himself.

A figure emerged from behind one of the pillars. He pushed back the sheet of plastic and walked his way. Why did this guy look so familiar? Tyler could have sworn he'd seen him before.

'Welcome angel,' the man greeted with his silky smooth, chameleon voice. He was the man who had been on the other end of the phone.

'Aren't you going to welcome me back as well angel?' the man questioned and then smiled evilly. 'Oh that's right. You can't. Clever little contraption there. Soundproof and painful. You can see and hear everything happening outside, but you cannot be heard in return. Perfect prison for someone as elusive as yourself. Don't think for one instant that I've forgotten your other most remarkable escape.'

That was it. He was the creepy man from the government facility he'd broken out of. "What is he doing here? And why is he looking at me like that?" he wondered, now starting to feel a little anxious.

The man retrieved a chair and sat himself down close by to Tyler's prison and stared at him. The last few weeks seemed to have been hard on him. From the state of his complexion, he looked as if he hadn't had the luxury of sleep for some time. His skin was a sallow, grayish colour. Not exactly healthy looking, but he didn't seem to notice. Either that or he wasn't concerned or didn't care. His eyes looked hardened and cruel. They were a oddly pleasant colour of gray accompanied with the creases at the edges of them. He had the appearance of a man who had seen many atrocities and in turn most likely contributed to a good percentage of them. He was used to seeing pain and dealing it. He was not a man Tyler was necessarily pleased to have watching over him.

'I can see it in your eyes that you remember me now. Yes, I'm back to see to it that you make no more miraculous escapes. The Brethren were not too pleased with the last one, but as your abilities were relatively unknown, I was pardoned. You seem surprised. I wonder why.'

It was true. Tyler was surprised to find out that this man also worked for The League of the Damned. But for a ruthless organization, he fit right in.

'Yes I am employed by what you view as your nemesis. Funny isn't it. For two forces with different modes of working, we are after the same goal with essentially the same end result. But me, I am a meager peon with no real understanding of the how's, why's and when's of this supposedly delicate operation, so I can only make simple assumptions. I used to one of the omniscient Brethren, but those windbags sit prettily cloaked in mystery while letting others get their hands dirty. No, now I am in charge of making sure you remain here and give us exactly what we need. How I do it is completely up to me.'

He began to laugh hysterically. 'Look at me rambling away like a bored housewife. I get his way when I'm overly excited. Always have. I suppose that's why I was let go from the CIA. Or maybe it was because of my ruthless techniques for extracting information. I guess I'll never know. It was so long ago anyway that it really doesn't matter. We're here now and you are my current job. So, are you ready to begin?' he asked, smiling like a mad professor about to embark on some suicidal experiment.

The man rose from his chair and walked off into the shadows. He was not a particularly tall man, average really. His frame was quite small and his muscular quality was not something to be feared. So how was he going to ensure that Tyler played nice and went along with whatever they requested?

'I'm sure you're probably wondering how such a weak, pathetic looking, rotten carcass such as I is going to be able to tame you, am I right?' he asked walking once again out of the shadows rather suddenly. 'It's going to be quite simple really. As I'm sure you have noticed, I have two advantages at my command. One is the fact that you are contained rather securely inside an electric cage...'

"So I was right," he thought. "The humming is from electricity."

'...Second is that I have your girlfriend at my disposal.'

Tyler's blood ran cold at the change in his tone. He went from sounding jovial and strangely friendly to cold and emotionless. The man was now slowly pacing behind Helen, running his hand down her hair and caressing her shoulders.

'Did you know that I went to med school before

getting involved with the government? No I suppose you didn't.' Tyler did though. He vaguely remembered Father Michael's crude description of the man. 'I was in the top five percent, which is why I assume they chose me. I probably wasn't their first choice, but that's all history now isn't it? I do remember them telling me that the one thing they saw in me that stood out from the other candidates was my complete disregard for life. Not my life of course. The lives of my patients. I would do what was necessary and whether they lived or not was no real concern to me. I did my job and if they survived great. If not, oh well. It didn't affect my emotional status as I pretty much don't have an emotional palette of which to paint all the moments of my life, just the basics really. Yes, it might sound callused, cruel and heartless, but there are enough bleeding hearts out there to console the grieving families so I don't have to. I was only paid to do my job wasn't I?'

The man took a moment to pause and look at Tyler and smile at the worried expression on his face. He relished the torment he was causing him. Ah the misery of lovers when the beloved was in mortal danger. He felt almost poetic in his verbal torture.

'I see you are beginning to understand what exactly I'm capable of. Being a licensed doctor and having no real conscience, I'm at liberty to exact whatever measures I deem necessary to ensure maximum results. But I think we should wait a little longer as she still has yet to be completely awake. What fun is working on a person who can't fully feel and appreciate what is being done to them?" he asked, smiling wickedly, his teeth like chisels. "Gives me time to prepare though doesn't it? You stay where you are, not that you have much choice. I'll only take a few minutes to set up.'

The man disappeared into the shadows and Tyler cringed as he heard something small and metallic clatter sharply to the ground. He wondered what was going to happen as he looked agitatedly around. He needed to get out, but from the looks of it there was no escape. He had his fire, but as he found out earlier, the glass absorbed it and who knows what it did with it after that.

He wasn't having much success planning an escape when the man came rushing back quite excitedly.

'You're not going to believe who we've just found lurking about?'

Sweat began to build up on Tyler's brow. "Could it be possible?" he wondered. A tiny glimmer of hope stirred within him. Could Kahit and Father Michael really have found him?

In walked a man he recognized. The large thug who'd been following him dragged in a limp body and tossed it on the floor between his cage and Helen. He couldn't tell who it was until the man kicked him over so he could get a better look at him. It was Mark! He'd barely given him a moment's thought over the past few weeks, but yet here he was lying on the ground. There was also something strange about the way he was dressed. Dressing in strange accessories was not out of the ordinary for him, but a feather cape was a little much considering the current circumstances.

The man nudged Mark again causing him to stir. He slowly crawled onto his knees. Tyler stared wide-eyed as he realized his brother wasn't wearing a feather cape at all. It was a pair of black wings. How he'd gotten them he couldn't understand. He knew he hadn't told him where the cocktail was. The only other person who knew where he'd put it was Helen and surely she would've known better than to tell him. Wouldn't she?

Mark groaned and slowly got to his feet. His head throbbed massively as if something had hit him really hard. He looked around and saw Erickson only a few feet away smirking mischievously. "It's gotta be his fault," Mark thought and instantly winced. Even thinking hurt. He grimaced slightly, closed his eyes and took a deep breath. He didn't want to look weak, especially now that he was forcefully brought before his brother's judging glare.

'This must come as quite the surprise to you mustn't it?' the man snarled amusedly. He was truly having the time of his life with this. One angel was chained in an inescapable prison while the other was shackleless outside. This was an episode for Jerry Springer if there'd ever been need for one about heightened family drama.

It did come as a surprise for Tyler. There was something going on here. Mark never just showed up by chance. There was always some purpose to his presence, and right now was no different. This time he wasn't sure whether he wanted to know it, but he didn't appear to have much of a choice.

'Do you want to tell him or should I?' the man asked. When Mark didn't respond, he continued. 'I'll take that as a no then.'

The man walked a little closer to Tyler's prison and then turned back to Mark.

'Is there any way to make it so that I can have a conversation with him rather than with myself and him just listening? It really makes this not as enjoyable for either one of us I'm sure.'

His devilish smile was a stark comparison to the look of pure hatred on Mark's face. Tyler had seen him angry before, but never anything like this. His knuckles were flushed white and his face was a deep crimson, the colour of fresh blood. It seemed as if the man was talking to him like he'd constructed the prison he was in.

'Of course there's a way,' Mark replied finally through gritted teeth, turning his gaze from the man to a disbelieving Tyler.

"It can't be true," Tyler thought. Was his brother really in league with this band of thugs? It couldn't be possible. He hadn't known about the plan beforehand

and here he was, standing in front of him. He was unshackled as well. It was all adding up, but he refused to believe it. Had it really come to this?

Mark walked over to the cage and pressed a cleverly hidden button on the base of the platform. 'You can speak now,' he said, his voice unmistakably filled with shame.

'What's going on Mark?' Tyler shouted, his rage now able to be released. 'Are you seriously a part of this? Why?'

'Of course he's a part. One of the biggest really,' the man hissed. 'It was his idea from the start. Naturally some additions had to be made, but it was he who supplied the idea for your capture.'

There was so much Tyler wanted to say, but he just couldn't get the words out. He opened and closed his mouth like a fish on land gasping for air. He was so angry and at the same time confused that Mark would be working for the same people he was working against. What would drive him to resort to such measures?

Mark stood there in tortured silence. This wasn't exactly what he'd envisioned when breaking out of his cell. He wasn't exactly sure what he was going to do. The only way out of this was to tell the truth. Honesty wasn't really his strong suite, but right now it was imperative to be explicitly truthful. So he was.

'Yes Tyler,' he began slowly and deliberately, his voice strong and full of confidence. If all was going to be revealed, he wasn't going to go out with his tail between his legs. 'I am with this group. I was approached not long after you broke out of the government facility. My help was needed and who am I to deny assistance. All I was required to do was follow and keep watch. Not like it was exactly difficult work would you say?'

'But they're the bad guys,' Tyler sputtered, amazed at what his brother was saying. "They're not who you think they are.'

'And who are you to say if one is good or bad? Do you think that because they aren't what you perceive to be good that they're bad? The world doesn't revolve around the ideology of you Tyler. You're not exactly the authority of right and wrong in the world.'

'That's not the point. I know more about these guys than you do and they are not good.' It felt weird pleading with his brother to believe him. Sure, Mark had no reason to listen to what he said, but in this moment he felt genuine concern for him. If he stayed with this group, it would end badly for both of them. He needed to find a way to get through to him.

Mark stood there gloating as he watched his brother agonize. He knew his brother was right. He knew it from the moment he met them they were bad. He had felt it deep within him. It was like a cancer eating away at his aura. But he wasn't about to give in to his brother's pleading. There was something evilly amusing about watching him. Was he an evil person? Shouldn't he fit in with this group then? He should, but he didn't. He always felt oddly on the outside. Like he was a different type of evil. Less human but more arcane, almost of an elemental sort.

'Well,' he said smugly. 'If you are right and they are bad, I'm sure I'll find out soon enough.'

'Mark,' Tyler shout exasperatedly, 'this isn't some video game where if you screw up and join the wrong team you can just start over and things will be alright. This is real life.'

'How would you know what I'm thinking or how I perceive things? My life doesn't take place in some alternate fantasy world as you seem to think it does.'

'I'm your brother Mark. I know more about you than you think.'

'THAN WHY HAVE YOU NEVER ACTED LIKE IT?' Mark bellowed, causing the air in the room to stir dust. 'Never once have you ever cared about what

I've thought or felt. Never once have you showed any interest in my life until now because I'm not playing according to your gameplan. I am NOT you nor will I ever be you and I most certainly do NOT want to be you. You only care about your reality and yourself. Never once did you concern yourself over my welfare until now when you saw me. You are selfish, arrogant and childish. You think I don't know what's going on here? I'm the one who introduced you to the legend. I'm the one who set all this in motion. And yes, I'm the one who gave them the idea to capture you. Why all this is happening I don't know, but you were the ultimate prize. Not that I'm not just as good if not better,' he said as the air around them got considerable moister.

Wisps of water swirled through the air as he gathered the moisture in front of him. His agitation and heightened emotional status should have caused him to fall to pieces, but rather, his ability to concentrate was strengthened. The molecules wove an intricate web of liquid silk, which formed into a perfectly shaped sphere in the air in front of him. As soon as the lines came into the contact, they flawlessly melded together. He flicked the water causing it to ripple and change shape into a flock of birds, which flew around the room like they had minds of their own.

As the birds circled ever closer, one of them misjudged the distance to the cage and crashed into it, exploding into a burst of static lightning. Tyler flinched and stared as a few bolts of electricity snaked across the surface of the cage evaporating the remaining drops of moisture. Thankfully it happened on the outside of the cage.

Mark smiled wickedly at that occurrence. 'Now that was unexpected,' he said, amused at these new events. 'I've never seen what water might do to the machine if used in small doses. Quite beautiful really. You should know I invented that contraption you're in.

Surprised? You should be. I made it especially for you.'

Tyler rolled his eyes. It would've been more surprising if the thug had created it. So what if Mark created this thing. What worried him was that it had been created just for him. What did he mean by that? He had to be joking. He wished he was joking. Please let him be joking. Something inside him whispered the truth that he wasn't. It was a strange thing realizing you never really knew someone. He always thought his brother was predictable, always doing the wrong thing, giving the wrong answer, making the wrong friends. It'd always seemed like he was doing it to lash out, to be different. Now, in the light of everything leading up to this very moment, the truth whispered something different. It was like acid corroding the once irritating image of his brother, revealing something less desirable. Every move he made was calculated. He knew what he wanted and he had plotted out every possible outcome. He was like a master chess player with the gift of foresight. Everything he had done had led up to this point. Somehow it all connected.

Mark smiled widely at Tyler's glazed over expression. It seemed like he was finally piecing it all together. Now all he needed to do was break.

'While you come to terms with whatever it is you are realizing, I'll go ahead and answer the questions I'm sure you want to ask,' he said gaining confidence. 'Naturally you first want to know what I meant by saying it was made especially for you. You were always so transparent. I was told of your miraculous method of escape from the government building, so I set out to create a cage that not even you could break out of. Oh and yes I know all about your fire ability so that was also worked into the mix,' he added as he walked around the cage, admiring his creation. 'I first took fire resistant tempered glass and injected it with an electrical current strong enough that you wouldn't survive long after multiple attempts of trying to break out. I'll tell you it's one tiny weakness though. Once the electrical current is significantly disrupted there is a few second window where the current reloads. Even then, you would be too weak to break it before the current came back. The only way for you to escape would be for someone out here to sacrifice themselves by disrupting the current. That'd have to be after you got your hands out of the chains that is. They aren't protected in any special way so you should be able to manage that just fine."

'That's enough chatting now. My goodness you're as bad as I am.'

Both brothers turned to look at the man. They'd completely forgotten about him. Whilst they were talking, he had moved unnoticed from where he was setting up to right behind Helen.

'You two have taken up enough of my time and I must politely ask you to leave,' he said, pointing to Mark, 'so we can continue.'

Mark looked over to where the man had been setting up his station and it didn't take long for him to realize what was going to be happening. There were tools there meant for torture. Saws, blades, vials of strange liquid and unknown objects littered the table. A muffled scream caused him to turn away from the chilling display. The man had now placed his hand on her shoulder. Her panic filled eyes stared passed Mark to the table behind him. There was no need to guess what was going to happen if he didn't get her out of there and they both knew it.

'I'm not leaving here without the girl,' he replied firmly and resolutely. He may have ulterior plans for his brother, but he wasn't about to see someone innocent get hurt. He wasn't that callous.

'I beg your pardon,' the man replied, laughing loudly. 'I beg to differ young man. You would be good to remember whose side you're on.'

'I don't care whose side I'm on. I'm not leaving without her.'

'So be it. Erickson get rid of him,' he replied nonchalantly as he turned his attention back to the girl.

The thug was suddenly at his side. He'd appeared out of nowhere and gently, but decisively, placed his hand on Mark's shoulder.

'Come on. Let's go. You know there's nothing you can do.'

'Isn't there? This shouldn't be happening,' Mark responded, feigning his courage wavering a bit in his throat. Tyler's head snapped up as he heard his brother speak. He knew this tone. He always spoke this way when another of his friends ended up dead or in prison. He always got a bad feeling when he spoke this way. Always.

'No it shouldn't,' Erickson agreed, 'but when you're at the bottom end of the feeding chain, there really isn't much you can do.'

But Mark wasn't at the bottom of the food chain was he? Not anymore. When he sprouted his wings he became a higher being, more powerful in more ways than being able to manipulate elements. He felt emotions. He sensed weakness. He wasn't only physically more superior, but mentally and spiritually as well. If he was going to succeed, he was going to need to outwit the lug that was in his way. It was going to be so easy.

'You may be at the bottom, but I'm far from it.'

'What...' was all Erickson could get out before Mark debilitated him.

Mark grabbed Erickson's wrist and twisted underneath his arm bringing Erickson's arm tightly behind his back. He slammed him firmly against a column and as Erickson collapsed onto his knees, he delivered a stiff palm to the side of his face, knocking him out cold. A scalpel suddenly shattered against the pillar, missing his head by inches. He turned to see the crazy man staring at him enraged.

'What do you think you're doing?' he shrieked, throwing another medical tool at Mark, which he easily evaded.

'I told you I wasn't leaving without her,' he replied before advancing towards him. The man turned to ran away when he ran straight into one of the numerous pillars in the room. He stumbled back stunned before collapsing in a heap on the floor. Mark checked to make sure he was still alive before running over to Helen and removing her gag.

'What's going on?' she cried. 'Why am I here?'

'I'm not sure why you're here,' Mark replied as he tried undoing her bonds. They were really tight and the knot was so complex that he wasn't able to budge it in the slightest. He formed a knife out of water, froze it and used it to cut her free. The first try was no good and broke quickly. The second time he made it a lot sharper and sturdier and soon sliced through the last strap holding her feet together.

'Come on,' he said, grabbing her hand and tugging her towards the door. 'We need to get you out of here before those guys wake up.'

'We can't leave Tyler,' she sobbed, struggling to free herself from him. 'We can't leave him here. They'll kill him.'

'No they won't. They need him. You're the one they don't need. If you stay here they'll hurt, maybe even kill you.'

'They won't,' she said through her tears. 'They won't. They promised they wouldn't.'

'Of course they said they wouldn't. They'll lie to anyone they have to to get what they need.'

'He said you'd say that.'

'Who said I'd say that?'

'My father.'

'What?' Mark said, feeling as if he'd just been

slapped. Her father?

'Yeah,' she began. 'He said I just needed to do what they said and I wouldn't be hurt. All they want is Tyler to translate some scrap of paper for them.'

'No they don't,' Mark said. 'I translated that for them right after they got it. They want the staff from Tyler. It is the only thing he has that they want.'

'You're lying,' she cried, tugging hard trying to tear her hand from his grip. 'Let me go. You're hurting me.'

'I'm not lying to you. Now quit struggling. We need to get you out of here. I'll come back for him.'

'NO!' she screamed as she struck him with her fist.

The hit was so sudden that Mark had no time to deflect it. In surprise he released her arm and Helen tumbled backwards onto the floor. Before he could catch hold of her again she was up and running back into the room towards Tyler.

'HELEN STOP!' both Tyler and Mark screamed, but it was too late. The world seemed to slow vividly as she ran determinedly towards the cage. Tyler struggled in vain inside it while Mark struggled to find a way to stop her. This couldn't be happening. He was meant to save her not be the cause of her death. This wasn't what he had planned. He had to stop her somehow before the inevitable happened. He summoned everything in him and sent forth a coil of water to intercept her. She nimble evaded his attempt. Before he could bring the coil back around, she was standing in front of the prison.

'I love you,' she whispered, staring deeply into Tyler's eyes, before latching on to the front of the cell. The electric charge sent her reeling backwards and against the wall where she lay, still as death.

A strange sound gurgled from Tyler's throat as the precious seconds counted down while the electricity recharged. With his hands still bound, fire began swirling around him till it filled the entire cell. Despite the special measures taken to temper the glass from Tyler's fire, the heat growing from inside the cage became so hot that the glass cracked. The charge was moments away from replenishing itself when his prison shattered sending millions of melting shards around the room.

Mark stood still, paralyzed in shock. What had just happened? Helen had killed herself freeing him, but was it necessary? Had she needlessly just executed herself? He watched in horror as the fire around Tyler dissolved into the air and he stepped through the smoke off the platform and onto the cold cement floor. The man, who would surely have loved watching the unfolding of this scene, had mysteriously disappeared. The two brothers were completely alone, other than the unconscious body of Erickson and the unknown condition of Helen.

Tyler knelt beside the motionless body of his girlfriend and gently pulled a strand of loose hair away from her face. She looked so peaceful, like she was only asleep rather than a broken body barely clinging to life in the basement of some unknown building. Could life be any more unfair? He wanted to cry but his anger was so potent that the tear would have evaporated before they could leave the ducts. His skin tingled as he tried to control himself, but staring at Helen only made it harder.

'Tyler?' a voice whispered behind him. He knew that voice. It was the voice of all his problems. He turned and faced Mark, who was now looking as subservient as possible.

'This is all your fault,' he snarled at his brother.

'I had no idea this was going to happen. I swear,' he stammered, taking a few steps back. 'All they wanted was the staff. That's what they told me.'

'Well it looks like they lied now doesn't it?' he replied snidely. It was taking all he had not to attack his brother. 'Besides, do you really think I'd bring it with me? Do I seem that stupid? No, quite the opposite actually. If it hadn't been for your stupidity I wouldn't be standing here now would I? It's your fault I look like this, it's your fault I was kidnapped, and now it's your fault the woman I love is dying.'

'Tyler, what I may have done is not important right now. We need to get her out of here and to a hospital. There's still a chance she can make it.'

Mark went to walk around him, but Tyler blocked him and pushed him back.

'You don't get it do you Mark? Don't you see there's no point? You've killed her. You. By creating that prison and suggesting my capture to a group you knew was not good. Because of you, I now have nothing in this world.'

Tyler's expression was a mixture of hysterics and rage. It was as if his brain could not figure out how he should feel or what he should do. Mark could see he was going into shock. He wasn't thinking clearly and was starting to act uncontrollably. He was going to have to somehow calm him down and get him to think rationally so Helen could still have a fighting chance.

'Alright Tyler,' he said calmly, 'you're right. It's my fault. All of it. Because of me your entire life has changed. I am more than willing to pay for the consequences of my mistakes, but right now Helen is suffering because of me and if we don't act fast, she'll die.'

He tried once again to pass Tyler and get to her. His brother snarled with rage. He grabbed Mark by the throat and threw him backwards onto the ground.

'You will NOT touch her. You've done enough damage,' he said, his expression suddenly changing. It became menacing as if he made a decision, 'but you're right. You will pay for what you've done, but I think you should pay now.'

Mark rolled to the left and ducked behind a pillar, barely evading the barrage of fireballs Tyler sent towards him.

'Tyler!' he shouted, wrapping his wings tightly around him to keep them from getting burned. 'Think about what you're doing. This isn't going to change anything'

'Oh I have,' Tyler replied calmly, sending another barrage of fire at the pillar. 'It may not change anything, but it's what you deserve. Now come out and fight me like a man. Or are you going to hide like the coward you are?'

Tyler felt a momentary chill, which passed like it had never been there. Mark fumed behind the pillar. If it was a fight he wanted than it was a fight he was going to get. He emerged out into the open as calm as if there was no danger for him at all. Tyler threw a fireball at him and it dissolved into a puff of smoke a foot from his brothers face, but he didn't flinch. Tyler threw a few more but each one dissolved into smoke before getting close enough to even singe the hair on Mark's head. He began to get even angrier as he threw more and more and more.

'You seem to be forgetting something important Tyler,' Mark commented nonchalantly, extinguishing the flames ever closer to his brother.

'And what would that be Mark?' Tyler replied über-sarcastically.

'Well, as I have abilities with water and you have abilities with fire and we are next to a very large body of water which is saturating the air around us, your fire is not going to have much of an effect now will it? Or have you just not noticed yet?' he said as he extinguished the flame the split second it left his brothers hand.

He watched as realization filled his brother's eyes. He smiled dolefully. There was no way Tyler was going to win this, but he didn't want to fight him either. He hoped against hope that his brother would realize this and come to his senses, but from the look on his face, that wasn't about to happen.

Tyler straightened himself and winked deviously. 'Well then I guess we're going to have to even up the playing field now aren't we?' In a puff of smoke he was gone.

Mark stared, unsure of what had just happened, before rushing over to the area where Tyler had just been. Nothing. He had completely disappeared. "Where'd he go?" he wondered as he looked around the room. Ironic, Tyler calling him a coward and then vanishing. It was like he had performed one of those fake magician's tricks to make a quick getaway.

His wondering was interrupted by a groan. Erickson was finally coming out of the stupor he'd knocked into him. With Tyler being gone, this was likely the only opportunity he was going to get to save the girl. He rushed over to Erickson, who was now sitting up.

'Come on now,' he motioned to the agent, offering him a hand getting to his feet. He was a bit wobbly at first, but was soon stable. They went as quickly as Erickson's legs would let him over to Helen.

'What happened to her?' he asked. He may be able to stand by himself, but his speech was slightly slurred from being knocked unconscious.

'That's not important. The point is that she's still alive. I need to find Tyler. He isn't thinking straight. Can I trust you to take her to the hospital?'

Erickson sobered up instantly as he quickly realized how serious things had become. He nodded his understanding and bent down to gently lift the body of the barely living girl. He cradled her like an infant before turning towards the exit. With one last hopeless glance, he was gone. Content that she was now being given a chance to survive, albeit slim, Mark turned his attention to finding his brother.

He barely had the chance to turn around when he was sent crashing through the concrete wall next to him. Thankfully the walls were not that thick or stable. No wonder they were still under construction. He tumbled amidst the debris before rolling to a stop in the middle of the room. Tyler, who was obviously torn with grief, stepped through the hole in the wall and placed his foot against Mark's neck.

'Is she going to make it?' he whispered, hissing through gritted teeth, struggling to keep himself from falling apart emotionally. 'Do you think she's going to live?'

Mark tried to reply, but Tyler's foot was constricting his throat so he was barely able to breath. He tried pushing the foot away, but it was like trying to move the foot of a leaden statue.

'WELL IS SHE?!' Tyler screamed at him, spit flying everywhere and warm tears dripping from his chin.

He lifted his foot slightly enough that Mark was able to roll away. He got to his feet and said, 'I don't know if she'll live. It's still too soon to tell. At least she has a chance now. What were you thinking?'

'I don't know I don't know I don't know,' Tyler sobbed, dropping to his knees. 'It's my fault she's going to die isn't it? I don't know what's happening. What am I doing? I can't control myself. Help me Mark.'

The look in Tyler's eyes appeared so sincere that all Mark wanted to do was help him. He took a few steps forward and then stopped. What if it was some sort of trick? He would have to try and help him from there.

'Tyler,' he said, trying to sound as sincere as possible. 'You're feeling grief and going through shock. People have very different reactions when going through these powerful emotions. You just need to try and calm down.'

Mark watched as his brother's shoulders sagged and the tension in his body dissolved. He looked up at Mark who nearly collapsed in fright. His eyes were empty and completely black. He looked possessed, if angels could even be possessed.

'Tyler? Talk to me. What's happening?' he asked, backing away slowly. He had never wished to be somewhere else as much as he did right now.

Tyler's head tilted slightly to the side and he fluidly rose from his knees. He stared creepily and unblinking at Mark. Mark's eyes glanced momentarily towards the curved hallway not far to his left. Could he make it in time? Without looking, Tyler sent a cascade of fire at the hallway, completely consuming it and causing it to collapse. A maniacal grin spread across his face, like he had finally caught his prize and had just decided what he was going to do to it. In this case, it seemed to Mark that it was only going to end in his death.

Tyler's knees suddenly buckled as he began to transform physically. Sparks and wisps of fire began dancing across his shoulders and from his hair down his arms, leaping from his fingertips to disappear suicidally into the air. More and more of the wisps of flame began to come till the fire was dancing all over his body, engulfing him entirely in flames. Mark considered dousing him off as he watched him crumple to the floor, but something about the scene stopped him. He had the feeling this was meant to happen.

The fire soon expanded and Tyler stepped from the midst of the flames. Mark lost his breath. His brother's body seemed to radiate with fire, giving his skin a pale unearthly white glow. His hair danced and swayed in the breeze, resembling a dancing candles flame. His eyes were still black, but a reddish glow burned behind them, giving them the appearance of blood rubies or garnets. What entranced him the most were Tyler's wings. Where once they had been the most brilliant white, now they were alive in flame. Tyler had now been consumed by his element, a deity of fire. If there were anyway to save himself, Mark would either have to internalize his element or be really lucky.

'Let's dance,' Tyler said and shot towards Mark.

'Wait,' Mark cried out, but it was no use. Tyler was instantly upon him jabbing, punching, kicking with such ferocity that it took every ounce of stamina Mark possessed to keep up with him. A quick fake to the left and roll to the right gave him the chance to catch his wind and get some space between them.

'Very clever,' Tyler mocked, smirking at his brother. 'The sign of a good fighter is the ability to adapt to the fight he's confronted with.'

'And how would you know that?' Mark shot back, ready at any moment to defend and make any hits of his own. 'You've never fought a day in your life before this.'

'True,' Tyler remarked contemplatively. 'I guess you could say it was my intuition that told me. That and it was something dad used to say during training. Not that you would remember. Round two brother.'

He catapulted himself at Mark again, issuing new kicks, punches, uppercuts, bicycle kicks and other martial art related moves. It was like someone had turned on his inner Jackie Chan. Mark counteracted with a volley of jabs, slices, backhands, roundhouse kicks and other moves equal to his brothers'. One after the other they dealt and defended against the blows. Some met their mark while most were successfully deflected.

Tyler was impressed with his brother's resilience and ability to keep up, but he could see it in his face and eyes that he was losing steam. On the other hand, Tyler still felt completely energized. Somehow, his anger was fueling some inner fire that kept burning hotter the more he fought. He was going to win this fight. He knew it. Then he would put his brother in his place once and for all. He just needed to remain focused on that. Still, somewhere in the recesses of his conscience, he heard and felt a voice he recognized other than his own begging him to stop. He recognized the voice, but for some reason he couldn't place how he knew it. He couldn't let it stop him though. He had to remain focused. He had to do this.

Soon he saw his chance. Faking a side punch, he dropped into a crouch and took Mark's legs out from beneath him. As quick as lightning, Tyler was up and delivering a hammer punch to his chest, driving him to the ground and taking away his breath. He watched Mark struggle for a few seconds and then moved a few steps back and leaned against a wall.

'Come on Mark. You're not going to give up now are you? You've proved to be such a worthy adversary. I would hate to have defeated you after only round two. Although truth be told, I could have taken you out at any moment. Poof! All that'd be left would be a trail of ashes blowing in the wind. I'm sure it'd only hurt for a few seconds. I'd make the fire hot enough. Although, you really deserve to suffer as long as possible.'

While he spoke, Tyler watched him crawl onto his hands and knees and before struggling to regain his footing. There again came the voice in his head urging him to leave it be. The voice was really starting to become a nuisance, but he knew he couldn't get rid of it. Maybe it was the remaining bit linking him to the human race, his last speck of humanity before the creature took over. If so, he could do without it.

Mark staggered uneasily to his feet, unsteady as a drunk or a baby learning to walk. Tyler walked over and gave him a tiny shove. Not too hard, but enough to test his sturdiness. When he didn't fall over and even pushed the hand away, Tyler gave a little smile.

'There we go. That's my little fighter,' he goaded, as if talking to a child. 'Time for round three.'

He grabbed Mark and flew straight up into the air and through the ceiling. Floor after floor they ascended till at last they broke through the roof. By this point Mark was on the verge of unconsciousness and Tyler felt a smidge of panic. What if he killed his brother? Would that make him a monster as well? If Helen died, whose fault was it really? Mark for his part in the whole plot, or his for not getting her help once he was free? "What was going on?" Tyler cried in his mind. Fear and confusion gripped his heart. Why were these thoughts filling his head?

A sudden stirring brought him back to the fight. Mark's eyes fluttered a few times drowsily and then opened wide in panic. He jabbed Tyler unexpectedly in the stomach causing him to let go. Mark tumbled towards the ground for a few seconds before extending his wings and gliding away.

'Mark come back,' Tyler called after him, his reasoning suddenly springing forth. Letting go of his anger, the flames which encompassed his wings, hair and his inner being extinguished. 'What have I done?'

Chapter 24

It took Tyler all night, but when he finally found the hospital where Helen had been taken he was too late. He overheard two doctors discussing how she never really stood a chance. The damage had been so great that her body would never have been able to recover, especially after the shock set in. He'd thought hearing such comments would make his guilt recede slightly, but it didn't. He might have been able to prevent this, but his rage had stopped him from thinking properly and now he was paying the price. First his girlfriend, the love of his life, was dead and then he'd almost killed his brother. What was he turning into? Maybe the League was right. Maybe he was just an animal.

Getting in to the hospital was a lot easier than getting back out. He only had two options. He could either wait until night to sneak out or climb back through the air vents, how he had come in. Neither choice was going to be easy, but he at least had some clue to navigating the vents. As long as he was going up he was going the right way. Before hoisting himself back up into the shaft, he looked back to Helen's body, which he could barely see through the small window in the swinging doors. He couldn't help feeling a bit morbid because he had checked the morgue first in all the hospitals before considering checking any other part of them. Something inside him had felt numb, lost, gone forever and he knew it could only mean one thing: Helen was dead.

He stood on the roof framed in the moonlight. He sat there pondering in the darkness what the next step was to be. Someone needed to be notified about Helen's death, but as tragic and heart wrenching as it was, it was not his first priority now. She was beyond any help he could give her. He needed to exert his energy repairing something he knew he could do something about. He needed to find Mark.

He had no idea where to look first. He was lost in a foreign city and the only places he knew was the dingy motel he'd been shacked up in with Father Michael and Kahit, and the dock. "That's it!" he thought excitedly. The dock had to be where Mark had gone. If he wasn't there, then Tyler was at a loss, but it was a perfect place to start looking.

The building was dark and foreboding when he arrived there. The only light around it came from a single streetlight. All the others looked shattered or as if they hadn't worked for quite a while. Even with this near absence of light, he was able to see that the side door where he'd almost entered the day prior was ajar. He tried opening it more but it wouldn't move. Instead, he heard a grating sound followed by a whoosh of air. He stepped away from the door and turned to see a segment of the wall swung open revealing a secret passage. He eyed the entrance warily before curiosity took over and he entered it. After he stepped through the entry, the partition swung closed, sealing him in. It was pitch black and he was unsure where to go until he noticed a faint flicker of light below him. With any luck it'd be Mark.

He lit a small orb of firelight and moved it around a bit. To his right he found a narrow stairwell. He followed it down a few flights before entering a dimly lit hallway. He worked his way deeper and deeper down the corridor until at last it opened up into a circular chamber. He had barely walked inside when he was grabbed on either side and thrust into the centre of the room.

'Welcome angel,' came a voice from the shadows where a large, high, desk-like edifice barely concealed the figures of twelve people.

'Who are you?' Tyler asked, strangely calm, yet still defiant considering everything else that had happened to him over the last couple days. He knew who they were. These were The Brethren.

'It's of no real concern at this moment who we are. What are of more concern are you and your brother. We have to say we were quite impressed by the show of power you displayed at the site. Such possibilities. Such aggression. You could attain much in this world and we would help you if you would let us.'

Something about his voice sounded oddly familiar to him. He knew that voice, but God help him if he was having the time of his life trying to place all these voices he was hearing. He was barely able to control his own. So he asked.

'Don't I know you?' He took a few steps forward, trying to peer into the darkness. He knew he did, and then it hit him. 'Richard?'

'I always knew you were a clever lad,' Richard smirked, his face emerging from the shadows despite the gasps of shock from the other people.

Tyler was speechless. How could this be? Richard sat there looking smug and arrogant. "He'd known all along hadn't he?" thought Tyler. He knew he was the angel. Had he used Helen as a spy to get information or was she just an innocent bystander caught in the crossfire of two opposing rivals?

'Don't act so surprised boy. Shall I fill in the gaps for you then?' Richard began. 'Helen was not an informant. We'll just get that out in the air to soften the blow. Truly tragic what happened to her. Margret and I honestly loved her. She was always such a good girl. So innocent and happy, but as it is said in John 15:13, "Greater love hath no man than this, that a man lay down his life for his friends.'"

'Don't you dare quote scripture!' Tyler shouted, his voice reverberating throughout the room. 'You used her all the same though didn't you? You let them take her and use her as bait. How can you hypocritically sit there and quote scripture about love when you willingly sacrificed her? How can you call that love? You were her father!'

'You seem to forget the story of Abraham and Isaac. Required by God to sacrifice his only son as a testament of his obedience, he willingly did what was necessary. As soon as God saw his loyalty, he stopped him.'

'So you're trying to tell me that God commanded you to sacrifice her? Well it seems like he wasn't quite sure of your loyalty because he let her die.'

'That's where you're wrong my boy. If you can remember correctly, I believe you will see that in fact it was you who let her die. She would have been just fine, but she died for you and because of you.'

As much as Tyler wanted to close his ears and hide from what he was hearing he knew it was true. It was his fault.

'I really shouldn't tell you this as you obviously already feel bad enough, but I had assured her that nothing was going to happen to her or you. Such a shame,' he commented with a wave of his hand before disappearing back into the shadows.

'Enough!' Tyler exclaimed, his voice echoing sharply off the stone walls. 'I didn't come here to have more guilt laid on me than I already feel. I came here to find my brother.'

'And we are more than happy to help you find him,' replied a sickening, silky, barely masculine voice.

'Actually, he's been waiting here for you.'

'Let me see him. I need to talk to him.'

'Oh we'll let you see him alright. It's not for us to stand in the way of one's family, but be warned,' the man cautioned with a tiny hint of cynicism, 'talking is most likely the last thing that'll be happening.'

Tyler never got the chance to ask what he meant. Two panels in the middle of the platform where the faceless figures were seated silently slid open, revealing a medium sized opening just big enough for an average sized person to walk through. Moments passed in agonizing silence as he waited impatiently for whom he expected to be his brother to walk through.

He was on the verge of asking what game these men were playing when a clang resonated from the opening, like a knife clinking against crystal. He tilted his head in confusion as something catapulted out of the opening at a rate of speed he'd never seen before. Time suspended in that moment as a figure slammed into him, sending him crashing straight into the back wall. A cold chill spread across his frame as ice snaked over his arms and legs completely concealing his hands and feet, latching him securely to the wall.

'Time for your reckoning,' Mark hissed in his ear.

Mark floated backwards into the centre of the room as Tyler's head hung in agony, waiting for his senses to return. After a few minutes, he looked up and stared at the still suspended figure of his brother, now visible under the fluorescent lighting metres above him.

'Didn't see that coming now did you?' Mark smirked. 'I bet you thought you were the only one able to do extraordinary things. Sorry to burst your bubble, but you aren't. I'm more than just parlour tricks and reanimation. I'm just as capable with ice and water as you are with fire.'

Tyler stared wide-eyed as Mark began to transform. Inch by inch, the colour in his body drained, leaving his skin an iridescent whitish-blue. His eyes became a most brilliant opaque white with his wings resembling veiny fragments of blue-black, crystalline ice. From the inside out, his body seemed to sparkle like the sun on ice and snow. He was the epitome of his element, the god of ice.

'Pretty good huh? Want to see something else I can do?'

He extended his arm, fingers stretched towards him. Tyler marveled as long daggers of ice extended from Mark's fingertips. Soon the air was full of these dangerous shards, which resembled spears more than daggers. They dangled in the air, metres from his imprisoned body until one came sailing through the air stopping millimeters from his face.

'Impressive right?'

'Mark, I just came here to talk to you. I want to apologize,' Tyler exclaimed, trying his hardest to mask his desire not to be impaled by the ice spear.

'You want to talk now do you?' Mark responded sarcastically. 'I'm thinking it's a little late for talking. You should've considered talking before you nearly killed me.'

'You're right. I wasn't thinking, but can you blame me? Do you think you would've been thinking rationally under the same circumstances,' he tried reasoning as the spear nearly pressed against his skin, its chill freezing the sweat building on his brow.

'You've got a point, but then again, I've never been able to be like you. Attempting to consider how I would react if I'd been in your position would be a waste of time. I kind of prefer the current situation where I consider where I should send this spear.' Mark giggled as he stroked his chin thoughtfully. 'You know, ice is quite the perfect weapon. Once it's melted, the weapon's gone forever.'

The icy missile darted back and forth as his

brother contemplated on a good, vulnerable place to stab. 'Now. Where would be a good spot? The heart?' he wondered out loud, the spear moving from Tyler's head down to his chest. 'No. You have to have a heart in order to pierce it. How about the forehead?' he considered as the spear went back up to his head. 'No no. Too messy. Maybe the eyes. Very symbolic that,' he mocked, watching in glee as the spear split into two halves and rotated like drills barely a centimeter in front of Tyler's eyes.

'Mark you don't want to do this,' he cried out, trying to break free from the surprisingly not cold ice that held him bound. 'You'd be making a mistake if you did.'

Mark rolled his eyes and with a wave of his hand the two spear halves retreated to a much safer distance.

'You might be right, but give me one good reason for not running you through this second. And don't try reusing your lame excuse about me being your brother. Those words hold no weight in this court.'

Tyler thought for a few seconds about what he could possible say to Mark that would keep him from attempting to kill him. He considered antagonizing him, but that thought was fleeting as it wasn't the smartest idea considering he was the prisoner in this situation. He had nothing.

'I honestly don't have a reason. We both know I haven't been the best brother, but that's the only reason I have. "Blood is thicker than water," they say. Plus, we both know I'm just as powerful as you so I can't guarantee that you will come out of this any more unhurt than I will."

This was not what Mark wanted to hear. 'We'll see about that,' he growled as he sent the two spear halves speeding straight for Tyler's eyes.

The spear halves were only a couple feet away when Tyler blew out heavily. He jolted as cold water drenched his face and upper body. Mark was not pleased and began sending more spears towards him. Each one melted as the airspace around him heated up, the first ones into water and the latter ones into steam.

'Get ready to meet your match,' Tyler said as the colours began swirling around his eyes, painting them a mirrored obsidian black. Mark backed away slightly, readying more ice spears as the fire spread through Tyler.

He burst free from his icy handcuffs sending chunks of ice spraying around the room. Connecting with the power inside him came a lot easier this time around. Within moments he latched on to it and soon his whole being resembled fire. He was barely able to step away from the wall before Mark was sending more ice spears to assail him. None of them were able to get close enough before disappearing in a pitiful puff of mist.

'I see things need to get a whole lot colder to cool you off,' Mark quipped, attempting to be witty.

'Seriously?' Tyler mocked. 'Is that the best verbal attack you've got? This is a real fight, not some cheesy Arnold action flick.'

'Verbal attacks will be the last thing on your mind once I'm done with you,' Mark shot back.

'Bring it.'

Motioning over the remaining ice spear, Mark gripped it in both his hands and Tyler watched, impressed, as the ends lengthened turning the spear into a sturdy looking ice staff. He twirled it around a couple times like a martial arts expert and turned to advance on his brother.

Tyler moved to intercept him but could only get a few steps before his brother appeared in front if him. His speed was ridiculous. He jabbed and cut with the staff, but Tyler avoided each attack, mostly narrowly. He rolled away shooting off a few fireballs to keep Mark at bay, which he casually deflected with the staff. They both watched as a section of the staff fell off the end, tinkling harmlessly on the stone floor. Mark winked, grinning wickedly at him as a new end quickly grew back.

Tyler needed to find some kind of weapon or else he wouldn't last much longer. Mark's newfound power was staggering. Fighting with his bare hands was only helping a little and there was no way to create a weapon simply out of fire. He needed an alternative. Then he saw it. Across the room he caught a glimpse of two decorative swords hanging low on the wall. Successfully evading the new onslaught, he rushed to the wall and pulled them off. Fire ran from his hands down the blades and he turned, the fire's reflection dancing upon his satisfied face, ready to face Mark.

He spun the swords in his hands as the two brothers circled each other, sizing each other up. Now they were equally formidable foes, Mark with his ice staff and Tyler with his fire swords. Both could see it in each others face that neither was going to back down and if it came to dealing the death blow, both would be perfectly capable of doing it. What both of them didn't know was that just below the surface, both were wishing the other would admit defeat so they could end this standoff. As both of them were steel-willed and thickheaded, neither was willing to do so. The time for reconciliation had passed, just as Mark had told Tyler.

Mark made the first move, striking swiftly at Tyler's left calf, which he easily deflected, slicing off a third of the staff, which was instantly replaced. He then dealt a backhanded blow towards Tyler's other leg, following through after the swords melted the staff and replacing the melted end in time to catch Tyler solidly on the knee. He stumbled momentarily, nearly collapsing, but recovered quickly dealing a couple blows of his own.

He spun quickly bringing both arms up and driving them down, crushing through Mark's staff. Bringing the swords up again quickly, he swung them horizontally, slicing the staff into four pieces. Mark had barely a second to react to this sudden onslaught. Just as

Tyler was bringing the swords down once more, a thick shield of ice materialized on Mark's arm deflecting the swords while staying intact.

'Nice move,' Tyler sarcastically admitted, retreating back a few steps, letting Mark reorganize himself.

'Don't stop because of me,' he shot back snidely. 'We wouldn't want anyone to think you were compassionate now would we?'

'That's if there was anyone around to see us. From the looks of it, your posse hightailed it out of here leaving you to fend for yourself. Some friends you have.'

'Of course they left. Do you think they want to be caught in the middle of this fight?' Uncertainty wavered in his voice.

'Yeah. Keep telling yourself that,' Tyler mockingly laughed.

'I will,' he shot back and then attacked.

From behind the ice shield Mark pulled a thick sword. He took a swing at Tyler who blocked it and stared in amazement as the ice sword stayed intact.

'That's more like it,' he smirked giving Tyler a wink before pushing him back with the shield.

'Yeah?' said Tyler. 'Try this on for size.'

In the airspace in front of him, a glowing ember began taking on mass, growing into a large fireball. Mark's eyes grew as the fireball triggered in his memory what happened to the stone in the forest. Once the ball had reached the desired size, he raised it into the air and sent it spiraling towards his brother.

Mark had nowhere to hide this time. Planting his feet solidly on the ground, he angled himself with the shield and awaited the impact. Moments later the fireball collided with the shield nearly sending him crashing into the platform behind him. Instead, although it did jar his arms, the ball ricocheted off the shield, crashing through the wall close to the ceiling.

'It seems our arena has just been enhanced,' Mark smiled, viewing the damage. He flew up and out of the room into the darkness of the surrounding warehouse above their secret enclosure.

Tyler's head drooped and he shook it in tired annoyance. Why couldn't they resolve this like civilized people? It was like some medieval sibling rivalry, fighting a duel or a war because the other one offended them or some other trifle. They never ended well and he was afraid that this was going to end just as bad. Of course, it wasn't as if he was helping out the situation very much by fighting, but that was beside the point. He was mostly defending himself.

'What's wrong down there? Fire wings not able to fly? Such a shame,' Mark called down, followed by maniacal laughter.

'Ha ha very funny. Better get ready cause here I come,' he shouted back. 'So immature,' he muttered under his breath.

When Tyler emerged from the hole in the wall he couldn't see a thing. High above the ground, plastic covered windows kept the light to a bare minimum, coating the inside of the building in an inky blackness mottled with grey patches. The fire from his wings, hair and swords created a torch like effect, but kept the radius of the light to five or six feet at the most. If he expected to see his brother coming at him like the last time, he needed to find a way to get light into the place. Without burning the place down naturally. Arson was really not something on his to-do list.

A sudden rustle and clang to his left broke his concentration. He created a small fireball and sent it around, lighting up the area. He inspected the space left of him but found nothing. Chains clanged in the rafters above him and a door shut far to his right. An icy wind gusted through the room, causing the orb to extinguish and the flames on his swords to flicker dangerously.

'Come out come out where ever you are,' he called as if playing hide-and-seek. 'How do you expect me to fight you if I don't know where you are?'

'Magic,' came a voice from behind him. Tyler ducked to his left as a cool breeze blew dangerously close to his right arm.

He turned to defend himself, but saw no one. Mark had disappeared once again.

'You think this is funny?' he called out, his voice echoing through the empty rafters eliciting no response. 'How funny do you think it'd be if I lit this place up? Would you be laughing then? I don't think your ice would be strong enough to put out the blaze this place would create.'

'Go ahead and try,' Mark replied nonchalantly, suddenly appearing on his left. Tyler raised his arm quickly to deflect Mark's blow and latched on to his leg as he tried to disappear once again above him into the rafters.

'I don't think so,' Tyler grunted as he yanked Mark down, letting go as he crashed onto the floor. 'Let's keep this on the ground shall we?'

Mark rolled to his side and placed both hands solidly of the ground. 'If that's what you want, then we'll play by your rules. Come and get me,' he said before jumping to his feet and disappearing into the darkness.

'Not again,' Tyler sighed. He took a step in the direction Mark had went and found himself suddenly flying through the air. He landed with a loud crack on the ground. Underneath him, Mark had coated the area with a thin layer of ice.

"Clever," he thought, groaning as he picked himself off the ground. He warmed his feet to a high enough temperature to melt the ice as he walked. It was now a lot easier following his brother. The trail of ice glittered in the light of his fire. It led him through the maze of material inside the building, which he would no doubt have been bumping into endlessly.

The centre of the room opened up revealing an empty portion. It was lit up from light coming from a few windows where the plastic covering had torn free. It gave him the perfect opportunity to orient himself. To his left, the light revealed the most direct route out of the warehouse, leading most likely to the sliding doors he'd seen opposite where he had entered. To his right, the light seemed to stop suddenly, like hitting an invisible barrier. The space behind it simply vanished into the darkness, like black paint splashed on a used canvas.

A gust of cold wind swept by as a loud, high-pitched squeal sounded to his left. He turned sharply towards the sound, but immediately saw nothing. He looked around for a few seconds and then noticed a few sparkling lights from the lower portion of the wall. He cautiously walked towards the lights. As he neared them, he realized the lights were actually the lights from the neighboring dock and street shining through the narrowly opened sliding door. "Mark must have come out this way," he guessed.

He walked through the door onto the dock and found Mark standing at its edge, staring silently out at the ocean. He had released his icy façade and was standing there with his back to him. Tyler let his fire façade drop and tentatively walked towards him. Caution urged him to stay a safe enough distance away in case Mark had something concealed he wasn't aware of. He ignored it. He walked up next to his brother and leaned against the railing.

'I love the ocean,' Mark muttered as soon as Tyler made it to the dock's edge. 'It has such a calming affect.'

Tyler could see his eyes were closed as if today was some different day and they were not in the middle of some epic battle. "I wonder what he's thinking about," he thought, watching cautiously as Mark took in a few deep breaths. Was he planning something or was he really just taking in the majesty of the great blue wonder that lay reflectively before them?

'Do you wish things had just stayed the same and that I hadn't did this to you?' Mark asked, turning his head to look at him.

'Honestly?' Tyler replied.

'Yeah. Honestly.'

'I haven't really been able to give it much thought over the last couple weeks. If I haven't been breaking out of places, healing kids, traveling cross-country or finding mythical objects and supernatural abilities, I'm fighting someone and just trying not to be discovered.'

'I can understand that,' Mark muttered in reply.

'Although, after all has been said and done, I don't know if I would change it back. Your life is given to you to see what you'll make of it and how you handle the challenges given to you. This just happens to be the challenge given to me. No it isn't the easiest, but it could be a whole lot worse. At least I have powers.'

Mark laughed at Tyler's last comment. 'You're beginning to sound like me,' he said, grinning slightly.

'I won't lie. I'm also beginning to understand your obsession with fantasy and the supernatural. If more people were able to do the things we can do, there wouldn't be so much of a need for guns and stuff. You could just burn, freeze, bury or blow away your opponent.'

'So true,' Mark agreed. 'It would definitely make this world a different one.'

The two brothers fell silent and stared again quietly at the sea and listened as the waves lapped gently against the pillars holding up the dock. It was a moment both brothers had never expected to happen: they were beginning to understand each other. If not for the battle, it would have been a cause for celebration.

'Well,' Mark spoke quietly, unashamed sadness emitting from his voice, 'we best be finishing what we started.'

'You know, do we really need to? Is it really going to accomplish anything?' Tyler asked, equal amounts of sadness in voice. Neither wanted to continue on, but they knew it had to be done. Some medieval sense of honour. That didn't mean they couldn't possibly come to some sort of honourable impasse.

Mark considered for a minute and replied, 'we probably don't need to. As much as I'd like kicking your butt, you're right, it wouldn't accomplish anything.'

'You wish you could kick my butt,' Tyler laughed, smiling at him. 'That would never happen.'

'Are you serious?' Mark scoffed. 'I'm pretty sure you got knocked down more times than I did.'

'Yeah, only because of your trickery. If you'd been fighting fair they never would have happened.'

'You're crazy. First off I never did anything unfair. Second, laying traps has been used in warfare since the dawn of man. Come on.'

'Fine,' Tyler snapped. 'How's this for trickery?'

Mark pitched forward slightly as he felt something scalding hot strike him on his back. It wrapped around his chest, pinning his arms to his sides. He looked down and found a length of fire binding him. The heat mellowed to a mild burn shortly after ensnaring him. He smirked and rolled his eyes, causing a shiver of ice to ripple up his skin, extinguishing the flames.

'Very clever,' he called out. He ever so slightly began rotating his wrists churning the water below them. 'Check this out.'

The dock swayed wildly as a large wave struck it. A large spray of water cascaded through the air, separating the two boys. The tiny droplets solidified and abruptly changed direction, striking Tyler sharply stinging his skin. Mark burst through the spray, catching Tyler off guard as he deflected the pellets with an aura of heat. As Mark crashed through the spray, droplets of water and ice swirled around his hands solidifying into another staff.

Sheets of water wrapped around his body and face forming into protective armour.

Tyler twisted out of the way as Mark brought the staff down swiftly towards his head. The staff grazed his shoulder, ripping a patch of skin off. He stared bewildered as a small rivulet of blood trickled down his arm. Mark smirked and advanced to make his second blow. He jumped into the air and drew the staff back hard in a repeat of his previous attack. As he brought the staff down, he swore the blood on his brother's arm was snaking around his arm. In a flash, the blades were aflame as he brought them up in defense. The staff shattering into blood stained shards and Mark nimbly retreated.

They slowly circled each other, assessing their strengths and weaknesses. Tactically a close assault proved fruitless. Both of them had proven to be proficient at close range and hand-to-hand combat. Tyler was going to have to attempt a long-range attack in hopes that he could sneak something passed. Mark withdrew even further, giving some distance between the brothers. Just as he was touching down, Tyler swung his swords in a giant arc and slammed them onto the wooden slats of the pier. A 6-foot wave of fire came gliding across the wood towards him. Mark quickly formed another staff and brought it down over his head onto the pier, sending a wave of ice back towards the fire. The polar opposites met and dissolved in a hiss and puff of smoke. A wave of energy from their impact nearly knocked over the two boys.

'That was pretty good,' Mark shouted as Tyler stood silhouetted against the smoke.

'You think so? Watch this.'

Mark watched as the swords began to glow a brilliant ruby red from behind the wall of smoke. Tyler raised both arms and bowed his head as if saying a prayer. He sharply rasped their edges together, as if sharpening them, and cut them into the pier in one fluid movement.

The burning red from the swords drained from the cooling metal onto the dock forming a large circle containing both brothers. Mark watched as the two lines of red slithered across the ground until finally uniting.

'I don't know what to say,' Mark taunted, smiling big. 'That was truly much more impressive than I expected.'

Tyler ignored the taunt, smiling absently as he reached down for the swords. He pulled them from the wood and rose gently into the air. He moved towards the centre of the ring, his arms with the swords outstretched, parallel with the ground.

Mark watched in perplexed amusement not exactly sure what he was doing. If Tyler had been fighting any other person, they probably would have killed him by now, unless he was putting on a show. If that was the case the show was dragging and beginning to get boring.

He was about to express his annoyance when Tyler turned to him. 'Ready?' he asked. Mark didn't get a chance to reply before the ring erupted into a massive wall of flame. The blaze climbed like vines, arms and legs, climbing over each other reaching for the sky until the fiery limbs connected, welding together to form a giant dome. Mark was speechless at this spectacle. It truly was magnificent. Then the fire began snaking across the floor reaching out to take hold of Mark's feet and wings in an attempt to scorch and possibly melt him. He leapt into the air doing all he could to stay away from the blazing inferno, which kept him captive on all sides.

'Weren't expecting that now were you?' Tyler gloated as wisps of fire twirled around his arms to his fingertips, springing away into the sea of fire once it reached the apex. He couldn't help but be impressed at this new feat. If only Father Michael and Kahit could be there to see this. Wouldn't they be so proud of this accomplishment?

A faint sizzle stood out from the roar of the inferno. "Where's that sound coming from?" Tyler wondered. He looked over to where Mark was floating and found him looking quite calm with his wrists crossed, his hands resting on his upper chest, kind of like a standing corpse. His skin seemed to emit some kind of translucent light. It lapped against his consciousness like the waves on a beach. He felt his mind begin to drift off and had to poke the wound on his shoulder to bring it back.

'What're you doing?' Tyler asked him. 'Why aren't you trying to get away? Finding a vulnerable area and escaping? And what's up with your skin?'

Mark turned to look at him, his once again opaque and crystalline skin glistening majestically in the light of the inferno. 'I am,' he replied calmly. 'But you seem to once again be forgetting one important detail.'

'And what would that be?' Tyler asked arrogantly. What could he possibly have forgotten? Mark was probably just saying that to unnerve him and it wasn't going to work.

Mark's smile grew wider as he saw that Tyler really had forgotten. 'You've forgotten that I can manipulate water.'

'I haven't forgotten that,' Tyler spat back and then his eyes got wide. Suddenly it hit him what a vital mistake he'd made.

The sizzling sound quickly became louder and soon overpowered the sound of the blaze, which seemed to lose its courage. He watched horror-stricken as sections of the flame began disappearing, making futile attempts to reconnect itself. From the holes in the fire he could see a large shadow looming over the dome. A large drop of salty water splattered against his forehead. It was apparent now that his beautiful creation was soon to become naught. He could only stand there as the massive tidal wave rushed over the dome. In one swoop, the water extinguished the fire and sent him crashing to the dock. The water consumed everything in its path before completely obliterating a section of the pier. The water passed over Mark as if connecting with one of its own. It didn't take a rocket scientist to know that this was the final blow, deciding Mark as the winner of the battle.

Mark looked around impressed as the water flowed back into the ocean. His pride quickly changed to anxiety as he realized the destruction the wave had caused. A large chunk of the wharf was completely demolished leaving jagged teeth as the dock angrily bit back the water in a successful attempt to save itself. Along with the dock, his brother was also eradicated. Somewhere amongst the floating bits and pieces of splintered wood and angry metal should be the battered body of Tyler, but Mark couldn't see it anywhere.

The alarming sound of sirens sounded in the distance, invading the otherwise semi-peaceful countenance of the night. Mark needed to find his brother and fast. Their exposure would surely not bring good results. It wasn't as easy as he expected to find him. The sirens were nearly upon them when he finally did. At least part of him. Mark dove down and grabbed his brother's hand from the plank it was weakly clutching before it was able to disappear into the silent, unrevealing water. He awkwardly maneuvered Tyler's body until he was cradling him in his arms. He flew off into the wild, far away from the lights, just as the first police car arrived at the scene.

Chapter 25

Being dead was quite different from what Helen had been led to believe. It wasn't cold, and so far there hadn't been any bright lights or doors. She simply sat next to herself on a gurney in the morgue. It was a bit unnerving not being able to feel the cold, but she figured without her body, it was impossible to feel such simply things as cold or heat. It also made her sad.

She waited for a few hours, but other than a few doctors and nurses, no one came down to see her. Was she really that surprised? Her death was a result of a sacrifice to save her love. Her father probably couldn't care less. What about her mother? Did she even know? Was she also a part of this horrible group? Had Tyler survived? If so, where was he? Where was Mark? She mulled over these questions, but felt no more concern than if she hadn't thought about them. She simply felt no worry. It was a remarkable feeling not being concerned about the trivial things of mortality.

"I like not having to worry about stuff," she thought, smiling at feeling carefree. "Too bad it took dying to feel like this."

She was contemplating whether or not she could feel pain when a faint shift in the light caused her to start. It'd been a while since anyone had come down. She felt her heart flutter, which surprised her a lot, as Tyler walked through the door and stopped next to her. He flipped over the tag on her foot and his countenance fell. She watched as he struggled to hold himself together. She reached out to touch his face when he turned his gaze her direction. She retracted her hand as if someone has scalded her. "Can he sense me," she wondered.

He walked right up and stopped directly in front of her. She shuddered at his intense heat. It wasn't like real heat. It was like an unearthly energy that transcended beyond simple sensory perception. He looked at her face, right into her eyes and reached out, but his hand went right through her. He shuddered a bit, presumably because of the cold, and pulled the sheet back, revealing Helen's face. She took a second to get over the odd sensation of having his hand go through her before turning to look at herself. She looked peaceful and finally at ease. She smiled at her still body. She reached out to move a wisp of hair from her face, and was slightly saddened when her fingers couldn't hold on to it. Instead, she had to sit there and watch as Tyler did it, his hand trembling, full of emotion.

It truly is a pitiful sight watching a grown man cry, even if he is the one you love. He is supposed to be the one who is cried to, who comforts the crier. When he is the one who is crying, there seems to be something fundamentally wrong with it. Even when she was alive, she found it awkward seeing men cry. She was glad she wasn't alive to deal with this. No matter how much she loved him, consoling him would never have gone right. She just sat there watching him sob until he finally stopped. "Angels must have more tears than normal people, because boy can he cry," she marveled as he wiped his face.

He didn't stay much longer. He gently kissed her forehead and replaced the sheet. He took one final look from behind the swinging doors before exiting the morgue and disappearing forever. It was strange knowing she was not going to be seeing him again. It felt somehow wrong. Would she see him again? It was possible if she couldn't find a way to get to the afterlife. She shrugged and jumped off the gurney. She started to walk towards the door leading to upper levels of the hospital when a sharp knocking stopped her. "Where's that coming from?" she wondering, turning back to investigate. The only other door in the room led to the freezer where they stored the bodies. She reached out to grab the handle when the knocking came again. This time it scared her.

'Who's there?' she called out, edging away from the door. She looked around the room, but she was completely alone. Except for the dead bodies. And whoever was knocking on the freezer door.

When the knocking came a third time, she reached for the handle, but her hand went right through it.

"Now that's inconvenient," she thought, frowning at the door.

The knocking came a fourth time, this time sounding more urgent than any of the others.

'I'm trying,' she called through the door, 'but I can't grab the handle. I don't know how I can help you.'

She wasn't too happy about being the cause of someone's death. She began walking away to find someone when she heard the door click open. She turned back and found herself staring into a brilliant white light; more brilliant than anything she had ever seen. It was warm and inviting. Her senses tingled and she felt relaxed. She wanted nothing more than to fall into the light, which she did. Her senses were so overwhelmed by peace that she didn't even hear the door close behind her.

When her eyes finally adjusted to the brightness, she found herself walking on clouds, white, fluffy clouds. It felt like she was walking on a thick, but sturdy mattress. The clouds stretched for miles, forming mountains, hills and even foliage. She heard streams gurgling and felt a gentle breeze, which rustled the cloud leaves. If this was heaven, she never wanted to go anywhere else. Before long, she came upon a sign indicating the entrance to heaven lie not too far away. When she finally came to the end of the trail, she rubbed her eyes in disbelief at the sight of a large pair of gates made out of what looked to be pearl. Sitting to the right of the gate at a desk was an older gentleman with a beard that lay in a pile at his feet.

'No way,' she exclaimed, rushing up to the old man. 'Are you really Saint Peter? Keeper of the Pearly Gates? This is incredible!'

He just smiled as she laughed and giggled in excitement. He waited patiently for her to calm down before he replied.

'I am Saint Peter and these are my Pearly Gates. I am the final hurdle for those who have lived their lives worthy enough to pass through them. And who my dear, are you?'

'I'm Helen Saunders,' she replied, confident that she was going to get through the gates.

'Saunders you say?' he muttered, searching through the overly large ledger in front of him. 'Hmm. Hold on just a moment.'

Saint Peter turned around to the pillar next to him and opened a concealed compartment. He pulled out a phone and put it to his ear.

"Mm-hmm," he mumbled, listening intently. "Mm-hmm. Mm-hmm. Really? Are you sure? Ok, I'll see to it."

Helen stood there in confused silence. "What's going on?" she wondered. She should be in the book. Why shouldn't she? It was the book of the living, and she had definitely been alive.

'I'm very sorry,' Saint Peter said, turning back to

her. 'It appears that someone may have tampered with the Book of Life. Your name is nowhere in it. Being that no one comes to the gate unless they were at some point alive, it's clear that you were alive. We're going to have to dig into what happened to your name.'

'So what do I do until then?' she asked, not really sure of what was going on. 'Do I have to wait here?'

'No, no, my dear. You'll be taken to a waiting room. Once we've rectified everything, we'll come for you.'

Suddenly, the ground a few feet from her opened, revealing a staircase. A man poked his head above the rim and motioned for her to follow him. He led her down a couple flights and through a narrow corridor before finally stopping in front of a non-important looking door. He opened it and with a nod of his head, motioned for her to go in. Reluctantly, she complied.

The room was filled with people of all sizes, ages and races. Some were pacing, walking anxiously through the crowd, while others sat and stared in dazed silence. Those ones appeared catatonic, as if they'd been there quite a while.

'What is this place?' she asked a lady sitting at a desk by the door.

'This is the waiting room for those people not found in the Book of Life,' she answered jovially.

'How long do we usually have to wait?' she questioned, looking around nervously. She didn't think she was going to like being stuck in this room.

'Oh dear,' the lady replied. 'I can't really answer that. It depends on how long it takes to locate your records and determine where you belong. It could last anywhere from a few hours to a couple centuries.'

'Centuries?!' Helen exclaimed. She couldn't stay there for longer than a couple hours. There was no way she could handle this chaos for longer than that.

Seeing the worried look on Helen's face, the lady

consoled her. 'Now don't you worry. Every case is different. You might possibly be one of the luckier ones.'

How she was attempting to help her Helen was unsure. It wasn't helping at all. She turned away from the lady and searched for a place to sit. The only available spot was between a man who looked as old as death and a lady who probably never ate healthy in her entire life. She opted to stand instead. Time seemed to drag the longer she stood. She had no idea how long she'd been there and was seriously considering sitting down on the floor when her name was called.

'I'm here,' she responded, trying not to sound too eager.

'Could you follow me please?' asked an official looking man. She wanted to ask if everything had been sorted, but the look on his face deterred her. For the afterlife, it didn't seem so much of a happy place. She wished she could be back on the path leading to the Pearly Gates. It was at least nice there. After a short elevator ride, they walked up to another gate, this one not as lustrous as the Pearly Gates. More than one gate, and elevators, heaven was looking to be more complex than people realize.

Next to this gate was another older man with a really long beard. Like Saint Peter, he found nothing in his book about her. They went to another gate and even Hell, but there was still no record of her existence. She was a phantom. A ghost of some existence who believed it had really lived. It didn't make any sense to her. She knew she'd been alive. How could she have not existed to them?

The man made a short phone call by the fiery coral Gates of Hell before leading her through a mysterious new door. It had opened out of nowhere, close to them. This one felt different from the rest of the areas she had been to. It felt like despair. Like all hope for her was lost. It scared her. A lot.

'Where are we?' she asked as soon as they entered through the door.

'These are the Roads of Lost Souls,' he responded, gazing in disgust at the scene that lay before them. 'This is where those who can't be placed are stored, forever to roam, never reaching anywhere.'

Helen was dumbfounded. This couldn't be it. There had to be something else. She was sure there was someone they could find behind one of the gates that could confirm who she was, but he had already turned to go. He walked back through the door, which closed quickly behind him, forever sealing her fate. She was a lost soul, cursed to roam endlessly, never happy, never sad. She wanted to cry, but she felt no need to. So she began to walk.

All around her roads intertwined endlessly. Some of them connected to create new avenues to explore, but most just followed their course. She had to be careful not to smack her head on anyone. Some of the roads curled around hers and she once almost knocked heads with some guy who was also not paying attention to where he was going. Then she tripped. She'd been looking around her at all the twisting roads and hadn't noticed the foot sticking out into her path. As she stumbled onto her hands and knees, she happened to catch sight of a bare foot disappearing into a nearly invisible tear in the air. The edges were frayed like a sheet torn in two. If it hadn't been for the foot, she never would have noticed it.

The tear confused her. While the clouds had moved around revealing doors and elevators and such, they had never been breaks in the physical structure of the universe. How could someone rip a hole in the fabric of this spiritual world? Where did it lead? As she had all the rest of eternity to roam, she was going to have to find out.

A tangible world appeared as soon as she stepped through the tear. The ground was solid beneath her feet and everything around her was the shade of burnt sienna. From the look of it, she was now in some type of cavern or tunnel. It was wide enough for her to stand upright comfortably, but not to jump. If she did she would have really hurt her head.

She looked behind her find the tear but saw only solid stone. It was as if it was a one-way entrance. Seeing as there was only one direction to go, she began walking forward into the unknown tunnel. Being in a solid tunnel beat walking endlessly in the drab open space for the rest of eternity. At least this way she'd have some sort of adventure. Not that it mattered any. She would have been fine either way.

Burning torches hung from the walls but emitted no smoke. They were spaced just far enough apart that the light seemed to fade ever so slightly before getting brighter again. The walls were smooth and curved. The tunnel was formed like a tube, except the floor was more leveled out than the rest of it. "Too bad it's not at more of an angle," she thought nonchalantly. "It would have made an awesome slide."

Helen had been following the tunnel for quite a while when she began to hear chanting. She walked a little bit further and momentarily felt an odd sensation in her chest when she noticed an opening a short way in front of her. It opened up into a gigantic cavern filled with dripping stalactites, naturally vaulted ceilings and a giant lake in the middle. Stalagmites jutted dangerously from out of the still water like thorns. It was such a magnificent sight. She couldn't believe that something like this was hidden away somewhere in the afterlife. She felt the pang again, like some sort of stifled emotion was trying to break free.

At the edge of the lake she found a pier with a boat tied to it, unmoving in the lake. This struck her as odd for some reason. Then again, why wouldn't there be a boat on a lake. It would make the most sense to cross a lake with a boat. It was just odd that it wasn't moving. It looked like it was congealed into place rather than floating serenely like on a real lake. She shrugged her shoulders, got in the boat, untied it from the pier and set off.

In the middle of the lake she came across an island. From a distance she could barely make out the frantic movement of shadows of people dancing. An unearthly wailing echoed off the walls causing her to jolt. It was rather unexpected, but it soon mellowed down to the same melody she had heard earlier. At least she was finally able to locate where the chanting was originating from. She felt a bit awkward watching them, albeit from afar. It was like watching some pagan ritual, like a Native American rain dance. She almost considered just paddling around the island, but decided against it. Who knew the next time she was going to run into more people.

She maneuvered the boat over to a pier and tied it up. She got out and cautiously made her way over to where the people were dancing. It was such a hypnotic sight watching them move. The group of masked individuals was clothed in loose fitting white tunics bound around their waists with a red and black sash. Some of the masks were creepy, demonic creatures or broken faces with jagged edges, while others were more happy, cherubic children or smiling, doll-like faces. They danced around the fire, jumping, twisting, all in perfect unison.

The firelight had barely made contact with her skin when the group stopped dancing and turned to stare at her. Their bodies were bent in such grotesque positions that even the cherubic faces looked malevolent. After a few seconds in their frozen positions, as if choreographed, they formed two lines, which began circling her in opposite directions.

Helen was quickly losing hold of the indifference

she'd been feeling earlier. The sight of these cultish people stoked up a nauseating feeling which quickly morphed into fear. Who were these people and what did they want? She kneeled down into a crouch and made to run for the boat when they stopped moving, forming a complete circle around her. They linked arms and began swaying and chanting. They were so close together there was almost no chance of her breaking through them. Two of them broke arms momentarily to let an unmasked woman through.

'Welcome Helen, Goddess of the Night,' the woman hailed kneeling right in front of her.

'Welcome Helen, Goddess of the Night,' the rest of the group chanted as they too fell to their knees.

'Who are you people?' she asked, staring at them confused. 'What's going on?'

The unmasked woman rose from her knees and smiled warmly at Helen. 'We are your servants. We've been preparing and awaiting your arrival for a very long time.'

'What're you talking about?' she asked nervously. Something sinister was going on. She was beyond terrified now. She wanted to run, but her body wouldn't listen to her brain. Warning lights were going off in her mind as she listened to the lady talk, but her body didn't care. It had other plans for her.

The woman gently took hold of her hand and led her towards the center of the island. Helen willed her body to let go of the woman's hand and run, but nothing happened. Her brain raced wildly, but outwardly she followed her calmly over to a fire. It was glowing a sinister, unnatural green. The group formed a large circle around the fire and once again began chanting and swaying. The chanting was a chilling melody that sounded strangely familiar. It was different from the one she had heard earlier. This time it sounded like something she had heard in a dream. Something not real.

'What's going on here? Please tell me,' she asked, turning to face the woman who smiled knowingly. 'How do you know me and how did you know I would be here?'

'It's quite simple my dear,' the woman began. 'We've known about your existence since the dawn of time. Your path to us has been planned for eons. All we needed to do was wait.'

'How was it planned? None of this makes sense.'

'That's because it's not supposed to. Nothing on the Roads of Lost Souls makes sense. The appearance of this magnificent cavern from a tear in the fabric of space? How does that make sense? Getting your very existence erased from the Books of Life and Death? Doesn't make sense either, but that's how it is. Your role in the destruction of mankind makes even less sense, but that's your destiny.'

"Could this really be?" she gawked. How did any of this make sense? Goddess of the Night, destroyer of mankind, existence erased from the Books of Life and Death? Was it possible? Helen didn't know, but here she was, standing in a cavern that shouldn't exist speaking with a woman who'd been waiting for her for eons. It had to be right. Hadn't it? What other explanation could there be? No one else had been able to explain why she ended up where she had until now. Who else could she trust?

She stared the woman in the eyes and asked, 'If all this has been planned, what happens next?'

'Just wait,' the woman smiled, turning to look into the fire.

The woman began chanting along with the crowd and drew something shiny from her tunic. Before Helen could even react to what she saw, the woman grabbed her hand and pricked her finger with the knife. Helen tried to wrench her hand from the crazed woman but her grip was like iron. She shook Helen's hand sharply to get the few drops of blood to fall in the fire. Suddenly the fire shot into the air. It began to swirl, shaping into a tornado like tube. Faster and larger is swirled, the end of the tube elongating and snaking towards the group. Just as it was about to land back into the circle of stones from where it had come, the tube twisted and wrapped around her, engulfing her inside it.

She tried to scream, but her fear caught hold of her voice, rendering it useless. She tried thrashing about, but it was also useless. The fire had somehow solidified, suspending her in the air, holding her prisoner inside it. She began hyperventilating. She was going to suffer some endless torment. She just knew it. These people had tricked her and she had fallen for it. Then a gentle voice calmed her.

'Chosen one. Do not be afraid.'

'Who are you?' she cried, finally finding her voice.

'I am you. You are I. We are each other. You are the past. I am the future. Together we are the present. Do you see me now?'

An image slowly began to take shape in the rippling green flames. When the image solidified, she found herself staring at a reflection of herself. At first the reflection was her exact likeness, flowing, shoulder length sandy blond hair and lightly freckled cheeks. Then her image began to change. Her skin paled to nearly white and her hair darkened to an obsidian black. From her back two scaly wings unfolded, peeling away from her skin as if they'd always been there.

Then the fire disappeared, put out like a clapper on a candle. She felt oddly different. Stronger. Angrier. The woman brought a mirror over so she could see herself. Her mind registered that she should have been shocked at her transformation, but nothing surprised her anymore. A throng of gasping admirers crowded her, touching her wings and praising her. The woman gazed at her in sinister admiration.

'Now you are ready.'

Chapter 26

It was lightly sprinkling as the funeral precession moved slowly through the gates of the cemetery. Other than the muffled sounds of sniffling and the blowing of noses, nary a word was spoken. This was a tragic day and the loss of someone so young was not being taken lightly among the mourning. There were so many unanswered questions about how she had died and why she had been down there in the first place. Naturally, none of the questions could be answered and if they could, would the people truly be able to understand? Would they be able to comprehend the significance of the events leading up to her untimely death?

Father Michael did the best he could to alleviate some of their suffering. He delivered a powerful sermon in which he stressed the overwhelming depth of the encompassing grace of God. He trusted that in their grief, the people could find solace in the fact that Helen would not be in Hell. He knew that deep down all the people wanted to know was how such a travesty could come to pass. Even if he could give them an answer, it would never satisfy them. It was true he wasn't there when it happened, but he knew the other intimate details leading up to it. How surprised they would be to discover such dark truths, but the world wasn't ready for this knowledge. Tyler had almost been exposed through his healing of the boy, but even with so many eyewitnesses, this modern-day miracle was immediately tossed aside from the lack of tangible evidence.

As the throng reached the plot where she was to be buried, Father Michael positioned himself next to her tombstone and began to deliver his final sermon.

'In the epistle of John chapter 5, Christ spoke to the Jews saying, "Verily, verily, I say unto you, The Son can do nothing of himself, but what he seeth the Father do: for what things soever he doeth, these also doeth the Son likewise. For the Father loveth the Son, and sheweth him all things that himself doeth: and he will shew him greater works than these, that ye may marvel. For as the Father raiseth up the dead, and quickeneth them; even so the Son quickeneth whom he will. For the Father judgeth no man, but hath committed all judgment unto the Son: That all men should honour the Son, even as they honour the Father. He that honoureth not the Son honoureth not the Father which hath sent him. Verily, verily, I say unto you, He that heareth my word, and believeth on him that sent me, hath everlasting life, and shall not come into condemnation; but is passed from death unto life. Verily, verily, I say unto you, The hour is coming, and now is, when the dead shall hear the voice of the Son of God: and they that hear shall live. For as the Father hath life in himself; so hath he given to the Son to have life in himself; And hath given him authority to execute judgment also, because he is the Son of man. Marvel not at this: for the hour is coming, in the which all that are in the graves shall hear his voice, And shall come forth; they that have done good, unto the resurrection of life; and they that have done evil, unto the resurrection of damnation."'

Father Michael paused for a couple moments to let what he said sink into the minds of all those who heard him. He also stopped to get his emotions in check.

Helen's parents had completely disappeared and for some reason she'd named him as one of her emergency contacts. It'd been heartbreaking for him to find out she was dead. His thoughts instantly went to Tyler and how he was handling the situation. He had to know she was dead. Was he okay? He hadn't heard from him since the day he'd been abducted. The priest had been contacted about bringing the staff in a trade for Tyler, but then all this happened.

Once he'd regained composure, he continued. 'Helen was by far one the most innocent and humble people I've ever met. She nary had a harsh word for anyone and if she did, it was never given maliciously or to hurt them. She was always quick to forgive. She loved everyone and everyone loved her. Since she was not one of my parish, I would never have gotten the chance to meet her if it hadn't been for Tyler, her boyfriend, who sadly is unable to be here with us today. I'm sure his thoughts and sadness are such that we can understand.

'He introduced us and I could see right away that she was a special child of God. She made Tyler want to be better and it constantly frustrated him because he always thought he could never be good enough. He doesn't know this, but she confided in me once about their relationship. One evening, I was surprised to see her show up on my doorstep. We chatted for a few minutes before she stared me intently in the eyes. It was plain to see she was frustrated and explained that she never expected him to be anything more than himself. She knew he wasn't perfect, but she also knew that he had so much to give and that one day he would be a greater man than any mortal being. She saw something in him no one else saw. She forbade me to ever tell him and as he isn't here, I'm sure she won't mind me telling you."

A nervous amount of scattered laughter hobbled through the crowd before Father Michael continued.

'She was a genuine, caring person who embodied

the spirit of Christ. She gave everything to be the best person she could. I can say without a doubt that when she stands before those Pearly Gates to be reckoned by Saint Peter, he will not bar her way. The gates might even already be open upon her arrival.'

He finished his speech and they all stood in silence as her coffin was gently and slowly lowered into the intimidating hole in the ground. Once they removed the straps from the casket, Father Michael grabbed a shovel and sent the first load of dirt down into the hole. One after the next, her friends, teachers, coaches and teammates all paid their respects and sent down a shovelful of dirt as a final farewell to the beautiful and cheerful girl they had all known and loved.

Once the last of the crowd had paid their respects and slowly vacated the graveyard, Father Michael watched in solemn contemplation as the graveyard attendants finished covering the plot with dirt and then a fresh layer of sod. He couldn't help but wish Tyler had been able to be there. In some way, he could feel that in one of the surrounding trees, he was lurking, spying on the proceedings, listening. In his own way, he knew Tyler would pay tribute. He heard a sudden flutter of wings, but didn't turn around. If it was Tyler, he knew he was going to need his time.

Days passed slowly, but there was no sign of him. He'd simply vanished and made no attempt to contact the priest. Even Kahit couldn't pick up on where Tyler was. It was as if he was either too far away, wasn't thinking - which was naturally unlikely - or had somehow managed to find a way to keep Kahit from hearing his thoughts. None of those ideas made any sense so it was a complete mystery to both of them where he could have gone.

To keep themselves busy until his eventual return, they attempted to search through the secret library for any clues to where the second piece of the key could be.

As they had no way of accessing the clue, this was the only means by which they could try. Despite all their searching, and they looked through every single book in that room, they still came up empty-handed.

'Maybe we could go back to where they took him from. There could be some kind of clue there,' Kahit suggested spontaneously one day. It seemed like a good idea, but Father Michael shot it down right away.

'Not a chance,' he exclaimed. 'We need to be here when he returns, and you can't go there by yourself since one you are too young to be travelling alone and two you have no money. Besides, the likeliness of the clue we need being 'accidentally' left behind or lost there would be largely improbable.'

'Sheesh. It was only a suggestion.' Kahit moped and went back to checking in the books.

Father Michael stared at Kahit in exasperation. He wished he could tell him that he too wanted to go back to where Tyler had been taken and search amongst the wreckage for either a sign of him or, if lucky, the clue, but he couldn't. He needed to be rational even while every particle of his being was screaming that rationality practically existed no more. The fact that the legend of the fallen angel was becoming a reality was proof to that. No, they needed to remain calm and make the world believe all was well. One day the world was going to find out that all was not well and when they did, they needed to be ready. The fight for salvation was only just beginning.

A sudden crash brought both of them to their feet.

'What was that?' Kahit asked.

Before Father Michael could answer him, a shadowy figure sauntered into view and walked straight through the glass as if it wasn't there. It stopped in the centre of the room a few feet from the two. Father Michael's voice caught in his throat as the figure floated passed. He couldn't think or speak and his breath felt icy in his lungs. It was like the cold hand of death was gripping his lungs.

'Truly beautiful ceremony Michael. Quite moving really, but from you one could expect such,' the figure gushed, its sultry seductive voice invading his ears like the sweet smell of honey to a bear. 'You must tell me where you get your inspiration. And please don't say from God, because from what I've seen, the whole concept of good and evil is quite overrated.'

'Who are you?' Father Michael gasped as he forced the words out. They felt as if each one was a razor sharp sword being pulled from his throat.

A musical, high-pitched laugh nearly forced Father Michael to pass out. He knew that laugh, but it couldn't be. She was dead. He had seen her damaged body and knew with a surety she'd been placed in the coffin and buried. There was no way she could be back. It was utterly impossible.

'Oh Michael. That hurts. I thought you'd be happy to see me. Especially after such a most touching eulogy,' the figure replied, its voice filled with mock sadness. Then the figure laughed again. 'Oh silly me. I seemed to have forgotten to reveal myself. Its kind of difficult getting used to this whole angel thing.'

The veil of swirling darkness around the figure dissipated revealing a female figure with ebony hair. The empty blackness of her hair was so stunning that as Father Michael looked at it he couldn't help but feel just as empty. Her skin was unearthly pale in comparison to her hair. Her arms and the majority of her legs and feet were bare. Draped loosely, but elegantly, from her shoulders was a tattered dress made of what might be black velvet or satin. From her back had sprouted wings, much like Mark's. They were dark in colour, but as Father Michael took a closer look, he saw that they were veiny and featherless, much like a bat or dragon's wings.

When the mysterious female figure turned to face him the blood drained from his face. What he had feared was real. Helen had returned, but something about her seemed wrong. It was true she still mostly looked the same, but her eyes were cold, soulless voids filled with anger and rage. It was her, but it wasn't the Helen he remembered. Something had happened. Something not good.

She stared at the priest with a somewhat amused expression on her face. 'I see you are getting a dose of some of my new powers. Quite terrible aren't they?' she quipped, before releasing him from the chill.

Father Michael gasped and collapsed on the floor as warm air filled his lungs, pushing the painful icy air out. 'What happened to you?' he asked as he struggled to stand.

'Well aren't you just full of inquisitiveness?' she chattered, like talking to a questioning child. 'Its quite simple,' she replied as she ran her fingers across the red satin of the armchair leaving black scorch marks in the wake of her fingers. 'I entered the light like a good dead person and followed it straight to Saint Peter's gate. It took a while to show up but that was no big deal. What was most fascinating was meeting Saint Peter! Who would have thought he really existed as they said he did?

'There he sat at his large desk with an even larger book. He asked me my name, to which I replied Helen Saunders. He searched around for a while and proceeded to tell me I wasn't listed in the book. You can only imagine my surprise to find out my name, my seeming existence, was not recorded in the Book of Life.

'I was led to a room filled with many people. They told me it was the room for those poor people who'd somehow been overlooked. Some had been there so long they couldn't remember who they were. I had been there for some time when some official looking man came and retrieved me. He informed me that I was to be taken to another department to see if I belonged there. Place after place I went, but I belonged nowhere. I was even rejected from Hell and you'd think they would've welcomed someone such as myself with open arms, but as I wasn't on their list I was denied entry. As if I wanted to go there in the first place.'

She took a moment to catch her breath.

'In the end, I was sent to roam the never-ending Roads of Lost Souls. Do you know what it feels like to be eternally lost? Like nothing. You feel absolutely nothing. You have no emotion, no cares. It's awful. Anyway, it felt like I'd been there an eternity when I tripped on something. It was then that I noticed a small opening in the wall, quite hidden from sight so I'm amazed I'd been able to see it...'

Father Michael stared at her in disbelief as she described her story. She sounded completely loony, but then again she was here now so he wasn't sure whether to believe her or what. While he listened to her story, he still wasn't sure why she was there. Dead people don't normally come back, especially after a week of being dead and buried.

Helen stopped speaking and smiled at him. She got up fluidly from the chair, which dissolved into ash, and walked over to where the priest was standing.

'I can see that what I'm saying is quite unbelievable, even for someone who communes with angels and boys that disappear.'

Father Michael and Kahit gasped. Obviously she knew about Tyler, but how could she know about Kahit's disappearing. Only Tyler and Father Michael knew about that.

Helen laughed mockingly again. 'Oh you boys,' she cooed as she stared at Father Michael. 'I guess I'm just going to have to show you what happened to me.'

Before he could move to stop her, she placed her fingers on his temples and closed her eyes. With a gasp, his eyes rolled back into his head and he collapsed onto the floor. Kahit quickly rushed over to him, giving special heed to not touch her.

'Who are you?' Kahit cried as he cradled Father Michael in his arms. 'Why are you doing this?'

'Can't you tell?' she asked, looking at him coyly. 'I am the Destroying Angel, the Angel of Death, the Harbinger of Doom. I am the Goddess of the Night and the end of this world.'

Chapter 27

A sudden stab of pain in Tyler's head woke him from his otherwise peaceful, dreamless sleep. It'd been a long time since he'd been able to sleep continuously without nightmares and now, just as he was falling into unconsciousness, he was awoken by a sharp throbbing in his head. He rubbed his temples roughly and after a few seconds the throbbing subsided and he was able to get back to sleep. Just as his mind was sinking into the endless void of dreamless sleep, a tiny, almost transparent voice echoed in his head, 'help us' before dissipating into nothingness.

He bolted up straight in his bed slamming his head on the low hanging ceiling. He cursed loudly, his voice echoing just as loudly through the cavern. "Just my luck," he thought, rubbing his now constantly throbbing head. "First my sleep is interrupted and now this." He could have sworn he distinctly heard Kahit's voice begging for help. There was going to be a massive bruise on his forehead and he knew it. Why couldn't he just be left alone?

It'd been almost a week since he'd had any real contact with the outside world. Not since Helen's funeral. He'd been hiding in the dense treetops nearby her grave and had heard everything Father Michael said, including the justified lie about Tyler's whereabouts. He knew the priest knew he was there, but not like he was going to announce it to the group, not with him in his current state. Once the throng had trickled out of the cemetery and Helen was completely buried, he took to flight and disappeared, not turning back to see if Father Michael had seen him go or not.

In truthfulness, he had no idea where he was. He just flew in one direction until he was tired. He thought it was west, but it might have been northwest. Either way, it was fairly cold now. He was most likely in Canada, but he didn't know and really didn't care. All he was concerned about was the fact that he was alone.

Once he felt he'd traveled far enough, he scouted the area and located a series of caves in some secluded mountain region. He went in as far into the darkness as he could and slept. He tried to sleep was more like it. Every time he closed his eyes, visions of that terrible day appeared, as if they had been etched permanently on the back of his eyelids. For the first few days after she had died, the images were as vivid as if he was seeing them for the very first time. As the days passed, the images slowly began to fade. He knew it was going to take a long time to completely subdue the memory somewhere deep inside his brain. On the random occasion, he was able to close his eyes and not see them at all. During those moments where he couldn't sleep, for fear of seeing her dying face, he would forage through the forest for food, which he had to go pretty far to get.

It didn't take long before he could feel Kahit rummaging around in his head. It was something he had anticipated and hoped wouldn't happen. Not that he could really blame the boy. He and Father Michael were the only people Kahit knew. With Tyler gone, if something were to happen to the priest Kahit would be alone with no money or food. Regardless, Tyler wanted to be completely left alone. It took a lot of concentration, but soon he had built up a wall inside his mind to keep Kahit's wandering consciousness from finding out where he was. It wasn't until this moment that Kahit was somehow able to break through the barrier. Tyler didn't understand how the break could be possible. The only explanation was that something had happened. He knew he needed to get back and the faster the better.

It only took him a few days to get back to Rochester. He was thankful he'd taken a fairly consistent route there so it wasn't too difficult to find his way back. When he arrived on the outskirts of town, he nearly dropped from the sky in devastation. There was nothing left on the hill but a pile of rubble. Someone had destroyed the cathedral. A single firetruck was putting out the remaining stubborn patches of fire. The flames had a strange greenish hue to them.

His first fear had been for the safety of Father Michael and Kahit and secondly for the key. Were they still inside or had they gotten out safely? Tyler attempted to contact Kahit, but he got no response. He then tried to find his mental presence. He sent out a mental probe and was relieved to feel his presence and it felt calm. If anything had happened to him, he was at least doing fine now.

The first and only place he needed to look was the city hospital, where he had been taken on the fateful day he'd grown wings. He waited until the sun set before beginning his search. He decided to take the airduct route as he had done before in D.C. Before he flew to the roof, where the airduct opening was the biggest, he had a random thought. It might be easier to locate their rooms from the outside. That way once he got inside, he could navigate to them quicker. If they had been hurt by the collapse of the cathedral, the ICU might be the place they were taken to, so he tried there first.

The ICU was located on the second floor on the

south side of the hospital. Making practical use of the journey around the building, he flew to the second story and stealthily checked each room whose drapes were open, no matter how slightly. He found Kahit's room just after he turned onto the south side of the building. The boy was peacefully asleep. Other than a single chair, a nightstand, and a TV hanging from the ceiling, his room was otherwise empty. Rather than risk making noise climbing through the ducts, Tyler opted to tap at the window. It would also save loads of time.

At first he tapped meekly, rasping gently on the window as not to draw attention in case someone walked by. When it had no effect, he rapped quite sharply against it accidently causing the fragile pane of glass to crack. It worked though. Kahit stirred and opened his eyes and looked straight at him. At first he stared blankly, nothing registering. After a few seconds, his eyes grew wide and he nearly collapsed in the rush to get out of the bed.

'What're you doing here?' he whispered as he opened the window to let Tyler in. 'How'd you know we were here?'

'Well, after you woke me up from the first peaceful sleep I've gotten in weeks with your urgent cry for help,' Tyler chided after shutting the door quietly and placing a chair where no one could see him, 'I went straight to the cathedral, but found it in ruins. The only place I could think of you both being was here and it looks like I was right. Are you both alright?'

Kahit had already begun gathering his belongings and changing into a different set of clothes that Tyler had never seen before.

'We're fine, but we're not safe here.'

'What're you talking about?' he asked. The lights began flickering as an eerie silence filled the air.

'We need to go now,' Kahit whispered, grabbing Tyler's hand to lead him out of the room. 'Father

Michael's room is next door. We'll get him and then go.'

Kahit stepped out into the hallway, quickly checking to see if the coast was clear. When they found no one, they quietly slipped into Father Michael's room and crept to his bedside. Tyler let out a sigh of relief when he saw the priest was ok. It appeared that both of them had made it out before the cathedral had collapsed. They were just being kept there a few nights to be safe. Kahit gently shook the priest until he stirred. He had about the same reaction Kahit had when he'd first seen Tyler.

'What are you doing here?' he asked Tyler groggily.

'We'll talk about that later,' Kahit reproached. 'We need to get going. Something bad's here and we need to leave.'

'Does he know?' Father Michael whispered to Kahit.

'Do I know what?'

Tyler leered at the two who looked guiltily at each other and then back at him. It was like they were trying to hide a really dirty secret, but doing a very bad job of it.

'What's going on? Does it have to do with why the cathedral is no longer standing?'

Father Michael sighed and got up from the bed and began to change as he spoke. 'Yes it does Tyler, but it's something I know you're not going to want to hear.'

'Well you'd better tell me. Did a person do this? Was it Mark?' he questioned, the irritation and anxiety rising in his voice.

'It wasn't Mark,' Kahit answered when Father Michael remained quiet. 'It was Helen.'

Tyler stood there confused. She couldn't be back. It was impossible. No one can come back from the dead. Especially when they've been dead for over a week.

'I know what you're thinking because we thought the same thing,' Father Michael said quietly, 'but it's true.

She's back and she's no longer the Helen you remember. She's dangerous and back with a vengeance. Kahit says she calls herself the Destroying Angel. Here,' he said, tossing the staff he pulled from the closet to Tyler, 'Kahit was able to hide it from her and get it out of the cathedral before she leveled the place.'

Tyler couldn't believe what he was hearing. His love was alive again. Could she really be as dangerous as they portrayed her to be? She'd always been such a kind, gentle and loving person. What could have possibly happened to her in the after-life to change her so much?

As soon as Father Michael was dressed the three quietly left the room and began maneuvering their way out of the hospital. Tyler couldn't help but feel slightly unnerved by the lack of life and noise. It wasn't that late in the evening so there should be some activity somewhere.

Suddenly Kahit stopped. He'd been leading them through the building and they were almost out. An exit sign posted just above him had an arrow pointing them right. All they needed to do was go through the double doors and they would've reached their desired destination, but he had stopped for some reason.

'What's wrong?' Father Michael asked him. 'We're almost out. Why have you stopped?'

'Something bad's out there. Can't you feel it? It's like my soul is being crushed beneath a glacier.'

They all stared in trepidation at the double doors. Slowly, they all began to feel their life draining from them. Tyler felt dizzy from a strange lack of oxygen. The double doors suddenly parted and a shadowy figure passed through the opening into the corridor. Behind it, they glimpsed bodies with faces and limbs contorted in all manner of unearthly angles and expressions lying strewn about.

'It's her,' Kahit chocked as the shadow concealing the figure suddenly vaporized, revealing Helen. Tyler couldn't believe it. "It can't be true," his mind screamed, but his heart knew it was. She was back and she wasn't happy.

'Look who my old friends have brought me?' she crooned with delight. 'Just the person I've been wanting to see. You've not been easy to find young man,' she chastised, grinning at him evilly.

'Aren't you glad to see me?' she sarcastically whimpered when Tyler didn't smile back at her. 'No. I don't suppose so. This really isn't what you were expected now were you?'

'What happened to you?' he responded sadly.

'Oh it's really quite a long story and I'm sure these two can fill you in with the extra bits as right now I just can't be bothered reciting it again. Especially Michael,' she said wickedly, winking at the priest. 'Had you been there when I first arrived then maybe we wouldn't be needing to do this now would we? But no, you needed to go off on some soul-searching expedition and leave us here to fend for ourselves until you deemed it necessary to come back. So how's this for a welcoming party?' she growled.

The ground beneath her feet suddenly turned black and rotten. The black mold multiplied like a virus, quickly spreading a plague of death and destruction. Acrid fumes filled the hall as the decay began sucking the life out the otherwise lifeless walls around them.

'RUN!!!' Tyler cried dragging the other two back the way they'd come. 'We need to find another way out.'

'I don't know any other way out!'

'Well if we don't go through a door we're going to have to go through a window.'

The plague was beginning to gain on them as they searched for a new exit. For every step they took, the mold advanced a bit further. Plus it didn't help that whenever they found a possible exit, Helen would always appear and bar their way. She would laugh and blows kisses as she toyed with them.

They'd nearly made a full circle when they stumbled across the cafeteria. The doors were locked, but after a solid kick they crashed open and they went in. On the opposite end was a set of doors leading back into the kitchen that were already infected. There was also a fire exit, but try as they might the door wouldn't budge. It was like the doors had been made to protect Fort Knox. After Tyler torched the door, he was dismayed to find that it was only a dummy door, put there to pass safety inspections but never intended for use. Their only option was to try and break one of the large Plexiglas windows.

Kahit angrily grabbed a chair and slammed it into one of the windows. The only effect was the chair bouncing back, knocking him down onto the cold linoleum floor.

'What're we going to do now?' Kahit cried. 'There's no way out.'

'You two take cover,' Tyler ordered, 'and make sure you cover your heads. It's about to rain glass.'

He clutched the staff by one of the ends and ran to the window. He swung it in an arc, bringing it down solidly against one of the large panes of glass. A ripple spread from point of contact, running through the metal to the other panes. Tyler was barely able to make it to where the other two had taken refuge when the panes of glass began exploding. Glass sprayed around them like crystalline snowflakes. When the explosions stopped, everything was coated in and outside the room with a thick layer of jagged glass.

The clambered from their hiding place a ran to the window. Just as they were reaching it, Helen appeared once again trying to impede their escape.

'Why are you doing this?' Tyler shouted at her. 'Why're you trying to kill us?'

'Why?' she sneered. 'You seem to forget a recent

event where you let me die.'

'Of course I haven't forgotten it, but they had nothing to do with it. Why have them die for my mistake?'

'They'll have to die sooner or later anyway. Better now than having to suffer the pains of old age and senility.'

'But is it really up to you to decide? You aren't God and you can't play him.'

'You think I want to play God?' she scoffed. 'He can't even keep track of all the records himself. If he was so almighty then why was I rejected from both Heaven and Hell, doomed to walk the endless Roads of Lost Souls for the rest of eternity? He has no more control on the lives and deaths on this plane than he has on dealing with all those who have died. I might not be God, but I sure can give him a hand now can't I?' she said, laughing maniacally.

'Well these are three people who aren't going to fall victim to you,' he announced.

'What's that?' she ridiculed again. 'You think you can stop me, the destroyer of this world? And how do you propose to do that?'

'Like this,' he said, tossing the staff to Kahit. Instantly a large fireball materialized in the air in front of him. Before she had any time to defend herself he shot it at her. She gasped and disappeared in a puff of black smoke just as the flames licked her skin.

'Go!' he shouted, pushing the two towards the window ledges.

The two made it safely out and onto the grass beside the building. Tyler was just climbing out when a sudden chill clenched his heart and made him gasp. He looked down and found a hand gripping the left side of his chest.

'Nice trick,' Helen whispered in his ear, 'but mine are better. Time to bid this world farewell.'

With very little difficulty, she pulled him back into the cafeteria. She completely disregarded the fact that the building was beginning to collapse around them. She threw him across rows of tables as easily as if he'd been a crumpled piece of paper. He landed on top of a round table and bounced awkwardly off it onto the floor. He barely could catch his breath before she was once again at his side.

'Oh come now,' she taunted. 'Don't be all chivalrous just because I'm a girl. You really aren't making this any fun for me.'

He groaned and moved his lips to say something.

'What was that?' she smirked. 'You need to speak a little louder please.'

'You probably shouldn't underestimate me,' he said loud enough that she could hear.

'What.....,' was all she could get out before a dragon materialized in front of her. It roared and attacked, sending her crashing through the cafeteria wall.

He quickly and painfully got to his feet, hurrying back towards the broken windows. He made it halfway there before two veins of black mold shot passed him on either side. He jumped into the air, seconds before the veins met and turned the ground beneath him to toxic sludge. Staying in the air, he flew backwards to shoot fireballs back in Helen's direction. Each one barely made it out of his hand before it was extinguished in a puff of acrid smoke. The dragon appeared again as well, but it too dissipated into black ash.

'Very clever catching me unaware like that, but it won't happen again,' she promised as she advanced towards him.

He wished he had kept the staff with him, but found a mop that would hopefully make a suitable substitute. He would shortly be finding out as he turned to find her nearly upon him. He ran to meet her and began the attack. With the first hit the mop shattered, leaving a jagged stake in his hand. He attempted stabbing at her with it, but she gracefully dodged each one of his attacks. He finally couldn't take it anymore and attempted a close range attack with fire. She seemed to sense his motives and countered with a wave of black matter. The force of the impact sent them both careening backwards.

Tyler growled as he stood up. There had to be some way to defeat her. He checked his distance to the opening but found her dangerously close to it so making a run for it was out. So far his physical attacks had been relatively fruitless. His final option was to go into Fire God mode. He felt the heat spreading through his veins like a drug and prepared to make his final attack.

'What's this you're doing?' came an amused question. 'You're not going to defeat me that way you know. Shall I show you why?'

She was getting very obnoxious now, but a sudden unnerving stirring in the air caused him to turn. His fire seemed to falter as he watched her change. If she seemed angry before, that was nothing compared to the rage she expelled now. She had become all black with her eyes a brilliant shade of poison green. He felt his soul rotting simply by being in her presence. His fear took hold as he quickly realized there was no way out of there. This was the final stand and it was hopeless. He willed himself not to die like a coward. She might destroy his body, but he would never let her destroy his dignity and self-respect.

He cried out in rage as he ran towards her. He made fire whips, which he soon had to extinguish as the black mold ate them. He fought with a multitude of fire animals, but she obliterated them, strewing their ashes about and splattering their remains on the walls. He fought with fireballs but they too were of no use. Every tactic he tried was put down. He was exhausted and had nothing left to give.

'My turn then?' she asked, smiling evilly.

All around her the space seemed to darken. Her eyes brightened and then smouldered into a deceptive emerald green. All around him creatures appeared. His nightmares were coming to life and were going to tear him apart. It took every ounce of courage within him to summon his fire whips and defend himself. One by one the creatures attacked and were repelled. It wasn't until the last one was defeated that the darkness dissipated and he collapsed on the ground. In an instant Helen was by his side and he had no strength to push her away. She leaned in swiftly and gently kissed him on the lips.

'What's that?' he asked as he felt his chest tighten.

'That's the kiss of death,' she replied, a faint hint of sadness ebbing through.

'Will it take long?'

'Not long at all.'

A sudden whoosh sounded as part of the ceiling close to them collapsed in a blaze. Many of the splatterings of fire had come into contact with the black mold, erupting into a toxic fire that had consumed most of the room. Helen gave him one final look before evaporating in a breeze of black smoke. As the room caved in around him, Tyler smiled. The poison from her kiss had almost reached his heart and he could feel it. At least he'd made a valiant stand.

He breathed his final breath as the building came crashing down on top of him. Father Michael and Kahit watched in horror as the building was consumed in the blaze. There was no way Tyler had made it out alive. Could he have? Neither of them spoke as they watched the fire trucks arrive and begin to put out the flames. The pain of losing him was too fresh to speak, so they walked aimlessly into town.

A few days passed before the fire was entirely contained. Each day the two would come and then go away in sadness, hoping against hope that something would be found. When the fire was out, the rubble began to be removed. The priest and the boy had to sneak around back in order to reach the cafeteria. It was the epicenter of the fire and thankfully was mostly rubble-free. The two began picking through the ashes praying that they would find something, although finding a skeleton wasn't really what they hoped for.

After days of fruitless searching, Father Michael exclaimed excitedly, 'I found something.'

Kahit rushed over and took the shiny medallion from his hand.

'What is it?'

'It's the medallion Tyler found while reading the book I loaned him. I never really understood the significance of it until just now.'

'What does it mean?'

'Read the Latin,' Father Michael said excitedly.

'Um "Sententia incendia mos inguolo ex cinis cineris anhelo novus vita." What does it mean?'

'Though fire will kill, from the ashes breathes new life.'

Kahit looked confused for a minute and then his eyes grew wide. He too began to understand the meaning behind the phrase and it inspired hope.

'Does this mean he's going to resurrect?'

'It has to. It's the only possible meaning this could have. He's going to resurrect.'

'But when? How long do resurrections usually take?'

Father Michael shrugged his shoulders and looked back at the remains of the hospital. 'My guess is that we're just going to have to wait and see.'

Kahit glowered for a moment and then raised his head, looking more hopeful. He smiled at the priest who smiled back at him. Father Michael put his arm around the boy's shoulder and they watched as a mysterious breeze blew the ashes from the extinguished fire off into the distance.